Irreparable
HARM

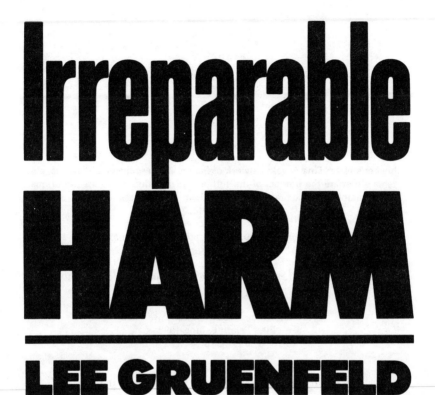

Irreparable HARM

LEE GRUENFELD

WARNER BOOKS

A Time Warner Company

Warner Books, Inc., 1271 Avenue of the Americas, New York, NY 10020

W A Time Warner Company

Printed in the United States of America
First Printing: June 1993
10 9 8 7 6 5 4 3 2

Library of Congress Cataloging-in-Publication Data

Gruenfeld, Lee.
    Irreparable harm / Lee Gruenfeld.
        p.   cm.
    ISBN 0-446-51713-5
    I. Title.
    PS3557.R8I77   1993
    813'.54—dc20   92-50526
                                                            CIP

Book Design by L. McRee

For Cherie

*Would that I had the world
that I could give it up for you . . .*

Acknowledgments

For technical, critical and moral assistance, I wish to express my gratitude to Martin Baum, Dr. Howard H. Crawford, the DBBHH, Maureen Egen, William Goldman, Robert Gottlieb, Irwin and Joan Goverman, Martin and Helen Gruenfeld, Harvey-Jane Kowal, Michele and Yossi Pinkas, Mike Simpson, Jim Stein and Mark Vezzani.

A special indebtedness is owed to Scott Klippel (attorney at law—Austin, Texas) and Dr. Bernard T. Ferrari (surgeon, lawyer, consultant—Los Angeles, California) not only for their many generous hours of technical assistance but for their friendship. I state emphatically that any errors legal or medical, whether purposeful or inadvertent, are solely my own responsibility.

Most of all I thank my wife, Cherie, for reasons far too numerous to mention but which include unshakable faith, unstinting support, unflagging love and mountains of pasta.

Primum non nocere
("First, do no harm")

—Traditional medical precept

PROLOGUE
Twelve Years Ago

CHAPTER

1

Jack Krakowitz was having a great deal of trouble figuring out the exhausted and panting uniform on the mat in front of him, which troubled him, because that made him one down instead of one up—not a good position for someone in his position to be in.

Krakowitz had seen lots of cops in his gym. He certainly realized that all human beings were unique (right thinking thought number one) and that simplistic attempts at categorization were unfair (right thinking thought number two). But the realities were otherwise to a jaded self-defense instructor. He was fully cognizant of the introduction to the Police Code of Conduct, and he meant no conscious disrespect for the intrinsic self-worth or the civil rights due every member of society—all of which caused him some small twang of guilt when he mentally lumped his students into three primary strata and varied his approach accordingly.

The scared ones he started off slowly. These were not used to violent physical contact and the surprising intimacy that always accompanied it. The transition to the physical expression of contempt rattled the scared ones, so he started with the basics: how the bad guys were likely to come at you, how to block, how to sacrifice a bone here or there to save your life, why mercy was for monks, not cops. Just the mechanics at first. Later he would do his best to give them some feeling for the attacker's rage, a simulated stream of venom to dull the shock of the real thing when it came.

The cocky ones he made sure to toss across the gym right away, and always three times. One time could have been luck, and his skeptical charges might scoff and call it a sucker punch, to be dismissed as entertainment. The second time, maybe it was the stress or the shock of the first one. *Let him get his breath, Coach, then let's see what you've really got.* Three times, though, and the point was made, no question, and the new recruits sobered up and paid attention. (He'd learned this lesson well when he'd soloed an airplane for the first time. Three takeoffs and three landings, the instructor had said: that way you won't lie awake all night wondering if your success was a fluke. Krakowitz taught the same to his police recruits.)

It was the third category of rookie that he liked, though: the dispassionate, businesslike, determined ones who pretended this was for real. They knew that when the time came, they'd be glad they had paid attention so they wouldn't have to think and create while dancing with a fellow human whose basic choice was to get away or go to jail, and who, like a thief who thinks nothing of ruining a forty-thousand-dollar car to steal a hundred-dollar radio, would as soon kill a cop as face a shop-lifting rap.

The one he had on the mat right now was about as deter-mined as any he'd ever seen.

This one had dripped sweat for over an hour, taking every-thing Krakowitz could dream up and coming back for more, learning with each fall and rarely making the same mistake twice. This was not a standard lesson, that much was clear, especially since this particular cop had special-requested the session, the third time this week alone, and it had been going on for months. There was a stalking relentlessness here, a veiled intent as to good or evil, very probably somewhere in the moral DMZ where most such driven undertakings usually reside.

Krakowitz gave the rookie an especially artful throw and

winced at the thumping sound as spine met mat. He waited a second and said, "So are you gonna tell me what this is all about?"

Amanda Grant brushed a sweat-plastered strand of dark brown hair out of her face, gulped some air and stared back at him, trying to look puzzled and feigning surprise. "Why?"

"Nothing, I guess, except that every cop hates this course, at least the ones who haven't been playing too long without a helmet. Women hate it most of all." He cocked his head inquisitively. "You come in for extra lessons."

Still breathing heavily, Amanda shifted position and rolled upright, trying to mask her labored gasps. "I like to watch men sweat."

Going to get nothing out of this one. She's getting off on the mystery, likes the drama. "Yeah, so I figured, except that you do all the sweating." *That was a little too quick*, he thought as he realized he had worked up quite the sheen himself. That wasn't the case when she'd started three months ago. She had made remarkable progress. He knew that she knew it, too, but if she was planning for trouble, he didn't want her overconfident, and she wasn't talking. Maybe . . . "Tell me something specific and we can focus the lesson a little." There: a little misdirection; attempt to be helpful, a partner in the conspiracy.

"The basics'll do for now." She glanced at the clock on the gym wall. "Gotta go to work."

———◆———

The daily patrol ended at four-thirty, and Amanda walked slowly from her car to the precinct house. She was still stiff from the workout with Krakowitz and not pleased with his suspicious questioning, although surprised it took him this long to get around to asking it. But that wasn't why her teeth were clenched or her shoulders so tense.

She was pretty, not beautiful, not in a magazine sense, anyway, but you could tell she'd also be pretty at sixty. Prominent cheekbones, widely spaced brown eyes, and lips not quite thin but somewhat shy of *full* might have lent her a moderately patrician air but for the softly rounded nose. In contrast with the shopworn, clumsy gait of the career beat cop, her walk rolled from the hips, betraying a practiced athleticism. Amanda took good care of herself, not out of vanity and not for anyone else, but just for herself, because it pleased her to do so. She was the picture of the modern, self-confident female whose self-possession was leaving her in great dollops with every step she took toward the station door. By the time she started inside, her clenched jaw was starting to hurt and her heretofore exclamation-point spine was devolving rapidly into a question mark.

It wasn't easy being one of the first female cops on the force, and "colleagues" like Dennis Murdoch didn't make things any easier. Amanda hated Tuesdays because that's when the beginning of his shift coincided with the end of hers, and their collegial exchanges were not the gentlest cap on her day.

"Yo, Amanda," came the shout from across the room. "Grant me my wish, Grant, you *know* what I'm talking about." She could sense his leer without looking in his direction and could feel it telegraphed around the room as it took hold like a brushfire. There were two brands of snickering: one that was willingly participative in her humiliation and the other that wasn't but was too cowardly to do otherwise.

Murdoch was a twenty-year man, with the promotion history of someone with half that tenure, and his voyage across the Styx of middle age was not a smooth one. He had raised to a fine art the traditional hazing of the rookie once he'd discovered Amanda, but that was two years ago, and the pledge period should have been over by now. But Murdoch was held in awe by some of the younger troops, and he felt compelled to hold court at every opportunity for the gathering of sycophantic tribute. These were fewer and fewer as the years passed, so each had to be milked well, regardless of the quality of the yield.

What galled Amanda more than anything was that Murdoch was actually a good cop, more than good, and some of his aura was deserved. Why he hadn't advanced more was a stationhouse mystery, subject to the typical rumors, which Amanda tried to ignore. He was the kind of cop she could have learned something from, and it wouldn't have been too difficult to let some of his less odious peculiarities slide, if only she didn't happen to be the target of nearly all of them these days.

Murdoch was particularly "on" today, hurling his schoolboy taunts like grenades as Amanda walked across the room. As the geometry of their positions made it inevitable that her back would soon be to him, she tightened the muscles of her buttocks involuntarily, as though to compress her well-formed bottom into some kind of shapeless, undifferentiated mass that wouldn't invite further gleeful insults from Murdoch. A wadded-up sheet of notepaper hit her square on the rump, and her artifice of disdainful contempt was shaken momentarily by the barely perceptible falter in her step. That she noticed at all gave Murdoch renewed energy, a small triumph, and Amanda a severe defeat. By the time she reached the locker anteroom her eyes were hot and wet and her nails bit into her palms from the strength of her balled fists.

None of this escaped Patrolman Robert Parks, who noticed that no tear left Amanda's eye. Her self-control was always a source of amazement to him, but he worried that a limit of some kind was being reached.

"Damn, Mandy, how long you gonna let this motherfucker carry on?"

She managed a smile, a little one to make sure the pressure of cheek muscles on her eyes didn't start the tears rolling. "The ghetto is showing again, Bobby." She loved to tease him whenever his emotions overcame his education and colored his language. Besides, it drew attention away from the embarrassment of her own brush with almost crying.

"Simple harassment suit, Mandy. Who's gonna deny it? Sonofabitch been hounding your ass"—it came out *"houndin' yo' ass"*—"since we got here."

Bobby's anger was genuine and growing, and it concerned Amanda, who knew he'd like nothing better than to handle it the way he had handled similar problems in his youth. "Let it go," she said, looking directly at him, and looking hard. They'd been inseparable friends since they were freshmen at the academy, both minorities, both declining full scholarships to more traditional schools. She understood the dilemma he faced with her: how to protect his friend yet respect her right to do things her own way. Amanda kept staring at him until acquiescence replaced ferocity in his eyes. "Trust me on this," she said, and he did.

Besides, he was going away, for a whole year, to train with the FBI as part of an exchange program to promote cooperation between the feds and local police forces. If she was not for herself, who would be?

She turned to face Murdoch once more before retreating to the locker room. Relays clicked and popped in her head. *Not yet.*

———●———

Amanda had cranked up the intensity level, and it wasn't clear to Jack Krakowitz who was giving whom a workout. He couldn't do anything to distract her, to spoil her concentration, and he wondered how quickly she could turn it on when she needed it. This was a gym; she knew he was coming after her. It wasn't real.

They worked for another half hour. Tired and worn, Amanda got to her feet after a fall and paused for a moment, hands on hips, to catch her breath. She felt Krakowitz's hand on her shoulder. "Amanda . . . ?"

Funny sound in his voice. She didn't remember hearing it before. His other hand slid around her waist. She started to say "Hold it," but his grip was tightening. She twisted around to face him, and his hands went to her buttocks. Eyes like ice, neutral. *Christ, he's strong.* She put her hands on his shoulders and tried to push him away, but it was like pushing a tree.

"Easy, baby, easy . . ." he breathed, his tone contrasting with the increased pressure he was exerting, and now she was starting to panic and her squirming became frantic and she managed to turn away from him again but it was like a Chinese finger puzzle: the harder she twisted, the tighter his grip.

She realized she was in serious trouble. The gym was empty (her fault—that's the way she wanted it), it was his territory, the world started to take on a sharp-edged aspect, she noticed how their feet made indentations in the mat. She felt a heat between her temples and sensed a sob welling up in her chest, and now she was pounding ineffectually at his knuckles.

Then suddenly his hands were off her, and he spun her around violently to face him. His eyes bored into her own, and he was mad. "What the hell is the matter with you?" he screamed, and her heart sank because this declaration of a debt owed was not what she expected from Krakowitz. She had actually gotten to like him over the past few months, like him a lot, respected his professionalism and his respect for her privacy, and now? "Four months we been at this and at the first sign of real trouble you start thinking with your crotch!"

What the hell was this, now?

"Dammit, Grant, don't tell me all of this was because you like wearing sweat suits. What's the good of it all if you go to pieces when the real thing happens? Why am I wasting my time with you?" He shoved her back as he took his hands off her shoulders, and she staggered, not so much from the push as from the chagrin she felt. She realized suddenly how much his approval meant to her, and there had to be a way to save this situation, however lamely it might come off.

"That was all to teach me a lesson?"

"No," he shot at her sarcastically, "because you got a great ass." Her eyes grew large and she tried to keep the crinkles from forming, but it was impossible and it was only a question of who cracked first, and soon they were both on the mat, laughing helplessly. They ended up sitting against the wall, very close together, wiping away a few remaining tears.

"It's about Murdoch, isn't it?" Jack asked.

Not willing to break their new bond, Amanda said, "Yes. Is it that obvious?"

"People are starting to think he's going over the line with you, but I really don't think he'd do anything serious."

What do you call what he's been doing? she thought but did not ask aloud.

Jack continued, "He's really not a bad sort, just a little troubled. He's got a good record, good connections on the street, the veterans know he's reliable . . ." Under Amanda's gaze Jack

realized he had said more than he meant to, a suspicion that
was confirmed when Amanda picked up on it.

"Why the violins, Jack? The guy's a greasy pig, and I don't
give two shits if he's good to his partner or his mother. He's
been on my case for two years, and people are talking more
about me than him now."

"I just don't think he's any real danger, that's all," Jack half
mumbled to himself, slightly petulant. He was now clearly
uncomfortable, and as Amanda realized he didn't understand
what she was up to anyway, she looked for a way to drop it.

"Hey, do I really have a great ass?"

"Yeah, you do." Jack thought, considered, evaluated, and
decided he liked this cop. "For a woman, anyway."

It was Amanda's turn to get uncomfortable, especially as
Jack turned his eyes fully toward her. She wanted his trust and
friendship. "I'd heard a rumor," she said.

"No rumor." It wasn't lost on her what a risk he was taking,
especially on the kind of police force that tolerated behavior
like Murdoch's.

She bent over and kissed him lightly on the cheek, then
got up wordlessly and headed for the locker room. Krakowitz
watched her go, knowing she was different but not sure how,
knowing this would not be the last he would hear from her.
Or *of* her.

CHAPTER
2

Christ, she was really getting to hate Tuesdays. Some people's lives revolved around their families, some around drugs, some around the up-down ticks of the Dow Jones index. Amanda's revolved around the Tuesday afternoon shift change. *Dialysis visits couldn't be this bad, she mused, and at least there's a point. But this . . .*

She leafed through her messages until she found herself reading the same one over and over, not comprehending. A damp rug hung over her mind, sapping her powers of concentration. She forced her eyes to the blue-lined slip of paper, moved her lips as she read until she caught herself.

She felt more than saw Murdoch; he was a wall cutting off her air supply. She stopped trying to pretend to read the message, realizing that the simple act of standing there was hardly a strong deterrent to this well-established ritual.

"Yo, Grant . . ." A strong smell of stale-beer breath and cheap cologne would have completed the scene, so her mind made up for their absence. Need to pump up the motivation. *If not now, when? If I am not for me, who will be?*

She felt his fingers start a wiggle on her back, just underneath her rib cage. The tickling could never be technically called sexual, which would eliminate one kind of formal charge, but it was designed to make her react in an undignified, little girl fashion. Good design.

She had asked Captain Rowan for a schedule reassignment that would have made these little interludes unnecessary. To her great astonishment, he'd instantly said no, without questioning the reason for the request. To her look of surprise he'd added, "Handle it, Grant," and stared her down.

The involuntary convulsion that resulted from Murdoch's rib attack made her turn around and step back. She was now staring him full in the face. This was new to Murdoch: she had barely acknowledged him in the past, trusting that her studied inattention would bore him and put an end to it.

Everyone else in the room knew it was new, too. She kept staring at him, knowing that the thousand-watt klieg light of public attention was flush on him. Murdoch drew his eyebrows up in mock surprise, made a little O of his mouth and drew his head back. "Well, well, what have we here?"

Amanda continued to stare into Murdoch's eyes. Muhammad Ali used to do that. Always blustery, blowing verbal hot air in all directions simultaneously. Just before the bell he went silent, drilling you with his eyes, frighteningly focused. Scared the hell out of you, shook up your plans, your timing. *If not now, when?*

It shook Murdoch up now, but not very much, just long enough to check around at his buddies for support and change the script a little. He put out his hand in the traditional Stop sign, palm forward toward Amanda's chest. "Easy, Officer. What'd I do?" Like a motorist stopped for speeding. The smile was a leer now, and his hand continued its journey to Amanda's chest, slowing only when it was inches away.

He turned to his audience again, with a questioning expression on his face. *Do I or don't I? Thumbs up or thumbs down for the bested gladiator?* He didn't count a lot of "yes" votes on the faces he could see from this angle. None, in fact, and this was disappointing, but it could give him a way out of the hole he was beginning to dig for himself.

But while he was contemplating his next step, the movie changed directors. Without warning Amanda stepped into his hand, so it now lay flat against her sternum. As Murdoch's head started to turn back toward her, she slapped both her hands over his palm, pinning it in place, just above and between her breasts. Any hopes Murdoch might have had about this potentially pleasurable acquiescence were forever dashed when Amanda leaned sharply forward, bending his wrist backward and forcing him immediately to his knees. A twist of her shoulders turned his arm inward, bringing his head sideways to the floor and exposing his not inconsiderable bottom to general view as well as to a solidly planted instep kick from Amanda's standard-issue patrol boot.

His unceremonious position on the dirty station-house floor afforded Amanda any number of choice options for further damage, all of which she declined for the moment. She knew that everybody figured she had caught him unawares, offguard. It was a sucker punch, probably just luck. By itself, it didn't really mean anything, like a 3 and 0 count that told you only that the batter could see, not that he could hit. She tallied it up on her mental balance sheet: one.

She also knew the great pig was not about to dust himself off and walk away. Her move was supposed to enrage him, make him more dangerous as well as careless, and it worked. He rose slowly, deliberately, careful not to stagger or in any other way betray surprise or shock. It took him a good half second to come to the conclusion that chivalry in the face of humiliation was no virtue, and he rushed at Amanda, holding back his damaged left wrist and leading with his right.

Still aware that actually punching a woman was probably not the best image builder available, he shoved her hard with his outstretched right hand, pinning her helplessly against the wall, pinioned and flailing like a freshly mounted butterfly.

At least that was the plan. What happened instead was that Amanda flicked his right hand aside, spinning at the same time so that her back was to him. She stretched her right hand way out in front of her. Murdoch wondered at this curious move even as the space between them narrowed. His curiosity was satisfied when Amanda pulled her arm back like a catapult launcher on an aircraft carrier, her precisely aimed elbow slamming into his solar plexus. This action deprived him of the ability to breathe, which ability he had always tended to take for granted, up until now. He considered this as he once again hit the floor.

Two.

Not enough. Maybe that was a lucky shot, too. Maybe the landing gear was particularly cooperative that day. Maybe Murdoch wasn't bringing out the heavy ordnance because, after all, she was a woman and an amateur. She had only one chance to get this right. She waited while Murdoch gathered himself, allowing him full recovery time for the third takeoff and landing.

Some part of Murdoch that he was no longer on speaking terms with elected to forget everything he'd ever been taught about this kind of situation. His eyes dashed off an incoherent wire and sent it to Amanda. A cooler, more studied and considered approach might have disrupted her irretrievably, but the wounded and desperate animal before her caused her little concern.

With surprisingly little planning, he rushed straight at her and was only mildly diverted by the fact that she let him come right into her. Even better, she dropped backward obligingly, even grabbing his collar to make sure he fell on top of her. This was interesting in itself, but not as much as the fact that her right foot was planted squarely in his belly. As they neared the ground, Murdoch was momentarily weightless, and thereby purchaseless, whereas Amanda had all of Mother Earth behind her for traction. She took advantage of this imbalance by pushing her foot up and back with all her might, while still holding on to Murdoch's collar. The laws of physics intervened cooperatively, and Murdoch's forward, rolling momentum was translated neatly into the parabolic arc being traced by Amanda's foot.

That foot, being connected to Amanda, stayed with her. Murdoch, on the other hand, being connected to his belly, went with *it*, and did so until the wall behind Amanda made further travel infeasible. His space intersected the wall's when his head and feet were inverted, and he slid to the floor, his hands scrambling frantically to break his fall with themselves rather than with his head.

Three

Amanda was on her feet by now and, in what traditionally would have been her moment of glory, felt real fear for the first time. Not because of the thoroughly disposed-of heap that lay breathing heavily behind her, but because the whole show would be wasted if they thought her a freak or someone nobody would ride with for fear of pulling her hair trigger, or if they threw her off the force for stomping the daylights out of a fellow cop.

That nobody in the room knew how to act became obvious, and she wished for a second that she could hand everybody a script that would tell them what to do, so it would turn out her way, and—

"Goddaamnn!" thundered from somewhere behind and to the left of her, interrupting her rapidly escalating anxiety. She turned to where the thunder seemed to originate, which turned out to be the doorway to the locker room, which turned out to be where Bobby Parks was standing alone. He was yelling "Goddamn!" over and over, with a ghetto/rap/bebop flavor that rendered suspect his cum laude college degree, and now he was whooping and hollering in unbridled glee, his eyes screwed up to tight slits by the rapturous grin, jumping and dancing in Amanda's general direction until she realized he was heading for her.

"Come to Poppa, baby, goddamn that was beautiful!" followed by more whoops, and his bear hug knocked her breath out as her feet left the floor, and he spun her around, still laughing and yelling. God, she was going to miss him.

By now cops were smiling all over the place, shaking their heads and slapping their foreheads as they turned to walk away and get on with work; except for the few that high-fived Amanda or punched the tops of her shoulders with both fists or actually kissed the top of her head. The more intimate and forward, the better she felt, because they knew her line wasn't frivolous or arbitrary but reserved for clods like Murdoch, who, nobody seemed to notice, was still snuffling and scratching about, trying to figure out if it was better to get up or maybe just stay down for a while.

Her triumph was complete when Captain Rowan walked in, quickly sized up the situation, and said directly to her, "Got any idea what's wrong with Murdoch?"

———————●———————

Nobody made a move to help him, not because they preferred to prolong his pain, which was considerable, or his humiliation, which was nearly unendurable, but because to do so would diminish Amanda's victory and blunt the drama. His solitary suffering was an integral part of the newly established *gestalt*, and coming to his aid was not worth the price of being the spoilsport taking the sharp edge off the game.

Murdoch rolled himself stiffly to a sitting position. His eyes watered, only partially from the sting of his badly cut lip. Before him was the prospect of getting to his feet, staggering off to the lavatory to clean himself up, and somehow getting out of the station house with some last fragment of his dignity intact, while knowing that even a partial fade from everyone's memory would take months.

Amanda watched from a distance, hidden by the half-closed locker room door. Her brow furrowed as she saw the tremble in Murdoch's lower lip, realizing that he was trying to stop himself from crying. She wondered if all her training couldn't have been better spent learning to hurl verbal rather than physical punches. He'd never actually hurt her physically, or even touched her, not counting the occasional spitball and his camel's-back-breaking tickle. A few weeks trading creative profanities, and maybe both their self-esteems could have been preserved.

Instead she was a hero, and the broken and bleeding man before her was dying the thousand deaths of the coward. Murdoch was on his feet now, and he straightened his back, ignoring the blood from his nose and lip. When he was certain that his step would be sure, he walked as normally as his aching body would allow, staring straight ahead, and left the station house without a backward glance. His bearing left little doubt that he would be back on duty tomorrow, on time and with no complaint. His only recourse to ensure self-preservation was to demonstrate that he could take it, take his medicine, and let the matter drop.

Amanda winced at the limp from his bruised and battered leg, doubtless sporting a great contusion where it had hit the wall. Laws protected the criminal from locally administered street justice, but nothing protected Murdoch from the righteous indignation of an insulted colleague. Her ability to assault him with impunity was an integral assumption of her plan, and, undoubtedly, his ongoing behavior toward her would be modified to her benefit. Tears sprang to her eyes for the first time since she'd joined the force, and she wondered what eating his dinner would be like tonight, and brushing his teeth, and would he awaken in the middle of the night to some stabbing pain that set in only after the shock had worn off, and while he was up, would he remember what happened and slowly get over it, or would his heretofore harmless derision of her explode into outright hatred?

BOOK 1

CHAPTER
3

Pamela Jacoby had not had a good day, primarily because it was a perfectly normal day, and perfectly normal days sucked, or so she thought to herself for the thousandth time.

Moreover it was hot, and her uniform was plastered to every square inch of available skin, except where the Kevlar vest lay claim to its own private field of vulnerable epithelial cells. The bulletproof vest was a conspiracy by men to keep women in girdles and by women to teach men how girdles felt. It was the cop's hair shirt, a religious talisman to keep them focused, concentrating, never forgetting that their lives were in constant danger. *Yeah,* she thought, *from heat prostration.*

"Officer Jacoby, have you got a problem with your vest?" Captain Amanda Grant had asked in the locker room shortly after Pamela had joined the force.

Pamela had been at the end of her shift, chafed and irritated in body and soul, and mindful of her superior's ever-perfect diction. She shot back sarcastically, before she could stop herself, "Yes, Captain. My tits are too big," while casting a not inconspicuous glance at Grant's considerably less ample bosom, which given the relativity of their anatomies still allowed the captain respectability in that department.

Amanda had then walked over to Pamela, opened her shirt

and unfastened the vest stays. An inexpertly suppressed half
laugh gurgled in her throat. Pamela looked up crossly as
Amanda said, "Oldest trick in the book, and I didn't see it
coming." She picked up the intercom phone, dialed two digits,
waited and then said, "O'Malley, this is Captain Grant. I'm in
the locker room with Jacoby. . . . Very funny, so now get her
the female model, you shithead."

Jacoby had stared openmouthed as Amanda walked off shaking her head. Then she sputtered, "Captain, are you gonna let
him get away with that?"

Amanda turned slowly, stared hard at Pamela, and said,
"Handle it, Jacoby."

"Handle it? Whaddya mean, handle it? How the hell do I
handle it?"

Amanda continued staring for another second, then turned
away, leaving Pamela angry and confused. *Not everyone's like
you, Captain,* Pamela thought, *not everyone can handle it or
even know what to do if they could.*

———◆———

The memory came back every time she took the horrible
thing off, as she did now at home. She had been too tired after
a late-ending shift to change at the station house, so she had
stopped there only long enough to check out.

The relief was instant, like taking off ski boots at the end of
a difficult day schussing above your ability. Her beat-up skin
was another gift from Grant. "No air conditioners in the patrol
cars. Robs power."

As she reached behind for her bra clasp, her eyes fell on
the portrait of Lieutenant William Jacoby, "Wild Bill" to his
friends and colleagues. The first man in every door, the one
guy you wanted behind you in a pinch. Her breasts fell gratefully out of the hot, sticky cups and into the cool air from
the window fan, and she eyed the picture as she undid her
hair. It fell in soft waves around her shoulders. Beautiful hair,
blond, but quiet rather than brassy. Her favorite asset, one of
the only things she did not feel inferior about but kept tightly
tucked beneath her cap so no one would see. Some days

she didn't wash it, kept it deliberately mousy so they'd keep their eyes off her. It didn't work; she knew it but didn't know it.

Why do I do this? Why am I a cop? The photograph started to fill her with the familiar sadness.

Pamela Jacoby had probably been the only senior in Benjamin Franklin High School with a portable police scanner. Other girls smoked dope, gave clumsy head to the football stars, and listened to heavy metal with scholarly concentration. Pamela listened to the scanner, even during breaks at school.

Her father had taught her all the codes, official and unofficial, that police officers used to communicate with one another. There was no practical way to scramble the signals, so they scrambled the language instead and broadcast in the clear. Once when a code 10 shot out over the airwaves, Pamela cut her afternoon classes, ran nearly three miles to South Eighteenth, and was the first civilian to happen on a hostage situation at the local branch of First Federal. Her expert eye caught a glimpse of the "perps" inside, and she ended up on the evening news as the only witness who actually spotted one of them. It was the only thing that saved her from a week of detention for cutting the classes.

Her math teacher had called. He didn't think Pamela was a hero. He missed her in class, saw her on television, and thought himself terribly clever for putting these disparate clues together. He got Pamela's mother first, who was immediately contrite and dripping with apology, until Lieutenant Jacoby figured out the gist of the conversation and grabbed the phone. Mother, as usual, put up no fuss but let him handle it.

"Who the hell is this?" he barked into the phone. "Yeah, well, listen, Mr. Math Teacher: she was the only one who could give the police a description of the scumbags that hit the bank, and now you want to give her a load of crap about missing a class?"

Mr. Math Teacher didn't know Wild Bill personally, but he knew who he was, and he was smart enough not to miss the menace in the voice. He mumbled something lame about not having caught that part of the news, which, while illogical, appealed to Jacoby's street savvy.

"Okay, then, that's the end of it, right?" It was an imperative, not an interrogatory, and Mr. Math Teacher's street savvy, such as it was, saw fit to drop the matter.

But Jacoby couldn't brag to his daughter about the little victory because Pamela, as usual, was elsewhere. She had hardly spoken a word to him in over a year, during which time she looked for every possible excuse to be somewhere else. The atmosphere in the house had grown intolerable, for all the typical and atypical teenage reasons, and Pamela's hatred for her father was surpassed only by her love for him, the whole enterprise complicated by an unreasoning admiration. He was a cop, after all, and she loved cops, especially good ones, and he was the best, even if he did have to report to a woman who wasn't as good, even if that woman was her idol, Amanda Grant.

It figured that it was a beautiful spring day when the code 3 flashed through her earpiece. "Officer down! Officer down!" the panicked young voice yelled unprofessionally.

The cool, calming voice of the dispatcher came back immediately, "Give us your twenty. Ten-twenty, right now."

Pamela could picture the dispatcher, hands gripping the mike stand, teeth clenched, trying to keep the anxiety out of her voice so the beat cop could get a grip and do this right. Also knowing that the automatic dispatch-recorder was sucking it all in, to be played back endlessly in the obligatory pursuit of blame.

"Burrito Barn at ... uh ... at Briggs and Dakota, and we need an ambulance, need an ambulance damned fast!" *Jesus,* thought Pamela, *it's the Choke 'n' Puke just three blocks away.* Her friends around the lunch table realized that Pamela had gone off somewhere in her mind. She waved their inquiries away furiously and closed off her free ear with a hand.

The frequency was filling with voices, out of control. The greater wattage of the dispatcher dominated, and the activity died down for a second as she said, "Pipe down, dammit, we know there's an officer down, we know the twenty. If you

don't have anything useful to add, shut up and clear the freq!"
Amazing, Pamela thought, *what happens when a woman who knows what she's doing asserts herself,* and this dispatcher knew what she was doing. Pamela's friends didn't understand her smile.

But then she went rigid, her eyes suddenly focusing to infinity, and she felt something vital drain out of her spine. "It's Wild Bill! It's Wild Bill! He's been hit" the faceless voice yelled. Pamela felt herself start to stand, holding the table for support, when her knees let her down.

Karen Griffin jumped up quickly and grabbed her arm. One of the more sensitive among the ditsy crowd that Pamela associated with, Karen said softly, "Oh, God, Pam . . ."

Pamela looked at her briefly, but Karen could tell she didn't see her, and now Pamela found her legs and they were carrying her toward the door, and Karen said, "Pam, d'you want me to go with you?" but Pamela couldn't hear her between the voices in the radio and the voices in her head, and now she was running and the voices on the radio got scarier and soon she was rounding Briggs and then she was there.

It was all the blood that struck her first, how much there was. She had read police reports, of course, but "pools of blood" meant nothing on paper. Now they meant her father's life, lying not in his veins, but on the sidewalk. Her first, blind thought was to scoop it up, quickly before it soaked into the concrete, to pour it back into her father, and each handful would make him stronger and he wouldn't need all of it just most of it, and *why was nobody saving his blood?*

The EMS detail was already backing off, if not entirely physically, then certainly emotionally, seeing that the case was hopeless; and while that ran contrary to all standing orders and medical protocol, they had all seen rear-entry, large-caliber spine and belly wounds before, and they knew that only the Almighty Himself would even know where to start to reassemble the pieces of His shattered handiwork. Better to give Jacoby a moment with his daughter than to deny him that right by a show of heroic futility.

She ran toward him, reached the police barrier and ducked

under just as another patrol car pulled up and Captain Grant stepped out. Pamela twisted to evade a uniform that was reaching out to grab her, but Amanda barked, "Let her go!" at the cop, and Pamela nearly gasped in gratitude as she dropped to her knees in front of the father she had spurned all these months.

"Daddy?" she asked softly, a test of his aliveness.

Jacoby's eyes opened and looked at his daughter. Life sparked feebly as he grabbed her hand with one that had been trying to hold his intestines in where they belonged, the one that now dripped with half-congealed blood. His eyes continued to look at her as best they could through the badly mangled face that held them in place. He squeezed her hand and tried to speak. "Pamela . . ." Funny gurgling sound, sort of a rattle, small rivulets of blood and foam on his lips.

She was supposed to tell him not to speak now, wasn't that proper? But she wanted him to speak.

"Pamela, I'm sorry. I'm sorry. . . ."

She felt him dying. She knew there was little time. How could she forgive him in that space of time? Worse, how could she relive the last year better, treat him better, make her shamefully bad behavior go away? There had to be a way. This situation was unacceptable, totally impossible.

"Pamela . . ." a little weaker this time.

Oh Christ, oh Christ, there has to be a way, it can't end this way. So handsome, so kind, such a good cop, such a good father. And me the worst daughter that ever lived, making this hero's life miserable, and now he's going and I can't take anything back.

And then he was dead.

Pamela's world went black. She felt her insides leave her, blow the air out of themselves, roll up into a little ball and reenter her body, which was now so much hollow and dark space. She felt gentle hands on her shoulders, pulling her away. What remained of her attention saw Captain Grant approach her father and stare down at him. The captain's shoulders slumped, and her normally iron back curved unnaturally under the weight of her building grief.

Amanda kneeled down and took Jacoby in her arms and hugged him, her neck against his broken and bloodied head. She rocked softly for a few moments, then stopped, picked up her head and looked into his blank eyes, and softly kissed his forehead.

She got up slowly and looked around at the gathered police officers, these macho men who worked for a woman. Somehow the death on duty of a colleague had subdued the swagger, and they were in awe of their captain, her normally impeccable designer skirt and blouse now soaked in Jacoby's blood, her eyes filled with tears she was not ashamed to let them see. *This is the first cop killed on my watch,* her eyes told them. *I do not take your lives for granted.*

They never found the ones who killed Jacoby.

———•———

Pamela was naked now and forced herself out of her reverie and away from the photo. Madness lay in that direction. It always had. That was its drawing power, like biting down on a sore tooth. But now was not the time for tempting her sanity. Now was the special time.

She went to the stereo and put on a soft-rock relic of the sixties she never experienced. A few capfuls of bath oil in the tub and both taps on full, a medium shot of Rémy in a crystal tumbler. Well, maybe not crystal, but very nice glass. She tucked her hair back up, but looser and more comfortably this time, and got into the tub.

The oily water found her pores and went to work, neutralizing the effects of the scratchy uniform, the leaden vest, the lines left by the holster carrying her .38 police special. She wiggled her toes to feel the friction between them dissipate. Feet, the cop's bane. Standard-issue shoes seemed purposely designed to maximize pain and long-term damage.

After a while she ran her hands over her knees and then soon found the inside of her thighs.

She could never remember how she came away from the Burrito Barn, just the blackness that shrouded her thoughts. She remembered the ambulance and thinking how pointless it would be to ride with her father, who, after all, was already dead. It was only when she contemplated seeing her mother that she realized the ambulance ride could provide a blessed delay to that event. *Mother.* Sure to be a blubbering, helpless blob of shot nerves and overweening dependency. With Pamela, of course, as the target for that dependency now that her tower of strength was gone.

A fruitless line of mental discourse, certainly, but Pamela could never forgive Mother for being the useless, subservient wretch she saw her as, and how Mother likely saw herself. What other interpretation could she arrive at?

Fat lot of help you were when I needed you, Mother.

It was all a confused swirl to Pamela now, though, as her carefully constructed perspective of their complex familial intertwinings unraveled, came together in a new knot, unraveled again. She found herself at her house just after the other cops' wives started showing up, in a ritual well known and well rehearsed among cops' wives, firemen's wives, test pilots' wives. They came to console but mainly to bathe in the relief that it was someone else this time.

They consoled her nearly to death—"poor, poor Pamela"— and presented her to Mother, who delivered a tear-soaked hug, but Pamela was blind by then and felt her mother only as a burned-out husk of a former human being, unworthy of a reciprocal gesture. The other wives looked on in horror at this cold display but chalked it off to shock, conveniently ignoring the expression of contempt on Pamela's face. *Too late, Mother. Too late.*

She then found herself wandering alone through the streets of her neighborhood, reliving it all, until she stood in front of the precinct house. It was after two in the morning already, and she noticed it was cold. Unlike her own house, the station warmed her soul. She hadn't been there in over a year but had been a welcome guest beforehand. Cops on the beat kept asking why she didn't come by anymore, and she could only flash the standard, enigmatic teenage places-to-go-people-to-see smile and walk on.

She stepped in and immediately felt the veil that had

dropped over the place. After all, this wasn't New York or Bogotá, where police officers were gunned down like so many toy soldiers. Here it was like a small African tribe, where a loss was mourned for a year. She glanced at the desk sergeant, a crusty veteran who had no idea what to do or say to her except wave and salute by touching finger to cap, which she appreciated. A professional.

She found herself in the booking room, and then in the detective ready room, with its low-walled cubicles and file cabinets occupying every available square foot. The light in the glass-walled corner office drew her, mothlike, and she headed for it. Inside she saw Eddie Papazian slumped in a chair, head leaning to the side and resting on his hand. He was talking softly, rubbing the side of his head slowly with one finger. On the couch nearby was Captain Grant, shoes off and legs curled under her, listening intently to every word.

Captain Grant had composed herself quickly at the scene. "Where's his partner?" she had demanded of the air, and someone pointed her to a nearby patrol car where Eddie sat, helpless and dazed. Amanda walked over to him. "Eddie . . ." He looked up blankly, but he focused quickly when he saw who it was. She had to get the statement out of him fast, before the events dimmed and the memory of his eyes took on the taint of his subconscious. But he was alive, and Jacoby was dead, and she had a duty to keep him going and keep him strong. Eddie was a good officer, and he had just lost his partner. To a cop that was like losing a spouse, only worse, because there was always the intimation of fault.

"Let's you and me talk," said Amanda, deliberately dropping the grammar to increase the familiarity. Then to the cop at the wheel, "Precinct house."

Pamela had wanted to go to Eddie, of whom she was very fond, but she was in too much shock to think clearly. Besides, now Eddie belonged to Captain Grant, and this was official business.

On the low table between them was a tape recorder, a mostly empty bottle of Jack Daniel's, and two partially filled glasses. The tape recorder was off.

Amanda looked up, startled to see Pamela shivering outside her office. Then Eddie spotted her, too, and stopped talking. He stared until tears returned to his red and swollen eyes. Amanda turned to him and said something Pamela couldn't hear. Eddie nodded slightly, and Amanda beckoned for Pamela to come in.

As Eddie swiped futilely at his eyes, Pamela walked up to him and put her arms around his neck and hugged him gently. She was sure that Eddie knew nothing of her troubles with her father. As he returned the hug, fiercely, Amanda noticed Pamela's dry eyes and chalked it off to trauma. Pamela looked at the bottle, then at Amanda, who got a third glass out of the end table, set it down and said with good-natured sternness, "Short one, okay?"

Pamela realized that Captain Grant had been sitting for hours with Eddie, letting him dissipate his pain and getting his statement at the same time, compassionately stopping the tape recorder when his reminiscences were personal and not relevant. "Eddie was telling me about when your father taught you to shoot a thirty-eight police special," she said gently, with a smile.

"Yeah," was all Pamela could manage. *He was quite a guy.*

———•———

The hot water had backed off to a more comfortable warmth, and the music and brandy were conspiring to relax Pamela in spite of herself. Her hands on her thighs slipped and slid as the oil worked into her skin, and she felt the familiar, distant tinglings as they worked their way up her legs. She parted her knees a little farther and stirred as the warm water touched the skin between her legs.

Memories invaded her mind from the sides, images of uniforms and blood, screaming confrontations and tearful reconciliations; lies upon lies, as much the fault of the believers as the liars. She touched her right breast with her left hand, circling and rubbing before settling onto her nipple, at first small and wrinkled, now coming to life from the images and the friction. She cupped the breast fully and squeezed it to herself, working the nipple with two fingers.

Her other hand teased her pubic hairs preparatory to the longer journey. She spread her legs as far as the tub walls would allow and gently kneaded her large outer lips, letting the oil do its magic. If only men knew the sheer bliss of extended foreplay, what lovers they'd be, and all of this would be unnecessary. The music surrounded her, a song about a handyman.

The tingling in her belly changed to a lower, deeper frequency and started spreading. Her left hand abandoned her breast to join the fray below, two fingers spreading her lips apart, a finger from the other hand starting a teasing insertion. Her hips began an involuntary pulsing, like riding a horse at slow canter, as her pelvis tilted rhythmically to meet her probing finger. She adjusted her cadence until it matched the sloshing of the water in the tub.

Soon her finger was well inside, then two fingers, pushing at her walls, exploring the mysterious twists and turns. She could feel the difference between her own natural juices and the bath oil. Her own were better, more viscous, the ideal combination of lubricant and friction.

She gave vent to her standard fantasy now, the one about big men who don't want to know her or love her, just to fuck her, and against whom she was powerless, only the recipient of brutal, mindless pounding.

She saved the best for last, spreading her lips wide and exposing her swollen clitoris. The warm water touched it and sent a current racing up her back. She brought a finger close and started her favorite game: seeing how barely she could touch it and still feel it. The slightest, glancing contact was electric, and the finger inside her worked faster without her even realizing it. She teased herself, working her finger around the little button, touching it only accidentally now and again, until she couldn't stand it anymore, and finally rewarded herself by placing the tip of her finger full on it. Her back arched and a gasp escaped her throat as she began rubbing lightly with a steady rhythm that matched the finger inside her.

The low-frequency tingle was everywhere now, and the fingers inside her and on her clitoris were becoming frantic as her breath shortened, grew raspy and labored, her eyes parting slightly. The vision switched suddenly, and the big men were now kissing her face, kissing her eyes, admitting that they loved her madly, had loved her all along, wanted to take care of her and protect her. The rhythm slowed almost to a crawl, but her hips were going way up and way down in huge, mighty swings, and then the train was on the tracks and the orgasm hit her like an avalanche and the moan in her throat was a low, animal, frightening thing that echoed the slamming in her groin, the big men admitting to the last that they loved her and wanted her forever.

CHAPTER
4

The previous evening's magic carpet ride ground to a shuddering halt with the onset of dawn. Onanism was supposed to be one of the few real free lunches left, the one great pleasure with no bad side effects, no red eyes or sour stomach, no pounding head or leaden tongue or burned-out brain cells, not even acrimonious contention with the injured party, which there always seemed to be whenever anyone was having any serious fun. Nope, doing your own was free of defect (guilt aside), the perfect pleasure, the one thing *they*, whoever *they* were, couldn't rob you of, even if you were in prison, even in solitary (*especially* in solitary).

Unless, of course, you happened to be seeing a therapist; and not just a therapist, but a psychiatrist, a certified M.D. trained *in absentia* across the generations by der gute Herr Doktor Freud, who invented the art in the days before left and right brains. Because if you were under the care of a psychiatrist, you told him everything, including the bad stuff. Especially the bad stuff; it was the bad stuff that brought you to him in the first place, not the good stuff; hell, if you only had good stuff you wouldn't be seeing him at all, so: especially the bad stuff.

Pamela knew that the first duty of a good psychiatrist was to help you understand that there was nothing really very wrong with your bad stuff. *Your shit's not you, Pamela: it's your shit. It is only the detritus of your tortured subconscious, the tip of your schizoid personality that happens to show, while the rest, the real you, lies lurking beneath the surface. The tip (that is, your shit) merely gives us clues as to the deep-water piece, which is what we're really after, because once we uncover the rest of the iceberg, the shit (that is, the bad stuff) will disappear, wafting out of your psyche on the light breeze of revelation. All of which you'll do yourself, Pamela. Not me, I just watch* (for a hundred thirty-five per fifty-minute hour).

Which doesn't make it any easier to keep talking to your male shrink about the fact that you're playing with yourself all the time. Not just the occasional giggly relief when you have been *sans nooky* for a long time—in her case, a very long time. Not just the infrequent and half-conscious semidream in the middle of the night that lets you fall back asleep and not really remember for sure in the morning whether you did it or not.

No. You have to tell the supercilious bastard the truth. But even then he just knows that you do it a lot, he doesn't know how good you really are, an Olympic-class wanker, chronic and skilled, with a library of detailed fantasies custom-tailored for any situation, and with a gallery of large, rough men to play their scripted parts. Long, slow lingerers for when there's plenty of time; quick, efficient get-'em-offs for when you're in a hurry; entire Saturday afternoons of rolling thunder in between hits of Maui-wowee trimmed from the last bust. (What's the perp gonna do, tell the judge, "Hey, Yer Honor, wait a minute, there was a whole kilo there when they popped me"?)

And he responds in a clipped, professional monotone, more intent on letting you know he is not shocked than on trying to figure out what it all means. After countless hours of listening to you drone, cry and babble, he knows by now you're not a lesbian, knows you haven't dated since Buchanan was president—and those last few attempts were disastrous.

Pamela dreaded these sessions. She would have dropped them long ago if Captain Grant hadn't insisted on them as a condition of her acceptance onto the force and gotten the insurance carrier to pick up the cost. Fringe benefit of Daddy-the-dead-hero.

She was locked into that most ancient of psychoanalytic conundra, the conflict between really wanting to get well (*really and truly, Doc, whatever it takes, I'm ready*) and desperately wanting to please the shrink. Theory had it that the only thing that pleased a shrink was getting better, but Pamela, like most patients, didn't believe the shrink would wait around for that if he thought that she was a depraved and useless piece of human jetsam, unworthy of association with polite society. So she constantly chose between showing him enough shit and showing him the real shit, and pretending to "work through" terrible internal strife that she didn't even know existed until he got her to find it herself by essentially doing nothing. If she thought she was suppressing things before, it was nothing compared to what she was now holding back so Dr. Ferrin wouldn't think she was as scummy as *she* thought she was.

Except that, deep down she knew that he knew. She knew that Dr. Brixton T. Ferrin understood exactly what she was doing, exactly what she was, what she felt and what was wrong with her, but also that he was damned if he was going to just come out and tell her, because that would ruin everything, that was not the way Sigmund F. taught it. So they danced around the issues a good deal, that was obvious; what *wasn't* obvious was just what those issues were. She really did not know, although she sensed them hovering just out of reach, with no way to jump over the wall for a peek.

What he already knew about her was bad enough. Here, in the artificial terrarium of his office, on his couch, it was open season on disgusting and shameful exposition. (Anachronistic as the couch was, it did mean that she didn't have to look at his face when she confessed, which was what she felt she was doing; it also meant that there was an official start and end to therapy: she lay down and it began; she got up and it was over—like turning an electric toothbrush on and off.) But God forbid she would ever run into him in a grocery store or in a restaurant, knowing what he knew! And if he was with other people? She'd melt like the wicked witch into a puddle of noxious effluvium and never congeal into a person again.

Fortunately, Dr. Brixton T. Ferrin was relatively new in town, which was one of the reasons she'd picked him, and he seemed to be a relative recluse, which she discovered after they'd started and which was just ducky with her. The more he stuck to his burrow, the less real he seemed as a person, and that suited Pamela just fine.

———◆———

These thoughts did little to brighten Pamela's day, and the impending tug-o-war with Dennis Murdoch didn't help.

Murdoch had calmed himself a good deal in the years following the legendary takedown by Amanda Grant. She had kept him on the force after she became the first female police captain. This seemed to many an obvious ploy to demonstrate sportsmanship, fair play, and whatever other qualities the self-help best-sellers of the hour were swearing were impossible for women to achieve because they never played baseball. But when asked, Amanda always gave the same answer: He's a good cop, and he learned his lesson.

The lesson Murdoch learned apparently did not include a class on how to not hit on other women cops, still Murdoch's favorite pastime. He'd softened his act, certainly, and there was nothing clear in the regs about attempted fraternization with your fellow officers, just as there was nothing clear about what constituted excessive aggression in that regard. The mystery, however, was one of statistics, not technique, because Murdoch had never managed to cadge a single date with any cop in twelve years of trying, and yet this deterred him not in the slightest. Moreover, he seemed to gravitate deliberately to the most inaccessible females, using lines and styles studied in their nonpersuasion.

All of this history was lost on Pamela as she entered the station house, the imminent pas de deux now more of a ritualistic annoyance than any real threat. Perhaps she had missed its transition from tense to merely tedious, but that did not help much in relieving the accompanying anxiety.

"Yo, Pam," lightly and familiarly, from off to the left somewhere. She rolled her eyes before turning slightly.

"Dennis, what a surprise, how nice to see you."

"You too. What's cookin'?"

"What's cookin'? You're asking me what's cookin'?" She bent one knee slightly and folded her arms. "I'm a cop, Dennis. We're both cops. The same thing's cookin' today as was cookin' yesterday, and the day before that, and y'know what? It'll be cookin' again tomorrow."

"Whoa, hey, take it easy, will ya? It was just a simple question. Christ, I don't give a shit *what's* cookin'; I was just makin' conversation." He walked away, mumbling "Sheesh" and shaking his head slowly.

Pamela stared after him, dumbfounded. *Now what in the hell was that all about?* "Hey, Dennis . . ."

He slowed and turned halfway back around.

"I'm sorry. It's been a shitty day."

"Hey, no problem," he said, smiling as he walked back briskly. As he approached, his smile grew less benign, and by the time he reached her he was all slime again. He top-to-toed her and sneered, "You wanna make it up to me, sweetcakes?"

This turnabout pushed more of her buttons than it should have, and she spat "Go to hell" with as much venom as she could muster on short notice, which was just enough to make him laugh. She was thankful that Amanda's long-ago course on manners was still effective in keeping Murdoch in some semblance of behavioral check, but she wished fervently that she could administer some of her own justice as well. She wished, but not hard enough to do anything about it.

Besides, she was off to see the shrink and didn't need any more complications that would require a report.

CHAPTER
5

Excerpt from transcript of Pamela Jacoby clinical therapy session 46, April 27, 4:00 P.M.; analyst Brixton T. Ferrin, M.D., Ph.D.

Tell me more about your father.
Oh, Christ, not again.

Tell me.
Shit, Doctor, we've been through this a million times, I mean, shit, it's starting to sound like a grade-B movie on the life of Freud. Can't we just move on?

Move on to what, Pamela?
Can't we get back to what's really bothering me instead of this bullshit?

What's really bothering you?
I'm unhappy being a cop.

Why?
I just hate it.

Why don't you quit?
  And do what?

Do anything. You're young, single: take a chance.
  I can't.

Why not?
  *I just can't, dammit. It's what I trained for, it's what I
  am.*

What you are?
  *Well, not what I am, but what I do. It's what I do, just
  like you're a shrink.*

Why did you become a cop?
  Are you kidding? Again?

Tell me.
  *Seemed like the thing to do at the time. They shot my
  father. They never found the perpetrators. He never
  finished, so I'm finishing it.*

Finishing it for your father.
  Yes.

Finishing what?
  It. Him. Finishing him. Finishing it for him.

Why? You weren't even talking to him at the time.
  That was a mistake. I loved him and I hurt him.

Should have talked to him [mumbled]. Yes, talked to him,
should have done that [almost unintelligible now].
  Doc? [Silence.] Doc?

Sorry. Why weren't you talking to him?
  Were you thinking about your own father?

Yes. But I resolved my grief.
  Doesn't sound like it.

I didn't say I don't get sad once in a while. That's normal.
To dwell on it and have it ruin your life is not. But let's
get back to your father. Why weren't you talking to him?
  *He didn't understand me, he didn't understand what
  was going on. I adored him but couldn't tell him.*

And your mother?
  *A nobody, especially compared to him. Terrified,
  mostly. No spine, let him get away with anything,
  everything.*

Did you masturbate last night?
  [Silence.]

Did you?
  [More silence.] *Yes.*

Tell me more about your father, Pamela.
  What?

You masturbated.
  So?

Talk to me about your father, say anything at all, any
remembrance.
  *We've been through this, Doctor, this is bullshit, I
  mean, for Chrissakes, all right, I want to sleep with
  my father, okay? I. Want. To. Sleep. With. My. Father.
  I thought we got past that.*

You said the words, but we didn't get past anything.
  [Silence.]

Pamela?
  Big man.

What?
> *My father. Big man.*

Big?
> *Big.*

CHAPTER
6

Dr. Brixton T. Ferrin was counting the ceiling tiles (5,148) for the third time. The totals he had gotten the first and second times didn't match, so the third time would have to be a tie breaker. The first time he'd counted the horizontal ones first, then the verticals, and multiplied. The second time he'd started with the verticals, which were harder because there were fewer light fixtures to use as references. If the third total was different from both the first and second, he'd have to start again and try to remember the extra six tiles that wrapped around the vent in the corner. Or maybe that's what had thrown his first count off. . . .

He already knew how many people there were (253) in the rows that he could see from his seat, near the back; how many stacks (38) of brochures; how many blondes, brunettes, and redheads (13, 22, and 2, respectively); and that the air-conditioning fans came on every fifteen minutes and stayed on for nine.

It wasn't so much that Ferrin was a big-city snob newly ensconced in a lesser metropolis that bored him, but that plenary sessions of the local chapter of the state medical society— by the very rules of logic—had to numb the minds of the vast majority of attendees. Specialists were interested in their specialties, but you couldn't address a general audience with a specialty topic because most wouldn't track along at all. So you picked a general topic that everyone could understand but only the generalists really cared about, and since there were only a handful of those, most of the rest were nearly driven to screaming from boredom, which they suppressed out of professional courtesy. Simple logic. Particularly applicable to the early speakers, like Ferrin, who had failed to properly consider the penalty for their participation and now regretted it.

For a psychiatrist of Ferrin's caliber to listen to a general practitioner drone on about the importance of bedside manner was like Albert Einstein attending a class on long division. The lecturer's sincerity notwithstanding, the oversimplifications and unsubstantiated platitudes grated on the surface of Ferrin's erudition. Seemed like a nice enough guy, though.

Later (seemed like days), at the traditional postmeeting finger-food trough, he spied the GP, wrestling indecisively with which facet of the triangle-shaped taco chip to dip into the guacamole. Ferrin took a deep breath and stepped over, but not before a surreptitious, confirming glance at the "Hello My Name Is . . ." badge just turning into view. "Dr. Nostrand?"

Jake Nostrand looked up quickly, having settled on the point of the taco chip as the neater alternative, albeit less capacious than the wide side. A response was called for, despite the mouthful at risk of inadvertent ejection. But Ferrin laughed and said, "That's okay, don't worry about it. I'm Brixton Ferrin. Just wanted to let you know how much I enjoyed your talk." Ferrin's slow speech and slightly British accent complemented the elegance of his bearing and made Jake's pedestrian predicament all the more pronounced.

Jake took advantage of the proffered hiatus to clear his alimentary passage, and responded, "Oh, well, thank you, thank you very much. I appreciate your saying so."

"I'm a psychiatrist, so obviously your topic was of great concern to me."

"Yes, I would imagine so. But I would have thought you'd find my perspective somewhat, uh . . ."

"Simplistic?"

Nod.

"Well, of course."

Surprise on Jake's face at this frankness.

Ferrin went on: "But you're a GP, not a psychiatrist. You're supposed to be aware of the basics and incorporate them into your practice. If you tried to practice psychoanalysis every time you checked a pulse, you wouldn't be doing your job, what?" Smile.

"Exactly, exactly, that's the whole point, Dr. Ferrin."

"My friends call me Brix."

"I'm Jake. I apologize if we've met before, but I'm pretty sure we haven't."

"No, I'm fairly new around here, and frankly, not much for meetings. But I rather suppose if one is a speaker, one must attend."

Jake laughed and leaned forward conspiratorially: "Hey, I feel the same way. I only caught the last half of your talk, but it was fascinating."

Ferrin doubted it. "Why, thank you."

"By the way, your name looked awfully familiar when I saw it on the agenda. I heard a Ferrin lecture on psychoactive drugs when I was interning. By any chance . . ."

Ferrin blushed slightly and flashed a sheepish grin. "I'd rather you kept that quiet, eh?" he offered in a stage whisper while looking back over his shoulder in exaggerated fashion. "Didn't go over so hot with the stuffed shirts in the London School."

Jake smiled and raised his eyebrows. "I bet it didn't," he said, "but I heard you here, I mean in the States . . ."

"I came over as a postdoc. My father—" His voice caught. "I came over with my father. I did some lecturing to enhance our income. My father worked two jobs to get me here, to put me through school. He . . . passed away some time ago."

Jake was anxious to relieve Ferrin's discomfort, get him back to a safer topic. "Are you doing any research at all these days?"

"As much as a solo practitioner can get away with without a lab or facilities. I do try to dabble now and again."

"Like in what?"

Ferrin shrugged, as though reluctant to get into it but willing to answer a sincere question or two. "Well, one of my interests is in a little known therapeutic theory. It's called complementary neuroses."

The interest on Jake's face was readily apparent. "That's a new one on me. What is it?"

Ferrin seemed to consider for a moment before reaching a decision. He looked around. "Why don't we have a seat?"

Jake leaned forward again, pleased to be in the company of a moderately prominent specialist and unwilling to let the opportunity pass. "Got a better idea. Let's get out of this shit-hole and get a drink."

Ferrin look mildly startled, thought for a moment and replied, "I quite agree." Jake grabbed him by the elbow, and the co-conspirators snaked their way to the exit.

———•———

"It's more than a theory, actually," began Ferrin when they were comfortably tucked into a corner booth, drinks in hand. "The problem is that the basic psychoanalytic process has changed very little since Freud's time."

"How so?" asked Jake.

"The premise is pretty simple: The individual human psyche is so incredibly complex that when you put two people together, the complexity is multiplied into a hopelessly tangled mess. If you try to psychoanalyze somebody, the psychological makeup of the therapist becomes as important a factor as that of the patient. If I'm a mess, and you're a mess, how do we know where my mess ends and yours begins?" Ferrin paused and sipped his vodka tonic.

Jake considered this for a moment. "I always assumed that the therapist was trained in technique, in interpretation, and was therefore in a position to make sense out of things the patient couldn't."

At this Ferrin started to grow animated. "Yes, yes, but let's look at what's really going on. It's not just a patient blabbing away to a blank wall. The patient is *interacting* with the therapist, responding to prompts and questions, and all the time is painfully aware that this other human being is hearing shameful and disgusting revelations that the patient would as soon never think about, much less talk about. How'd you like to tell me you once caught a peek at your German shepherd's bare bottom and got an erection?"

Jake, glad he didn't have a dog, understood. "So the therapist's own set of problems is also a factor in the doctor-patient relationship."

"Exactly. And the difficulty is knowing whether it's the psychiatrist's neurosis or the patient's—or both at the same time, for that matter—that is at the center of the discussion at any given moment. Is the doctor really seeing your problem as it truly is or only as he perceives it through whatever happens to be troubling him at the moment?"

"Neurotic psychiatrists? Kind of like a fat dietitian."

"Psychiatrists are hardly immune to the slings and arrows of personality deficiencies. Good Lord, they have the highest suicide rate among all professionals."

"So . . . ?"

"So," continued Ferrin, "Freud was well aware of this little problem. And he was clever, make no mistake. He figures, well, there's no way we're going to clean out the psychiatrist's mental junk pile, so let's go to plan B: we'll simply analyze him so thoroughly, make him so aware of his own sea of troubles, that it will be easy for him to distinguish whose junk is on the table at any given moment."

"Sounds reasonable. Only . . ."

"Only what?" prompted Ferrin.

"Only now that you've got an artificial brick wall created, where's the therapy?"

"You're getting to the heart of the matter. Freud's basic thesis was that revelation is cure. The minute you recognize and understand the nature and source of the problem, it goes away. Dredge up the psychic mud and confront it, and you can pay your bill and walk away free."

"Which is why people stay in therapy for years?"

"It's worse than that," said Ferrin, an angry look coming

over his face. "The patient starts to build a huge, overwhelming dependence on the therapist. All of his new defenses have been carefully constructed in concert with the doctor, whose own inadequacies and problems are strewn in amid the newly laid concrete. This is normal, and not necessarily bad, but let me ask you this: How do people choose a psychiatrist?"

Jake pondered this for a moment. "Recommendations from friends, from doctors? General reputation?"

"Right." Ferrin looked pleased, which pleased Jake. "So one of your friends tells you about this terrific shrink, who happened to be great for someone suffering from anxiety over a history of heart trouble in the family, and you take your German shepherd problem to him without realizing he's been having a go at his poodle for ten years."

Jake laughed as Ferrin continued. "Is this the chap you want as the template for your psychic reconstruction?"

"Well, golly, Brix, I guess not," said Jake, drawing out the words slowly, chiding Ferrin for the obviously rhetorical question.

Ferrin looked away, slightly chagrined, and smiled, but with his mouth only, not his eyes. "Sorry. I do tend to get a little carried away." Then, with some excitement creeping back, "But you do see the point, don't you?"

"I do, actually: it makes sense. But now what?"

"That's where complementary neuroses comes in," revealed Ferrin. "There's no way around the fact that two people are going to have to interact in the therapeutic process. So"— Ferrin paused for effect—"why not pick a therapist whose particular psychological makeup is the one most appropriate for helping this particular patient?"

Jake looked up at Ferrin. "What, are you kidding? Are you going to have a national registry of each psychiatrist's personality disorders? Maybe a computerized matching service?"

Ferrin laughed now. "Well said. No, of course not. What I'm talking about is a therapist who is not a therapist, but another patient."

Jake waited for him to go on. When he didn't, Jake said, "Excuse me?"

"If I could put the patient in close proximity with someone whose strengths complemented the patient's weaknesses, someone whose ability to cope was evident not just for an hour or two a week, but all day, every day . . ."

Jake listened, riveted, as Ferrin continued. "Better yet, what if that other person himself was a patient, and one whose problems were a close inverse of our original patient's?"

Jake finished for him. "Then they'd be helping each other, all the time. And it would be a fair deal."

Ferrin sat back, satisfied. "And that's the idea behind complementary neuroses."

Jake was mesmerized by its simplicity. "Is it real? Have you ever tried it?"

Ferrin relaxed a little and took the last sip of his drink, signaling the waiter for another. "Yes, with some success, at least in conjunction with traditional therapy." To Jake's look of surprise he responded, "There still seems to be a need to discuss the process in addition to just participating in it. We're still talking about a very complex set of issues, and the psychiatrist plays an important role in trying to sort it all out. And, oh yes, there's one little detail I forgot to tell you."

"Oh, boy. Here it comes."

"The patients don't know what's going on." Jake knitted his brows in confusion as Ferrin continued. "We get them together and we don't tell them why. Otherwise, the artificiality of the situation takes over. They start clocking progress and get mad at each other if they don't like the rate of improvement."

"Doesn't sound very ethical. I mean, should you be manipulating people like that?"

Ferrin seemed to take offense. "Did you ever give a hypochondriac a placebo? Did you ever call a patient's wife and tell her to let him play golf an extra day a week because you thought he was stressed out, or prescribe Ritalin for a hyperactive kid, or give someone a tranquilizer before a minor procedure and tell him it was an antibiotic?"

"Hey, I get the picture," Jake protested good-naturedly, holding up his hands defensively.

Ferrin smiled. "We do it all the time, Jake. It's our job, if you think about it."

Jake knew he was right, although the degree of deception still bothered him somewhat. Nevertheless, he was fascinated by the whole concept and unwilling to let it drop. "Listen, I'm getting hungry. Why don't we have dinner and talk about this some more?"

Ferrin glanced at his watch. "I don't know. . . ."

"C'mon, you've been in town nearly a year and don't know anybody yet, time to do some networking. Besides, I'm buying."

Ferrin considered and said, "In that case, how can I refuse?"

After they had ordered, Jake started in without preamble. "Can we do it here?"

Ferrin was startled. "Sorry?"

"Your theory. Can we work it here?"

Ferrin put down his drink and grew thoughtful. "To tell you the truth, probably not."

Jake couldn't hide his disappointment. "How come?"

"At my old practice, we were a tight group in a large city. We knew each other, consulted frequently. It was relatively easy to zero in on good patient candidates. Here, I don't know anybody, really, and nobody's clicked in to the concept." He looked directly at Jake. "It wasn't without controversy, you know."

"Neither was your drug research. Nothing is when it's radical. But the idea is so good, and when you get right down to it, there's not a lot of risk, is there, and—"

"Hey, take it easy," Ferrin said, smiling, "you just got a whiff. There's a lot more to it, a lot—"

"What are the parameters?" Jake interrupted. "How do you know when the match is right?"

Jake watched Ferrin, hoping he'd go a little further, play this out. His professional life didn't offer a lot of excitement or opportunity for innovation. Ferrin seemed to be sizing up Jake at the same time and seemed, once again, to come to a decision.

"I've got this one patient, a cop, female, twenty-two years old. Her father had been a cop and she adored him beyond describing, but when she was a junior in high school, all hell broke loose. Typical story, actually. Screaming, yelling, storming out of the house. She stopped talking to him altogether. It tore him up, and she knew it, but somewhere inside she was enjoying the ability to have that kind of effect on him. He was a hero in the police department, so she tells me, and she had the power to make him miserable."

Jake followed intently. "Not unusual. I've got patients who tell me things like that all the time. Most of them usually grow out of it, though, and have some kind of reconciliation."

Ferrin's eyes grew sad. "Yes, well, there was just one little problem. Pamela's father was shot during a robbery attempt. A simple, minor-league police intervention gone terribly wrong. Pamela heard it on the scanner she carried and made it to the scene before the ambulance arrived. Her father died in her arms, apologizing to her for what she believed was essentially her fault. She was seventeen. She'd made his life miserable for nearly a year, and now he was dead and he went out apologizing to her."

"My God," Jake whispered.

"I couldn't begin to list all the things it did to her. She even thought it was her fault he got killed. Didn't have his mind on what he was doing."

Jake, unused to these situations that psychiatrists hear all the time, momentarily lost his concentration as he considered the plight of this deeply troubled woman, until he found himself and said, "So what would the complementary personality be?"

Ferrin grew thoughtful, then started slowly. "The parameters would be relatively straightforward, I would think. Pamela was traumatized during a critical stage of her development, a period of great confusion and change." As he spoke his tone became more clipped, almost professorial. He was back in his element. "The experience resulted in scars that are very deeply rooted, to the point where they almost don't relate to the original cause anymore. A good counterpart would be someone with a relatively stable childhood who had matured into adulthood in a more normal fashion, but who then suffered a trauma that, while devastating, should have been dealt with in a more normal manner." He realized that he had been lecturing, caught himself, and stopped.

Jake was growing excited. "Is that it? Is that all?"

"No, not by a long shot. Pamela feels bound and constrained to follow a path in life, and she has no control over it. She hates being a cop, feels honor bound to be one by some strange logic I won't go into. To do otherwise would involve a degree of psychological risk, and she never takes such risks, at any level.

"Her complement would be someone who lives life on the edge, for reasons as compelling as Pamela's fear of risk, taking chances all the time but desperate for some real stability."

Jake had more questions than he could contain. "But police work is risky, isn't it? I don't get it. And would the other person have to be some kind of wild daredevil?"

"First off, police work isn't risky to Pamela. The physical danger pales next to the mental risk of not following in her father's footsteps. I'm even afraid she might try to get shot in some sort of bizarre expiation. As for the other person, it wouldn't necessarily have to be a daredevil. In fact, the best thing would be somebody smart enough to have largely figured out how to suppress the dangerous behaviors, but who was constantly agonizing over the urges."

By now Jake could hardly restrain himself. "Look, Brix, I've got the guy. Is that okay, that it's a guy?"

"What?" Ferrin appeared to be caught unawares. "What are you talking about?"

"The complement, the 'other.' I've got the perfect guy." Jake had his hand on Ferrin's arm and was squeezing.

Ferrin appeared to find Jake's excitement ingratiating and started laughing. "You trying to break my arm? What guy? I thought we were just having a hypothetical go here."

"But why not? What's the harm? You said there was little risk and—"

"No, you said it, not me."

"Well, is there?"

Ferrin grew serious but couldn't shake Jake's enthusiasm. "I told you, it's not so simple, you've no training in these things."

"Fine, fine, I know that, you're right. Only let me tell you about someone."

The waiter showed up and, as the hour was early, had time and began a more elaborate than necessary presentation. Ferrin stifled a smile as Jake said impatiently to the waiter, "Just set it down, wouldja?

"Student of mine, back at the medical school," Jake began once the obtrusive waiter had departed. "Very bright, very driven, very low on funds. . . ."

———◆———

Okay, the bones of the wrist, upper row: Simple Souls Crave Peace. Scaphoid. Semilunar. Cuneiform. Pisiform. Bottom row. Troubled Times Often Mean Unrest: Trapezoid. Trapezium. Os Magnum. Unciform. Or was it trapezium, trapezoid . . .

"F'Chrissakes, watch it, goddammit!" the angry voice raked at him. Mackenzie Graham jerked back quickly on the black-knobbed lever at his side and brought the turning cab of the crane to a shuddering halt. A half dozen steel I-beams four stories above the ground swung back and forth precariously, their immense weight tilting the cab slightly each time they reversed direction.

Shaken out of his memory exercise, Graham looked out the cab porthole to see his supervisor, Charlie Danocek, staring in at him angrily. *When the hell had he climbed up?*

"D'hell is wrong wit' you, anyway, Mac?" The "Mac" was less related to his nickname than to the fact that Danocek called *everybody* "Mac."

"Nothing. Didn't see you is all."

"Bull*shit*. You keep your mind on that crane or you're gonna kill somebody one of these days, and I don't give a flying fuck *who* you know, get me?"

Mac sighed and hung his head but quickly raised it back toward Danocek. This was no time to assert himself. If it wasn't for this job that Dr. Nostrand had gotten him, he'd be out of medical school, selling knitwear. And if he didn't memorize eight more pages of *Gray's* goddamned *Anatomy* by tomorrow morning, he'd be out anyway. What the hell, the money from the job was barely enough to cover expenses, so what was the use? But you never knew what could pop up. It paid to keep options open until the very last. Besides, Danocek was right; he did screw up.

"Sorry, Charlie. Won't happen again."

"Damn well better won't."

Mac fought the temptation to correct the grammar.

Danocek went on, "Take a blow, I want to talk to you anyway."

Mac pulled the braking lever up until it ratcheted into place, clicked the safety latch over the release, and climbed out of the cab. Danocek was on the ground by now, and Mac backed his way down the rungs on the side of the giant crane.

Danocek took off his hard hat and wiped his wrist across his brow, which Mac noticed hadn't been sweaty. Nervous gesture. Strange for a guy like Danocek, who never seemed unsure of himself. Mac felt a warm sensation start in his chest as the thought that he might get fired occurred to him.

"We got a little problem, Graham."

Not Mac? *Oh, please, God, please, don't do this to me.* He was in his fourth year, only nine months to go. It was bad enough having to make up third-year material, bad enough in general, but when you were the best student in the school? Memorization wasn't his strong point anyway. He had a natural gift for medicine. His professors knew it, the school administration knew it; why else would they let him make up a basic course? But if he got canned, holy Jesus . . .

"You know that little twerpy guy that's been snooping around here the past few days?"

Mac looked at him dopily, not comprehending. Danocek went on: "The short geezer with the stupid hat, bow tie . . . ?"

Short geezer? The little man who'd been walking around the site? Don't tell me that little scumbag is a crane operator, that he's got a better connection than mine, that he's gonna get my job!

"Well, he's a union organizer. Been bothering some of the boys, planting bullshit in their minds. Some of 'em are starting to ask questions."

What's this? Union guy? What's this got to do with me? "Yeah, so?"

"The company don't like him hangin' around, causin' trouble."

The first trickle of relief beckoned to Mac from a distance.

"We need to make him go away, gentle-like, no big trouble."

The relief became a small stream, growing as Danocek's words opened the valve. Mac was back on the bus, as grateful as a spared lamb, ready to sacrifice his soul for this terrific company. *Ask it of me and it shall be done.*

"We want you to drop a load of beams close enough to scare the shit out of him, but far enough away that there's no real danger, but close enough that he won't mistake the message."

Mac stared at Danocek for a second. "Forget it," Mac said, and turned to walk away. *Who needs this shit?*

"Graham, don't be an asshole. The guy won't get scratched, and the company will be real grateful."

He stopped, turned. "Grateful?"

Now Danocek had him, and he worked it. "About five grand worth." *Just about enough to finish school, you spoiled wienie,* he echoed Mr. Thornton in his mind. The owner of the company had called his big-deal medical school dean brother-in-law and asked about Mac's financial status.

Having lost some of his self-righteous bravado, Mac asked, "No danger?"

"None. I'll handle it myself. I'll be on the lot and watch your load. Whenever the guy walks onto the site, the rest of the boys will drift off to the sides. That way, when the bang comes, the guy'll be alone and he won't miss the point. When he's well clear, I'll look up at you, tweak my ear or something, and whammo." Danocek clearly relished the image of fifteen thousand pounds of steel slamming to earth from six or seven stories high.

"Whammo," Mac repeated absently.

"Whammo," Danocek said again. "Union guy catches the next bus; Graham heads to Easy Street."

"And if I don't?"

Danocek pursed his lips, stuck his hands in his pockets, and turned to inspect a mound of dirt.

"Whammo," said Mac.

Jake blinked his eyes several times to bring them back into focus, as though reorienting himself to the here and now.

"I've pieced a lot of this together over time, you understand. Maybe the details aren't that important . . . ?"

"No." Ferrin shook his head without taking his eyes off Jake. "No, tell me everything."

Jake lifted a shoulder and dropped it, then stared off again. "He and Danocek had gone over it dozens of times, which was out of character for Danocek. The signal, the position, the configuration of the beams on their tether to minimize the spread when they landed. Mac even came up with the idea of the knot, a friction hitch he remembered from the Boy Scouts. Strongest knot imaginable while under tension, but reduce the pressure and it gives like wet tissue. It was common in construction for quick lifts because you could tie a wire without unhooking it first. Illegal, but it saved time."

————•————

But Mac's hands sweated anyway, and he couldn't make them stop. Now here was the little putz coming onto the site with his pamphlets and his harangue. Mac tried to hate him but couldn't. Despite his best snob instincts, Mac knew the workers were getting a raw deal, that the union would probably be a blessing or certainly could entail no worse than what the laborers were getting now. What was so terrible, except a little less profit to the company? Two fewer rooms in the boss's house? Five thousand dollars less to be able to throw at flunkies like Mac for bullshit pranks?

On to business.

The union guy had walked through the lot about forty times in the last three days, but never where they needed him. He looked perfectly positioned to Mac on any number of occasions, but Danocek gave no sign. Now, with the guy in sight, Mac slapped at pneumatic one to start the big flywheel turning, hauling a massive load high into the air. They'd been using the friction hitch for all loads these past few days, and Mac had been extremely gentle on the controls to make sure he kept the tension constant. He slowly turned a knurled control-panel knob, and the cab started an almost imperceptible rotation to the right.

The guy headed straight for the center of the site. Danocek stopped what he was doing, dropped his clipboard casually to his side, and glanced up at Mac in the cab, which was perched on the running ledge above the lot. The other workers started slowly drifting off, which did not escape the attention of the union guy, who maybe wondered if the owners had issued a warning. Par for the course; he'd get to them regardless. He looked discreetly to his left and his right. He never looked up, though. He kept walking.

Danocek held up his index finger, and Mac slowly brought the cab's turn to a halt. It was barely noticeable, and the beams high overhead remained steady.

Mac fixated on Danocek's finger so hard that he had to move his head and eyes a few times to bring it back into focus, and then it was gone and Danocek was tugging frantically at his ear.

Mac grabbed the brake lever and threw it completely into release, then just as quickly back into full brake. The cable above the beams went slack for a split second, before the brake locked the big flywheel back into place, but it was just enough time for the knot to lose its grip.

The great steel structural members, so implacable and majestic while firmly packed together in the air, now looked like so many shafts of wheat as they began their inexorable submission to the laws of gravity. Mac noticed in particular the surprising lack of sound, other than the occasional mild clang or click, as the beams tumbled and plunged earthward, the silence belying the enormous force that was building up in direct proportion to their ever-accelerating speed.

The steel didn't seem so much to strike the earth as pour into it. The great cloud of dust that rose as the column of beams disappeared obscured the ground at the point of impact, and only the terrifying shudder that spread outward from ground zero betrayed the enormity of the weight that had fallen.

Mac fixed his eyes on the spot that last held Danocek,

but he couldn't tell through the dust if he was still there or not.

As the light brown haze of dirt began to dissipate and settle, men on the fringe began a slow walk toward the mound of beams, which looked as though it were smoking in the aftermath of a fire. As the men approached, they picked up speed. Mac tried to bore his eyes through the haze to find Danocek.

Inexplicably, as the men neared the beams, they slowed again, then stopped, staring, transfixed and immobilized. Mac felt a trembling beginning in his shoulders. He looked back at Danocek's spot, now clearly in sight, but there was no one there. Several men in the middle of the site were now staring at the crane, at the cab. At him. The trembling grew more pronounced.

The laborers near the beams were reanimated now, shouting and scurrying and making the kinds of arm-waving, useless motions that possessed people helpless in the face of catastrophe, but who nevertheless were driven to do something rather than stand idly by. A siren went off atop the supervisor's trailer, whose doors opened and disgorged several men in short-sleeved white shirts and brown ties. Mac noticed that the ties were too short, didn't meet their belts, which were partially obscured by their overhanging bellies anyway. All kinds of details occurred to him now as his mind kicked into self-defense overdrive and sought to divert him from the slowly dawning horror.

He was paralyzed. Quick, transient currents of hot lava appeared and disappeared in his arms, legs, chest. He could barely make out the voice behind him, coming through the porthole of the cab, until a rough hand grabbed his shoulder and squeezed, painfully.

"Don't say a word. Not a word." The hissing voice struggled its way through clenched teeth. "Not to anybody. Just look like you're in shock and keep your mouth shut."

Mac turned as best he could and stared into Danocek's face, searching for some evidence that it had been an accident. He found none, just Danocek's eyes digging into his own, eyes full of evil, devoid of compassion, all business.

"We'll take it from here."

Then new faces were at the porthole, most sympathetic, but not all, and then he was out of the cab, and then there were policemen, and Mac couldn't speak, could only stare dumbly, and then there was an ambulance and a hospital and a shot of something in his arm, and then there was darkness.

———•———

He swam up out of the murk into the light dropping from a half-open venetian blind. He moved his eyes to the left, and they fell on the shelf of medical books by his bed.

"Hey."

Mac turned his eyes toward the sound, and they fell on his anatomy instructor, who was also his friend, sitting by his bed on a chair turned around, arms resting on the chair back.

"You look like hell."

Mac stared stupidly, still swimming beneath the tranquilizer. "I killed a guy, Jake," he mumbled softly.

"They said it was an accident. A knot slipped or something."

Mac closed his eyes against the pain of the memory. "Who said?"

"The guy that brought you home and called me. He left an envelope."

Mac looked to where Jake was pointing and saw a plain envelope, bulging against the rubber band that surrounded it.

"There's gonna be a hearing. He says you'll have no problem. The papers are probably in the envelope."

———•———

Jake idly pushed a few vegetables back and forth on his plate, not looking at Ferrin.

"I sat with him outside a committee room at the county courthouse, waiting for him to be called to tell his side. He was going to have an attorney with him."

"An attorney? At a grand jury hearing?" asked Ferrin.

The psychiatrist's knowledge of procedure surprised Jake. "No, that's not allowed. This was to be only a preliminary courtesy meeting."

"Why?"

"Good question."

———◆———

"Don't like this company-appointed lawyer business," Jake said to Mac. "Who the hell's he representing, you or the company?"

Mac, who had been silent for most of the morning, looked up suddenly. "I'm going to tell them the truth. Everything."

"You're innocent, Mac. Why make more trouble for yourself? These guys look like hardball players."

"I killed him, Jake."

"It was an accident. Or at least it was as far as you're concerned. How could you know they meant it that way?"

"I knew. And I knew before it happened."

"What?" That shook Jake, and he couldn't conceal it. "I don't believe it."

"I must have. All the signs were there. Union guys don't scare so easy. Danocek's an evil scumbag. I knew that, and so did everybody else. And five grand for a little joke?" He looked at Jake.

"I think the guilt has you all twisted, friend. If you keep this up, you'll have yourself thinking you aimed the beams on his head."

"I'm going to tell them the truth. . . ." Jake felt the conviction in Mac's voice. "Let them sort it out."

Jake's protest was cut off as the committee room's doors opened. He and Mac stared as the assistant DA strode out, followed close at heel by three union representatives, who were red-faced and angry, shouting in his ear. The ADA held up his hand absently, flicked it back and forth in a dismissive motion, and kept up his stride. As they disappeared down the hall, company president Ed Thornton walked casually out of the room, amid a group of immaculately well-dressed attorneys. He was looking at the floor but cast his eyes upward from beneath hooded brows, straight at Charlie Danocek standing at the opposite end of the hallway. The brief moment ended, and the group disappeared down the main circular staircase.

Danocek walked toward Jake and Mac and stopped directly in front of them. "It's all over, Graham. You can go home."

Mac stared, dumbfounded. "What the hell are you talking about, Charlie?"

"The ADA said there's not enough there to bring charges. Union guys couldn't convince him it wasn't a coincidence. Says going to the grand jury would be an embarrassment."

Jake brightened and grabbed Mac's shoulders. "That's terrific! What a break!"

Mac continued to stare at Danocek, who said, "S'matter, kid? Get up, go home, go be a doctor."

Mac wouldn't let Danocek's eyes go. "How did you know, Charlie?"

"How'd I know what?"

"You weren't in there. You didn't hear. How'd you know what they decided?"

A cold cloud came over Danocek's face. "Look, Graham, don't fuck with me. Go home." And he walked away.

Jake nudged Mac's elbow. "C'mon, let's get the hell out of here. It's over."

CHAPTER 7

"But it was far from over," said Jake, who had resumed eating and was forking the last mouthful from his plate.

Ferrin had touched virtually nothing of his own meal. He stared transfixed as Jake, delighted by this rapt attention, recounted the tale. "How so?" Ferrin asked without taking his eyes off Jake.

"Mac disappeared. Ran away. It was months before I heard anything at all about him, and then it was bits and pieces of pretty sordid stuff. In and out of jail on petty offenses, minor drug dealing, that sort of thing. He'd left the envelope with the five thousand. Never touched it. I kept it in my office. Then one day about a year after he left, I got a call from him. He needed the money, and he sounded desperate.

"I met him at a bar in one of the seedier neighborhoods in town. I hardly recognized him. He was dirty, smelly, dressed like a bum. He'd grown a beard, and there was a wild look in his eyes. He had a contusion over his left eye and several lacerations on his lower lip.

"I hadn't seen him in over a year, and he never even said hello. Just asked where his money was. I took out the envelope, he grabbed it, then he turned and walked away. Say, aren't you gonna eat?"

Ferrin reached for a pack of cigarettes in his jacket. "No, no. Not really hungry, actually. What happened then?"

Jake took a sip of wine. "That was the last I heard from him until about six months ago. I got a call from a police station in a little town not too far from the medical school. They had Mac in lockup, and he had asked for me instead of a lawyer. I drove half the night and got there about four in the morning. The desk sergeant told me that Mac had beaten a pimp half to death. The pimp's lawyer was screaming for justice, and an arraignment was scheduled for nine that morning. The pimp was in jail, too.

"They took me to see Mac. He looked even worse than before. When he saw me he started crying, bawling, like a little kid. It was my first experience with someone who'd reached rock bottom. There was just no more rope left.

"When he'd calmed down, he told me about the fight, and it sounded like a pretty good case for self-defense. I spoke to the lawyer, and when the DA showed up we proposed that everybody just walk. That was fine with him, and I took Mac home."

"Where is he now?" asked Ferrin, holding a gold lighter to his cigarette.

"He's got his own place. He went into therapy, and I guess his intelligence got the better of him. I got him a job as a physician's assistant. Hell, he's better than half the doctors I work with. He's putting his life back together and doing a damned good job of it.

"But he still has nightmares, he's still lonely, still finding it difficult to connect with other human beings." Jake paused to let it all sink in, hoping that Ferrin would be intrigued.

Ferrin took a long, slow inhale of his cigarette, looked at Jake, and asked, "Do you think he knew?"

"Knew? Knew what?"

"Do you think Mac knew that he was going to kill the union organizer?"

Jake stared at Ferrin, unprepared for that particular question. "I . . . I don't really know. I always just assumed he didn't. Why, is it important?"

Ferrin ground out the cigarette. "Not necessarily."

"So what do you think?"

"About what?"

"C'mon, Brix: about putting your patient and Mac together?"

Ferrin sat back in his seat and tucked his chin into his neck, shaking his head slowly.

"What's the problem?"

Ferrin grew thoughtful. "It's a hell of a responsibility to do something like that. Is Mac still in therapy?"

"No, that ended. He was one step ahead of the therapist anyway and felt he'd do better to go solo."

"That's a bit of a complication, then. Look, Jake, I appreciate what you're trying to do, and Lord knows it would probably do my patient a world of good, but I don't think so. Please don't be offended."

"I don't offend easily, doctor. For example, you keep referring to me as a GP, and I'm an internist."

This seemed to upset Ferrin's very British sense of protocol. "I am sorry, Jake," he said. "I didn't mean—"

"Look," said Jake, disappointed and unwilling to give up, capitalizing on Ferrin's momentary discomfort. "Will you at least think about it? It doesn't have to be elaborate. Let's just introduce them and let it go. My wife and I see Mac on a more or less constant basis; I'll keep my eye on things."

Ferrin pondered this for a few seconds. "Yes, I'll think about it." The capitulation, however noncommittal, seemed to ease his embarrassment slightly. "I promise."

CHAPTER 8

Pamela swung her legs out over the side of the couch and sat up slowly. Elbows on knees, she dropped her head into her hands for a few moments, rubbing her temples and then the back of her neck. She stared at the floor.

"I want to prescribe something for you," said Dr. Ferrin.

Pamela looked up through half-closed eyes, wishing she were asleep, or could fall asleep, or do anything other than sit here in the afterglow of her latest romp with the demons. She grasped at this conversation as a welcome diversion from her own thoughts. "Like what?"

Ferrin got up from the leather wing chair and walked around his desk, taking a seat in his session-is-over-now chair behind it. He pulled out a prescription pad and began writing. "It's a very mild sedative called Xanax, barely noticeable but very effective."

Pamela was surprised. Central nervous system depressants of any strength hardly meshed with police work. "Do I really need it?"

"Most of the time, no," Ferrin said as he completed the slip and tore it off the pad. "But we're getting to the point where you need to start thinking about involving yourself more in social situations, and those will be stressful at first. Think of these as 'dating pills.' "

The subtext was not lost on her, nor was the vague anxiety that accompanied even thinking about dating. A response was appropriate, but Pamela was not about to get into a conversation over the relative merits of sleeping with a man rather than with her fantasies, not face to face with Ferrin, anyway, not with her session officially over. She reached for the prescription slip, but Ferrin did not hold it out.

"So what good am I going to be floating around on downs when I'm supposed to be sociable?"

Ferrin smiled indulgently. "You'll hardly notice them at all."

"Then why take them?" She knew she was being difficult, but her natural intelligence always got the better of her. Failures of logic were intolerable and had to be dealt with at all costs. And even though Ferrin had spent most of their first half-dozen sessions letting her know that overintellectualization was a smoke screen and had to stop, he was also a sucker for logic and knew better than to condescend to Pamela in these situations.

"Essentially, if you're sitting on the edge deciding whether to fall over or not, these will tend to push you back to safety."

He was still holding the slip back, and by now Pamela had let her hand drop.

"You're going to need a checkup first. The drug has one or two interaction precautions, rare ones, but I'd feel better if we did a bit of a look-you-over and a blood analysis."

"Is all that necessary?"

"No . . . if you happen to know offhand whether you've got elevated liver enzymes."

"But I get an annual physical through the department. They know I have a liver, don't they?" Pamela hated physicals, especially from male doctors, and in her first year with the department she had located the only female doctor approved by the department for police physicals. But Pamela figured the ugly dyke must have had it in for good-looking women or was just in a bad mood, because she'd had Pamela in tears by the time she'd finished with her poking and prodding. "Is all this necessary?" Pamela had asked.

Hard glare. "You catch the bad guys and let me be the doctor, okay?"

And last time, with the physician Captain Grant had recommended, she was so anxious she couldn't pee and had to carry back her urine sample later in the day.

"They don't know what to look for, and I doubt you want to tell them." The fact of Pamela's therapy was a private matter between herself, Grant, and the insurance carrier, the last of which occasionally made certain exceptions for the captain, who coincidentally sat on the committee that selected insurance providers.

Ferrin could sense Pamela's anxiety (as he could most things about her by now) and sought to allay it. "The physical part's only blood pressure and the like. What we really need is the blood sample." Pamela seemed to relax as he went on. "I've got a friend, a GP—I mean an internist—in town. I've told him a little about you." At Pamela's startled glance he added quickly, "A very little. Don't worry, he sees a lot of my patients. He's a very nice chap, most sympathetic. You'll like him, I promise."

So long as he doesn't touch me. Or at least not too much. "Okay. What's his name?"

"Jake Nostrand. Here's his card, and I'll start you off on some physician's samples as soon as we get the results."

All I need is for Captain Grant to think I'm on downs, thought Pamela. *Christ, I thought all of this was supposed to be making me better.*

———•———

"So lemme ask you something," she said, looking over the diplomas on the wall, trying to alleviate her tension as he wrapped the cuff around her arm. "How come a guy who goes to Harvard works as a sawbones in a one-horse dorp like this?"

He smiled, taking no offense, squeezing the bulb a few times until the cuff gripped her arm. "How come the class valedictorian becomes a cop in the same dorp?" He laid the stethoscope on the skin below her elbow and eased off slightly on the valve.

"Touché," answered Pamela, touched by his easy manner

and relieved that Ferrin had told him very little—and only the good stuff.

"Actually," Jake went on, "all I ever wanted to do was be a doctor here, and not a specialist, either. I love the work, and I was born here, so . . ." Helpless shrug of the shoulders as he opened the valve fully, letting the remaining air hiss out. "So what's your excuse?"

Pamela was warming up to him, but nowhere near sharing anything of note. "Long story, actually," leaving it at that and hoping he wouldn't press it.

He took her hand. "Open." She flattened her fingers, and he laid the round, metal end of the stethoscope in her palm. "Close," he commanded, and she wrapped her fingers around the cool metal, the rubber tubes and earpiece dangling freely.

"This something new?" she asked him. He ignored her for the moment and stepped around to her back, where he laid his hand on her skin and began rhythmically rapping with his knuckles, head bent close to listen.

"Secret Malaysian palm medicine." He came back around to her front. "Open," he said crisply, and she let her fingers relax. Jake picked up the stethoscope, stuck the ends in his ears, and without warning reached inside Pamela's open collar and laid the metal against her bare skin. She gasped involuntarily, expecting a freezing sensation, but felt only a gentle warmth.

"You sly devil!" She smiled in amusement. "I bet you have a lot of kids as patients."

Jake smiled back. "I do, but it's the adults that're the worst when it comes to cold 'scopes. Take a deep breath." Conversation ceased as he listened. "Speaking of children, lemme ask you something," he said. "I do a few turns a month in the pediatrics ward at County General. The worst that's the matter with a lot of them is that they're bored out of their skulls."

"And?"

"And, I bet they'd get a kick out of a good-looking lady cop. Any chance of a visit? Don't you guys have some schoolkid presentations, 'cross at the green, don't take candy from strangers,' or something like that?"

Pamela was flattered at the invitation and surprised at how much she wanted to accommodate this charming and modest doctor, a Harvard M.D., who simply liked to practice family medicine. "I imagine we could come up with something."

"Terrific!" He seemed genuinely delighted. "I'll have one of the staff give you a call to set it up. You can button up now, we're done."

Pamela looked at him, puzzled. "Aren't you supposed to draw some blood?"

Jake slapped his forehead. "Oh, hell, I almost forgot. Glad you reminded me." He fished in his venipuncture kit for the necessary tourniquet, vials, syringe and related paraphernalia.

"So who can I expect will call, just so I recognize the message?"

"Name's Mackenzie Graham. Goes by Mac. You'll like him a lot."

CHAPTER 9

An earthquake, that would do the trick. A nice little 6.5 or thereabouts. Not enough to kill too many people, but sufficient to knock down power lines, buckle a few streets, break lots of windows—that sort of thing.

Pamela took the tissues out from under her arms and rolled the deodorant carefully just in the middle of each armpit, then raised her hands high and walked around, letting the breeze dry the liquid.

Hurricane would be good. That would be good. Bit of flooding, lot of dangerous lightning, lots to do, what with boarding the place up and such.

She walked back to the mirror, arms still raised, and looked for telltale white spots. She grabbed a towel and swiped at a couple that weren't there.

Industrial explosion! Perfect! Panic in the streets; investigate immediately before the evidence grows feet; general call for available cops, wherever they may be.

She changed her bra for the third time. Great tits indeed, but no sense sticking them in his face all night. Go with a looser one. Walk away from the mirror, then turn quickly, catch yourself by accident. *Damn, too flabby now.* She put the first one back on, then changed it again and resolutely pulled on the green blouse with small pink flowers.

Her list of disasters depleted, Pamela sat down and slumped in the chair. Unless she set the apartment on fire—a concept whose attractiveness was increasing by the minute—she really was going out to dinner with Mackenzie Graham.

She eyed the bottle of pills Ferrin had given her the week before. Couldn't have come at a better time.

"I do not want you depending on these," he had admonished her sternly. "If you know you're going to be in a situation that makes you nervous, take one a half hour or so beforehand. At no other times."

Right. Like she had control over when things happened to her.

She hadn't tried one yet, but like the net below a tightrope walker, it was nice to know it was there. She dropped the little bottle in her purse and went back to worrying about how she looked when she chewed, whether she would spill wine when she drank, what she would do if, God forbid, they ate Italian and she got a spot of sauce on her blouse—oh God, what if it were right on her chest, what would she do, start swiping at it with a wetted napkin . . . ?

"Stop!" she yelled out loud as she banged both fists on the countertop.

The doorbell rang.

She thought of the icy calm that was supposed to fall like a shroud over the boxer when the bell finally rings after a year of training, the cessation of tremors in the bullfighter's hands as the caged beast is released into the arena. She could barely move her legs and thought her earrings would fall out from the vibration in her shoulders. Then she was at the door.

"Hi." Smile.

"Hi yourself." Smile.

It suddenly occurred to Pamela that maybe this person at her door was every bit as nervous as she was. He had hardly been Cary Grant at the hospital, which was important, because as far as Pamela was concerned, nonthreatening was the greatest compliment she could pay a man at this particular point in her emotional development. Her street cop's savvy told her that Mac's awkward advance had been a setup by the good Dr.

Nostrand, since Mac's behavior was clearly not entirely self-directed.

No matter. He had been sweet, deferential, polite, and, well, he had been a *gentleman*, a term Pamela never thought she would use in a complimentary fashion, but that was what had made her agree to this outing. Not bad looking, either, but her practiced eye had some trouble categorizing his physical features. Just shy of a full six feet, but looking taller; his cheeks and the skin beneath his chin slightly convex, as though hastily filled out from a longer, gaunt state. Not unlike a convict recently sprung, although that comparison didn't occur to Pamela, taken as she was by Mac's eyes. They were dark brown almost to the point of black, sunken deeper than was truly compatible with the rest of his face, as though they had evolved that way in later life under the force of events rather than genetics. Now, although their intensity had been replaced with resolve, they still betrayed great strength of will, despite an occasional furtive, flickering glance at nothing at all.

He was intelligent as well, and she'd felt a bit silly at the hospital affecting the singsong, "Romper Room" vocal style appropriate for addressing little kids, but he had given no hint of derision, and she had eventually relaxed and found herself enjoying her performance and his enjoyment of it as well.

That was then. Now, she faced him across the doorway and it dawned on her that for the next three or four hours her life was out of her control. Barring the afore-contemplated menu of natural disasters, she was fated to close proximity with a stranger, with no graceful way out. Conversation was not her strong point, except with other cops. Charming repartee, yes, but Ferrin had succeeded in convincing her that her rapierlike wit was a cover-up, so now even this one social skill was denied her, and her arsenal of remaining psychic weaponry was as outdated as dueling pistols.

And it was not clear that Mac was going to be able to hold up his end of the kind of conversation that ensured that nothing really got said, which was the only kind of conversation Pamela was ready for. The central fact of her life right now was the balloon in her stomach that threatened to inflate at any given moment with anxiety or unnamed dread and expand until it took over everything. Great dinner chatter with a first-time gentleman caller.

Ferrin had been vociferous on this point. "The problem with the last two decades was that people thought honesty meant saying whatever happened to pop into their head. More people's feelings got sacrificed to this self-indulgence than we can imagine. If you tell you're in therapy, he'll look underneath every sentence you utter. Wait. Wait until he gets to know you without the clutter of trying to second-guess your motivations. Then it won't make a difference." He had then tried to soften the moment with an attempt at levity: "Besides, if he doesn't like you and you never see him again, you'll be sorry you mentioned it." The joke didn't work because the thought had already occurred to her.

So the cop and the physician's assistant were going out to dinner, a goodly portion of which would be spent groping for some commonality. Gunshot wounds were a possibility.

"You look different out of uniform," he ventured with a shy smile.

"You too." *Wrong bra, dammit, I knew it.* She drew her shoulders back imperceptibly as she stepped aside to let him in. "Not too flattering. Occupational hazard."

"Actually, I'd never realized how sexy police blues could be."

At that she shot her shoulders forward and bent her stomach slightly, surely removing a good six inches and two cup grades from her bustline, which now hung in space between them like an unspoken challenge. *But if I turn, he'll be looking at my ass, of which I am mightily proud, but why didn't I wear a loose skirt, and* STOP! she yelled to herself again.

"Well, thanks," she said, blushing. It then occurred to her that she had been wearing her bulletproof vest during her presentation, so how could he have found the uniform sexy when he hadn't even gotten a decent eyeful? Hair? No: tied up under her cap as usual. *Could only have been my ass.*

"This is a beautiful place," he said as he surveyed the room. "I don't mean this the way it's going to sound, but I somehow didn't expect it to be so . . . feminine."

"You were expecting maybe a gun collection?" *Too witty. Back off.*

He laughed easily, though, and said, "In some sense, I suppose so. Such are the stereotypes we're brought up on. Is this your father?"

Whoops. "Yeah, shouldn't we be going?"

The abruptness caught him off guard, but he recovered well. "Sure. Hope you like Italian," he said, reaching for her jacket and helping her on with it.

"Love it." *Oh God.*

———●———

Pamela's demons started circling toward the end of dinner. She and Mac had, as was obvious to them both, danced around their respective pasts in a herculean effort at small talk. Mac learned that Pamela's father had been killed in the line of duty, Pamela learned that Mac had left medical school because of "some problems related to money," but each of them was sufficiently sensitized to suppress curiosity over details. *Remarkable*, thought Mac, *how those who suffer most are most considerate.*

But the demons had held back only while there was time enough left to not consider the après-dinner options. Pamela was now torn between ordering dessert, which she didn't want but would buy her another twenty minutes, and declining. She went for the raspberries, plain. Pick them one at a time, space them right, and they could be here until morning.

Then the berries were gone and the demons were growing impatient for their turn at bat. She ordered another cappuccino, decaf this time (no sense fighting the Xanax she'd taken in the bathroom). So how would this go: *How 'bout a little nightcap? Got time for a glass of wine? Could you use a cup of coffee? I've-had-a-very-nice-time-good-night (slam)?*

The demon stared up at her out of the empty cappuccino cup. *Tick-tock.* Mac's change had come back (he'd paid with cash), and the tip was inside the vinyl American Express folder. His napkin was folded up and on the table. So was hers. The waiter had thanked them (twice).

"Shall we?" Mac asked, rising.

She pushed back her chair and stood up. The waiter, motivated more by turnover than manners, helped her on with her jacket. Then she was walking, then out the door, and somehow in his car. "Why not have a look at my place?" he asked casually. "Besides, I fix a better cappuccino than they do. How does that sound?"

Sounds fucking terrible is how it sounds. "Sounds good."

It was about twenty minutes away, only a mile from her own apartment. She felt the pressure in her chest mount as they drove along in relative silence. *This would be so much easier if I didn't like the guy.* Then she could tell him to bugger off and never see him again, but Mac had been charming and friendly, and it had really been fun, somehow.

As they came to a T in the road and turned right to his place instead of left to hers, the pressure reached her throat and knees at the same time. A distant keening began in her head, and the dance of streetlights as they reflected off the surfaces of the car went from patterned to random, then back to more coordinated, but this time the dance had a purpose, dark and forbidding.

Pamela raised her hand to rest it on the armrest in the door, but it felt removed, detached, and she watched it as if it were a small animal with a mind of its own. The rhythm of the tires over the cracks in the street became a chant, a dirge, and the very air in the car became diabolical. The need to get away, to get out, started and grew quickly. She could feel the sharp edge of panic at the periphery of her awareness and didn't trust herself to speak.

"How long have you lived here, Pam?"

What? "What?"

"Just curious how long you've been around. Were you born here?"

This can't be happening. I can't do this. "Yes. Listen, would you mind very much taking me home?"

Missing only a beat, Mac said, "Sure, no problem."

Even through her turmoil Pamela could tell that something more was called for here. You didn't just throw something like that into the air and let it hang there. "I really had a very nice time. . . ." *Is that enough?* Why had she ended the sentence on an upward inflection instead of with the declaratory finality that would have spared her further effort? The distant keening was in danger of becoming a howling and drowning out further conversation. "I'm glad you asked me."

"I enjoyed it, too."

Good, now she was free, could relax, take it easy. Mac was a gentleman after all, wouldn't press her. Back to normal. Somebody else's fingers on her right hand drummed softly, and she was certain they were about to leap up and go for her throat. The trees reached out and grabbed at her as Mac swung the car around and headed in the opposite direction. The howling was a tornado now, and she hoped that Mac wasn't saying anything because there was no hearing him through this.

They pulled up in front of her building, and she drew herself together. "Thanks so much, Mac. You don't have to see me in."

"You sure? I don't mind."

"Not necessary. Hey, I'm a cop, remember?" Big smile.

"You know, I almost forgot that."

Yes, well, this is just great, but . . . "Well, good night."

"Good night." She started to walk away. "Pamela, can I call you again?"

"Oh, yes." Easy, now. "I mean, yes, I wish you would." *I really do, too, but can we please end this now?*

"Great. Sleep tight."

"You too, Mac," she called over her shoulder, and hurried on.

———◆———

"Take it slow, Pamela, take a few deep breaths. I'm not going anywhere."

She held the phone away and tried to stop the choking, then brought the mouthpiece back. Then, between sobs, "It was horrible. It was the worst thing that ever happened to me. I'm still a mess, I can't feel my own legs, I feel like I'm going to get crushed and disappear . . ."

"You won't disappear, I promise. I *promise,* Pamela. This is a normal response, there's nothing surprising about it. It'll get easier next time."

"Next time? Are you crazy? No next time, not ever. I've had it. This was insane, Doc, I swear to God I thought I was losing my mind. I still do. I've been home over two hours and I'm still spinning. Should I take another pill?"

"Try not to. Trust me, Pamela, ride it out and it'll be fine. None of this is unusual, believe me."

"How could you have known and not warned me?" she asked angrily.

"You wouldn't have gone. You wouldn't ever go."

"You're damned right," she snuffled, knowing that her anger at Ferrin was just a displacement of her own self-loathing. "And I'm never going again."

"Okay, it's not important now."

"Will you stay on the phone with me for a little while?" It had taken her twenty minutes to get him on the phone in the first place. What the hell could the heartless sonofabitch have been doing at this hour?

"Of course, Pamela. I'm here."

My prince. My anchor. "Wait'll the insurance company gets *this* bill," she joked weakly through her tears.

"It's just between you and me, Pamela," Ferrin replied gently, settling in for what he knew would be a long night.

CHAPTER 10

Heard you were out yesterday, Jacoby. Anything serious?"

Captain Grant felt she had a personal stake in this young police officer. She actually hadn't liked Wild Bill Jacoby very much. Not at all, if truth be known, which it wasn't to most people who knew her. He was a good enough cop, but Amanda felt his reputation for bravery wasn't entirely deserved, although Lord knew he did his best to cultivate it. What had bothered her the most had been his attitude toward Pamela.

The young girl had been a favorite around the precinct house, full of questions and in almost reverential awe of policemen in general and her father in particular. Amanda knew that Pamela's view of Wild Bill was inflated, but what little girl saw her father any other way, especially a big man, and a cop, and somewhat of a local legend?

Jacoby seemed to like the adulation, but there was an uncomfortable edge to his treatment of Pamela. More like a dog than a daughter. He demanded loyalty but seemed to have no capacity to share it.

Shortly after Amanda got her gold shield, Lieutenant Ted Wilanowski parlayed six months of intensive investigation into one of the largest drug busts in the county's history. He had worked in tandem with the DEA, the FBI and a state-level enforcement agency, but he was generally credited with masterminding the operation, using information from street informers he had been cultivating for years.

The afternoon of the bust, Pamela came running into the station house, portable scanner in hand, and raced past the desk sergeant directly into the detectives' bullpen, where Wilanowski sat surrounded by a horde of officers.

"Teddy, Teddy, is it true?" she asked breathlessly, eyes bright and wide, blasting right through the crowd until she was face to face with him. "Did you nail 'em? Are the feds gonna let you have the collar?" All of fourteen years old and tossing off lingo like a veteran.

Teddy laughed for the first time that day. Not until that very moment had the significance of his achievement truly dawned on him. "Hell, yes, it's true, and hell, yes, I get the collar!" he cried, picking her up and planting a kiss on her forehead. It was a wonderful moment for her.

Until Jacoby, who had been sitting in a silent, jealous funk for the past half hour, picked that moment to ask, "What are you doing here?" in a tone strongly reminiscent of his interrogation style, which, like that of most closet bullies, was not a pleasant one.

Pamela had no idea what was coming. "Hi, Daddy! Isn't it terrific? Isn't it great—"

"Did you cut a class?" He looked at his watch. "It's only one o'clock, did you cut a class?"

"Daddy . . . ?" Of course she cut the class. She cut class whenever something big came over the scanner. She was a straight-A student, president of the Honor Society, a cheerleader, the whole damned school administration knew her special passion and winked at it, she was a shoo-in for the college of her choice, so what in the hell was he on her about?

"Get out of here," he snarled. "Get back to school and I'll deal with you later."

There are few things more delicate than the psyche of a fourteen-year-old girl. It is a fragile structure at best. The bullpen turned into an arena, an amphitheater, seating thousands in tier upon tier, all looking at her, naked in the spotlight of her humiliation. To stand still was agony, to turn and leave ten times more so.

Wilanowski put his hand on Pamela's shoulder and said softly, "C'mon, kid, Pop's right. I'll drive you back to—"

"Get your hands off her," Jacoby spat.

"Hey, c'mon, Bill, I'm just gonna—"

"She ran here, she can damn well run back. I said take your hands off her."

Wilanowski raised his hands in the air and looked at Pamela helplessly. She never remembered afterward how she got out of the station house. She never came back until the day her father was killed.

And now here she was, herself a cop, still in need of someone else's solicitous protection.

"No, not too serious," Pamela replied absentmindedly, appreciative of Captain Grant's concern but not wishing to go into it.

Amanda fumbled around in her jacket pocket. "Have you got a quarter?"

"Huh?" said Pamela. "Uh, hang on, I think so." She opened her desk drawer and reached for some coins in the paper-clip receptacle.

"Good, I'll let you buy me a cup of coffee," said Amanda, turning to walk out toward the vending machine.

Pamela followed, not unmindful that Captain Grant's coffee typically came from the pot kept brewing especially for her and served by the desk jockey right outside her office. Talking to the captain was like talking to Ferrin, except that it was comfortable, painless and about forty other varieties of preferable.

"I had a date two nights ago," Pamela said when they were seated by themselves in the patrolmen's ready room.

Amanda seemed genuinely pleased. "Well, that's wonderful. I'm really glad." Then, in a conspiratorial, somewhat girlish whisper, accompanied by a sidelong glance, "How'd it go?"

Pamela felt the tears before she could stop them. She swiped at her eye with the back of one hand. "It was awful," she said through a forced but mostly failed smile.

Amanda suppressed the desire to put a hand on Pamela's shoulder, to wipe her face or offer some other supportive gesture. Pamela's weepy histrionics were a bad model for women police officers, and being mothered by the captain would not help. "Why? What could have been so bad?" She sat upright and added, "Any trouble?"

"No, no, nothing like that. Jesus, are you kidding? That would have been a relief, then I could have decked the creep."

They both laughed as Amanda prompted, "So, what was so terrible?"

Pamela calmed a little bit after their shared joke. She had been in the station house the day of Amanda's rite of passage via Dennis Murdoch, and she hadn't stopped talking about it long after Amanda had nearly forgotten it.

"He was a nice guy, a really nice guy, and we were getting along just fine. . . ." The tears started again, and she dropped her head. "And then on the way to his apartment I got this anxiety attack. It was so awful . . ."

She was unable to continue, and Amanda didn't press it, letting Pamela find her own time. "Anyway, I was up all night, and I think I was seeing things or something, but I couldn't sleep." In fact, she'd tried to turn off the light, but as soon as the bulb darkened, the room had exploded in swirling lights, so she'd switched the lamp back on. "I called my shrink and I guess he talked to me for a long time and then I felt better only soon it was light outside and I still hadn't slept so I bagged it." She looked up at Amanda and added, "I think I have a lot of sick days left."

Amanda smiled at this concern for procedure. "The last time I had a date like that was when some bozo practically tried to rape me."

Pamela was startled by Amanda's candor. "Wow. Did you teach him a lesson?" she asked expectantly.

"In a manner of speaking: I married the creep."

Pamela's eyes grew wide, and then she threw back her head as they both laughed.

"So now what?" asked Amanda. "Going to give up?" It was a loaded question.

Pamela looked at her thoughtfully, then said, "No. I'm not going to give up," making the decision even as she announced it.

Amanda withheld the obligatory "Atta girl" and merely pursed her lips slightly, looking directly at Pamela, the subliminal approval coming across more strongly than any words could have conveyed. "So," she said as she started to rise. "Better luck next time."

Pamela stared after Amanda as she walked away, full of admiration for her easy grace and the time she took to care. "Hey, thanks, Captain." Amanda waved her hand without looking back.

———•———

Excerpt from transcript of Pamela Jacoby clinical therapy session 49, June 16, 4:00 P.M., analyst Brixton T. Ferrin, M.D., Ph.D.

Not so hot, huh?
That's one way of putting it.

Tell me.
I couldn't believe it when he actually called me after that first disaster. The guy must be a professional masochist.

Maybe he just liked you. Maybe to him it wasn't such a disaster. After all, all that happened was you went home a little early.
Maybe. Anyway, he called me and I agreed to go out with him again.

And . . .?
The rest, as they say, is history. Same damned thing happened.

Did you take a pill?
Yeah. I wonder what the hell it would have been like if I hadn't.

Probably not appreciably different.
> Damned if I want to find out. Doctor, I can't take
> much more of this.

Yes, you can.
> I can't. Can you give me something stronger?

I could, but sleepwalking through your date on Stelazine
could hardly be termed a triumph.
> [Silence.]

Trust me on this, Pamela. We'll get through it together.
> Yeah, right. You go out with him next time.

That sharp tongue again.
> Sorry. All right. You know I trust you.

Atta girl.

CHAPTER 11

Variation on a theme of recurring tragedy: a double date this time.

With Dr. Nostrand and his wife, no less.

Pamela was used to thinking fast. Like a drug addict or closet bulimic, her ability to create instant excuses for any situation had been honed to a reflex. She was so good she sometimes believed herself. While it always made her feel bad to lie to people she cared for, the intellectual victory of successful dissembling usually made up for it. And she didn't care for that many people.

She had been at the top of her form when Mac had called.

Mac: "Thought we'd take in a movie and dinner with Jake and Jennifer Nostrand."

Pamela, with lightning-fast thought and effortless creativity: "Sure, sounds good."

Why was he still trying? He couldn't be that horny, as evidenced by his tolerance toward her behavior, which all else aside ranked close to ten on the Queen Victoria scale. They'd given up all pretext of having sex, although it was in the air, like a facial disfigurement or an indiscreet passing of wind, palpable and painfully evident but never discussed, by mutual assent.

The thought had occurred to her that maybe Mac just liked her, enjoyed her company. She was an excellent conversationalist, which she had discovered in his presence. Maybe Ferrin didn't appreciate her wit, but Mac seemed to, and those countless thousands of hours spent alone reading an eclectic selection of books lent substance to her discourse, a light left undiscovered under the bushel of her day-to-day occupation.

But she largely dismissed this thought, the force of her subconscious slapping a lid on any delusions of self-worth. Having spent a good many years in the careful construction of a pitiable self-image, she was not about to let the part of her mind responsible for such things give up easily on all that work.

So she turned instead to the more satisfying worry about the implications of an evening with the Nostrands. Reducing the problem to its essentials left her, in true binary fashion, with two possibilities.

The primary issue could be one of personal interaction. Dealing with Mac one on one carried a galaxy of complications familiar to anyone undergoing psychoanalysis. The simplest head movement or snippet of a sentence or hand gesture was a candidate for microscopic examination of the most exacting sort, circling back to the immediately previous clues, multiplying logarithmically until neuronal gridlock forced a clearing of the slate and a restart.

This was tough enough with one other human being, but three? Mathematically this equated not to multiplication, but to raising to powers, an escalation of complexity too daunting to take seriously. ("Sure, sounds good." *Grab the reins, Pamela!*)

On the other hand, that analysis might miss the point totally. What if the problem was simply being alone, exposed, naked and defenseless, with just Mac, unable to amortize the vulnerability over a larger population? Was it not possible that she would find comfort in a crowd where she was only twenty-five percent of whatever was going on, instead of a full half? As an added bonus, the scene might be more easily manipulable to engineer a more graceful end to the evening that would avoid the inevitable question that hung between her and Mac.

Playing with this alternative, Pamela considered that the Nostrands and Mac were already close friends, which had actually been a bit of a surprise the first time that Mac had mentioned it. Moreover, Jake knew that Pamela had problems of some sort, although she was banking on Ferrin's sense of professionalism and integrity in withholding specifics. Of course, Jake was a physician and in theory was consulting on her case. Still not so bad: she was going out with Mac, not Jake, and surely Jake had said nothing to Mac, else why would he be dating her? But that aside, she was the outsider at the party, and the Nostrands had to know something was going on (or, more correctly, not going on). Wasn't that why Mac had arranged the get-together, to take the pressure off? Only, what kind of tactic was that, with her in the spotlight while three normal people gloated and relaxed their way through the evening at her expense . . . ?

Victory! She'd managed to concoct disaster at the end of every possible road and had worried herself into a froth before the evening even got under way.

Damn, she was good.

———•———

She hadn't had a better time that she could remember.

Jennifer Nostrand was fascinated with the concept of a female police officer and, with the same kind of candor that Pamela had noticed in Jake, peppered her with endless questions, never considering for a moment whether they were appropriate. Pamela found herself taken by this unselfconscious innocence and before she could stop herself was regaling the other three with anecdotes and relishing the spotlight.

"So this big yahoo stands behind me, reaches both arms around in front and puts his hands over mine while I'm holding the gun, and he says, 'You put that little doohickey up here right on the target and look down this little doohickey here, and squeeze—don't pull—the trigger,' and he squeezes my hand at the same time and gives me this big smile.

"And I say, 'Gee, Sergeant, what do I aim for?' and all these other cops are standing around smiling and laughing, so the big yahoo laughs, too, only he doesn't know that all these other guys already know me, and he says, 'Aim for the circle there on the right,' and I say, 'You mean where the bad guy's heart is supposed to be?' and he says, 'Yeah, where the bad guy's heart is supposed to be, sweetie, but you just try to keep them all on the paper.'

"So I say, 'Gosh, Sergeant, I'll sure try,' and he walks back behind the barrier. I reach for the crank and send the target back about another fifty feet, and his eyes get real wide, then I put down the police special and pick a forty-four Magnum off the rack, and he starts to look a little pale, then I take a two-hand stance and fire off all ten rounds within about an inch of each other in the circle.

"There's dead silence, right? The rest of the guys can hardly keep it in any longer, and with the straightest face you can imagine, I say, 'Ah, shit, Sarge, I'm sorry: I'll try to spread 'em out more next time.' "

She found their laughter immensely gratifying, oddly reminiscent of her fellow officers' that day at the range. She felt like they were on her side and was surprised at the degree to which she seemed to be opening up.

The waiter appeared with dessert menus, and Pamela was startled to hear herself say, "Hey Mac, I thought you told me you make a wicked cup of cappuccino?"

Mac looked up, surprised, then said, "I do. Why don't we head over to my place?"

Pamela, still vigilant and self-protective, creatively came to her own rescue. "That'd be fun, and then maybe Jake and Jennifer can drop me off afterwards."

"That's easy. Let's do it," said Jennifer.

There, now Pamela could relax, as the question of the parting arrangements had been solved.

They rose and headed for the door. As they neared it, a parking attendant came through it and toward them. Jake turned to speak to Mac at the same moment the attendant veered slightly, brushing Jake with his shoulder and slightly upsetting his balance. "Hey—" Jake began as he recovered his step.

The attendant turned slightly but kept walking. He was taller than Jake, taller even than Mac, and much more massive than both of them. Dark eyes looked out from under hooded lids, an effect complemented by a thin mustache and goatee. A gold earring with a Maltese cross hung from his left ear. "Hey what?" he threw over his shoulder with disdain, without breaking stride.

Jake, too smart to make anything of it, turned back toward the door.

"Hey, asshole," said Mac, facing the attendant, stopped and with his feet slightly apart, hands at his sides.

"C'mon, Mac," said Jake, resting his hand on Mac's arm, which felt like a lead pipe except for the bristling tension he could feel through the jacket. Mac stayed silent.

The attendant stopped and turned, slowly and with exaggerated drama. "Excuse me?"

Mac stared at him, unblinking, looking alert but very unafraid. "What part of 'asshole' didn't you understand?"

The attendant, incredulous of this display of bravado in the face of his *prima facie* physical superiority, and not unmindful of the two attractive women looking on with fear, started back toward them. He hesitated only slightly when he noticed Mac slip the shoe off his right foot. "I'm gonna fuck you up, scumbag."

"Wanna bet?" Mac's nonchalance was starting to have an effect on the attendant. He realized, as did Pamela and the Nostrands, that Mac was dangerous, although none of them knew exactly why at the moment. Only later would they realize that it was because Mac was completely unconcerned about getting hurt and equally indifferent to any long-term damage he might cause his adversary. Such a combination implied a ferocity of belligerence that could easily compensate for any technical shortcomings. And something about removing that shoe created doubts about those.

Jake was the first to realize that the attendant, not Mac, was the one in serious trouble. He stepped between them, which halted the attendant, whose relief was obvious though he tried to hide it. At that moment the owner of the restaurant appeared.

"What's going on here? Why's everybody standin' around? Billy, what're you lookin' at? Did you find the guy's car?"

Billy started to hand a set of keys to the owner, who didn't take them. "Give 'em to Mr. Anderson, not me. S'matter with you today? Table seven."

Billy cast a last murderous look at Mac, as if to congratulate him on his great fortune at being rescued, and started for the interior of the restaurant.

The owner turned back toward the foursome. "I'm sorry, the kid, sometimes he, ahh, I don't know . . ." His finger made a twirling motion toward his head. "You gotta problem with your foot, mister?"

"No," said Mac, slipping his foot back into the shoe. "No problem."

They turned to leave. "Good Lord, Mac," said Jake. "What was that all about?"

Mac shrugged. "Kid needed a lesson, 's all."

"What was with the shoe?" asked Pamela.

Mac turned to smile at her. "Didn't want to waste his teeth when I took out the rest of his face."

"What a perfect gentleman!" exclaimed Jennifer, giving them all a laugh and helping to relieve the tension. "Don't you carry a gun, Pamela?" she asked.

"Have to. Regulation. But if I'd'a pulled it out, I probably would have had to use it on Kung Fu over here," she said, pointing to Mac and setting off another round of laughter, "and then there wouldn't have been any cappuccino, which, in case anybody's interested, I still want."

———◆———

Driving up to Mac's house, even with Jake and Jennifer in the car behind, she could already feel the familiar stirring, a remote sexual longing mixed in with lurking terror, the two by now so frequently paired that distinguishing between them was becoming difficult. She needed a minute to get a grip on herself.

Once inside, she headed for Mac's bathroom, went in and turned on the light, looked at herself in the mirror, and spotted a small stain on her blouse. Fretting over how long it might have been there, she wetted a corner of a washcloth and began dabbing at it until it seemed to disappear. Now left with a conspicuous wet spot, she swiped at it with a dry towel, blew on it and waved her hand rapidly back and forth in an attempt to dry it, glad of something mindless and distracting to occupy herself

While that was going on, she went to the toilet as well, still blowing on the spot, got up, flushed, straightened out her skirt, poked at her hair, took one more look at the barely noticeable stain, opened the door and walked out not feeling any more relaxed than when she'd gone in.

"My turn," Jake said as he approached the door, cutting off any ability she might have had to go back and hide in the bathroom, which would have been awkward anyway. She walked stiffly back into the living room as the sound of hissing steam drifted in from the kitchen.

"Sit down, lady," Mac said as he entered, carrying a tray with four cups of expertly prepared cappuccino. "You're in for a treat." He set the tray down and picked up two large shakers the size of tin cans. "Cinnamon. Chocolate," he said, indicating each in turn.

"Very professional," said Jennifer. "I hope it tastes as good as it looks." She looked at Pamela and patted the cushion beside her, cutting off any hope of a retreat.

Pamela took the offered seat and hoped her discomfort didn't show. She started talking silently to herself in harsh tones. *Goddammit, I'm not going to screw up this evening. I'm not. Get a grip. Get a grip. Get a grip. . . .*

"You okay, Pam?" Mac asked with a smile. "It probably won't kill you."

She managed a smile back and feigned a plantation accent. "Ah declayuh, no man evuh cooked fuh me befowah," she said, fluttering her eyelashes.

Jake came back and sat down beside Pamela, effectively pinning her in place and rendering moot any possibility of escape. *Get a grip.* She looked at her cup but could see only a sea of boiling caffeine ready to incite her nerve endings. Mac's expectant eyes brooked no refusal, and she took a first tentative sip. It was good. Very good.

"Hey, buddy," said Pamela. "Do I detect a wee drop o' the grape?"

"Actually, my cappuccino tastes like shit, so I drown it in brandy."

Laughs all around, Pamela's mostly from relief. Nothing like a little alcohol to soothe the savage demon.

The talk turned to Jennifer, a lawyer and newly made partner in a mid-size firm. Pamela marveled at her poise and the kind of self-confidence that allowed this impressive credential to go unmentioned thus far this evening. They talked about Jake's practice, some recent interesting cases, Mac's progress at the hospital, the latest scandals in county government and other topics of no particular moment.

The longer the conversation went on, the more amazed Pamela became. This felt good. She sneaked a glance at Mac and wondered if she should push it or just let well enough alone for now and not take chances. Deciding to stay at this point would be uncomfortably obvious, anyway. Still, the thought at least carried less fear than it normally did.

Progress.

CHAPTER
12

The fingernails were a dead giveaway, the vital clue that cracked the case wide open. The world's greatest detective had scored yet another impressive triumph.

"Nice night, Annie?"

"What? Hey, Pam, how ya' doin'?"

"Great. Really good. Helluva night, was it?"

Annie del Gatto looked at her quizzically. "What're you talkin' about?"

"It's the fingernails, Annie."

Del Gatto looked down at her nails. "Yeah, so?"

"No polish. You always wear polish."

Slower and more drawn out this time: "Yeeaah, sooo?"

"So whenever a lady who wears polish doesn't wear polish, it's because nobody takes care of her nails when she's with somebody all night. There's no opportunity, and there's no means, so what good is motivation?"

Still holding her hands out in front of her, del Gatto cracked a big smile. "Hey, that's good, Jacoby. Damned good. What're you, buckin' for a gold shield?"

Pamela, pleased at del Gatto's good-natured reaction, held up her own well-manicured nails. "No, just some of that means and opportunity."

She envied Annie, who joked about her sexual exploits easily and apparently without a trainload of emotional baggage. She tried to picture Annie with her new beau, an assistant DA (Annie never dated cops—"Don't shit where you eat," she always said). She imagined them getting into bed without a lot of awkward preamble, with the lights on, kissing and talking for a while, fondling each other as the mood struck. She envisioned Annie's hands running over his body, maybe playfully avoiding the good parts before attacking them with a vengeance, him getting hard, both of them breathing heavier, and then coupling, smiling, maybe—did anybody ever smile while doing it? What a lovely thought. . . .

"Jacoby!" Someone was rapping knuckles on her head. Captain Grant. "You in there?"

"Oh . . . oh, yes, Captain, I'm sorry. I was just—"

"Never mind." Grant was already striding away, and Pamela ran to catch up. "Emley and Murdoch just nailed some creep knocking over a video store on Highway Twelve. Could be our little friend," she said, referring to a series of recent robberies of the cash-intensive video rental outfits in town. A lot of volume and transactions too small for credit cards added up to a tempting target for petty criminals. The sophisticated security systems were designed to protect the merchandise, not the till, as the hapless owners were just beginning to discover.

"Seems he did a bit more damage this time, too. Grab a car and let's go check it out."

Amanda sat in the front seat with Pamela and read the file on the previous robberies as they started the drive across town. When she was finished she settled back, turned to Pamela and asked, "So how've you been doing lately?"

Best to start off noncommittally and see what level she was asking on. "Not bad." No more than that. Not about to blurt it all out at the slightest provocation.

Amanda turned back to the windshield and stared out in silence.

"Better, in fact." C'mon, Captain, don't quit yet.

Amanda turned back. "How so?"

"Well," Pamela began, checking both rearview mirrors and

turning her head to look out the right rear window, so the captain would know she was keeping her mind on business. "Remember my first date with Mac Graham?"

Amanda smiled and replied, "How could I forget it?"

"Yeah, I know what you mean. It happened again, actually, but then we doubled once and it was nice. Really nice."

There was a time to dance and a time to shoot, and Amanda hadn't gotten to her captaincy by failing to distinguish between them. "So skip all the bullshit and tell me: Is he any good in the sack?"

Pamela nearly swerved off the road. "What? Captain!" she cried, but smiled in embarrassed amusement.

"Look, you've been living like a nun for so long, tell me that a little rumpy-bumpy isn't on your mind." They were fast approaching the video store, and there was little time. Amanda knew from long experience at interrogations, police performance appraisals and courtroom testimony that shock wore off quickly, leaving the substance of witnesses' recollection exposed and ready without the traditional useless preliminaries. Besides, this was fun: she'd never seen the silver-tongued Pamela at a loss for words.

Pamela's shock rapidly devolved into dismay as the truth of Amanda's words sank in. "Are you kidding? I get horny flossing my teeth."

Amanda's laughter lightened the atmosphere. "Nice guy, this Mac?"

"Oh, he's wonderful, Captain," Pamela gushed involuntarily. "He's about the nicest guy I ever met, he's smart as hell, he doesn't push. I don't know why he puts up with me."

"Maybe he just likes you," Amanda said, realizing the futility of those words even as she spoke them. The depths of Pamela's insecurity were not to be breached by mere logic, no matter how powerful the evidence.

"I'm sure he does," she said, not really believing it. "But for how long?"

"Maybe if you're lucky, he'll dump you before you get a chance to find out." A little harsh, but they were only a few blocks away.

Pamela, looking fragile and longing, said with a small choke in her voice, "What? I don't get it."

Sure you do. "Why don't you just let him like you, Pamela? Don't ask so many questions. There aren't any answers anyway." To Pamela's silence she added, "All the analysis is always done by the failures. It's chemistry, not mathematics. I'm more in love with my husband than the day we got married, and you know what? I don't really know why, and I don't really care. If I'd asked myself all those questions, I'd still be asking them and would have missed out on some great years."

As surprised as Amanda herself was by her spontaneous monologue, it was nothing compared to Pamela's amazement. Her embarrassment was acute, not so much at her captain's speech, but at the realization of its essential truth and her comparatively lame and self-generated predicament.

The moment was broken as the video store came into view, surrounded by flashing blue lights and yellow tape strung between orange traffic cones to keep the curious at bay.

Bobby Parks walked up as Pamela pulled the car into a waiting open space.

"Hi, Jacoby. I think this is the guy, Captain. Same MO, only a little rougher this time." He pointed to a shattered front window and a fallen cash-register station leaning partway out. "Got a little annoyed when he couldn't get the drawer open. Kid sitting over there with the ice pack took a swing at him."

"I'll never understand why people want to be heroes for a few dollars," said Amanda, shaking her head as she got out of the car. "Like he's supposed to risk his life for a handful of somebody else's money."

"Where's the guy?" Pamela asked.

"In Murdoch's car," answered Bobby, but Amanda was heading for the injured clerk.

"You all right, son?" she asked him.

The clerk looked like a high school part-timer, big, probably an athlete, soon to be a local hero. He looked up at Amanda without answering.

"This is Captain Grant," Bobby said to the boy. How many times had he explained to the uninitiated who this lady with no uniform was?

"Oh," said the boy. "You look like a lawyer."

"You trying to insult me, kid?"

He smiled. "No, ma'am. I'm okay. Banged my head trying to catch the register. I let it go when it headed for the window, and slipped."

"How'd we get the guy?" Amanda asked Bobby.

"When he was on the floor, Superman over here grabbed his ankle and knocked him down."

The clerk grinned at the left-handed compliment and looked at Amanda for approval.

C'mon, Captain, thought Pamela, *don't puncture his balloon just because you know he was stupid.*

Amanda stared at the boy for a second, then said, "You did good." The smile on the kid's face could have warmed a small planet. "So where is this creep?" she said, looking up.

They walked over to Murdoch's squad car, where the suspect sat in handcuffs. "Read him his rights?" she asked.

Murdoch's partner, Al Emley, answered, "Yes'm, did it twice."

Amanda leaned down to the open window. "Do you understand your rights?"

He was young and didn't have the look of a practiced criminal, although he wasn't about to be intimidated by this lady. He shifted his eyes to look at her with contempt, not even turning his head to her, then returned his eyes to their forward stare. Amanda grabbed a fistful of his hair and twisted it hard so that he had no choice, and when his face, contorted with sudden pain, was pointing toward hers, she squeezed a little harder and said, "I asked you a question."

"Yeah, yeah, I understand," he pleaded. Amanda gave it another second, then let him go, standing up and turning her back to him.

"By the book," she said to Murdoch and Emley.

"You got it, Captain," said Emley, not unintimidated himself.

As Grant and Parks stepped off to the side to confer, Murdoch wasted no time starting in. "Well, hello, little darlin'," he said to Pamela.

"Great to see you as always, Murdoch."

"S'matter, 'Dennis' not good enough for you, now that you're riding around with the captain?"

She resented the condescending allusion and said, "She might ride with you if you took a bath once in a while."

"Well, why don't you come over and give me one, baby? Eight o'clock all right with you?"

She felt a rising need to jab Murdoch a good one. "So happens I've got a date tonight, big shot."

"Ho, ho," Murdoch came back, buying some time to put his thoughts together. "Y'mean with that twerp I saw you riding around with last week?"

This was new. She didn't have time to respond before Murdoch continued, "What're you gonna do, hold hands?" he said with an obvious and deserved reference to her reputed but misunderstood celibacy.

Like a boxer who spied an opening, Pamela looked right at Murdoch, took a step forward and, within full hearing of his partner said, "No, asshole, I'm gonna take him home and jump his bones, and by morning he's gonna think he's seen God."

Murdoch looked like he'd been hit by a falling safe. To Pamela it was most gratifying to see his jaw hanging open and his hands where he'd left them, unable to move. Emley roared, bent nearly double with his hands on his thighs, shaking his head in delight.

As Pamela turned to go, she glanced at Amanda and Bobby, who had been standing on the other side of the car but had stopped talking as the verbal battle took shape. Amanda was staring at Pamela, eyebrows raised in surprise, an amused expression on her face. Pamela held her eyes briefly and smiled, answered in turn by a tilt of Amanda's head and a slight purse of her lips, which might or might not have signaled approval. Pamela treated Murdoch to a little extra wiggle as she walked away.

Murdoch was recovering and said to Emley, with surprising venom, "Fuck her. And fuck her boyfriend."

"C'mon, Dennis," said Emley, "it's no big deal. Why don't you lay off and forget about it?"

Murdoch was watching Pamela walk away, hatred in his eyes. "Fuck 'em both," he spat.

His back was to Amanda and Bobby, and he didn't know they were listening. Bobby turned to Amanda with a questioning look, but Amanda was at an equal loss and just shook her head slightly. When Murdoch turned around to get into the car, Amanda expected a look of shocked surprise when he spotted her. All she got was a long, hard, murderous stare, betraying feelings he had probably been bottling up since the day she had emasculated him so many years ago. Pamela's psychic bludgeoning was likely no less painful, albeit for a smaller audience.

Murdoch's look sent a small shiver through her, and she realized she had unconsciously taken a step toward Bobby.

CHAPTER
13

Pamela was having trouble remembering if there were special things you did to prepare for going to bed with someone. Was it supposed to be like an undercover sting operation, well planned and (she eyed the bathtub longingly) well rehearsed? Or was the idea to adopt an air of casualness and pretend the consummation was serendipitous?

One thing was for sure: If she worked herself into a frazzle, she'd tighten up like a vise and ruin the whole thing.

Into the tub.

One of the great scientific hypotheses promulgated in the cheerleaders' locker room had been the notion that sexual nervousness could be ameliorated by, as Jill Carruthers had put it, "doing your own but keeping the train off the tracks." Pamela had looked at her stupidly, and Jill had translated condescendingly. "You play with yourself, see, only you don't come, you stop short." To Pamela's wide-eyed expression, she added, "Glow lasts for hours. Helps later when the real thing happens." This from Carruthers, who was no small authority—as an impressively large percentage of the male student body could verify.

Pamela figured she'd find out soon enough. Had a certain logic to it, anyway. Besides, she could only brush her teeth and comb her hair so many times. She visualized Mac, instead of the usual suspects, and was surprised at the speed of her arousal and the willpower it took to stop.

There was a sexist edge to her intention that hadn't escaped her notice. She had been holding Mac off for weeks, and now she'd come to a unilateral decision that affected them both. What right did she have to assume that he would be a willing party?

This moral pang lasted a good two seconds, about as long as it took for her to review the percentage of her high school trysts who were unwilling. No, there would be no last minute reprieve by Mac's surprise noncompliance.

She felt resigned and more than a little excited and reached over to her handbag for the hundredth time to make certain she had her pills.

———•———

Mac had chosen a spy movie, one of a basic crop of thrillers whose primary distinction was more the elimination of boredom than the presentation of art.

What was a surprise was an unexpectedly tender and explicit love scene between the hero (a Bulgarian expatriate on the run from corrupt KGB apparatchiks) and a striking brunette sent by the CIA to seduce him. Lit only by candles, the scene's eroticism was out of all proportion to the technical definitions accepted by the motion picture ratings board.

Given his brief but interesting relationship with Pamela, Mac found himself growing uncomfortable as the scene progressed and wasn't quite sure what to make of her slight but definite movement toward him. As the on-screen consummation approached inevitably, Pamela reached over and took his hand in hers.

In deference to what he perceived in Pamela as a delicate sensibility of unknown but possibly pathological origin, Mac had exercised remarkable restraint since they'd started dating. He had surprised himself, given his background of easy conquests. He could hardly remember a week in his postpubescent life where he hadn't enjoyed the connubial pleasures of a woman, at least prior to his shameful incarceration and rescue by Jake Nostrand.

He was horny as hell, and the close proximity to a pretty, curvaceous, sweet-smelling blonde was not making his life any easier. Which presented a dilemma just now, because he would have been perfectly happy to take her right there in row sixteen, but he wasn't sure that even putting his arm around her might not be misinterpreted or, stated another way, interpreted correctly. This latest gesture from her was either an invitation or a test, and if there was one thing Mac knew about women, it was that, like experience, they were very hard teachers: they gave you the test before they gave you the lesson.

What was also important to him was that he truly liked her. He could go out and get laid anytime but kept choosing to be with her, for no other reason than he enjoyed it, even if she was a head case. So he put his arm around her and held his breath, and she laid her head on his shoulder and he breathed in her perfume and they both relaxed into each other. It didn't last very long, thankfully.

"Hey, sailor," she whispered in his ear. "Wanna take me home?"

"Nah."

She slapped his arm, and they got up and left.

———•———

Pamela had been begging her father to take her horseback riding for months. Now she was standing beside this beast that was twice as big as she had imagined, stamping its feet and shaking its head back and forth, great shuddering waves passing down its sides.

She allowed herself to be hoisted into the saddle, gripping the horn until her hands hurt, squeezing her legs together to hold tight to the horse. The first few steps terrified her, and she held herself stiff-backed, which only increased the awful jarring and thumping. The half-hour introductory ride was horrible, and she hung on out of desperation and out of the certainty that Wild Bill would give her hell if she copped out after all her begging.

What she also knew was that familiarity would bleed out the tension, and, whether it was two or twenty rides later, at some point she would relax and learn how to ride.

She reflected on this on the way to Mac's house. It might be romantic someday, but all she really wanted for now was to get through it without freaking out, get used to it and worry about enjoying it later.

It had seemed a little easy in the movie theater, and it was getting more difficult now in the car. There was no turning back, the moving finger having irrevocably writ, and there was no mistaking the acid rising in her throat. Mac held her hand and kissed it occasionally. Pamela clutched her handbag and prayed.

Once inside, Pamela said, " 'Scuse me a second," and headed for the bathroom. She closed the door and gripped the towel rack as tightly as she could to try to settle her trembling hand. She opened her handbag and took out the bottle of pills, shook one into her hand and looked at it for a second, then tapped out a second one and quickly tossed both into her mouth. The only glass in sight was a plastic cup in a toothbrush holder, and figuring they were going to swap bacteria one way or another, she filled it with water and downed the pills. She stared at herself in the mirror, but the image staring back held no useful information, so she turned, took a deep breath, then a deeper one, and stepped out.

The lights were down low, and two candles were burning in holders on the table. Mac had a bottle of white wine in a bucket and two glasses and was setting them down on the table as she emerged. "You figuring to seduce me with wine?" Pamela asked.

"Why, you need it?"

"Damned right I need it," she answered, smiling.

"Me too," said Mac as he poured.

"I doubt that."

"You'd be surprised." He didn't need it at all, but he guessed that a little shared nervousness might make Pamela feel less like a fraternity pledge at an initiation rite.

"Cheers." They clicked glasses and drank. After an awkward

silence Pamela looked directly at Mac and said, with the usual acerbic edge to her voice now completely gone. "Look, I'm really nervous and I don't know what the hell I'm doing. You don't know what to do because I've been acting weird since the day we met."

As Mac's shoulders began the preliminaries to a disappointed sag, she continued, "So why don't you just sort of take charge here, okay?" and watched him brighten noticeably, then grow serious.

He stepped to her and put his hands on her shoulders, then slid them down to her arms. "Are you sure?"

Of course I'm not sure, you big idiot. I feel like I'm standing at the edge of a cliff with drops on both sides and wolves biting my ankles. "Yes."

He bent his head and kissed her, pressing the length of his body into hers, literally growing dizzy at the warm wetness of her mouth, the plush feel of her back under his hands, the swell of her breasts against his chest. She had put her arms around his neck and responded hungrily but not hurriedly. For all his sexual exploits, he never would have believed that a simple kiss could feel like this, and it suddenly became important that their lovemaking have nothing of the frantic about it. He wanted it to take forever.

He pulled back and looked at her, his arms still around her. She looked back, waiting. He knew that this was the time for him to take charge, demonstrate his strength and control, and by his careful and skillful mastery of language perpetuate the magic he knew they both felt. "Gee whiz."

Pamela smiled and nodded slightly. "Gee whiz."

They kissed again. Then again. It was getting better.

They were still standing in the middle of the living room. "If I'm taking charge, I say we need music," said Mac, leaving her and walking to the wall unit.

"Something slow and bluesy," said Pamela.

Mac looked over the shelves and reached for a CD, turning on the stereo and opening the plastic case. "This one always reminds me of whiskey and cigarettes at three in the morning at some thirties nightclub." He pressed a button on the stereo, and a drawer slid out silently. He placed the disk in the drawer, pressed another button to close it, another button to start it playing, and yet another to have it repeat automatically. He waited for the muted trumpet and piano notes to drift out of the speakers, then turned the volume down lower.

He came back to Pamela, took her hand in his, and said, "Come with me." She was at a loss for a snappy comeback and followed him toward the bedroom.

He stopped and said, "Just a minute," then went back and picked up one of the candles, returning with one hand cupped in front to protect the flame from the breeze of his walking. He looked at her and said, "I want to see you."

In the bedroom he kissed her again, then let his hands drop down over her buttocks. She pressed closer to him, and he unbuttoned the back of her blouse. The touch of his hand on her skin was electric.

Too electric. It felt like a hot spark and wasn't altogether pleasant. It made good company for the rising bile in her stomach. *Oh, God, dear God, please, not now. Not now.*

Now her hands were on his buttocks, and then she pulled the back of his shirt out of his pants. There were no buttons left on her blouse, and she stepped back and worked her hands through the cuffs and let the blouse drop on the floor. She turned her back to him and raised her hair, and he undid the clasp of her bra. She turned back to him without taking it off, and he slid the straps off her shoulders and watched her breasts spill out of the cups, her nipples erect and the skin around them lightly bumped from the sudden cold.

His own shirt was now off, and he stepped forward and kissed her again, the touch of her bare flesh arousing him mercilessly. There was no way around the erection that now pressed against her, and she undid his belt. Then, by silent assent, they stepped apart and continued undressing themselves. Pamela turned her back to him, not so much out of her own modesty, but because his now freed erection was standing straight out in space, and there was nothing for him to do until she was ready.

The sight of her bending slightly to take off her pants, accentuating the curves of her full bottom, was more than he could bear, and he hugged her from behind, his penis nestling comfortably between her cheeks as he licked her neck and took her breasts in his hands. Pamela tilted her head back and reached behind him, rubbing the backs of his thighs and moving her bottom slightly. The gnawing in her stomach had reached her chest, and her ability to fight it was weakening.

She walked toward the bed without looking back at him and started to turn back the covers, then reconsidered and lay down on top of them instead. He looked at her for a long moment, then lay down beside her. As they embraced she reached down and teased the skin around his thighs and belly, finally grabbing him full on, and—impossibly—feeling him grow even larger under her touch.

His hand was between her legs, opening her gently and beginning a slow rhythmic motion. She parted her legs to accommodate him, and the slipcover started clawing at her back. Unpleasant currents in her midsection were now competing with the erotic flashes coursing through her body, and as she pushed up toward Mac's probing hand and spread her legs farther, the tingling began in her head and she had worried about her tightness and would she be dry as a bone, though she could feel Mac's finger in her now, slippery and effective, making her wider and bigger, and she wondered how long she could keep the demons at bay and maybe we'd better hurry this up.

She let go of his erection and reached around to his buttocks, and she lay flatter on the bed at the same time, an unmistakable signal, surely, and Mac got the message and picked himself up over her and now he was inside a little and gently, gently, as it got more slippery, he went deeper until his full weight was on her and he was fully in her and it felt good to be filled up like that, smothered in his kisses, his hands now free to knead her breasts and toy with her nipples and—

say, this isn't bad, not bad at all. Zowee, I did it! I'm doing it!

and Mac's penis is a live thing, worming around inside of her, then it occurs to her that it is alive, of course, what else could it be, except that it seems to have a mind of its own, and she didn't know that one of those things could turn to the left and take a look and then turn to the right and do the same thing and—

hey, wait a minute, feels like little hands growing out the sides and running little fingers along her walls, feeling trapped and trying to claw their way out. *This isn't right* and now serious panic comes in for the next dance and she notices herself shoving away at Mac, noticing his eyes like pinwheels, turning, his mouth twisted into an ugly snarl, teeth flashing bright sparks of light. *This* really *isn't right* and then she quickly realizes that she must be hallucinating and fights to regain control of herself. She hears Mac somewhere in the distance calling her name and asking if everything is all right—*all right? all right? why shouldn't it be all right? why is he asking me that? can he see this, does he understand?* and she finally realizes not only that she is going crazy but that she is in danger of losing it all, losing Mac, losing her mind

and she has to get out—*now*—before it all crashes around her. She manages to disengage him, and won't remember exactly how later, and starts dribbling apologies but he is so good so kind (mostly scared to death but she can't see that through her own terror) and asks for no explanations just is she okay. *Sure, sure, fine, only listen, I have to go to the bathroom now, okay? No big deal, just—need—to—get—to—that—bathroom*, but he tugs at her, reluctant to let her go into such a dangerous room, what with all the drugs and razor blades and the hundred ways you could really hurt yourself in there but she *really* has to get in there which is to say *out of here* so she fixes a choking smile and tells him not to worry, *don't be silly, just a little anxiety, that's all, is that so hard to understand, Mac?* and at her intimation that he might not be the understanding guy he thinks he is, he lets her go.

The bathroom isn't much fun, either; it's hard to relax when the walls are bulging in and out and the soap is doing the rumba but Pamela is nothing if not disciplined and she tells herself it's all an anxiety-induced hallucinatory experience—

wasn't that what Dr. Ferrin called it?—and knowing that makes it a little better.

Like hell it does. What she has to do is get out of this house and fast, very fast, because every second trying to sound moderately sane in front of Mac costs her more of her sanity and it isn't exactly totally absolutely one hundred percent crystal clear how much is left in the till—

And now the demons come and they look like her father which doesn't make a lot of sense because she usually pictured him as an angel, and why is this particular demon with her father's mustache tugging her ankles apart and why is there something all of a sudden so terribly familiar about that . . . ?

And then more demons come and one of them looks a lot like Dad but this particular brand of demon seems to come a little damaged, a little shot up, with its face half gone and its guts oozing out of a gaping wound in its belly and an enormous feeling of euphoria comes over Pamela because this is one prick bastard demon that isn't going to get her anymore, the little fuck. *Good for him, good for him, I hope it hurt like hell to get shot, the little fuck. Boy it sure does look a lot like Dad and so do those wounds, but it was terrible when the demon got busted up and great when Dad got hit—*

no no no no no I got it backward (must be going crazy) it was terrible for the demon but great for Dad. . . . Ah, no, still something wrong there what could it be. But that particular thought leads to a wallop of nausea and I really really really need to get out of this house but can't let Dad (I mean Mac) see me this way or he'll never let me go and if I stay one more minute Dad (dammit, I mean these beasties) will be at me again and I'll never get out.

Dredging up every shred of control she ever had throughout her whole life and rolling it into this one moment, she opens the door and does the hardest thing she's ever done by far, which is to speak normally while the demons shriek in the bathroom. "Mac, listen, it's hard to explain and I'll be okay in the morning it was just a little too much too fast and would you mind terribly if I just went home now, okay, because I really feel, well, just a tad shaky, yes, that's it, just a tad shaky and so will that be okay, please?" It wasn't bad, maybe a little too long and a little loud (but she had to make herself heard over the din from the doorway behind her), but it seems okay and now she will be safe.

Almost. Mac's concern is a terrible thing, a grenade on her footpath out of here. "Sweetheart, are you kidding? You look just awful, how can I let you go? Let's get dressed, I'll fix you a drink, no harm done. . . ."

Now she's in real trouble. Doesn't he realize how impossible, how totally and utterly unthinkable it would be for her to stay? Raccoons stuck in traps who chew off their own limbs have it easy compared to how badly she has to get out of here, and this dear, sweet man is not understanding any of this and she has to pull this off and keep him at the same time because this was going to work one of these days, she just knew it.

The demons in the bathroom are hysterical with laughter at her predicament. "At least let me drive you home, Pam." *Oh, this is just great, yes, I'll spend the next fifteen minutes in a four-wheeled coffin, trying to explain, and these little shit-heads behind me will sit in the backseat, playing with their enormous dongs, just like they're doing now (Christ, look at the size of those things, almost as big as Daddy's) and that will settle me down for sure,* and just then it gets worse and she gets desperate and it's getting a little hard to tell where the wall ends and she begins. She hears Mac but can't understand what he's saying, she feels him pull her clothes back onto her, she sits on a chair, she gets up, she sits on the couch, she gets up, she drinks some coffee but it tries to steal her intestines so she throws it up and somehow someway she has to get him to stop. *Now.* It all seems to take a very long time (too goddamned long) and now she's getting mad and she kisses Mac good-bye at least she thinks she does and tells him again and again she's really okay at least she thinks she tells him because he doesn't answer and now she's out the door, and the cool air helps for a second and she looks up and sees Dr. Ferrin's face glowing in the sky but that only lasts for a second and then it winks out and so does the light in Mac's living room and then it's gone and only a vaporous Cheshire cat of glowing plasma remains and then it too is gone.

And she's walking, turns left at the Andromeda galaxy and

now she's home and her neighbor smiles hello and Pamela mumbles something suitably innocuous and steps quickly inside and she thinks about calling Mac but can't because of the little green bastard sitting on the phone holding his outsize dick and leering at her. Then she thinks about calling Dr. Ferrin and the little green bastard jumps away.

CHAPTER 14

Ferrin heard the phone from his driveway but could not tell how long it had been ringing. It rang seven or eight more times by the time he got into the house and made it to his study. He picked up the phone and said, "Hello?"

"Oh, you bastard, you bastard!" the hysterical voice assaulted his ear. "Where the hell have you been, I've been calling forever!"

"Pamela, calm down, take it easy, take a few deep breaths."

But the rasping sobs coming through the phone betrayed her inability to stop and inhale. "I . . . oh, Jesus, Doctor . . . oh, Jesus . . . I can't . . . I don't know . . . I don't know what's me, what's happening, oh, God, I'm losing it, losing it bad . . . please, please . . ."

"Pamela! Pamela, listen to me: Are you calling from home?"

"Where the hell were you, Doc? Where . . . I called, I called, you didn't answer . . . why didn't you answer?"

"I wasn't here, Pamela, I just walked in." He tried to keep his voice calm to avoid adding to her hysteria, but he had to find out where she was. "Are you home, Pamela?"

"Home?"

"Yes, are you calling me from home? Where are you?"

"Home."

He couldn't tell if she was mindlessly repeating his question or answering it. "Where are you, Pamela?"

Silence, then, "I'm right here, can't you see? Right here." More silence. "This is my apartment, isn't it? So I'm here, right here."

Bingo. "Pamela, I'm coming to your apartment, do you understand? Will you be all right until I get there?"

"Oh, yes. Oh, yes, please come, please come fast, Doc, right away. You're really coming, right, you're not lying to me?"

"I'm really coming. I'm going to hang up now and—"

"No! No! Don't hang up, oh, God, Doc, don't hang up, don't leave me, please . . ."

Her paranoia was like smoke he could feel coming through the phone. He was experienced enough to know the futility of trying to get her to believe he would really come. "I'll be there in ten minutes," he said, and hung up. It was better to have her sweat the next few minutes than to stay on the phone all night trying to convince her that he was being truthful.

———•———

Pamela knew Ferrin was on his way. There was no doubt in her mind that he was leaving his house, getting into his car, turning the key, backing out of the driveway. She knew with an ineffable certainty that he would be there shortly. She knew with every last fiber of her being that it was a cosmic truth that in however many minutes remained of the ten he promised, Dr. Ferrin would be walking through that door.

She just didn't believe it.

And even if he did come, there were too many of them even for Ferrin to stop. It was too crazy even for the doctor. He'd probably see them, too, and then have his own set of problems to worry about and wouldn't even bother with her. And then it would get worse, not better, and it would have been preferable to not even have him there, so maybe he'd smack his car into a light pole, and what if that happened, then he'd never get there and she'd disappear into a black whirlpool and . . .

Stop! Stop it!

Not a chance. Her panic knew no bounds now. They were going to get her, they had the advantage, they had the power. . . .

They had the buzzer.

The buzzer ate into her brain, and she clamped her hands over her ears, but it started working in through her eyes, and she couldn't cover everything at once.

The buzzing was more insistent now.

Wait.

Wait a minute....

She jumped up in sudden realization and ran to the intercom on the wall, which was blaring urgently. It was Ferrin calling from downstairs. As she reached for the button she stopped: What if it wasn't him? What if it was more of *them? Stop!* She jabbed at the button before she could think.

He came through the door, but it wasn't him. It looked like him, but she was too smart for this. His eyes were like burning coals, sinister, malevolent. She could feel her own eyes start to burn from the radiated heat. "Stay away from me," she said as she backed up and felt for the arm of the couch behind her.

The Ferrin-thing came closer and showed her his satchel, filled with instruments of torture, pain and death. The bulge in his pants was pulsating like a beating heart, and she was suddenly aware of her own slickness, the shameful vestige of rape following weeks of skillful and manipulative seduction.

She fell backward onto the couch, and the Ferrin-thing came closer, whispering words of comfort and reaching into his bag. She was terrified into numb paralysis now as he said, "Pamela, take off your pants."

Her swirling dread transformed itself into resigned obedience under the power of his spell. She was in her bathtub, the oil was around her, the music played softly, she'd been there for hours, and the desire she had conjured up crescendoed to new heights. "Your pants, Pamela. They need to come off."

Oh, bliss. The ultimate fantasy, too awful to contemplate before, was now hers in the flesh. This must be the bad Ferrin, arisen from the doctor in his sleep. She unbuttoned the top of her pants, pulled the zipper down. She was lying back on the couch, her eyes closed. She reached inside her pants and peeled off the top, and when she was exposed she could feel the heat pouring out from between her legs, and the desire was a flame now. Could he see the wetness, feel the engorgement as blood rushed in? Her need for him following the evening's earlier malignant brutality was all-encompassing.

But when her pants were only as far as her knees and she thought she would burst if it took much longer, the Ferrin-thing asked, "Where are your pills, Pamela?"

What was this? "Pills?" The god of all living creatures was disappearing into the galactic maelstrom between her legs, and he was going to give her a pill?

"The pills I gave you, Pamela. I can't give you anything else until I know what you've already taken. Where are they?"

She stared at him dumbly. Would he put a Band-Aid on an amputation? Shoot elephants with spitballs? She gestured toward her purse and watched him reach in and bring out the little bottle. How could she possibly begin to explain the colossal inadequacy of what he was contemplating?

She parted her knees slightly. "I'm dying," she whispered.

"No, you're not," said the Ferrin-thing, but it reached into its bag and withdrew a dirty and rusted arrow, filled with poison. Pamela rubbed the tops of her thighs anxiously, studiously avoiding her crotch, her lust now at the boiling point. The Ferrin-thing started for her. He was going to put the big, filthy arrow inside of her. Not good. This wouldn't do at all. It was all turning dark.

She put her hand into her underpants, blocked herself with it and squeezed her legs together. The sensual slickness turned to gravel and scraped her until blood ran out and over her legs. The arrow was coming closer and she reached out to stop it but the Ferrin-thing grabbed her hand and locked it in an iron grip and with the other hand stabbed her with the arrow, held it there and then pulled it out, taking muscle and bone and sinew with it until the two rivers of blood met and threatened to drown her, and she sank beneath the waters of a red sea.

———◆———

Ferrin waited until she stopped writhing and her breathing became more even and less labored. He wiped the tiny spot on her leg with an alcohol swab and put the hypodermic back in his bag. He went into the bedroom and pulled the comforter off the bed and carried it back to the living room, where he finished taking off Pamela's pants and covered her. He took out his address book, thumbed through it until he found the right page, walked to the phone and dialed.

"Hello?" Jake Nostrand said groggily.

"I'm sorry, Jake, did I wake you? This is Brix Ferrin."

"I guess so. Must have just nodded off. What time is it?"

"Little after midnight. Had a little problem and thought it best to let you know."

Jake was fully alert now. "What? What happened?"

"I'm at Pamela Jacoby's apartment. She had a date with Mac tonight, and it must not have gone very well."

"According to Mac, it hasn't been going too well for her altogether, since they started."

"So she tells me, but I really thought she was making good progress. I don't know what happened, but she called me a little while ago in the middle of a full-blown psychotic episode."

"You're kidding me. I didn't know she was that bad off."

"The potential was there, and she'd come pretty close a couple of times recently, but nothing of this magnitude. Paranoia, hallucinations, inappropriate affect, the whole picture."

"Where is she now? Is she okay?"

"She's sleeping on her couch. I checked how many of her pills she had left, then gave her twenty-five milligrams of Thorazine intramuscular, so she'll be out for a while. But listen, Jake, you've been talking to Mac. Is there any possibility he tried to force himself on her?"

Jake took a moment to answer, to make sure Ferrin understood that he was not reflexively jumping to his friend's defense. "None, Brix. There's no denying the sexual tension he's been feeling, but he's really very taken with her, maybe even in for the long haul. He felt everything would happen in its own time."

Ferrin looked over at Pamela. "I don't get this, although for sure it's got a large sexual component."

"What now?"

"I think she'll be all right in the morning. Probably feel like a truck ran over her, though. Doesn't look good for Doctor to spend the night with beautiful young patient, so I'm heading home."

"Are you sure it's okay to leave her?"

"She'll be fine."

"Brix," Jake started hesitantly, "did I jump the gun with this little experiment? I'm gonna feel like shit if I did anything to hurt that girl."

"I wouldn't beat myself up about it. Worst case, all we probably did was hasten the inevitable. Maybe this will give me the opportunity to make some real progress with her."

This was small comfort to Jake, who sensed that Ferrin was trying to ease his guilt and soften the consequences of his presumption. "Yeah, maybe. Well, good night, Brix."

"G'night, Jake. Don't worry too much about it. It'll be okay."

CHAPTER 15

The shipwreck was barely visible in the murk, obscured not only by the darkness at this depth, but by the silt-laden consistency of the water. The pressure was so great that it was like struggling through honey, and the notion of swimming up past the wreck to the chimes was mostly futile, even if she could locate the source of the sound.

The masts were heavy with lichens and barnacles, which seemed to add even more weight to the surrounding water. What remained of the sails was bathed in a ghostly and frigid light. Great, dark shapes glided past, slowly, but by choice, not because of the syrupy water. She wondered why they moved so effortlessly, in contrast with her huge efforts to move only inches.

The chiming was very far away but seemed to have gotten closer, so now she could tell that it was intermittent, not steady. A spot of light that might have been the sun appeared high above her. She was alone, and her eyes were closed, but it caused her no concern that she could see the wreck and the spot of light anyway.

The chimes grew more insistent, and irritating, and she was closing in on assigning them a definite direction. They came from off to her left, exactly opposite the direction of the light.

Arms and legs quivering with fatigue, she increased her effort and found that the higher she went, the less burdensome the water became. The spot grew brighter as the sound grew louder, but the disparity between their relative positions grew more pronounced as she rose, almost accelerating now. The ringing assaulted her ears, and the light was so bright she closed her eyes tighter, to little avail.

She clamped a hand over her face and the light dimmed, and when it no longer hurt to do so, she risked a peek through her fingers and saw brilliant flowers of scarlet and indigo, arrayed in a repeating pattern that started at her cheek and receded into the distance until they touched her foot. They looked familiar. She'd seen them before, countless times, but where?

On her couch. The one she was lying on. The ringing was shrill and more than unpleasant now, and the sun pouring in through the partly opened window hurt her eyes, so she closed them again. But the phone wouldn't stop, so she blinked hard several times and then forced her eyes open. Looking at the clock was out of the question, but the height of the sun told her it wasn't early morning.

She tried to turn her head, and it obeyed creakily, paying her back with a wave of dizziness. She turned it back and was dizzy again, but less intensely and for a shorter period of time. Back and forth a few more times cleared her focus a bit more, and she risked raising an arm, then opened and closed her fingers a few times, then reached for the phone.

The end of the ringing was blessed relief and gave her the strength to hold the receiver to her ear, hoping that whoever was on the other end would speak softly. She tried to say hello, but nothing came out, so she worked her jaw up and down a few times, cleared her throat and tried again.

"Hwah?" was what she managed.

"Pamela?"

"Hawah?" Two syllables. Definite improvement.

"Pamela, it's Jake Nostrand."

"Jayh?" She cleared her throat a few times, holding the phone close so he would know she was trying. "Jake?"

"Yes, Jake. Are you okay? You sound lousy."

"That a profeshull daya-nosis?" Tough to be a wiseguy in this condition.

Jake, on the other hand, was relieved at her attempt at wit. "Tell me how you feel."

Pamela was coming around rapidly. "God, I don' know wherra start. Gimme a secon' t' sit up 'n' I'll be back to you."

"Hold it for a second, Pam. Is Mac there?"

Mac? Here? What could he possibly mean? Bits and pieces of the night before started coming back to her. *Ferrin. He was here and gave me a shot of something. Or did he?* She peeled the cover off her leg, saw the small bandage, and sighed with relief. At least her mind was back. She remembered thinking Ferrin was a monster and was surprised at how lucidly she was able to look back and realize that she had been hallucinating.

"Pamela? Pam, you there?"

"Yeah, Jake, I'm here." Then she remembered Mac.

"I need to know if Mac's there."

The question made more sense now. "He's not here, Jake, he's probably home slashing his wrists."

Jake laughed and said, "Another great night, huh?"

Pamela smiled at the understatement and realized that Mac must have been giving Jake some hint of her odd behavior. "Let's put it this way, Doc. If I were he, I'd pack up and head for another planet."

"Ah, c'mon, it couldn't have been that bad."

"Yeah, you're right, only bad enough for Dr. Ferrin to have to come over here and pump enough tranq into my leg to kill a horse."

"So you remember at least that much."

"What much? What do you know about it?"

Jake hesitated before answering. "He called me from your place, said you were schiz'ing pretty badly."

"How come he called you? Schiz-what?"

"Doctor talk. Maybe a psychotic episode, but sure as hell a whopper of an anxiety attack."

A dull headache started to form. "Then you know I came home alone. Why would you think Mac was here?"

"He hasn't shown up at the hospital yet, so I thought maybe he was worried about you and stopped by."

"No, and I don't blame him. I was horrible, Jake, really horrible, so awful . . ." She started to snuffle.

"I don't think so, Pam. And neither does Mac. He likes you, y'know. I mean, really likes you." He sounded almost desperate.

She smiled in spite of the pain. "It's okay, Jake, really, it's okay. It's just not gonna work. Doesn't mean it wasn't worth the try." *Wish I really felt that way,* she thought.

"This is great, you sitting there feeling so miserable and trying to make me feel better. I'm supposed to be the doctor, remember?"

"Don't . . . Hey! What time is it?"

"About eleven. You on today?"

She stood up suddenly, before she had a chance to consider what an abysmally stupid idea that was.

"Pam, you there?"

She waited for the room to stop whirling around, then said, "Yeah. Whew, never knew standing up could be so much fun. What the hell'd he give me, anyway?"

"It's called Thorazine. Knockout drops. You slept for about twelve hours. You might want to consider taking the day off."

She'd already taken half of it off, and the thought of sitting home alone with herself was worse than that of going to work. "No, I'll be okay."

"Do you have any idea where Mac might be?"

"No, although I wouldn't be surprised if he's out prowling a bar or two. I really wasn't much fun."

"Don't give up, Pamela, please. You're stronger than you think."

No, I'm not. "Thanks, Jake. I gotta run."

"Sure you'll be all right?"

Hell, no. "I'll be fine. When you find Mac, tell him . . ."

"Tell him what?"

"Nothing. Nothing. I'll see you, Jake."

———◆———

The phone rang twice before someone answered it. "Duty sergeant."

"It's Jacoby."

"Hey, kid, we were about to send out an APB. Captain's been asking for you."

"Great. I'll be in about noon."

She made a pot of coffee using espresso beans and took a stinging cold shower while it brewed, using a shower cap to avoid wasting time drying her hair. Running the soap over her body made her remember Mac's gentle touch, and she stuck her face into the cold stream of water to keep from crying.

The burning hot coffee felt good going down, and her body felt stronger even though her head still seemed to harbor a mild buzzing and a slight, otherworldly feeling. She walked to the phone to pick it up and put it back where it usually sat. Ferrin must have moved it next to her after he knocked her out. Setting it down, she spotted the note. "Call me as soon as you wake up." It was signed "B. T. Ferrin." *I sure was swell to him, too*, she thought, picking up her cap and walking out, aching with the need to call Mac and apologize and not knowing where he might be.

Mrs. McGillicutty opened her door as soon as Pamela opened hers. "Are y'awright, Pammy?" she asked in thick brogue, worry in her eyes.

"All right?" asked Pamela.

"Y'looked tarrible when y'came in. Parfectly tarrible, and then the doctor an' all. Y'seem awright now, tanks heaven."

Pamela remembered seeing her neighbor on the way in. Must have been awfully rude. *Anybody else I screwed up last night?* She smiled her brightest smile. "Must have been something I ate. I feel a whole lot better now."

Mrs. McGillicutty smiled back. "Y'look fine. Off wi'ya to pertek the citizenry now, eh?" she said, gently shooing her on her way.

———◆———

Murdoch was the first thing she saw as she entered the precinct house. *You bother me now and I swear to God I'll shoot your dick off*, she thought, meaning it. But he made no moves, only stared at her with a hard and impenetrable glare, followed by a glance at the clock above the duty desk, now showing quarter past twelve.

She picked up her messages and sat down at an unused desk, leafing through them and ignoring the meaningless squiggles she couldn't see anyway. She felt a presence off her left shoulder. "Must have been one hell of a night."

Pamela turned her puffy and red eyes and pointed them toward Captain Grant, who dropped her smile and said, "Whoops."

Pamela clenched her jaw to keep her lower lip from trembling, which worked but also helped the tears form in her eyes. Amanda looked around the crowded room, looked back and said, "Outside."

They got up, made it across the room, through the back door, and down a small set of steps to the service alley behind the station. Amanda looked around carefully, pulled a pack of cigarettes out of her inside jacket pocket and started to pull one out.

"Captain!" said Pamela before she could stop herself.

Amanda ignored her, lit the cigarette with a disposable lighter and took a long drag, closing her eyes in the process. As she let the smoke out, she opened one eye, held up the pack and asked, "Want one?"

"Yeah." Pamela took a cigarette as Amanda held out the light. "So Mrs. Clean has a vice?"

Amanda smiled. "Two a day, that's it. Is that what they call me?"

"No, as a matter of fact. I gotta sit down," said Pamela, settling onto a step.

Amanda sat down sideways one step higher and on the opposite side, looking down at Pamela. She took another hit on the cigarette and asked through the exhale, "So whadja do to the poor guy this time?"

Pamela laughed and thought again how effective the captain's straightforward style was. She inhaled on the cigarette and looked away. "I really did it this time, Captain. A four-alarmer."

Amanda smoked and kept silent, looking away, letting Pamela find her own time. Pamela remembered a line about how anybody's troubles were tedious after fifteen minutes, and she wondered how long she could count on this attention before Grant got bored with her and figured enough was enough.

"Everything was going so well."

"Everything?" Amanda prompted with what would have been a leer in a man.

Pamela looked at her. "Everything. It was nice, really nice. And then I got hit by a truck. Right in the middle."

Amanda tucked her chin down and looked up at Pamela as though peering over the tops of bifocals. "In the middle?" she asked in a low, comic voice.

"*In flagrante delicto*," replied Pamela, using official vice squad phraseology for "caught in the act."

"Oh, dear," said Amanda.

"That's one way of putting it." She took another drag. This wasn't getting any easier. "I pushed him away and tried to leave, but he was afraid, afraid for me, and he didn't want me to go."

She looked at Amanda, who had a funny look on her face. "No, no," Pamela said. "He was scared. He even put my clothes on me, if you can believe that."

"Quite a guy, your Mac."

Pamela looked away again, wistfully. "He is." Another drag. "He was. I've had it, Captain, no more. I was so embarrassed and ashamed. I could never even look at him again." She was crying now and hung her head in her arms. "I called my shrink. I thought I was losing my mind, I mean really losing it, not sort of losing it. He gave me a shot and the lights went out. That's why I was late. I'm sorry."

Amanda reached over to take the smoldering cigarette out of Pamela's hand. "Don't worry about it."

Pamela looked up at Amanda. "I can't make it, Captain. I'm not getting better, I'm getting worse. I was doing fine, y'know? Just fine, really, making progress, until I met this guy, and I told Ferrin I didn't want to go out with him and he kept badgering me, telling me sooner or later I had to take the chance, and he wouldn't let it go, and it kept being bad except sometimes it was good . . . so good . . ."

Amanda didn't try to stop her but let her go on until the

heaving stopped. She was having trouble reconciling how this intelligent and lucid woman could keep breaking down so severely and recovering so completely. Even now, as Pamela sat crying, there was no hint of mental instability, just profound sadness and resignation.

Pamela had finished for the most part, dried her eyes, and recovered. "Just two?" she asked Amanda.

"Well, most of the time just two," said Amanda, reaching inside her jacket.

After they lit up Pamela leaned back and said, "I don't get it. I really don't get it. I was afraid, sure, and nervous as hell. But I really wanted this guy, not just in the sack, but maybe a lot more than that. And I just can't stop myself from freaking out. I don't know why. It doesn't make sense to me."

"These things rarely do," said Amanda. "I think we'd better go in."

Pamela took a last hit and ground the cigarette out on the step, then got up and walked back in behind Amanda. As they came in sight of Amanda's office, they saw two patrolmen in anxious conversation with Amanda's secretary. One of the patrolmen spotted Amanda and pointed, and his partner and the secretary turned to see them walking in. As they got closer the patrolmen stopped talking and stared hard at Pamela, unable to break their eyes away, until Amanda slowed and stopped. The two officers then reluctantly looked away from Pamela, toward Amanda, who said, "What?"

One looked down and started fiddling with his cap, and the other asked, "In your office?"

Amanda only stared at him. He looked at Pamela briefly, then he looked back, nodded his head toward Amanda's office door and said, "Please, Captain?"

Pamela turned to go back to the desk where her messages waited. Amanda led the way into her office. When they were all inside, the secretary closed the door, then a second later opened it, came out, and closed it behind her, looking offended.

Pamela sat down and tried to go through her messages again but looked up and through the glass panel of Amanda's office. One officer was still staring at her as the other one spoke, then

Amanda turned suddenly and looked right at her as well. *A couple hours late, what the hell was the big deal here? I bet that creep Murdoch is making a big deal out of this. Gonna look bad if the captain plays favorites. Christ, what else today?*

But Amanda had turned back toward the two officers and was now going behind her desk to sit down, stealing a look at Pamela, who noticed it and didn't like it. Amanda reached for a yellow pad and began jotting notes, asking questions, jotting more notes. Two detectives whom Pamela knew walked into the room, looked at her without saying anything, then looked away quickly when she caught them and headed for Amanda's office. She motioned them in before they could knock, and they entered with one last glance at Pamela, who was starting to feel the first tremors of anxiety. What in the hell was this all about? *Easy,* she said to herself, *probably just the last remnants of the raging paranoia from last night.*

After what felt like hours but was only twenty minutes, all four of the men in Amanda's office got up and walked out, casting furtive glances at her but refusing to look head-on. She watched as Captain Grant turned her swivel chair sideways, laid her head back on the chair and stared at nothing for about a minute. She then sat up, stood, looked directly at Pamela and beckoned with a wave of her hand.

Pamela stood on weakening and shaky legs, with no idea what could possibly be going on but filling with the certain dread that whatever it was, it wasn't about being late for work. She noticed that the room had gone quiet as she made her way across the fifteen miles to the captain's office and stepped in, closing the door without needing to be asked. "What's going on, Captain?" she asked in a small and frightened voice, taking a seat.

Amanda raised her head quickly and looked outside her office, where a dozen pairs of eyes that had been turned in their direction rapidly averted themselves at her rebuking glance. She got up and dropped the blinds on the interior window, blocking the inside from any prying eyes. She sat on the chair next to Pamela, facing her squarely, and looked into her eyes for a moment.

"Mac's dead, Pamela."

Pamela's eyes didn't flinch, and her facial muscles betrayed no emotion. They also betrayed no comprehension. The impulses that ran from her ears to her brain rejected the message and sent it back for retransmission. Amanda knew better than to think she needed to say it again. She took Pamela's hand and waited.

Somewhere deep in Pamela's eyes something flickered and died, then tried again. She blinked once, twice, and furrowed her brows. "Dead?" she tried hoarsely, and cleared her throat and swallowed. She shook her head very slightly, and the look in her eyes remained puzzled. She now understood the word and was trying to interpret it in the context of some reality she could relate to instead of the one that it was really in.

Amanda was nodding her head, tightening her grip on Pamela's hand. The answering tremble told her that meaning was starting to sink in, and she could sense Pamela fighting for control. She would keep herself calm and answer questions without subterfuge, to avoid adding to Pamela's confusion.

"How?" asked Pamela, more out of reflex than the desire for information, but once she had the question out, it became important to know. Very important.

Amanda hesitated only briefly before responding. "He was murdered." She watched Pamela's eyebrows rise and her back stiffen, knowing that it was sinking in, thankful that there was no sign of the kind of blanket denial that might have signaled a potentially irreversible psychic meltdown. "Sometime after you left. He was hit on the head, probably while he was sleeping . . ." She left the sentence unfinished, which Pamela caught.

Pamela was coming around, was actually more comprehending than Amanda thought. "Oh, Jesus . . . oh, Jesus . . ." She felt herself start to slip but considered Captain Grant's half-completed sentence and fought for composure so the captain wouldn't withhold vital information. *There was more? What could be more? What was more than death?* Pamela looked at her and waited.

"They cut off his genitals, Pamela. We think he bled to death. We'll know more after the postmortem."

A cloud moved in front of the sun, dropping the temperature with surprising suddenness. What had been colorful paled to a slate gray as though covered with a fine layer of volcanic ash from a silent, unseen eruption. Pamela watched the office grow dark as the murky waters crept up around her and claimed her for the second time that day, sucking her back down, painlessly, into the soft, warm womb of welcome and beckoning nothingness.

BOOK
2

CHAPTER 16

She came to with surprising rapidity, roused by the cool, wet towel on her forehead. Lying on the couch in Captain Grant's office, she found herself looking into Bobby's eyes and instantly remembered the news that had drained the blood from her head. A small current of portending dizziness rustled quietly but was soon gone. It was replaced by a stranger feeling, very far away, a wisp of translucent gauze too insubstantial to scrutinize.

Bobby smiled and said, "Hiya, kid." He was rubbing her wrists.

Pamela smiled back. "Hey, Lieutenant. Some hard-ass cop, huh?"

He stopped rubbing and said, "We're always hard when things happen to other people. Makes us feel tough as hell. It's only when it happens to us that we remember we're mortal."

She grabbed his hands for support and pulled herself up to a sitting position. The little feeling was on the move now, and Pamela could tell it was significant, but still not what it was. The towel started to slide off her forehead, and Bobby caught it in mid fall. She saw Captain Grant getting up from behind her desk and heading over to the couch.

"Sorry to hit you with it like that, but I didn't think you'd want me soft-soaping it."

"No, no, you're right. It was all just so . . . I don't know, just so much."

"Well, you've had your share. Feeling any better?"

The little feeling was no longer little, and it danced up from somewhere deep inside her. Its edges were starting to clarify, and Pamela didn't like it, didn't like it at all. It just wouldn't do, and she needed time to sort it out and fight it. "Much better. Really, okay. Look, this is a little embarrassing, my being in here like this. Would you guys mind if I just had a minute to myself?"

Bobby rose immediately and said, "Sure, no problem. Pamela, nobody out there thinks you're a wimp. They understand. It's okay, okay?"

"Okay. Thanks."

When they were gone, Pamela lay back again and closed her eyes, giving full freedom to the unwanted emotion building at an ever-accelerating pace. Her legs and arms felt light, and her whole body suddenly felt free of a pain she never knew she had, like an air vent that drew attention to its annoying sound only by shutting off. Her lungs seemed to take in more air than usual, and she felt so alert that lying down was unnecessary, so she sat up, and that was when she was first able to put a label to the feeling, and it filled her with shame.

Relief.

She pictured Mac and tested her reaction, waiting for the shock and horror to set in and rush to her head, then she realized it wasn't coming, and while there was a sprinkling of sadness and regret, mostly there was just . . . relief. A terrible and oppressive pressure was gone, and she became aware of how filled with ceaseless agitation her days had been of late, fighting to sort out her feelings, to overcome her myriad deficiencies, to behave appropriately and not lose her mind in the process.

Now it was over. Mac was dead, and she couldn't get past her near euphoria to grieve for him. Like a drunk newly fallen off the wagon, she felt filled with strength and resolve. *Just let me off the hook for a while, dear Lord, just one more drink and I know I can do better next time.*

She stood up. No dizziness, and her legs felt strong. Her eyes were clear, and familiar objects in the office took on a new brightness and clarity. Amanda had seen her rise and came back in carrying a glass of water.

"Thanks," said Pamela. When she sipped the water, her mind went back to a Girl Scout hike in high school. They had walked in the sun for over three hours with empty canteens and happened upon a small, clear stream. Pamela had knelt and dipped her cupped hands into the icy water and brought some to her lips. It had felt as though she were drinking life itself, and she could feel not only the liquid slipping down her throat, but every bend and turn as it coursed throughout her body.

This glass of water felt the same way, and she tried not to let it show. There ought to be some guilt associated with this, she thought, and it wouldn't do to look too happy before her boyfriend's body was even cold.

"Pamela, I've got to ask you some questions. About where you were, at what times . . ."

Pamela's eyes grew wide, and the color that was returning to her face threatened to leave. "Captain, you don't think . . ."

"No, no," Amanda said quickly. "We know it wasn't you. But you're the only one who can help us nail down the specifics of the hours prior to the, uh, crime."

Pamela relaxed a little and said, "Oh, yeah. I'm sorry. Not thinking straight, I guess."

"Understandable. But I want this while it's fresh in your mind. You'll probably wind up going over it several times if the investigation drags on, so we might as well get started, if you're up to it."

Pamela now had a way to turn her disgraceful sense of well-being into an asset, by sublimating it into a calm professionalism. She took a deep breath, which she didn't need but would look to Captain Grant like heroic resolve, and said, "Let's do it." She sat down on the chair in front of Amanda's desk.

Amanda walked around behind the desk and sat down, pulling a pad of yellow paper to her and picking up a pen. "Where were you before you got to Mac's house?"

"At a movie. It wasn't very good"—small lie, no harm—"so we left in the middle."

"About what time did you get to the house?"

"I'd guess pretty close to ten."

"Let's try to keep some of the intervening details between us for now," Amanda said, smiling conspiratorially. "I don't see that they're relevant, anyway."

"Thanks," said Pamela, trying to maintain a cool exterior.

"Did you notice anything unusual between the movies and the house? Anybody following you, anybody hanging around the house, phone calls while you were there, noises, anything?"

Pamela was surprised by the question, then understood that Amanda was fishing for indications that someone might have been lying in wait for them. She tried to think hard and said, "Nothing I can think of. Things got pretty wacky for me, Captain. Afraid I'm not much of a reliable witness."

"You're a trained cop, Jacoby. Some of these things are instinctive after a while. Think. Anything at all."

She tried. "I'm sorry, there just doesn't seem to have been anything."

"Okay. What time did you leave?"

"God, I don't know, maybe around eleven?"

"How do you know?"

"I don't. I just guess I was there for about an hour. No, wait, it couldn't have been that long, or maybe it was, maybe longer. Shit, it's all so blurry. I have no goddamned idea. That's gonna look pretty funny, isn't it?"

"I'm afraid so. Is there any other way to establish a time? Did you see anybody? How did you get home?"

"I walked. It's only about a fifteen- or twenty-minute walk."

"Did you walk straight home? No stops?"

"None. And I walked pretty fast, so it was probably closer to fifteen minutes."

"Did you say hello to anybody or see anybody you know walking?"

"No. Wait. Wait a minute. On the way into the apartment. Mrs. McGillicutty, a neighbor across the hall. I must have been unsteady on the stairs and made some noise. She opened the door and asked if I was all right. Must have thought I was drunk."

"Good. Very good. That'll help if she can remember the time."

"There was also Dr. Ferrin. I called him, I think I told you that, and he came over."

"There should be a phone record of the call. Do you remember how long after you got in you called him?"

"Almost right away. Well, not quite, he wasn't there at first, but I kept trying. It felt like hours before I got him, but I don't think it was really that long. Do you have to interview Mrs. McGillicutty? I'll never hear the end of it."

"I don't see where we have a choice, but we'll try to keep it light." Amanda hesitated. "One last thing for now, Pamela."

"Go ahead."

"What was Mac wearing when you left him?"

Pamela grew uncomfortable but was determined to see this through. "He was naked. He helped me get dressed but never bothered to himself. Captain . . ."

Amanda looked up from her pad. "Yes?"

Pamela looked straight into her eyes and, with all the control she could muster, said, "I want in on this investigation."

Amanda was startled and said, "You must be kidding. You know better than that."

"I thought you said I wasn't a suspect."

"Technically you are a suspect. How could it be otherwise? Besides that, you're probably the last person besides the killer to see Mac alive, which makes you a material witness, and you also had a nasty shock. Hardly a good candidate to investigate the crime."

"But it wasn't me, you know that. And I know a lot about the hours leading up to the actual event. How do we know I didn't miss a detail somewhere? If I'm on the team, I can be on the alert for relevant details and might remember something important."

Amanda seemed to consider for a moment, then caught herself and shook her head. "Forget it. The DA would go nuts if I risked a case like that."

In a last attempt to convince the captain, Pamela said, "How about this: Put me on the team, but no solo work. Anything I do is with another cop or detective, no exceptions, and no access to evidence. How could anybody have a problem with that?"

"About a dozen different ways." But Amanda seemed to soften. "Let me think about it. Work on your statement until you hear from me." She handed Pamela the yellow pad with her notes. "And no patrol duty."

———◆———

Pamela left the protective cocoon of Captain Grant's office and aimed for an empty desk, conscious of the sudden quiet and uncomfortable stares. She kept her eyes straight ahead, took a seat, found a pencil in the desk and tried to concentrate on the yellow pad and how to begin her narrative.

Straining her eyes to her left side without moving her head, she saw Mike Atkins, a veteran investigator from the DA's office, break away from a small group and start in her direction. She was fully prepared to put the pencil through his heart. The group broke up and drifted apart.

"Jacoby," Atkins began. Pamela looked up. He seemed to change his mind about what he was going to say. "How you doin'?"

On her guard, Pamela answered warily, "Okay?" more as a question than an answer.

Atkins reached out and tweaked a few of the hairs near her temple, two or three light tugs. "You got friends here, lady." As she stared at him wordlessly, he went on. "I mean, sure, everybody fucks around a lot, but that's just fucking around." He paused again, then said, "Don't ride this out alone, Jacoby. It's too big, too much. You got family here. You don't need to be tough."

Pamela continued to stare at him, too overwhelmed to speak. Then he said something that she hadn't even considered, that Captain Grant hadn't even considered—or possibly had chosen not to mention. "This shithead that did your friend. He probably knows who you are."

Pamela finally spoke. "Will he come after me?"

"Who the hell knows? Until we get some handle on his motivation we know jack shit."

"What do I do?"

"Not much. Don't drive yourself crazy."

That's a good one. She kept her face immobile.

"Change the locks on your door. Vary your habits, like the routes you drive, the times you do things like shop, come to work, shit like that. The captain will let you vary your schedule, that's standard operating procedure."

"Thanks, Mike." Pamela looked away with a stricken expression. "I mean it, thanks a lot."

"Just don't go apeshit, Jacoby. A few easy precautions, but don't go apeshit. It's just 'til we nail the sonofabitch."

She looked back at him and nodded.

CHAPTER 17

I want this one by the book. No mistakes."

They'd all heard this speech before and were well aware of the captain's attitude toward sloppiness in making a case. It had become standard procedure to read every suspect his rights twice and then repeat them every time somebody new questioned him, and to do so in the presence of another cop. Chains of custody were maintained with legible signatures and photocopies of property room tags. All interrogations were videotaped.

But they'd never heard it like this before. Amanda looked at the four people in the room in turn, to make sure the message sank in, took root and stayed at the forefront of their thinking as the investigation progressed. She knew the risks of getting caught up in the drama of the chase, the adrenaline high as disparate pieces of evidence begin to coagulate around a central theme like iron filings arranging themselves around a magnet, the subconscious belief that solving the crime equates to convicting the criminal. She knew it did not equate, and she felt that the depressingly low rate of convictions following grand jury indictments owed less to the merits of professed innocence than to the inadequacy of proferred evidence. The most successful defense attorneys were not the masters of serious investigation and the incontrovertible alibi, but of the technicality and dubious precedent. Their great victories occurred in the quiet isolation of the pretrial motion rather than in the public spectacle of the damning cross-examination.

That wasn't going to happen here. "Nobody plays shrinking violet, either," Amanda continued. "We're our own severest critics, or somebody else will be. Any problems to start with?"

"Just one," Mike Atkins piped up, pointing at Pamela. "We've got our only suspect on the investigating team."

Pamela, silent up to now, turned sharply toward Atkins, startled at this betrayal after his tender scene in the ready room. He turned to her. "No offense here, Jacoby. I don't have a problem with it, but the DA's gonna throw a shit fit, and any defense attorney with half a brain is gonna grind us into pulp. They can claim tampering, influence, compromising our objectivity, all of that."

Amanda nodded and said, "That's true, but it'll only make a difference if our case is weak, and I just don't believe that's going to be true. And there are some rules." All eyes turned back toward Amanda. "The DA's agreed to let us run the investigation."

Atkins nodded in confirmation, as this was not unusual when it involved one of the police department's own. Normally the DA's office would be in control.

"Lieutenant Parks is in charge of the case," Amanda continued. "I'll let him tell you."

She sat down, and Bobby stood up. "Jacoby's not on the team, she's an observer. No solo interviews or site visits, no evidence exams. We're hoping that she remembers a detail, or that something we turn up sparks a memory, and maybe she can keep us from going down useless roads."

More nods from Atkins and the other detective.

"And there's another thing, as you pointed out, Mike. We don't know anything about the killer, who he is, where he is, why he did it." He looked at Pamela. "We don't know how Jacoby fits in, or if she fits in. . . ."

Atkins looked at Pamela while he spoke to the rest of the

room, finishing Bobby's sentence: "So we want her around a lot of cops all the time."

"Exactly," said Bobby.

Atkins looked back toward the front, but not before sneaking a wink at Pamela. "That's good thinking."

As the atmosphere relaxed, Bobby turned toward Detective Joshua Schuyler and said, "Let's start with the scene. You just came from there, Sky. What've we got?"

Schuyler stood and pulled a notepad out of his jacket pocket. He glanced nervously at Pamela, saw only her steady stare, and made a quick decision to just play it straight. "Victim you already know, so I'll skip the ID. Found lying on his back on the bed in the bedroom, by a doctor guy he works with, name of Nostrand."

Pamela blanched but kept still while Schuyler continued.

"Hit once on the forehead, just above and in front of the right temple. A fireplace poker was found nearby, and the wound seems to be consistent with the handle end, not the part you poke the fire with. Makes sense, anyway, because it's heavier and the leverage is better and you could get a better whack out of it." He caught himself suddenly, realizing how detached and callous his delivery was, and looked at Pamela.

"Just keep going, Sky," she said.

"Yeah. Sorry, Jacoby. His genitals were cut off and appear to have been crushed. They were at the foot of the bed. No other apparent mutilations or marks on the body. The ME is Judson Goverman, and you know how careful he is: won't give a preliminary on cause of death, even off the record, but they've got a spatter guy coming in from the state lab today." He was referring to an expert in interpreting the patterns made by blood as it left the body under force and created patterns on nearby walls, tables . . . and sometimes ceilings.

"So we don't know if he was dead when the cutting started," said Amanda.

"That's right," answered Schuyler, "but he was at least un-conscious, 'cause there was no sign of a struggle. There's blood everywhere, but it laid down clean. Except that it was wiped."

"Wiped?" asked Pamela.

"Where there were prints," explained Bobby. "What was wiped?"

"The floor, mostly, and the poker. And the bathroom."

"The floor I get," said Amanda. "He probably walked through the blood. But why the bathroom?"

"Best we can figure right now is that he took a shower before he left, to get rid of the blood," explained Schuyler. "There were traces still in the tub, but he wiped the bathroom floor clean."

"Where he was standing," added Bobby, "and he probably wiped the tub itself. Any hairs on the towels?" He knew that Captain Grant wanted to use the present situation to sharpen his skills and validate her faith in the FBI exchange program. He had been its inaugural participant years ago and its strongest supporter since. It never hurt the cause to demonstrate its value from time to time.

"None that I could see, but they're on the way to the lab. One's just damp, but the other's soaked in blood. Probably used on the floors."

"Sounds like a professional," said Atkins.

"No," said Bobby, shaking his head. "It doesn't fit. It's a crime of passion, not a hit. Unless . . ."

"Unless what?" prompted Amanda.

"Unless he wanted to send a message."

Schuyler held up his hand, palm outward, and said, "Lemme give you the rest before we start in."

A knife was found in the tub, wiped clean, and matching a set in the kitchen. The details accumulated like petals falling from a dying flower. Mac was naked. The phone was on the hook. Each fact complicated the puzzle even as it clarified it. Schuyler told them that the negative comparison process was under way, where samples of Mac's hair, prints and blood were taken so as to separate his from others lifted at the scene. Then they would "cartoon" the remaining prints against all of those in the computer, not just those of suspects. There were no signs of forced entry, but both the front and back doors were found unlocked. Pamela found the recitation soothing, distracting, a litany of abstract items each of which increased her distance from the actual, hard fact of what had really happened: some person, with a face, had looked down at Mackenzie Graham, beaten his head in (*What did it sound like?* she would ask herself much later), mutilated him with a knife and then probably watched while his life spurted out in spreading deltas of blood that minutes before had pumped through his capillaries. As Schuyler spoke and they all asked questions, the essential horror receded to the horizon in front of a wave of evidential flotsam not about Mac, but about a victim; not about Pamela, but about a witness before the fact; not about the stealing of a life, but about a violation of Penal Code 242-7.

"Doors unlocked?" queried Amanda, looking at Pamela.

Pamela looked at the rest of the group. "He never locked them when he was home. I don't know exactly why, but he was always taking little chances like that. . . ." Her voice trailed off, and her eyes relaxed to focus on a distant point.

"Like what?" asked Atkins, bringing her back.

"Driving too fast, no seat belt, wising off to guys twice his size. Little things." She remembered him deliberately provoking the parking attendant. Taking off his shoe. Standing there, unafraid.

"What do we have on time of death?"

"Nothing too useful yet. Goverman got there at about eleven this morning and guessed six to eighteen hours. When he guesses you can make book on it. They got a good coagulation fix from a deep sample in a depression in the sheets. Should get us close within an hour, maybe less." Schuyler stopped and looked up. "That's the basics for now. They're still working the scene, and we'll get more, plus the stuff from the lab."

Not letting anything interfere with the efficiency of their activities nor drawing unnecessary attention to Pamela, Bobby was brisk in his tone to her. "Jacoby, give us all the logistics you can remember. Do it from memory. You can leave out the steamier details," he added lightly.

"Hey, no fair," said Atkins with an exaggerated pout, and Pamela flipped him the finger.

Although momentarily stalled without the draft of her statement to refer to, Pamela was concise and articulate in her recounting of the movements of the night before and was feeling good about her even-voiced and dispassionate delivery.

But somewhere in the middle Bobby interrupted, shaking his head. "No, stop. You're giving us your notes, not your memory."

Pamela looked at him. "I don't understand. The notes were from my memory."

"Then we can read them. I want you to think, hard."

Seeing only confusion on her face, Bobby decided to try a different approach, one of the best seminars in the FBI program coming back to him now. "Jacoby," he said, and stood up. He turned to face her, then sat on the desk and opened his jacket. "What were you wearing?"

"Wearing?" she asked, but Bobby only stared at her. "Uh," she continued when it was clear he wasn't going to help, "black slacks, green silk blouse."

"Shoes?"

"Black leather sandals."

"What was he wearing?"

"Sort of a faded denim jacket, dark blue jeans, moccasins."

"Did his shoes make noise when he walked?"

She had no idea what this was about but went along, especially as she saw the others settle back in their chairs, deferring to Bobby and letting him have the floor to himself for now. "No, I don't think so. Well, yes, sort of a tapping sound."

"Did they make that sound when you walked up the stairs to his front door?"

"No, it was more crunchy, like there was dirt on the steps."

"Did he use a key to open the door? Who went in first? Were the lights on?"

Pamela was beginning to catch on, and she closed her eyes. "The door was locked, and there were no lights on. He pushed it open and let me in first, then reached around before the door closed to turn on the foyer light. He pushed the door closed but didn't lock it."

"Interruptions while you were there?"

"None. No phone calls, no visitors. No unusual noises."

"Did you go to the bathroom? What did you touch?"

"Doorknobs, both sides of the door. Toilet handle, and the seat, too. You men always leave it up." She opened her eyes and smiled at him.

He smiled back but motioned for her to close her eyes again. "Did you use a towel?"

"Yes, face and hands. Touched the faucets, too, both of them. I left the towel neat, like I found it."

"Take a shower? A bath?"

"No."

It went on. Nobody else interrupted, but Amanda and Atkins both took notes furiously. About half an hour into it Bobby asked if she ate or drank anything.

"I think so," Pamela said hesitantly.

Bobby raised his eyebrows.

"I think maybe I threw it up."

Bobby said nothing, waited for her to go on.

Pamela looked pleadingly at Amanda, who said, "She had an anxiety attack, Bobby. Massive one."

Bobby looked at Amanda and then back at Pamela.

She tilted her chin up and met his look. "I've been in therapy." When Bobby didn't respond she went on. "I didn't handle my father's death very well, and now I don't handle men in general very well. Mac was the first serious relationship I've had since high school, if you can call anything in high school serious."

"People in high school think they're serious," said Bobby.

Pamela was surprised by the remark, and it encouraged her. "I kept freaking out all the time, I kept trying anyway, last night things got pretty heavy, and I lost it."

"Lost it?"

"I just couldn't deal with it. I was so tight I couldn't even drink the coffee, and I think I threw it up. I started seeing things, and finally I knew it was no use and I left."

Bobby went back to all business. "What was he wearing when you left?"

"Nothing. He was naked."

"Did you make love?"

"Started to. Never finished."

"Did he?"

"No."

"Are you sure?"

"Yes."

"Was he awake when you left?"

"Yes. No. Yes, I kissed him at the door and then left. I think. Or a little time later, I'm not sure how long."

"Okay." Bobby stalled, the tip of his index finger tapping his chin. He didn't want to lose the spell, and even though he was fishing he knew there might be something important here. "Okay. Was the light on when you left?"

"Yes, but I don't remember either of us turning one on. It must have been on from when we came in."

"Now, when you—"

"Wait. The light went out as I was walking away. The light in Mac's living room."

"Are you sure? Are you positive?"

Pamela thought back to that moment, to the colored lights dropping from the trees, the moon as bright as the sun, and the stars connected each to the other by silvery filaments, but all obscured by the pressure in her head that had a shape and a pulsing glow of its own.

She dropped her head and looked at her hands, folded tightly in her lap. "No, I'm not."

Bobby got up and walked over to her. "Hey," he said quietly, his face still expressionless but softer somehow, his hand extended. "You done good."

"I guess you did, too," she said, taking his hand.

Having done all he could with Pamela, he resumed command. "Sky, you stay on top of the ME and the labs. Pull it all together and keep reporting on it as we meet. If anything really hot crops up, call it in to me directly. Time of death is number one priority."

Schuyler nodded and asked Amanda, "Can we put the punch on it?"

"Doubt we need to. Goverman doesn't get a lot of murders, and he'll clear the decks. But I'll put in a call just to let him know we're nervous."

"We've got approximate times from Jacoby, with possible

corroboration from a neighbor and phone records to her doctor. Run those down, and as long as you're in the neighborhood, grab a couple of uniforms and do a canvass. Suspicious cars, noises, the usual. And be cool: they know there was a murder, but they don't know the details. Let's keep it that way for a while."

"It's possible the place was cased," added Atkins, "so how 'bout we go back a few days?"

"Do that. I'll talk to her doctor myself." He turned to Pamela. "Jacoby, you and I'll visit with Mac's buddy, what's his name again?"

"Dr. Nostrand. Jake. How come?"

"The guy that found him?"

"Yeah. How come?"

"We don't know enough about Mac's background. Could be important. And you'll need to release your doctor." He looked around. "Any questions?" There were none.

"Let's hit the streets."

———•———

As they left, Pamela pulled Amanda aside. "Captain, what does Parks mean, he's going to talk to my doctor? I mean, that's pretty private stuff. *Really* private. What does he mean, 'release'?"

"Don't worry about it. Your sessions are privileged communications. All we want are the timing details. Nobody's going to get at your secrets."

"Y'sure?"

"That stuff's between you and your doctor. Don't worry about it. 'Scuse me a second. Parks!" she yelled, and walked off toward the front door.

Bobby wheeled around and stopped, eyebrows raised in question.

"The autopsy's important," Amanda said as she walked up to him.

"Hell, yes. There's a lot to corroborate in what Jacoby told us."

"Right. So cover it yourself."

He stared at her for a moment without speaking, then said, "What the hell for? I'm no ME, I won't know what he's—"

"Be there," she said. "Talk to him, listen to what he says, but most of all make sure he's going after the right stuff, stuff that'll shed some light on whatever theories we come up with."

"Listen, Mandy, I just don't think—"

"It wasn't a request, Lieutenant," she said as she turned to leave. "Besides, most of that FBI business was in the classroom, wasn't it?" She was halfway across the floor now. "Do you good to get dirty a little." Then she was gone.

CHAPTER
18

I gotta tell you, Doc, I thought that business with a couch was an old joke. Do your patients really lie on this while they talk to you?"

Brixton Ferrin laughed in appreciation of Bobby Parks's straightforward style. "As a matter of fact, they do."

"How come?"

"Several reasons, really. For one, it's relaxing and helps to put the patient at ease. Second, and perhaps more important, they don't have to look at me."

"You're not so bad looking," said Bobby, eyeing him up and down playfully.

"Awfully good of you to say so," Ferrin returned in kind. "In truth, people find it much easier to discuss difficult topics when they don't have to look another person right in the eye," he said, looking Bobby right in the eye.

"I guess you're right," said Bobby, returning the look without flinching, then flinching. "Now you've got me self-conscious. I wasn't even thinking about it until you mentioned it."

"Common reaction. Interesting also how we use the phrase *self-conscious* in negative terms. To be self-con-scious is to be embarrassed, just the opposite of what we're trying to do here, although I can tell you that being conscious of yourself can be the most uncomfortable feeling of all sometimes."

"So the couch helps."

"It does. Care to try it?" asked Ferrin, gesturing toward the furniture in question.

"Hell, no," Bobby said as he threw up his hands, palms outward. "Never get me on that thing."

Ferrin grinned and leaned back in his chair. "So sit here instead," he said, indicating the chair in front of his desk.

"Much better," Bobby said when he was seated.

"I must warn you in advance, Lieutenant," began Ferrin, adopting a more serious tone. "I won't divulge anything about my patient without her permission."

"There's no need to invoke doctor-patient privilege here. Pamela is not a suspect, at least not a real one. She's even been assigned to the investigation, although a lot of people are not too happy about that."

"I'm not concerned about her relationship to this case, although Lord knows I hope you catch the killer with all speed. I only care about her privacy."

"Understood," said Bobby, nodding emphatically. "It's just that we know so little at this point. We're pursuing all avenues just trying to get any information that might give us some kind of a bead on the guy, and we're fishing." He paused and looked at Ferrin.

"And?" prompted Ferrin.

"And, maybe you can help."

"How?" Ferrin asked cautiously, putting his hands together as if in prayer and touching his index fingers to his lips.

"Look, Pamela says she was whacked-out the night of the murder. She's hazy on details and timing and isn't making a very good witness, but she's trying. She also doesn't seem to know a lot about Graham, like they've been dancing around each other for weeks."

Ferrin stared at Bobby without speaking but opened his hands slightly as an invitation to continue.

"So we thought maybe she told you something significant in therapy, something about their relationship that might shed some light on things but that she may not think was significant enough to tell us." He paused. "Okay, well, maybe not about their relationship, but about him, that wouldn't be a violation of anything, would it?"

"It might be." Ferrin looked thoughtful. "I want to help you, but I can't get into anything that might compromise her rights."

"But something about *him* doesn't have anything to do with *her*. So what's the problem?"

"The problem, Lieutenant, is that whatever Pamela Jacoby tells me is filtered through Pamela Jacoby. Not the policewoman, but the patient. It's done in the context of her therapy, not a criminal investigation. I'm not interested in Mackenzie Graham, only Pamela Jacoby, and I'm only interested in her perceptions of Graham insofar as they reveal something about her, not him. How she describes him to me says a good deal about her, how she perceives men, what she notices, what she ignores, what she finds pleasing and what terrifies her. These are secrets, Lieutenant, and they belong to her, and she comes to me because not only do I try to help her understand their meaning, but because she knows that they never leave this room." Ferrin had grown animated during his monologue and by the end was leaning far forward. He became aware of this as he finished and looked surprised to find himself half out of his seat.

Bobby saw it, too, and thought it best to lighten the moment. "Gee whiz, Doc, no need to sugarcoat it; go right ahead and feel free to express yourself."

Ferrin stared at him for a second, then slumped back on his chair with an embarrassed and self-deprecating laugh that Bobby found affecting. "Sorry. It's just that this is such a vitally important part of the process. It's tough enough trying to get people to open up. Imagine if they thought there was a chance anything could get out."

"I understand completely, and I should be the one who's sorry. What you explained just never occurred to me."

Now it was Ferrin's turn to be disarmed. Expecting an ill-considered and inelegant argument, he found instead a reasoned apology. He saw right through the transparent technique to soften him up but acquiesced in spite of himself. "Can I help another way?"

"I do have some logistics to confirm, mostly routine, about the night of the murder. Let me ask you some questions."

"Go ahead. I can answer anything about my own movements."

"Good. As for Pamela, I can tell you what she's already told us, and you can either confirm it or not, all right?"

"Fair enough."

"You went to Pamela's apartment that night, correct?"

"Yes. She called and asked me to come."

"About what time was that?"

"I'd say the phone call was about, oh, maybe quarter of twelve or a little after."

"Why did she call?"

Ferrin hesitated. "She was troubled."

"How so?" asked Bobby.

"Let's just leave it at that."

"She told us that she'd had a date with Mac, they went to bed, started doing it and the roof fell in. Things get unclear after that, but somewhere along the line she got dressed and walked home." He stopped and looked at Ferrin, who appeared startled.

"She told you all of that?"

"Yes. Basically true?"

"Why, yes. I'm surprised she was so forthcoming."

"She's a professional," said Bobby. "Her boyfriend was murdered and mutilated, and she wants the sonofabitch that did it to fry. How long did it take you to get to her place?"

"About fifteen minutes."

"Did you see anybody on the way over?"

"I'm afraid I don't understand."

"The time is important, Doctor. The medical examiner can only get so much accuracy. We need to fit as many pieces together as possible. We can get phone records with the exact time of the call, but sometimes calls don't show up, especially local ones."

"Ah, I see. I don't recall seeing any . . . Wait. A neighbor, Pamela's neighbor."

"Tell me."

"She came out of her flat as I was knocking on Pamela's door. She asked who I was and I told her, and she said Pamela looked dreadful. Yes, that's how she put it, 'dreadful.' Then Pamela called out for me to come in, and the neighbor tried to look around me into the flat as I opened the door, and I said something to her. She looked a bit offended and went back into her own place."

"And this would have been, what, around twelve-fifteen?"

"I imagine so. Something like that."

"What was the matter with Pamela?"

Ferrin bristled at the question, as though his lecture had gone unheeded. "I told you. She was troubled."

"She said she thought she was going crazy, seeing things, stuff like that."

"Basically correct."

"She said you gave her a shot."

"A tranquilizer. Powerful one."

"Did she tell you anything that might help us? Did she mention anyone else, see anything, did Mac act strange, was there a phone call, anything?"

Ferrin rubbed his forehead, lost in thought. "Truthfully, she said nothing like that. She'd had a significant trauma, she was in a great deal of pain, mentally, and I gave her something to calm her and make her sleep."

"But you saw her in therapy after that. Did she say anything then?"

"I'm sorry, Lieutenant."

Bobby started to lose his temper, as much at Ferrin as at himself for failing to shake Ferrin's obstinate adherence to protocol. "Jesus Christ, Doc, I've got a fucking lunatic on the loose somewhere and you're standing on ceremony here."

Ferrin was not intimidated and hit back as hard as Bobby. "Look here, Lieutenant," he said sternly, slamming his fist onto the desktop. "Let's not give each other advice on our respective professions. I will not have you going back to your team and announcing some bit of information that could only have come from Pamela via me. You catch your killer and I'll handle my patient, and don't come back expecting me to violate confidences."

Bobby sat back, defeated, knowing that Ferrin was well within his legal rights and also trying to wrestle the balance between Pamela Jacoby's right to privacy and his obligation to the public trust.

Ferrin broke into his thoughts. "There is one thing you ought to know, and the only reason I'm telling you is that you'll probably find out anyway. Pamela's meeting Mac wasn't an accident. His friend Jake Nostrand and I arranged it."

"She already knew about Dr. Nostrand." He noticed that this seemed to be news to Ferrin. "I don't think she knew you were in on it. What's the big deal?"

"It's one thing if your friends set it up, but your psychiatrist? She would have spent all her time trying to dig underneath it. We wanted it to be natural, to be . . . nice, I suppose. If she thought it was part of her therapy, it never would have worked. As it happened . . ." His voice trailed off, and he looked toward the window, out into the distance, in rueful contemplation.

"Well," said Bobby, rising. "I don't see the point in telling her now."

Ferrin looked back at him gratefully. "Thank you," he said, then got up and came around the desk, offering his hand. "I'm sorry I couldn't be of more assistance, Lieutenant. Doesn't mean you shouldn't continue to ask."

"I understand," said Bobby, taking Ferrin's hand. "You shouldn't think I won't keep trying."

"Fair enough," said Ferrin, and walked him to the door. He seemed to consider something for a long time, then said, "Incidentally, I wouldn't be too concerned about her being on the team."

"Oh? Why's that?"

Ferrin paused and watched a look of distant awareness start to appear in Bobby's eyes. He could see him jump hopefully to the conclusion that Pamela Jacoby's psychiatrist was professing her innocence. He stopped it cold. "Don't read too much into that, Lieutenant. All I'm saying is that she's much tougher than she looks, in a lot of ways."

Bobby nodded slightly. "I'm glad. These aren't easy days. She sure seems pretty together about it."

"Shan't last," Ferrin said with casual confidence. "The enormity of it hasn't set in yet."

"I was afraid of that," said Bobby. He squirmed uncomfortably. Ferrin noticed and knew there was something else on his mind, but he stood quietly and let him find his own time.

"Doc," Bobby began, "have you got a couple minutes more?" He shifted position once again. "It's not about Jacoby."

"Certainly," said Ferrin, reaching into his sweater pocket for a cigarette and indicating a living room chair.

Bobby sat and cleared his throat. "Have you ever seen an autopsy?"

Maintaining a poker face was a professional skill, but Ferrin could not hide his surprise at that question. "Of course," he answered, sitting down on a couch. "Required in medical school. Why do you ask?"

Bobby leaned forward and asked in lowered tones, "What's it like?"

———◆———

He swung the squad car around in a tight U-turn, stopping just outside the station house door. Pamela opened the car door and stepped in. Bobby glanced at the outside rearview mirror, then once over his right shoulder, and pulled out.

"Quite a guy, your Dr. Ferrin," he said without looking at her.

"You didn't stay very long," she said, then added warily, "Get anything useful?"

"No," Bobby answered testily, and was instantly sorry because he knew it wasn't Pamela's fault. He tried to soften his tone. "One thing you don't have to worry about is that guy spilling any of your innermost nasties."

She stayed silent, knowing there was a question hanging in the air somewhere but unwilling to acknowledge it just yet. She thought that her earlier public testimonials to her weaknesses and failings were sufficiently revelatory to warrant a stay on further such indignities, but she was smart enough to know that detectives were relentless in the face of a major crime. That relentlessness could easily metamorphose into storm trooper mode if the case went badly and they were desperate for leads.

"I tried to get him to tell me about Mac, but he wouldn't," Bobby continued. "He said that all he knows he got from you, so it would invade your privacy for him to say anything."

"But I told you everything I could remember," Pamela protested. "What did you think you'd gain from Ferrin that I didn't already provide?"

"You didn't tell us very much about Mac."

"But I don't know that much. We didn't spend a lot of time comparing histories."

"So maybe you told Ferrin something that would be useful, only you don't remember or you don't think it's important. If we had your transcripts—"

"No!" Pamela interrupted, a tinge of hysteria in her voice. She quickly regained control. "Listen, are you kidding or what? You got any idea what goes on between a person and her therapist? How'd you like me to stick a tape recorder under your bed some night you're having a hot dream and talking in your sleep?" When Bobby didn't respond she continued. "This isn't fair, Bobby. You're asking the impossible and it's making me look uncooperative and it's not fair."

Bobby considered for a few moments and then said, "Okay. Maybe you're right. But we have so little to go on, and sooner or later the rest of the guys are gonna start getting antsy for information, however weak the links."

"I'm telling you, there's nothing there we can use." They were pulling up in front of Jake Nostrand's house, and as the car drew to a stop Pamela said, "Nostrand set me up, you know. With Mac. I'm almost positive."

"So you said."

"He doesn't know I know, though. He's so sweet, he was just trying to be helpful. Probably eating himself up over it now."

"Why not let him off the hook?" asked Bobby.

"How?" she replied. "What do you mean?" But they were already up to the front door and Bobby had rung the bell.

Jennifer Nostrand opened the door, barely noticed Bobby and looked at Pamela. Her eyes started to moisten, and it was obvious she'd spent time telling herself not to do just that. Her composure crumbled visibly, and she put her arms around Pamela, her words muffled. "Oh, Pamela, I'm so sorry. . . ."

Pamela hugged her back, avoiding Bobby's eyes, and said, "It's okay, Jenny. Really."

Jennifer drew back and looked at Pamela, still holding her arms. She saw strength there, and determination, and she resolved not to let her own feelings interfere with Pamela's efforts to maintain her grip. Jake appeared at the door, and Pamela was dismayed at his appearance. He seemed thinner, paler, and his clothes, normally not much to look at anyway, appeared even more disheveled than usual.

"Hiya, Jake," Pamela said with a forced cheerfulness that didn't fool anybody. Her smile faded, and she said, "Christ, you look worse than I do."

Jake smiled with his mouth but not his eyes, and stepped back so Bobby and Pamela could enter. As they did so, Jake said, "I don't know what to do. I don't know how this works. We're his only family here, and we have to clean up, look after his place. But they're still investigating, and we can't go in, and if we do, I don't know what to take, what to leave, or what to do with anything." He looked at Pamela helplessly, his confused eyes pitiable.

When they were all seated in the living room, Bobby took out his notebook and said, "I know this is difficult for you both, but somebody's still on the loose out there. The physical evidence isn't very helpful, and we've got to get smarter about Graham so we can start looking for connections." Jake was still looking at Pamela. "Do you understand?" Bobby said directly to him in a commanding voice.

The question brought Jake around, and he said, "Yes, Officer. We'll be as helpful as possible." He looked back at Pamela. "There are a lot of things about Mac you didn't know, Pam. Eventually you would have learned everything, but it didn't seem important at first. Did he tell you we were friends at medical school?"

"Yes," said Pamela, "but not much beyond that."

"Doctor," said Bobby, "let me make a suggestion. We sort of need it all, rather than just filling in what Pamela doesn't know.

Why don't you start telling me about Mac, and assume I know nothing, which is pretty much true."

"Yes, I see," said Jake. "Well, where to begin . . . ?"

"Why not start with telling us how Mac ended up here?" prompted Bobby.

"Tell them about the accident," Jennifer said.

Jake described the death of the union organizer that had driven Mac from school and away from his friends and family. Under professional questioning from Bobby and a more personal interrogation from Pamela (who could not have guessed the scope of Mac's ignoble flight from things human and decent), Jake tried as best he could to reconstruct Mac's odyssey. Most of it was rumor, some came from late night, alcohol-fueled excursions into Mac's memory, some from the police officers who took Mac in and, sensing something unusual that set him apart, agreed to release him into Jake's custody with a minimum of fuss and paperwork.

Is there anyone not running from his past? thought Pamela. *Are we all bound inextricably to a set of starting conditions, like the lead weights under a jockey's saddle, the handicap we can never discard and whose presence we are forced to accept as part of the game?* She felt a deep sadness at the impact Mac's death was having on Jake. She sensed that there was a strong element of guilt as well, and she was starting to understand what Bobby had meant before Jennifer opened the door, about letting him off the hook. When Jake didn't go on, she looked at him and said, "I know you engineered our first meeting, Jake. At the hospital."

Jake was startled and failed to contain his surprise. "You did? When?"

Pamela smiled and said, "I suspected it all along, but wasn't really sure until just now." Jake's uncertain look prompted her to go on. "I never mentioned it because I wanted it to be real, and anything else, even something as simple as your scheme, would have spoiled the illusion. It was wonderful of you, Jake. None of this is your fault."

This seemed to give him small comfort. "There's one other thing," he said.

"Yes?"

Jennifer broke in and finished for Jake. "He was falling in love with you, Pamela." At Pamela's surprised look she went on: "He really was. He didn't say it in those words, but we knew. He wanted to give you all the time you needed to get used to things, to the two of you. He was in no hurry. He wanted it to work."

The look of surprise on Pamela's face was still there. She looked back at Jake and said, "That wasn't it. That isn't what you wanted to tell me."

Now Jennifer looked bewildered. "No," said Jake.

"You wanted to tell me Ferrin was in on it, too."

Jake was extremely discomfited by now and said, "But why didn't you let on that you knew?"

"Because," answered Pamela, "it was less embarrassing to just let it lie. I didn't want to spend time with you all in therapy, talking about relationships. I just wanted to have one." She continued to derive strength from the near mania attendant to her newfound relief, and it was important to her to make Jake and Jennifer comfortable, to "let them off the hook," as Bobby so aptly put it. They were her last link to Mac, her only link, really, to a fantasy life no longer available to her in reality. "I know what Ferrin was trying to do, and it was right. It would have been right." She didn't really believe that, but it was an illusion worth hanging on to.

"He told me about a theory called complementary neurosis. Still experimental, but I wanted to use it to help Mac. Ferrin refused at first." Jake's hands lay still in his lap. "I pressed him. After a week, he finally gave up and agreed."

Jake stood, walked over to Pamela, leaned over and hugged her, hard. He had come to think of her as strapping and healthy, but now she felt fragile, like an abandoned sparrow, and as his guilt and mortification started to give way to a more rational and manageable sorrow, he felt protective of her in a fierce and paternalistic way. She was his last link to Mac, too. He owed them both.

CHAPTER 19

Assistant District Attorney Scott LaBelle, not normally given to dramatics, stopped in his tracks and threw a shocked look at Amanda.

"You can't be serious, Mandy," he said.

"I am serious," she retorted.

He was practically sputtering. "She's the only material witness, f'Chrissakes! How can you have her on the case?"

"Because we need her. Information on the victim is sparse. She's practically all we've got except the Nostrands, and they don't know much, either."

LaBelle tried to calm himself in order to convey thoughtfulness rather than hysteria to Captain Grant. "You need her or she needs you?"

Amanda asked cautiously, "What do you mean?"

LaBelle looked in both directions, then lowered his voice. "I heard she's half a bubble out of plumb."

"She's had some problems. She sees a therapist."

LaBelle was not without compassion. His record of successful convictions was due in no small part to his deep rapport with policemen in general and this captain in particular. The cops trusted him because he sometimes sacrificed the niceties of protocol to achieve a greater goal, and his advice on procedures to strengthen cases was welcome and received without offense. Over time, Amanda's troops had come to believe that the answer to crime was not more cops, but more DAs, that caseloads and crowded dockets were a greater detriment to the administration of justice than any other single factor.

So they listened when he spoke, because the times that they didn't, before they got to know him, they occasionally watched suspects walk on technicalities that could have been avoided. He never rubbed it in, but the offending officers withered under his glare.

"Mandy, you've got to listen to me on this one. Her presence could be extremely prejudicial to our case once we bring it."

"But she had nothing to do with the crime," Amanda protested.

"Of course not. We all know that. But picture a suspect in court with a good lawyer. Try to anticipate his closing argument. 'Ladies and gentlemen, this police officer, a psychiatric patient, goes to bed with the victim. That same night he is murdered and sexually brutalized. She has no alibi, she needs a tranquilizer to calm her down, and she winds up on the team investigating the murder, where she has the opportunity to tamper with evidence, give false testimony and deflect the investigators away from the truth.' I might as well phone in my own closing."

Amanda held her ground. "If I believed we were going in weak, I'd worry about it. But we'll go in strong or we won't go in at all. And we've taken steps to keep it clean."

LaBelle slumped against the wall, shaking his head, knowing Amanda's mind was made up. He changed subjects. "They're calling it a fag murder in the DA's office."

"Why?"

"Genital mutilation seems to be a common theme in crimes of homosexual jealousy," he answered. "My homophobic colleagues have a way with words."

"Interesting," Amanda said half to herself as they started walking again. She led the way to a small conference room, where Parks, Atkins, Schuyler and Pamela were already assembled.

"Hey, Libel," said Atkins. "Captain let you have a hall pass today?"

Schuyler chimed in as well. "Thought this was an important case. How come we get the B team?"

LaBelle unbuttoned his jacket and dropped into a chair, throwing his arm over the back in exaggerated nonchalance. "If you knuckleheads could stay off the sauce for five minutes in a row, I might get to go fishing once in a while instead of baby-sitting."

He looked at Pamela, knowing enough not to embarrass her with public expressions of sympathy but suddenly uneasy with such light-hearted banter in her presence. "Hi, Jacoby," he said gently, with a small smile.

"Hi, Libel. Nail any bad guys lately?"

"Not this week. You?"

She shook her head. "Not so far."

Amanda stood at the front of the small room and started the meeting. "I've asked the assigned ADA to get involved early because this thing could get complicated. He's already given me grief about Jacoby."

LaBelle continued to look at Pamela. *Nothing personal*, his look said. *I understand*, said hers.

"He'll give us advice on how to minimize the damage, but it's our call until we have someone to charge."

LaBelle looked at Amanda and nodded. "I've been dealt worse cards." He paused for effect. "Lost every one of 'em, too." The laughter in the room helped to ease the tension.

Bobby nodded to Schuyler, who rose to update the team on late developments. "We're pretty certain the killer took a shower. There was blood everywhere, but not a trace leaving the house. No hairs on the towels except Mac's, which is pretty weird. We're still checking on that."

Atkins broke in when it was obvious Schuyler had nothing else. "Preliminary spatter analysis says Mac was alive when he got cut." He looked at Pamela, then quickly turned away. The unspoken protocol among the team was business as usual. Pamela appreciated it. He read from a sheet of paper. "Splash patterns indicate an arterial spray aimed up and to the left of victim's position. Force was sufficient to establish that the heart was still beating. Victim was lying on his back and was not moved after the knife attack. Sounds like he never knew what hit him."

He paused. "There's another thing. There's a pattern on some wrinkles in the sheet that hit from the side opposite where Mac was lying."

Bobby broke the silence that followed. "I don't get it. Somebody else?"

"No," said Atkins, "the blood was the same. It took Goverman a few minutes to figure it out. The guy was standing on the left side of the bed, which was the direction of the spray. The blood hit him and bounced back. There's a blank spot on the floor a few feet away where he blocked the spray."

"How sure is Goverman?" asked Bobby.

"Very. He had the spatter guy figure the velocity of the spray. Left side was about seventeen meters per second, which tallies with an artery cut. Right side was practically straight down, and slow."

"So the killer got soaked," said LaBelle. "That's why he took a shower."

"That seems to be the deal," confirmed Atkins. "And while we're at it, the victim was only hit in the head once, for what that's worth. No medium-velocity impact stains anywhere"— the kind that would have been produced had a blunt instrument been used a second time, on already bloodied skin.

"Then there must have been somebody walking around with bloody clothes on at some point," said Bobby. "Even if he tried to wash them, they would have been soaking wet."

"What about the neighborhood canvass?" Amanda asked Atkins.

"Nothing," he said. "No cars parked in front of the house, no suspicious characters, nothing. We did get a confirmation of Jacoby's timings, though." He consulted his notes. "The neighbor, Ms. McGillicutty, says she saw Pamela come in somewhere around eleven-fifteen or eleven-thirty. She was more certain about Ferrin showing up, because the 'Tonight' show was already over. She would put that at about one-fifteen."

"That's a little later than Ferrin remembered," said Bobby. "He said about twelve-fifteen, but he wasn't very sure. Anything from the ME on time of death yet?"

"Yeah," said Schuyler, flipping through his notepad. "Midnight, plus or minus an hour."

Atkins whipped around and looked at Pamela. "Guess that lets you off the hook, kiddo," he said with a grin. The subject of Pamela's being a suspect had not been discussed openly, and Atkins's ill-timed address of the topic, however well meant, did not generate the mirth he expected.

"No, it doesn't," Pamela said to him quietly, her classroom knowledge of police forensics, recently acquired, clearly exceeding his own.

Bobby explained. "The 'plus or minus an hour' is equal probability across the range. Eleven o'clock is as probable as one o'clock. It only tails off on either side of that."

"Whoops," Atkins said sheepishly.

"It's not an issue, anyway," said Bobby. "We're in trouble. We're running on fumes."

"What about this Murdoch guy?" LaBelle asked of no one in particular.

The room grew silent. Pamela broke the stillness. "Dennis Murdoch? What about him?"

LaBelle looked at Amanda, then at Bobby, who finally spoke. "The night we nailed that guy knocking over video stores? You drove Captain Grant to the scene."

"I remember," said Pamela. "What about it?"

"You had some words with Murdoch," said Amanda. "Embarrassed him in front of his partner and some other cops. You thought it was funny, but he didn't."

A frown crossed Pamela's face. "Hardly sounds like a reason to kill my boyfriend."

"He's not had a lot of luck with women around the precinct," said Amanda.

"That's one way of putting it," LaBelle said to her.

"He's been harassing women around the station for years.

But it's not that bad, at least not since you explained the rules to him, Captain," said Pamela to Amanda.

"This was different," said Bobby. "I've never seen him that angry. It's hard to explain. It was just different. Worse."

"There's talk around the precinct about him," added Schuyler.

"What kind of talk?" asked LaBelle.

Schuyler looked uncomfortable. "Nothing specific. He's a little weird. Good cop; damned good, in fact. You know that, Libel."

LaBelle nodded his head. "That's true. But I also know what you mean. He's secretive somehow."

"Let's not get carried away here," warned Amanda. "I know we're in trouble, but let's keep cool, okay?"

"Can't hurt to check him out," said Atkins.

"No," Amanda said firmly. "Not unless there's more than apparent sexual jealousy, which is what I think his little outburst was all about." She changed topics quickly. "I think we should call a police psychologist in, see if we can't get some kind of a profile."

"The county's helped us out before," said Bobby. "I'll put in a call."

Amanda shook her head. "No. I'll do it."

CHAPTER 20

Excerpt from transcript of Pamela Jacoby clinical therapy session 51, June 28, 2:00 P.M., analyst Brixton T. Ferrin, M.D., Ph.D.

Can you remember anything else?
It's so hard. Everything was buzzing. I don't know what was real and what wasn't.

That's not important. Just talk.
But that won't help the investigation.

That's not my concern. I'm trying to help you. Maybe we can sort it out together.
I think I've told you pretty much all I can remember. It's so hard.

No, Pamela. It's too easy.
What are you talking about?

You've spent our last two sessions talking about the murder, the details, the case. It's been easy. I've let you avoid dealing with yourself.
[Silence.]

It brought back memories, didn't it?
Memories?

Of your father.
What are you talking about?

They both died violent deaths, just when you needed them
most.
*Needed my father? You're the one that's crazy, not
me. I didn't need him.*

Yes, you did. You needed him badly. But what you needed
was for him to be somebody else.
Who?

Somebody you could love.
I did love him.

No, you didn't.
*What are you talking about? Why are you doing this?
I spend countless hours with you hmmm-ing me to
death instead of telling me anything useful, and you
finally open your mouth and this shit comes out? I
don't get it. What the hell are you talking about?*

Pamela, we've waltzed around your father for months,
and we—
No—

—and we can't—
*No! Listen, this is bullshit, Doctor, there's nothing
going on in this stupid process so you dig out some
piece of psycho-mumbo-jumbo crap about my father
like it's a big-deal insight and toss it on the table.*

That's not—
*Forget it, Ferrin. This is bullshit. If we're going to
keep banging on this every time I come here, I'm
quitting. I don't need this, I got enough troubles....*

Okay, Pamela, okay. Please take it easy. I didn't mean to upset you.

[Sounds of muffled crying.]

Feel better?

[Short silence.] *I just don't think I want to know.*

How do you mean?

I think maybe I'd rather be all fucked up than get into shit that's better left buried.

It's not like a dead dog, Pamela. It doesn't stay buried. It's there all the time, and it'll haunt you and hurt you. [Long pause.] Time's about up.

———•———

She sat up and swung her legs out until her feet were on the floor. She didn't look up at him, but put her elbows on her knees and her face in her hands, rubbing her eyes.

"How's the investigation going?" asked Ferrin.

Pamela put her head back and looked at the ceiling before answering. "Lousy," she said finally. "They think maybe it was a gay revenge thing."

"Oh?"

"Because of the mutilation. Does that make sense?"

"It's the standard first conclusion."

"I've been thinking about visiting the scene. Maybe see something, remember something. I don't know . . ." Her voice trailed off. When Ferrin didn't respond she said, "It's like this great thing that's out there, waiting for me, always there. I'm supposed to be a cop. What's the big deal? Just another gory murder."

She looked at Ferrin. "I'm terrified. If I even think about it, I start to shake." She clasped her hands together and squeezed. "But I think I have to do it."

"Would you like me to go with you?" Ferrin asked.

Pamela turned to face him. "Do you mean it? Would you do that?"

"If you like. You might also like a mild tranquilizer before you go in, at least the first time."

"The first time?"

"Just to get used to the idea. Then, after the initial shock, you can go back, no drugs, and try to be a cop." He smiled warmly, and Pamela brightened.

"That's good thinking. I have to run it past Captain Grant first, though."

"Why?"

"I'm not officially on the team. No solo work. There'll have to be another cop."

"Is that necessary? I'll be there."

"You're not a professional. Cop, I mean."

"All right. Set it up and we'll do it together. But Pamela . . ." She looked up questioningly. "Next time, we're going to talk about your father. There's no getting around it anymore."

CHAPTER 21

Dr. Edan Tancredi studied his two visitors before speaking.

He already knew Amanda. She had taken one of his advanced courses and solicited his assistance on two other cases. She would have made a good Israeli woman, he thought: not afraid to be feminine, but not willing to take any crap from swaggering males.

The black was more interesting. Tancredi, son of an Italian father and Israeli mother, guessed he was fighting his past, overachieving to compensate for his anti-cop upbringing. The files said they had been in the academy together. They made quite a pair: it could not have been easy for either of them. At least they had their friendship holding them up.

Bobby stared back in wonder at the small man in an old brown suit, unruly tufts of white hair sticking out of both sides of his head. You might hardly notice him sipping coffee in a diner, he thought, except for the eyes. Bobby had seen eyes like that only once, on an FBI agent nearing retirement, brought in to mastermind the bust of a cocaine distribution network. Those eyes sucked in information, mixed it with hard-won wisdom and filed away the results for future use. Tancredi's were different from those only in their tinge of sadness, as though he had seen too much but wasn't allowed the luxury of unburdening to another human. Bobby knew something about his background as well.

Tancredi shrugged expressively, reaching for his pipe. "A homosexual revenge killing, so am I thinking." Slight Middle Eastern accent. "This you knew without me. A lot of mayhem?"

"No," said Bobby. "In fact, it appears the killer cleaned up after himself."

This seemed to interest Tancredi. Bobby knew he had been head of a covert operations subsection of the Mossad. His specialty had been the psychopathology of terrorism. His insights and his ability to unravel the convoluted neuronal dementia of the politically motivated criminal had led to the humiliating downfall of several notorious terrorists. The legendary Amalfi Al-Sahaad was captured in an expensive Iranian brothel after Tancredi figured out that his entire political agenda was geared around the women who would flock to him after spectacular acts of destruction. Al-Sahaad himself had no idea what drove him, but Tancredi uncovered it from a distance.

"Cleaned up? What means, cleaned up?"

"Wiped the scene, probably took a shower," said Amanda, studying his face, hoping for a brilliant observation that would provide a new lead.

"Please, lady cop, don't look at me like soon I'm solving your case before you leave." He had given her a hug and a kiss when she'd walked into his office. Bobby was surprised, but not as much as when his captain had warmly returned the affection.

"I didn't come all the way down here for your sloppy kisses, Tanc," she said.

"There was a time, believe me when I am saying this, when some women would have, you know. An interesting end to what is I am supposing a crime of passion." Amanda knew Tancredi filled in his thinking time with idle chatter. "The victim, he was alive when the cutting is started?"

"Yes, but not conscious."

"How?"

"Blow to the head. Probably while sleeping."

"You said he had sex with your officer, a female, but he is not finishing. Are you sure?"

"Of what?" asked Bobby.

"That he is not finishing?"

"The officer said he didn't. Is it important?"

"Could be. Changes the scenario. Who is the medical examiner?"

"Judson Goverman."

Tancredi rolled his eyes toward the ceiling. "A *putz*, but one of the best MEs. He needs to be telling us, did the victim ejaculate."

"Can he do that?" asked Bobby.

"He can do that," answered Tancredi. "Depending how much of his *schvanz* is left. Ask. Two rough possibilities."

Amanda and Bobby, realizing that he had switched tracks again, leaned forward slightly as he continued. "One, a diversion. A straight hit made to looking like a gay murder. The other, a final act of contempt from a jealous lover."

"I don't get the second one," said Bobby.

"If the victim is having a homosexual lover, he was bisexual. The victim, I mean, because he is dating your police officer, yes? That would mean that the lover maybe adopted the feminine side. After he kills the victim, how is he rubbing it in his face?"

Bobby nodded. "He cleans up. Like a housewife after a party. Taking care of business as though his lover's death didn't matter."

Tancredi leaned back and drew on his pipe. "Just so. Maybe. Just a possibility."

"We need to keep the gay angle under wraps for a while, Tanc," said Amanda. "We don't want to scare the guy away if he's around."

Tancredi turned his hands up in resignation. "It is hardly news. Common motif. . . ."

"But we haven't let the detalis out yet. We're going to try to keep it that way."

"DA's people already know," Bobby reminded her. He turned to Tancredi. "They're starting to refer to it as the fag murder."

"Enlightened bunch, your DAs," said Tancredi. "And a secret is a secret between two cops or DAs maybe when one of them is being dead."

"They don't mean anything by it," said Amanda. "It's just horsing around. And they're savvy enough to keep it in the family."

"Myself, I say dipping into the gay underground for some intelligence," suggested Tancredi.

Amanda smiled at him. "The what?"

"We still are treating them as outlaws, so they are acting like it," Tancredi explained. "A separate subculture, largely impenetrable."

"You're out of touch, Doctor," said Bobby. "In our little burg it's pretty out in the open."

At Tancredi's look of bewilderment, Amanda explained further. "Half the cops in town eat in the gay neighborhoods and send their wives to shop there."

Tancredi didn't smile. "All very admirable, I am sure. But I tell you this." He leaned forward. "There are many not so open. Maybe policemen in your own precinct, who knows? These are not living in the gay neighborhoods. These are scared people, frightened from discovery. They are even married, maybe, with children. Somewhere there is a subculture, beneath what you see. You would do well to go and see."

He leaned back, and Amanda and Bobby both felt a little less complacent about an attitude they had shared for years. As police officers they did not concern themselves with private matters as long as those matters did not run afoul of the laws they were pledged to protect. The rapport between the police and the gay community was founded on a simple, tacit agreement: We don't cause trouble, and you protect us. They liked having the police visible in their neighborhoods. It discouraged bored and insecure lowlifes from capricious violence toward them.

But Tancredi was right. The cops involved themselves only with the declared, not the hidden, and it was quite possible that the latter outnumbered the former. There had to be a network or, more likely, many networks.

"I've got one or two ideas," said Amanda. She turned to Bobby. "And I think we better talk with Dr. Nostrand some more and get a better handle on Mac Graham's activities before he arrived in town."

Tancredi nodded as Amanda spoke. She turned back to him and said, "Can we keep the lid on this for a while?"

The irony of asking that question of a former Mossad officer was not lost on any of them. "Not to worry. I am needing to do a bit more research before I issue a preliminary report, anyway."

As they rose to leave, Tancredi asked, "Mandy, how is your young officer?"

"Holding up remarkably well, I think. She's been in therapy, so she has someone to lean on."

"Yes," said Tancredi. "That is helpful. Watch her carefully, though. Sometimes the shock, it has a way of delaying itself, yes?"

"That's just what her doctor told me," said Bobby. "What might she do?"

"Who knows?" Tancredi said resignedly. "If I am that smart, I would be a police captain instead of a *putz* psychologist."

"I can't thank you enough, Tanc," said Amanda. "Please give me a call when your preliminary is available."

"Just a day or two for looking at some old papers."

———◆———

Amanda and Bobby walked into the precinct house after the drive back from the county facility where Tancredi had his office.

"I'll get onto Nostrand about more on Graham's background," said Bobby. "What are you going to do about this underground business?"

"I've got one or two calls I might be able to make," Amanda replied. "And Bobby: Talk to Jake without Pamela. No sense getting her more upset."

"Got it," he said.

When he was out of earshot, Amanda leaned down to the attendant outside her office. "Get me Jack Krakowitz on the line," she said quietly.

CHAPTER
22

He was prepared for the smell. Every description he had read, every account he had heard, had mentioned the smell. So he understood it and was prepared, as much as one could get ready for anything not actually experienced before. *No problem*, he told himself, and pulled open the swinging door and it hit him, and he pondered the immediacy with which his stomach started boiling and his head swimming. The smell wasn't *like* anything, not *like* the spoiled meat they'd compared it to, not *like* a slaughterhouse at the end of the day, not *like* anything, just uniquely its own.

It was the smell of death, of inglorious putrefaction. No veil of formaldehyde or disinfectant could mask the essential truth of that smell, that what had once walked and breathed was now a decaying husk, discarded like an obviated wrapper.

He shut the door quickly without passing through, spun around and leaned against a gurney to catch his breath. The gurney started rolling under his weight but stopped when it banged into a pay phone with a metallic clang. He couldn't tell if the smell was still there or if he only imagined it was, or was it on his clothes, maybe indelibly, for how could such a thing be truly removed? Or was it on his soul forever?

I can't do this, he thought.

"Ah, Lieutenant, you needn't have waited out here. Door's open, I believe." Dr. Goverman's voice pierced the fog that had clouded his mind.

"No problem," said Bobby, hoping the catch in his voice might be mistaken for the normal growl of not having spoken for some hours. He cleared his throat. "Not much for me to do in there without you."

"Yes, quite. Well, let's do it." Whereupon he threw open both double doors and marched through quickly, leaving Bobby no choice but to follow suit or let the doors slam back into the jamb with a revealing *thwack*, the same sound they'd made just a minute before.

He realized that the smell that had coldcocked him was only the barest hint of what it was going to be. It thickened as they walked, as palpably as if the temperature were dropping as they went along, which, he soon realized, it in fact was.

"Hope you don't mind the cold, Parks," Goverman said cheerfully. "Keeps things fresher for just a little longer, right?"

"Right." He kept up with Goverman's pace. "Hate to be here on a hot day when the air-conditioning goes."

Goverman laughed. "It's happened. Coupla times."

Jesus H. Christ, I wonder what the hell that was like. "How'd you take it?"

"Worked a lot damned faster, I can tell you that. Made up some new techniques in a helluva hurry. Any questions while we're walking?"

"Just one. Why do you do this?"

"Because I love this stuff."

"You're shitting me." Bobby reacted too fast to take it back.

Goverman laughed good-naturedly, enjoying Bobby's discomfort. "Not dancing around cadavers, no, although it has its moments. I like the puzzle. All the clues. Some right there to be seen, some hidden, others only when hooked up to yet others."

"Helluva price to pay to do puzzles, it seems."

Goverman turned his head to look at Bobby as they walked. "What price do you pay to do your job, Lieutenant? You see 'em while they're freshly dead or dying, drowning in their own blood, surrounded by the trappings of their own demise, often violent. Here? More clinical and detached, scientific, proceduralized. Like in medical school."

Bobby had no answer for that one, and they had come to the inner room. Coldest of all now, and not just the temperature. Harsh fluorescent lights, brighter than one would normally expect to find, hung in metal fixtures from the ceiling on short chains. Six of these, and under each one an aluminum table seven feet long, all empty except for one, the farthest from where they were standing.

Next to it stood a Latino youth, maybe twenty years old. He was writing on a clipboard and turned to them as they entered. On the table before him was a sheet, barely disguising the contours of a human form beneath it.

Bobby had stopped without realizing it upon entering the room, and now he felt Goverman's hand on his back, urging him forward. "You're in luck, Parks. Light duty today. Just the one, so we've got lots of time to do this right."

Swell, Bobby thought as he forced his feet forward. It felt to him as though the shrouded form were growing closer as it enlarged in his vision, rather than him going toward it. At one end of the table a piece of paper poked out from under the sheet.

"Manny, say hello to Lieutenant Parks. He's gonna observe."

Bobby was transfixed by the shape on the table and only saw the Latino's hand come toward him out of the corner of his eye, but there was no sound of greeting. He reached his own hand forward and looked at the boy. "I know you from somewhere?"

Manny nodded. "Sort of. You busted me about three years ago."

Bobby looked at him closely. "Yeah. Auto theft, or something small. Smith, right?"

"It is now. I made it up back then. Kept it."

"That's all behind him now," said Goverman.

Bobby nodded. "That's good. We ACD'd you out. Never saw you again, so you must have cleaned up." ("Adjournment in contemplation of dismissal," the judge had said after confer-

ring with the DA and the cops. ACD. Keep your nose clean
and stay out of my court, and we make this case like it never
happened.)

Manny shrugged, as though embarrassed to be off the streets
and responsible. Bobby looked around and noticed for the first
time how scrupulously clean the room was. All the instruments neatly laid out, no papers out of place.

"Best goddamned *diener* I ever had," said Goverman, using
the slightly antiquated funerary terminology to refer to his
assistant. A handler of bodies, an unofficial paraprofessional
pathologist, a narrow specialist who, after hundreds of procedures, and nothing but, often guided the licensed dissector to
small things he might have missed. *After a while, you see
patterns.* "Swears he can tell by looking at their faces what
they were thinking when they died."

"That so?" asked Bobby. "What was *he* thinking?" and then
thought, *Oh, fuck, hold it a second, don't—*

But it was too late, and Manny reached for a corner of the
sheet and flipped it forward, revealing Mac Graham's dead
face, pale, washed out, splotched with a blue purplish hue in
places where no life forces were left to stop his blood from
congealing in convenient cavities. Without hesitating, Manny
leaned over and looked right into the cadaver's face, holding
his pose for several seconds. The dead eyes were open and
looked back. Bobby thought they'd be milky, opaque, but they
were perfectly clear, with what appeared to be blood spots in
the outer corners. Manny stood back up, restored the sheet and
said, "Wasn't thinking shit."

Goverman, who'd made the first determination at the scene
that Mac was unconscious at the time of death, smiled. "Told
you." He was slapping on rubber gloves, and Manny held out
a pair to Bobby, who waved them off.

"I don't plan on touching anything."

"Suit yourself," said Manny. He pulled a shoe box down
from a shelf and held it out to Bobby. "Any preferences?"

Bobby took the box, which contained several dozen cassette
tapes, and looked at Goverman in confusion. "Music?"

"Why not? What would you like?"

Bobby selected a cassette and handed it to Goverman, who said, "Mozart! Never woulda guessed it," while Manny rolled his eyes upward in a gesture of contempt. "Kid's not a Mozart fan."

"Bullshit," said Manny. "I just heard that one fi'ty million times already." He reached up to a microphone hanging from the ceiling and pulled it down until it was about a yard above the center of the table. He pressed a button mounted on the wall over the head of the table, then said "Testing" while watching a small meter above the button. The needle flickered halfway across the dial in response to his voice. He slid a pedal under the table so it came to rest near Goverman's foot, then handed him the clipboard. Goverman pressed the pedal, and a light came on over the meter.

"Postmortem examination of subject Graham, Mackenzie, number eight nine four seven alpha, confirmed by positive ID on toe tag. Goverman, Judson, M.D., county path, presiding. Assistant M. Smith, Police Lieutenant Robert Parks also present without objection. Authorization certificate in order, no limitations." He tapped the foot pedal, and the light went out. "Ever seen a post before, Parks?"

Bobby thought for a minute, trying for a witty response to dampen the ME's obvious merriment at his discomfort. He said, slowly and thoughtfully, "You know, I can't remember, really. . . ."

Goverman looked at him sharply. "You can't remem—?" *How the hell can you not remember if you saw a goddamned human dissection?* He turned back to the table. "Okay, are we ready or what?" he said somewhat irritably.

"All set," said Manny. It was a good job, well paying and steady, and Goverman tried to teach him something once in a while. After the ACD, his mother, who had pleaded with Bobby Parks to give him a break (Bobby had checked the kid's arms and found no tracks), had dragged him from the courtroom straight to the employment center. "Medical pathologist assistant," his father had read from the bulletin board posting. "D'fuck is that?" Mama had answered, "Never you mind," in a tone that brooked no dissension. "Eight hours a day, civil service benefits, learn a profession: you just got yourself a job, Manolo."

He opened the tap above the stainless-steel basin that rested off to the side of the table. Water ran down into the bottom and disappeared down the drain.

Without preamble or warning, Goverman drew off the entire sheet at once, leaving only a small towel over the body's genitals and another on the head that Bobby hadn't noticed when Manny had exposed the face before. An opaque, green plastic bag about the size of a sandwich rested between the body's feet. He had been standing a foot or so from the edge of the table and now leaned heavily against the unused table behind him. Manny looked at him quizzically. *What the hell are you looking at?* Bobby thought. *What was it like your first time?* But still wanting to save face, he tried to say something meaningful. "Why's his face covered?" The privates he could understand, kind of.

"Respect for the dead," Goverman said, "if you can believe that in a place like this. Tradition of a sort."

The towel covering the genitals looked unnaturally flat. Bobby wondered why, then he remembered, then he looked at the green plastic bag again, then he heard Goverman.

"Subject is Caucasian male, age consistent with death tag listing. Gross physical abnormalities include anterior cranial trauma above the right frontal eminence and below the hairline, in the form of a starburst laceration . . ." He touched the forehead wound and pressed his fingers down several times. They bounced slightly, as though pressing on a damp sponge. "With instability of the cranium beneath, indicating a depressed skull fracture, and . . ." He reached down and picked the towel up off Mac's middle. Bobby turned away and coughed. "Absence of external genitalia by apparently nonsurgical means."

Goverman replaced the towel and continued in this manner, dictating a cursory examination of Mac Graham's body the last time it would ever be whole. He used a metal rule to measure lengths where appropriate, pressing it against the feature in question and dictating the results. Most of it was in highly

technical terms ("Teeth, gingiva, oral mucosa normal"), but
Bobby managed to catch most of it, trying to stay alert for
anything that might be useful in the investigation, knowing
the vast majority would be routine. The remnant of a small
hole in the left earlobe was interesting, maybe a highlight of
Mac's wilder years. Bobby kept his bottom on the next table
over, not wanting to risk getting too close lest he—

"Give us a hand here, will ya, Parks?"

They were turning the body over and could do it in one flip
instead of several turn-and-slides if he assisted. He got up and
approached the table. Manny had moved the green bag out of
the way. Goverman indicated a shoulder with his chin, and
Bobby reached out both hands and put them on the dead body
of Mac Graham.

It was cold. He'd never felt anything like it, and the sensation
made him stop involuntarily, the preservation of his self-image
momentarily forgotten. It wasn't until that very moment that
it finally hit him that this body would never breathe again.
That someone could be this cold had never entered the realm
of the possible in his mind. He'd heard it, of course, read about
it, but never touched it with his own hands before. He looked
up at Goverman, who had ceased his own strugglings with the
positioning of the body and was watching Bobby, watching his
eyes. He nodded gently, giving Bobby a few moments. Manny,
too, was not moving, only standing quietly.

Bobby realized his mouth was open, and he tried to close
it slowly without snapping it shut. "Jesus . . ." he breathed,
knowing he would never be the same. He'd seen dead bodies
before, many having died violently. But it was never like this.

"Okay, easy now," Goverman said after a decent interval,
and the three of them got the body facedown. Bobby stepped
back from the table, unable to take his eyes off the thing that
lay before him, until Manny touched his shoulder and pointed
to the rinse basin, handing him a clean towel at the same time.
He hadn't put on gloves. He held his hands in the stream while
Manny dripped Betadine onto them. After they were dry,
he reached for the gloves he had declined before and put
them on.

By that time they had Mac's legs apart and were continuing the examination. "Hey, c'mere and look at this," Goverman said.

"What?" said Bobby, firmly planted back on his table.

"Was your man homosexual?"

Bobby jumped up. "What are you looking at?"

Goverman tapped the foot pedal back on. "Circumferential scarring around anal canal evidences abnormal fissuring." He tapped the pedal off.

Manny put it less delicately. "He took it in the ass."

"Maybe," corrected Goverman, turning toward Bobby. "The anus is like your lip. It can split if subjected to too much pressure. Like during anal intercourse." He looked back at the body. "These are old, though. No recent activity, and it's possible there was another cause. Hard stool, say." He turned again. "Anything click here?"

"Possibly," Bobby answered noncommittally. "Can you tell how recently?"

"Nope. More than a year, but could be ten years. If it was newer, we could get more precise. Let's get him back over."

Bobby went back to the table. The back was much worse than the front, great, ugly splotches everywhere where blood had pooled when the heart had ceased circulating it. The towel over the middle stayed on by itself, held intact by the caked and congealed blood underneath.

"Okay, boys and girls, let's get to it," said Goverman, reaching for a razor-sharp scalpel lying on a sterilized tray. Tapping the pedal once again, he said, "Standard Rokitansky incision," and plunged the blade into the left shoulder, pulling it toward him until reaching the sternum, the edges of the cut splaying open, strangely bloodless. Then a mirror image cut from the right shoulder, meeting the other in the center of the chest. Finally, straight down from the junction, piercing skin and subcutaneous fat and muscle, carefully avoiding the body cavity proper for now, terminating at the pubic bone, until what had once been Mac Graham now lay split and exposed in a giant Y, first step in an unholy transformation from a creature of God into a pointless assemblage of parts.

Bobby glanced down at his watch. *Please, Ruth, please please please* . . . He noticed for the first time that the table beneath the body was not solid, but a series of aluminum slats separated by slight gaps. Manny had turned on another tap, and water ran beneath the slats down to a drain at the foot of the table. A scale for weighing organs hung off to the side, in the style of a street-side produce vendor, a pan beneath a round scale. A small work surface was attached to a track, mounted in the edge of the table, that could be slid along its length to wherever needed. *Don't let me down, Ruth.* . . .

Goverman was settling in for a detailed examination of the body cavity. "Doc, any chance of changing the order here?" Bobby asked tentatively.

Goverman looked back, surprised. "Might could. Why?"

Bobby cleared his throat and tried to keep his voice even. "There're some things we need to know about, uh, well, he might have been having sex that night. Sort of." He swallowed another chunk of something in his throat, unwilling to clear it again, make that noise for them to hear.

"Sort of?" Manny asked.

"Well, he, uh— Look, we need to know if he ejaculated, you know, shortly before he died. And if he didn't, can you tell if he was having sex anyway, that sort of thing?" His voice sounded hopeful, not just that the information was possible to gather, but that it could be done *now.*

"Sure, okay, we can try to check that out. What kind of sex?"

"What do you mean, what kind of sex?"

"He means," said Manny, "was he fucking, and what was he fucking, or anal sex, or oral, or animals, or—"

"Okay, okay. Uh, the straight stuff, I guess." He looked pleadingly at Goverman. "The officer involved—you know what I mean, Doc—says that they were doing it, normal—" He glanced briefly at Manny. "And then she got nervous and stopped it before they—he—finished. We don't know if it's important yet, but we need to check out all the details." He was getting tired of struggling. "So can you help out with that or what?"

"Sure," Goverman said easily. "Maybe. Let's have the jewels, Manny."

The green plastic bag went on the sliding work surface. Goverman used the scalpel to slit open the top. He reached inside.

Oh, fuck me, Bobby said to himself, and turned away. Manny cackled.

"Fourteen centimeters," he heard Manny say.

"Well, I'll be damned," said Goverman. "Right on the nose."

"What's that?" Bobby asked.

"Perfect average. Fourteen centimeters, stretched."

"Stretched?"

"Yeah. Held out and stretched, not erect, which is tough when you're dead. You have to extrapolate, though, because the skin loses elasticity postmortem. For as long as this guy's been dead, you add twenty-two percent. Some guy did a study, if you can believe that. Fourteen is standard, but you hardly ever see it. Usually bigger or smaller."

"Why's that?" asked Bobby, his curiosity slightly, but not by much, overcoming his revulsion.

"Averages don't mean a hell of a lot," Goverman answered. "Shit, on the average, everybody in the world's got one tit and one ball!" He and Manny cracked up over that one.

"Brothers got bigger ones," Manny said when he'd calmed down.

"I thought that was a myth," said Bobby.

"It's supposed to be a myth," said Goverman, "but the good Lord wasn't feeling politically correct that day."

Bobby was kneeling on the floor, rubbing his temples, wondering if Goverman and Manny's banter served the same purpose as his, to divert them from the enormity of what was really going on here.

"Don't fade on me now, Lieutenant," Goverman said sternly. "You asked for it."

Bobby stood and turned back. He looked at the bloody mass from a distance first, hoping that would ameliorate the shock as he moved in closer. Goverman was speaking for the microphone. "External male genitalia, brought in with the body, reported as located within close proximity. Includes penis, scrotum and two mature testicles. Lacerations at the base and a ragged edge at the top indicate incising started posterior to the scrotum, proceeding upward. Cute." He shrugged and continued. "Normal appearing as to systemic pathology, but gross evidence of crushing. . . ." He tapped off the recorder. "What'd the spatter guy say?"

"Splash marks around the floor where it was found were in a circular pattern," said Bobby, "some spray as far away as four feet."

Goverman nodded. "Stomped in place and left there, sounds like. Consistent with the trauma here. Gonna make it tough to get you answers."

"How come?" Bobby asked. Manny looked at him as if it were a dumb question. "I mean, exactly?"

"Get me a tube scraper," he said to Manny. "Here's the idea: If he started doing it, there should be prostatic and seminal fluids in the urethra. Those start flowing with arousal. But— and here's how we get specific—if he didn't ejaculate, there won't be any sperm in it. So if we can get a good sample, and it's got the right fluids and no sperm, it supports the story." Manny handed him a long, thin piece of metal about the size of a swizzle stick with what appeared to be a tiny cup at one end, mounted so that the bottom of the cup formed a rounded tip to the whole assembly.

As its purpose became clear, Bobby turned away again, not willing to witness the insertion and withdrawal that would ream the inside of the urethra, retrieving the required sample. Goverman continued speaking as he worked. "This won't work. Too dried up. Let's cut it up and go for the proximal, mix up what he's got in a little saline and have it analyzed in solution. Gonna need to get into it anyway, to check for sperm in the proximal vas deferens. If there's a lot, odds are pretty good it's been sitting there for a long time." He was into it now, happy, going after the puzzle. Bobby was fighting to keep from gagging, still not looking. *Goddammit, Ruth, I'm really getting pissed now!*

"While we're at it, we'll check the prostate and seminal vesicles for residual engorgement. Hey, remember 'blue balls,' Parks? Wanna see what that was all about?"

"No thanks," he managed to choke out between clenched teeth. "What about what he was doing? Any way to tell if he was inside her?"

"That's easy. Or would be without the mutilation. Scrape the outside of the penis and check for mucopolysaccharides and the like. Could even match some genetic stuff with the cop, if you want."

"Not sure that's necessary yet."

"Okay. Well, maybe our best bet is to check the proximal blood clots, see if some of it got mixed up in there. The rest is a bit of a mess, which isn't a big surprise. He got the arteries at the penile-pudendal junctions. That's how the room got so splashed."

Ruth! "How long is this all gonna take?"

"Gotta go to the lab. Couple days."

That's it. I'm outta here. Fuck Ruth. "Any reason for me to stick around, Doc?" The hopefulness in his voice was about as subtle as a fart in church.

Goverman considered toying with him some more and decided he was in a merciful mood. "Go on, get outta here."

"Good to see you, Smith, glad you got it together," Bobby called as he headed for the door.

"Hey, Lieutenant," Manny called out after him. Bobby stopped and turned. Manny was grinning broadly, his gloved hands invisible inside the cadaver's body cavity, palpating some unseen internal organ. "We even now, hah?"

Bobby gagged and bolted through the door, down the corridor and through the outside double doors. He sprinted for the pay phone without breaking stride, fumbled wildly for some coins and slammed them into the slot. The phone was answered on the first ring. "Dispatch." He wondered why it sounded tinny and hollow but forgot it quickly and started yelling.

"Ruth, you ugly bitch and a half! What the shit, you were supposed to beep me half a goddamned hour ago! Why in Christ's name—" He stopped, the sound of laughter coming through the earpiece. Not one person, but many. Still tinny and hollow. *I'm on a goddamned speakerphone!* "Ruth?" He could hear her laughter among all the others. "I'll kill you—" *Hold it. Still on the speaker.* "Pick up the phone, Ruth. Now!"

He heard a click and a sudden cessation of the surrounding

sounds. "Hello?" said a female voice, mirth still evident despite the effort to sound professional.

"You're dead meat, Ruth," he said. "I'm gonna cut your fuckin' heart out."

"Maybe," said Captain Grant, "but for right now, get back into the station, will ya?"

CHAPTER
23

Police files are awash with stories of friends, families and business colleagues who "had no idea . . . he was such a nice boy." The slowly evolving truth that little Johnny next door was really an ax murderer was startling in itself, but the recurring familiarity of this scenario had another, more ubiquitous, effect: the realization that anybody could be a depraved sociopath beneath the civil exterior, and that our everyday judgments about people close to us were not always suspect, but tiresomely clichéd. This fact of modern life had insinuated itself so deeply into the mass psyche that police investigators lend virtually no credence to pronouncements of moral fitness by witnesses describing suspects.

Such it was with Lieutenant Bobby Parks on the phone with Dr. Jake Nostrand.

"Impossible."

"How so?" asked Bobby.

"I was close to the guy for two years, Lieutenant. He had women hanging around him all the time. Half the time he never made it back to the dorm at night and the other half his roommate had to sleep somewhere else. I don't know how he found time to study."

"You said he was severely traumatized after the accident.

He disappeared, sank into a different life. You said you had heard stories."

"I never believed them," said Jake, his voice less strident. "They were just stories, probably blown up out of proportion by medical students hurting for some excitement."

"What kind of stories?" asked Bobby.

"They were third- and fourth-hand, Parks, like playing telephone when you were a kid. How could that kind of distorted evidence help?"

"It helps because it provides leads." Bobby played the string out, as he had so many times before. Smart professionals like Nostrand were easy, because they were suckers for logic. Morons were surprisingly difficult. They found it easy to stare at you and deny that two plus two equaled four. "The rumors themselves aren't useful, and we don't take them at face value. They give us a starting point, a place to go look, something to check that might lead to something else that might lead to something useful."

Nostrand's silence told Bobby that he was making headway. He pressed on. "A bank was robbed in town last year. Just a couple of blocks from you. A teller was slightly injured."

"I remember it," said Jake.

"The teller supposedly was badly rattled by the incident and disappeared. We couldn't find the guy that did it. Without a suspect we had no use for the teller's testimony, so we forgot about her while we tracked the guy."

"Yes, I do remember," said Jake. "Wasn't she in on it?"

"Kind of. There was a rumor going around the bank that she was living high on the hog somewhere. She'd been making four fifty an hour. Where'd she get the money? So we went after her instead. The bank employee who started the 'rumor' had gotten a postcard from the teller."

"From an island off Panama," said Jake.

"Contadora, right. She never heard of the place but probably figured they could use a little excitement around the bank, so she plays it up as the playground of the rich and idle. Turns out she was right.

"While the guy was lifting tens and twenties from scared

tellers, our little cutie was sweeping fifties and hundreds into an empty carton underneath her counter. She walked out with it three days later. We found her in the casino on the island, about a day ahead of the guy who pulled the job. We got them both."

"What was he doing there?" asked Jake.

"He got away with about seven grand, but he hears on the news that the bank was hit for over a hundred. He figured it out and went after her. It's little leads that add up, Doctor."

There was silence from the other end. Bobby waited it out. He was used to waiting.

"There were stories that he was involved with male prostitution," Jake finally said, with obvious pain. "I never asked him about it, because I never believed it. Mac was not homosexual."

"Male prostitutes often aren't, Doc." Bobby's tone was gentle. "Good money and good dope gets you past a lot of hang-ups. The cops who busted him said he'd beaten a pimp. His pimp?"

"They didn't say. I didn't ask."

"Okay, Doc. I take it there was no arrest record."

"No. Nobody saw a need. It was a walk-away deal and . . ." Jake hesitated.

"Go on," said Bobby.

"No offense, Lieutenant, but I think those cops were more interested in protecting the pimp than busting Mac. My taking him far away was part of the deal. Records were the last thing they wanted."

"I got it," said Bobby. "Gonna make my job tricky."

"You'll see them? Ask questions?"

"Yep. And I'll get answers. The last thing they need is a smart-ass out-of-town cop poking around wanting to know why there's no paperwork."

———◆———

Amanda lay on her back staring up at the ceiling. Her lungs hurt and her arm muscles were sore. A kink was beginning to develop in her left knee.

"There's something awfully familiar about all of this," she

said as she wiped a line of perspiration from her upper lip. She rolled onto her side and sat up, then got shakily to her feet.

Krakowitz came at her and went for her breasts. She put her hands in a praying position between them, then reached forward and outward, slapping his hands to the sides. She stepped in to him, grabbed his right arm and turned to her left, dropping her hips low and into his thighs, pulling his arm over her right shoulder. Off balance, he fell forward over her into a neat arc, and Amanda set him on the mat with a satisfying thump.

He lay there for a second and then flailed about and pounded the mat in ersatz pain. "Suffer, pig," Amanda said, and he went still, his tongue hanging out the side of his mouth.

Amanda slumped to the mat in a cross-legged position facing him. He rolled over onto his stomach and raised himself on his elbows. "You had a good teacher," he said.

"The best."

They waited a minute while their breathing moderated. "Don't tell me some suicidal maniac is making passes at the captain," Jack said.

"Not a chance. Past my prime, you know."

Jack looked her over and grunted in appreciation.

"Ever had Pamela Jacoby in here?" she asked.

"The girlfriend," said Jack, referring to the case that was on everybody's mind. "Yeah. Pretty, athletic. Quiet, though, and scared. Like she didn't want to be here."

"I'm not sure she did. How did she handle herself?"

"Pretty well. Not nearly as good as you. Technically thorough, worked hard, but scientific. No passion. Funny, too, because the good-looking women usually get pretty intense. 'Course they're more afraid of their fellow officers than of street creeps."

Amanda smiled. "You won't believe this, but our old friend Murdoch bugs Jacoby, too."

Jack raised his eyebrows. "In front of you?"

"Hell, no. And it doesn't seem to bother her too much. Except maybe sometimes."

Jack dropped his elbows and rested his head on the backs of his arms for several seconds. In all their conversations over the years, he and Amanda had never mentioned his little secret, even though they had become confidants of sorts. His gym had become somewhat of a microcosmic proving ground: Amanda and her first-line subordinates had come to rely on Jack's judgment of character during the rookie weeding-out process. How they behaved in his classes was often a moderately reliable predictor of field performance. The lesson had been learned with Tony Palladino, a swaggering wise guy Jack had pegged as a show-off who took unnecessary risks. Palladino tried to storm a convenience store hostage situation before the more experienced Tactical Patrol Force could arrive and had gotten his partner shot in the foot. Jack had been gracious. "Next time listen to me, assholes."

Now she had to bring it up, because they were trying to catch a murderer, probably a homosexual, probably in the closet, and she needed Jack's help.

"It wasn't Dennis Murdoch, Amanda," Jack said.

Her reverie broken, Amanda quickly replayed what she thought she'd heard in her head. *Couldn't be.* "Sorry, what?" she asked.

Jack got back up on his elbows and looked directly at her. "I know there's talk going around that maybe Murdoch had something to do with this. They say he's been hitting on Jacoby for months, then she goes and pisses him off in front of his partner about how she's getting rack time with some lowlife drifter, he gets mad, blah blah blah . . ."

Amanda was having trouble digesting all of this. Tancredi was right about secrets. How could this half-baked theory have gotten this far? It didn't add up, and it wasn't why she was here, anyway. But she needed Jack and would spend the time necessary to deal with his concerns.

"It's a possibility. What about it?" she said.

"What about it is, it makes no sense." He paused and locked his eyes on hers. "He's gay, Amanda." He stopped again to let it sink in. "Murdoch."

Amanda's head reeled, trying to process the new information, assess its magnitude and keep a straight face at the same time. She was supposed to say something, not sit there like an idiot, but no words made themselves evident.

Jack mistakenly took this for shock at the size of the setback to the case. "I know you guys are running on empty on this one, Cap, but Murdoch's going to be a dead end for you."

"Yes," she managed to mumble before realizing that this would be an inadvertent leak. She trusted Jack, but there were things about the case he obviously didn't know, and she was too confused for the moment to figure out whether they now made any difference or not. "Well, it wasn't a strong . . . I mean, there's really very little . . ."

Jack jumped in for the rescue. "Hell, you don't need to explain anything. Just wanted to save you some trouble and stop a good cop from getting hurt."

Oh, Jack, she thought, looking at him with affection. Not until the meeting with Tancredi had she realized what life must be like for him, especially in light of his unique profession. His career would come to a shuddering halt if he ever came out of the closet. She knew that now.

"So what was it you wanted to see me about?" he asked.

What indeed. There was little sense in pursuing that avenue with Jack. For all she knew, he and Murdoch were an item, though she doubted it: Jack's perspectives on the human condition wouldn't tolerate a Murdoch in his life. But if she revealed her mission to him, there was a chance it could drive Murdoch underground if he was the guy, the probability of which had just shot off the charts, unbeknownst to Jack, who thought he was doing Murdoch a favor. But did that still make sense? She needed time to think, to sort this all out.

"Just trying to understand Jacoby a little better. She's under tremendous stress, handling it well, but it can't last. If I can get beneath the surface a little better, I might be able to help her."

Jack wasn't buying her story but had no problem going along to get on a different tack. "Doesn't she have a shrink for that?" he asked.

"Jesus!" Amanda said loudly, with real indignation but also

because it led to a way out of this conversation. "Isn't anything sacred around here at all?"

"Not among cops, lady. It's in the training."

She slumped her shoulders, not realizing how tightly she had been holding them as the conversation progressed. "I wonder what the hell you all know about me," she said.

"Terrible things. Horrible. But your secrets are safe with me," Jack said with a smile.

———◆———

"Wow," Bobby said into the phone. "This could be a real break."

"Not so fast. I thought so at first myself, but there's a problem," said Amanda. She was on a pay phone, not willing to risk the airwaves.

She waited, and her favorite detective didn't fail her. There was dejection in his voice, which a moment ago had been nearly jubilant. "Oh, sure. Where's the motive?"

"Right," she said. "If all this pawing at women has been a front for Murdoch's real tendencies, then any sexual jealousy was bullshit also. Sure he was pissed because he was embarrassed in public, but that doesn't add up to murder."

"But hang on a second," said Bobby. "What if Graham and Murdoch were lovers?"

Amanda was taken aback. "Never thought of that. But rather a huge coincidence, don't you think? Where's the connection? I can't believe Graham was carrying on right under Dr. Nostrand's nose. He lived in their house for the first few months he was here. And you said Nostrand swore Mac wasn't gay. And even if he was, the scars are old."

"But what if it started before Mac got to town? He was living on the fringe, remember, and Murdoch's a cop. What if their paths crossed before?"

Amanda contemplated this in silence for a moment before responding. "Maybe. It's still a stretch. And I don't want Murdoch hurt by an investigation if it's wrong."

"Understood. Let's do this: I'll have Atkins and Schuyler try to put together a chronology on Murdoch and Graham.

Murdoch's easy, all his cases are in the files. We'll get what we can on Graham out of the cops that busted him last. Maybe if we match up dates and places, something'll jump out and give us a connection."

"I like it. But talk to your people first and make damned sure they keep it on the QT. Murdoch's a slimeball, but he's our slimeball and he's still a good cop."

"Hey, he always spoke well of you, Captain."

"Up yours, Parks."

CHAPTER 24

D'ya think we'll get like that someday, Larry?" Irwin asked his busboy.

"Like what?" He stopped unloading a tray and followed Irwin's eyes to the far side of the room.

"Those two. Purple Haze and his Electric Squeeze."

Larry searched but saw only a conservatively dressed couple, the woman mid- to late-thirties, trim and well kept, the man somewhat older and apparently less attentive to matters corporeal. Larry looked back to Irwin.

"Yeah. Those two."

Larry looked again. They sat opposite each other, seemingly miles apart on any of a dozen scales one might care to interpose on the scene. He seemed intent on the filet before him, she on the broiled fish (no sauce) on her plate. A bottle of wine and two glasses sat on the table, barely touched for being this late into the meal. Larry tried to imagine what banalities passed for polite conversation during so staid a repast.

"D'ya think?" Irwin frequently studied his customers, as though to willfully adopt a future by selecting from the various options presented to him in the cultural terrarium of Ernesto's Trattoria.

"God, I hope not," answered Larry. "Look at the fucker. Like he's gonna have a stroke or sumthin'." And, indeed, the man's fork had stopped halfway to his mouth, his eyes now focused intently on the nothing in the middle of the table.

"Holy shit," the man mumbled, inaudibly except to his wife, who pretended not to notice the cause of his consternation, which in fact was her foot, slipped discreetly out of her shoe, placed between his legs, and whose toes flexed up and down so as to rub ever so gently at his crotch.

"Mmhh?" Amanda said innocently, as though unmindful of the effect she was having on him. To stop a piece of steak on the way to her husband's mouth was a victory comparable to diverting a minor river. She made a point of smoothly continuing her own dinner, in stark juxtaposition to his failure to do the same. She reached over to the vegetable plate and set her hand down softly on a carrot, two fingers running up and down its length, then did the same to another she found more to her liking. She picked it up slowly, very slowly, and put out her tongue and licked the tip, back and forth. Slowly. Looking at him, she took it in her mouth, nearly all the way, put the length of her tongue underneath it and withdrew it, closed her mouth gently around it and took it back in again, then out.

Without taking her eyes away from his, she said, mumbling around the enfellated carrot, "There's a waiter and a busboy over there who think you're about to have a heart attack."

"I am," he croaked. "Which would be a damned sight less embarrassing than what I'm about to do to my pants."

"Shall I stop?" She smiled coquettishly, still silky smooth and in complete control, enjoying his discomfort and her power. Then she jerked upright, wide-eyed with surprise.

"It's up to you, sweetcakes," he said, turning back to his plate, his own newly bared toe commencing a separate exploration in her own nether regions.

Standoff. They looked at each other. Amanda spoke first. "At least I could stand up if I wanted to." She could feel his nascent erection graduating to the next class.

"Go ahead," he replied nonchalantly, and rubbed a little harder.

Amanda's eyes half closed, without her consent, and she put

her fork down carefully rather than risk dropping it. "Uhhh, nahh, maybe not," she said after a while. "Maybe later." She started with the carrot again, and when his foot stopped moving, when his eyes were riveted to her mouth, when she knew she had his full attention, she bit down hard and snapped the end off, chewing noisily before his shocked expression.

"Slut!" He withdrew his foot, and she did the same. "I don't know why I put up with you."

" 'Cause I'm the only one who could put up with you?"

He slapped his forehead. "That's it. I remember now. So"— he paused and softened his voice—"what is it?"

She rested her head on her hand, looking at her fork twisting idly in the fettuccine on her plate. "What's what?" she said without looking up.

He put down his knife and fork and leaned back, reaching for his wineglass and turning it without drinking, keeping his eyes full on her. She shrugged one shoulder lightly, glanced up at him and then back down. He waited patiently.

The busboy appeared. "Clear these away for you?" He looked at the man, who nodded without looking away from his wife. Larry, deciding that it would not be politic at this time to ask how everything was, worked quickly and turned away, rolling his eyes up for Irwin to see before walking away.

"Do you have any idea how much I love you?" she asked at last.

He waited before answering. "Of course. So what's not to love?"

She looked up. "Sometimes I wonder when it's going to burst. You'll turn out to be an escaped ax murderer or something, or you'll be boffing one of your clerks with a perky little ass, giant tits and no teeth. I don't know, something can take it away and then it'll be like we never happened. But even so, all these years, all those hours . . ."

"All that screwing . . ."

She smiled dreamily. "And other stuff." The version she had given Pamela of their sexual courtship was slightly censored. He had buried his head in her crotch and not come up for air until she had been to Neptune and back. At first she was scared and rigid and not sure she trusted him quite *that* much, but then it was clear that he was not only skilled but indefatigable, and that didn't make any difference, either, and she still resisted, embarrassed and afraid, and then she realized that he was *enjoying* it, and then that she was, too, and she figured, *What the hell, no graceful way to stop it, so let's see what all the fuss is about,* and the rest was a little hazy in her memory, just this cushiony bubble getting larger and larger and filling her up and suddenly there were tiny holes in it until the whole thing started to unravel with ever-increasing speed until it gave up and exploded in a shower of sparks and colors. . . .

"Hellooo? Yoohoo . . . ?" He was waving at her as one might to see if an accident victim were conscious. As her eyes refocused he said, "Well, I can certainly see why this is upsetting. Now what is it?"

When she didn't answer right away, he said, "It's that cop, right? Jacoby."

Amanda nodded. "She doesn't know. Any of it. She's so alone, and she has no idea how it can be, to be with someone." A tear formed in one eye. "And every time she tries, she makes it worse." She wiped at her face and looked around, chagrined, composing herself quickly.

He pursed his lips and looked away, pained at his wife's distress, at a loss for what to do about it. "What's this about me being an ax murderer?"

"Just that I don't want to be smug and complacent about us. I could be a Pamela Jacoby by the simplest finger snap of the gods. What makes me so special? Why do I deserve you?"

He took her hand and squeezed it. "Because you're an angel. And until I found you I was so much sand." Then it was his turn to look around in sudden self-consciousness. He turned back to Amanda. "Now, let's talk business: I'll be glad to sort out this little cop for you, say, a week from Thursday at the— nnhhh!" He winced as her reshod foot found the soft spot just below his knee.

The waiter appeared out of nowhere, pointedly making no remark about the fresh look of pain on the man's face. "Anyone for dessert?" he asked with as much pseudoeffervescence as he could muster. ("Sincerity is everything, kid," Ernesto had told him as though he'd made up the old joke himself. "When you can fake that, the rest is easy.")

"Sure," said the man. As he reached for the little menu, his wife reached for a carrot, a little slowly and deliberately, it seemed to Irwin, and the man looked at her, and she looked back at him, and the man said, "Uh, on second thought, just bring me the check." The wife brought the carrot to her mouth. "Quickly, son," the man said.

CHAPTER
25

Alberon Jolicoeur had bad feet, and he was superstitious.

Each of these facts taken alone was not very significant, and their juxtaposition in his mind at this moment would seem coincidental to the casual observer. They happened to be the only things he was thinking about these days, at least for the past several weeks.

He hadn't had his first pair of shoes until he was thirteen years old. Shoes weren't necessary on the island of his childhood, but the junior high school, ostensibly as part of its charter to prepare island children for the outside world, insisted on shoes, and all day long, too. They'd hurt the day he'd put them on, and he'd wondered if maybe they came in different sizes, but, as his mother had explained, if they were good enough for his older brother, Etienne, they were good enough for him. They'd never stopped hurting.

As for superstition, Jolicoeur wouldn't have called it that. What made his religion any more deserving of that particular criticism than any other? Catholics wore crosses around their necks, Jews kissed little pieces of paper on door frames and Muslims' toilets never faced east. If he killed a live chicken once in a while, so what? Did that make him worse than white people who had other people kill theirs for them?

So here he was, standing on his burning feet, guarding the scene of a murder, the spirit of the dead undoubtedly swarming around his head, waiting for the opportunity to snatch him to the bosom of the voodoo high priest, Baron Samedi. At least it was the day shift. He'd told Lieutenant Parks in no uncertain terms that he'd quit before he took nights, and the lieutenant, knowing Jolicoeur had the eyes of an osprey and the strength of a division, had relented.

He saw the car approaching and pushed back from the wall he had been leaning against. He watched it pull up to the curb and waited for its passengers to disembark. When they didn't do so, he got nervous. When they still didn't do so, he un-snapped the safety cover on his holster and folded the flap back behind and under his belt.

Then both doors opened simultaneously and the driver and passenger got out. Jolicoeur let out his breath and waved.

"Ho, Jacoby," he yelled amiably, his singsong Creole accent apparent even in a few syllables.

She looked up and seemed to search for the sound. *Strange,* he thought fleetingly, *as I am the only one here.* Then she spotted him and managed a weak smile and a wave.

"Hey, Al," she said in a quavering voice, far different from the one he was used to. He didn't recognize the driver but knew who it was. He wondered why he came around the front of the car and took Jacoby's arm. *Still upset,* he figured, although he'd seen her around the station and thought she was holding up fairly well.

"I'm Dr. Ferrin," said the driver, extending his hand.

Jolicoeur took it and said, "Okay. Remember, please, touch no thing." He said it as two words. "And I stay with you, yes?"

"I understand," said the doctor.

As he spoke, Jolicoeur watched Jacoby staring at the door-way. She hadn't said a word after her initial greeting, nor looked at him. She held a tight grip on the doctor's arm. When he started forward, she seemed to hesitate for a moment before following him. Jolicoeur opened the door and stepped aside as they entered.

He watched her eyes settle on a single candlestick and a

mostly full bottle of white wine sitting in a bucket of water. He'd had plenty of opportunity to look the place over. He knew there was a matching candlestick in the bedroom. He saw it only for an instant, from the doorway, before the rest of the scene registered in his mind and made him turn quickly away. He hadn't gone near the bedroom since, had in fact asked the forensics guys, the ones who paraded their unemotional professionalism in the face of such abomination, to close the door behind them when they left.

Now he watched her eyes rise toward the bedroom door, hoping foolishly that maybe she'd decide not to go in there, knowing full well it was the only reason for her visit. Lieutenant Parks had told him to keep her in sight at all times. Maybe there was a way to do that without looking at the sheets, the walls. Maybe if he angled his head around the doorway and she kept only to this side of the room . . .

"Can I touch the doorknob, Officer?"

Jolicoeur looked at him blankly. Did the doctor expect to dematerialize through the walls like the wizard Samedi?

"I'll leave prints," the doctor explained.

"Ah, no, I mean yes, yes, you will, Doctor. No problem. They have done all the printing they are going to do. What they have not yet they will not have. But in the room, no hands, please."

The doctor's authoritative nonchalance was normal, but Jolicoeur was keenly aware of Officer Jacoby's trepidation. "Jacoby," he said gently, "some water?"

She turned in his direction and seemed to see him for the first time. He noticed that her pupils were very wide, almost completely dilated, and the whites were moist and glassy. There was fear in her eyes as well, not simple apprehension but deep dread. It was the kind of terror he'd seen in voodoo initiates fallen under the baron's spell in the more secret ceremonies. He drew back involuntarily.

"That would be good, Officer," he heard the doctor answer for her. "Thank you."

He fetched the water from a portable cooler in a paper cup. Jolicoeur brought his own so he wouldn't have to draw any from a house where such an abomination had occurred. The doctor took the cup and gave it to Jacoby, who obediently took a small sip and handed it back. Then the doctor walked down the hall and opened the bedroom door, without hesitation, and looked in. He took a moment, then turned and came back.

"Come, Pamela," the doctor said, and led her down the hall. They paused at the doorway, the doctor letting her take her own time about it. Her legs had grown unsteady, and Jolicoeur suddenly feared for her more than for himself. Besides, he had his orders. He started forward.

Jacoby took a step and looked into the room. Jolicoeur wondered what it had looked like to her the last time she had seen it. He heard her draw her breath in sharply, in a choked and rasping gasp, and saw her stagger backward, stumbling over the carpet edge. He jumped toward her, but the doctor had caught her and held up his hand toward him, and he stopped short.

Jacoby was taking broken and labored breaths now, and the doctor was looking at him and motioning him away. The doctor let her gather herself, then helped her up. He kept her facing the room and then pulled her forward. This seemed unnecessary to Jolicoeur. Wasn't the point made? Why go on with it? But he kept his silence and observed.

With one hand on the jamb for support, Jacoby walked unsteadily through the doorway and into the room. She was starting to disappear from his sight, so he followed, but not past the doorway. Her trembling was visible now, and the doctor was speaking.

"What do you remember, Pamela?" he was asking. She didn't answer, only stared at the blood-soaked bed, where the rumpled and stained sheets still held the unmistakable outline of a body. "What do you remember?" he repeated, and her eyes moved toward the wall, where vertical streamers of dark red dropped from a spiked oval of dried blood. She turned her head and found the single candlestick, the wax from the spent candle gathered in neat folds at the base. She fixated on it, and the doctor shook her, gently, then thought better of it and stopped.

Jolicoeur noticed that Jacoby had become very still, but there was something very disquieting about it, and he had trouble figuring out what it was. The air in the room was palpably heavy and seemed to have a syrupy consistency. He let his eyes drift to the bed and forced them to stay there. He saw the blood not as isolated pools and splatterings but as an organic whole, one interconnected thing, part of a system as it had been when it was all inside the victim.

He looked at Jacoby, who was still locked on to the single candlestick. She hadn't moved, and everything started to look familiar to him. The blood, a candle, a figure frozen in marble . . .

That was it. Jacoby wasn't simply still, she was frozen. Even in the dimly lit room, Jolicoeur's sharp eyes could pick out the individual hairs wisping from the back of her neck. Not one of them moved, not a glimmer in the light they reflected from the single lamp. It was impossible to hold oneself that still voluntarily.

Jacoby had become a zombie. Jolicoeur had never actually seen one, was not completely convinced they were real, but imagined suddenly that this was what they might look like. He'd seen young women in similar states of mesmerism during the dark rites, but never one this unmoving.

He didn't like this, not one bit. He wasn't educated enough to recognize catatonia, but he didn't need a degree to know that something was very wrong with Jacoby.

"Pamela," the doctor said softly.

Jolicoeur looked at him. *Talking to the undead? Crazy Western doctor!*

"Pamela," the doctor said again, louder this time.

We need a priest, thought Jolicoeur. *It has gone beyond whatever this white fool thinks he knows.* The thick air in the room started to compress further.

"Pamela!" the doctor said sharply, and soon the array of ripples on the back of her jacket started to shift slightly. The pattern of light on her hair changed. She turned back to the bed.

Her immobility started to give way to small vibrations in her hands and head. She looked at the bed, but it wasn't with the same fixation. Her eyes darted back and forth, as in the REM sleep of the actively dreaming, except Pamela's eyes were open. She shifted her feet to retain her balance as small, spasmodic jerks attacked parts of her at random.

"Talk to me," said the doctor, and he took a step toward her, his mouth near her ear.

Her trembling was now so bad that she had difficulty standing upright. She started crying, but it was an eerie sound, an animal mewling high in her throat, the kind of crying a child might make if she were afraid of bursting into full sobs. It was a struggle for control, fought by giving in slightly in hopes of deferring the larger battle.

She managed what sounded like an attempt at speech, but her back was to Jolicoeur and he couldn't make it out.

"What?" the doctor asked. "What did you say, Pamela?" Jolicoeur couldn't tell if the doctor really didn't understand or just wanted her to repeat herself.

"Blood," she said with some more clarity, though it was still a garbled murmur. "Blood. Everywhere." *What is she talking about now?* Jolicoeur wondered.

"Whose blood?" asked the doctor.

"His." Her arms were outstretched, palms up, the fingers curled inward, postured like the Pietà Madonna. She was holding something imaginary. Jolicoeur could feel its weight. One fist clenched and released, clenched and released again.

"What are you holding, Pamela? What's in your hand?"

Jolicoeur went into the room but didn't take his eyes off her. First the back of her head, then her face as he circled around her slowly, coming to a stop on one side of her and several feet away. Tears streamed down her cheeks, her mouth tensed in the rictus of a silent scream, her red-rimmed and swollen eyes reduced to slits under the pressure of her torment.

"Him," she breathed as she looked at her right hand. She opened her fist. "He's dying. There's so much blood."

Jolicoeur felt a shroud descend over the room, over Jacoby, threatening to sweep her into a deep hole. Nothing about this felt right. "Doctor," he began, "don't you think that perhaps—"

"Shut up!" the doctor spat at him.

He was immediately intimidated but looked at Jacoby again and said, "I am sorry, sir, but she is so—"

"Listen, dammit, do your job. Let me do mine." Jolicoeur backed off.

Jacoby looked as though she hadn't heard a word of the exchange. The doctor turned his attention back to her and waited until the sharp words receded under the weight of her anguish. By the time he spoke, the continuity with their earlier dialogue had been fully restored. Jolicoeur felt the shroud just above them, and he was afraid for her.

"Did you love him, Pamela?"

She looked confused for the first time. "Yes," she said resolutely, then the resolve began to wither and die. "No. I don't know." The crying sounds began again.

"Did you tell him?" the doctor asked.

"No. So much blood . . ."

"Where is it coming from, Pamela? Where is the blood coming from?"

Jolicoeur looked at the bed. *What goes on here?*

"From him." She was staring, but not at the bed—at something else, something far away. Her eyes focused closer, at the bloodstains on the wall. "He's dying. His blood is pouring out and he's dying." A note of hysteria began to creep into her voice. "It's my fault," she said suddenly.

"Why, Pamela? Why your fault?"

She was stepping back and had a fierce grip on the doctor's jacket that wrenched the fabric, but he ignored it. "Why?" he insisted.

Jolicoeur was thoroughly frightened now. Jacoby appeared ready to explode. He stepped back into the doorway and pulled his radio out of his belt, keyed the mike and whispered several words into it.

She closed her eyes completely and tilted her head back. "He was in me," she cried, and started to crumple, no longer able to stand.

"Who, Pamela? Who was in you?" The doctor's voice was insistent, relentless. "Tell me, who, dammit, who?"

Jacoby didn't seem to hear him. The radio crackled, and Jolicoeur turned away and spoke rapidly into it, then turned back. They were both on the floor now, and the doctor was screaming almost directly into her ear. "Who, Pamela? Tell me!"

Jolicoeur watched as Jacoby opened her eyes and seemed to grow still for a second. The shaking had subsided to minor tremors. He was aware of her breathing, which had steadied slightly but was starting to get faster and deeper. Her shoulders were rising and falling with the effort. She looked at the doctor, held his eyes for a long moment.

"Who?" he asked again.

Her breaths came in loud panting now, and Jolicoeur could feel his own panic rising with hers. She looked at him suddenly, and her eyes were frantic, wild, searching for something. She looked at the bed.

"Who?" the doctor asked, and a feral moan started in her throat, stayed in place, circling. "Who?" The moan strayed from its starting point, and the sound bored into Jolicoeur's brain. He'd heard something like it before, when he was young, but he'd forgotten it until now. The sound stopped abruptly as Jacoby drew in an impossibly large breath until the veins stood out on her neck and her hands dropped from the doctor's coat as all her energy left her extremities and gathered deep within her body.

"Who?" asked the doctor for the last time, and Jacoby screamed, a piercing wail of purest terror that went on and wouldn't stop. Jolicoeur put his hands over his ears and squeezed his eyes shut, but the awful shriek penetrated anyway and found his soul, went to its source and burned there.

The sound changed to a guttural sputter as Jacoby sucked in air, then exploded again as she released the confined horror in paroxysms of uncontrolled screaming. Jolicoeur reached the limit of his endurance and started to bolt from the room, but the doctor's voice caught him before he reached the door.

"Help me, Officer," he was saying. Jolicoeur fought down his fear and looked at him. Jacoby had her arms wrapped around herself, her legs tucked up so that she was in a tight

ball. The doctor was hugging her, rocking slowly. The screaming was starting to subside into heaving sobs, and Jacoby's
head was on the doctor's chest. "My bag. It's on the backseat
of the car."

"I am not supposed to leave you, Doctor," Jolicoeur said.

Ferrin looked up at him beseechingly. "Please. She's in a
great deal of pain. I won't move." Jolicoeur looked at him,
deciding. "I promise," the doctor said. "Please."

Jolicoeur ran from the room, down the hallway and into the
sunlight. It was like leaving one world for another. He found
the bag and rushed back into the house to the bedroom. The
doctor was where he had left him.

When Ferrin saw him, he gently laid Jacoby down on her
back. Her distress was obvious and acute and seemed to have
transitioned from the outward expression of her pain to a more
inward and enclosed, recirculating resignation. She still held
herself tightly and seemed oblivious of what was occurring
around her. She did nothing that led Jolicoeur to believe she
was hearing anything they said. He wondered if she would
ever come back.

The doctor was unbuttoning her pants. When they were
loose and he started to pull them down, Jolicoeur looked away.

"I need you here, Officer," the doctor said. "Please hold her
legs still."

Jolicoeur turned back and knelt at Jacoby's feet, trying not
to look at the bikini briefs or her bare legs. He gripped her
ankles and pinned them to the floor. He noticed the stark
contrast between her pink legs and his ebony hands and wrists,
now pure black in the dim light of the room. He'd never
touched a white woman before. In his fascination he didn't
notice that her legs were still rolling back and forth.

"I need her thigh to be still," the doctor was saying. "This
is no time to be shy, Officer."

Jolicoeur put one hand on her knee and pressed it to the
floor, which locked the whole leg in place. The doctor had
prepared a syringe, and as soon as her leg stopped moving, he
plunged it into the fleshiest part of her thigh. Jolicoeur had
never seen an injection delivered like this and was startled

and started to pull back, but the doctor said in a slow and soothing voice, "Easy, easy. It's Thorazine. Have you heard of it?"

"Yes, Doctor. They give it to crazy drug people when we bring them to the hospital. From the dust of angels. But I never see it go in. It goes in the leg?"

"It's the fastest way to make it work." Jolicoeur saw Jacoby start to calm even before the doctor withdrew the needle. By the time he had a small bandage over the puncture, her head had lolled to one side and her breathing had steadied. Her leg went limp in his hands, and he let go. The doctor dropped the syringe in his bag and closed the cover. Then he looked at Jacoby and gently brushed away several hairs that had matted to the sweat on her brow.

The doctor, himself looking drained and exhausted, looked at Jolicoeur. "She wanted to try to remember something about the night of the murder."

Jolicoeur nodded. "She and him . . ." He cocked his head toward the bed but didn't turn around to look at it. He tapped his two index fingers together.

"Yes," said the doctor, looking down at her, talking as much to himself as to Jolicoeur.

"But it was like Jacoby was in the movie pictures. She look at the screen and tell you what she see."

The doctor smiled at him. "That's a good way of putting it."

"But same movie or different movie?"

The doctor looked back down at Jacoby. "I don't know. . . ."

The sound of a car drifted in through the door. Jolicoeur stood and looked down the hall, but the sound waned and died as the car drove past.

"I called in to precinct," Jolicoeur said. "Sorry. I became frightened."

"I don't blame you. Imagine how Jacoby felt." Ferrin knelt down and started to put his arms underneath the sleeping woman. "I need to get her in the car." Jolicoeur saw that the doctor weighed barely more than she did and wouldn't make it.

"Wait," said Jolicoeur. He stepped forward, bent over from

the waist and slid his arms under her back and knees. Effortlessly he gathered her up and held her to his chest. Her body
felt fluid, and her arms dangled awkwardly. The doctor picked
them up and folded them across her chest as Jolicoeur carried
her back into the corridor and then out of the house. They laid
her carefully in the backseat of the car and secured her with
both seat belts.

When they had finished and the door was closed, the doctor
stood up and seemed to really notice Jolicoeur for the first
time. He looked into his large brown eyes, still wide with the
vestiges of fear and lack of understanding, and realized the
effort it must have taken for him to maintain his composure.
He was sorry he had been harsh, but it was necessary. Now he
wanted to smooth it over.

"She'll be all right . . . Al, is it?"

"Yes, Doctor. For Alberon."

"You were very helpful, Alberon," said the doctor, grabbing
his upper arm and giving it a reassuring squeeze. The rock-
hard triceps beneath his hand barely yielded. "I'm going to
take her home. She'll sleep for a while and then she'll be all
right. Don't worry."

"Okay," he answered, and looked at her through the car
window.

The doctor walked around the front of the car and got in,
started the engine and drove off slowly, waving once back to
Jolicoeur, who answered by touching his finger to his cap. He
turned to go back to his post when he heard another car approach from the opposite direction. It pulled up to the curb,
and Captain Grant and Lieutenant Parks got out.

"What's going on, Al?" asked Parks.

Jolicoeur looked embarrassed and lifted his shoulders
slightly. "I am sorry, Lieutenant. I got scared. Jacoby was inside, with the doctor. Everything okay now."

CHAPTER 26

Oh, he was just leaving," said the female voice on the speakerphone. "Wait and I'll see if I can catch him."

"Thank you," said Amanda. Detective Schuyler appeared outside her office and motioned to his watch.

Bobby held up two fingers to Schuyler and silently mouthed, "Two minutes," then thought better of it and waved him into the office.

"We were just catching Tancredi on his way out," said Bobby, pointing to the speakerphone. "His secretary's going to try to get him back."

"Good. Jacoby hasn't shown up yet, anyway," Schuyler said.

"Anything interesting in the background checks?" Amanda asked while they waited.

"Interesting, yes. Connected, possibly," Schuyler answered, some frustration evident in his voice. "About sixteen months ago, Murdoch was working liaison with the feds on a dust lab out of state."

"I remember," said Bobby. "They were shipping through our bus terminal, and he wanted in on the case. Always had a thing about drug runners."

Schuyler nodded. "That's the case. They had everything except how the money got cleaned. There was one bar that the technicians hung out in, and one of the feds spotted a few of them going in empty-handed and coming out eight or nine beers later with little paper bags."

"A drop," said Bobby.

"So they figured. Murdoch went in on cover to watch. Turns out that Graham was running for a single-shingle bookie at the time. Had his own table away from the bar, and Graham would come in two, three times a day and turn over receipts. At least that's what we got off the fed information sheets."

"Are we sure it was Graham?"

"Pretty sure. The snitch knew him already and told the feds, mostly because the bookie was known trouble. But you know those guys: it didn't have anything to do with their case, so they filed it and let it go."

The voice crackled over the speakerphone. "Caught him at the elevator. Be right with you."

"Thanks," Amanda said into the microphone, then turned back to Schuyler. "Go on."

"So the feds finally pop these guys in the parking lot, and what's in the little bags? Beer."

"Beer?" said Bobby in confusion.

"Beer. For a midafternoon snack. No grocery stores in walking distance, so they bought a few extra in the bar."

"And Graham?" prompted Amanda.

"Tough to say. The feds got flustered and embarrassed over the beer thing, so they busted the lab right away. The technicians split, the bookie found a new bar, Murdoch came home . . . Tap city."

"Shit," Bobby said through gritted teeth. "Are we running it down?"

"Yeah, as a matter of fact, there's a—"

"Hallo, lady," Tancredi's voice rasped over the tinny speakerphone.

Amanda smiled. "Hi, Tanc. Sorry to drag you back. I've got Parks with me and Detective Schuyler."

"I apologize," said Tancredi. "I am heading out and already I am late."

"We won't keep you long, Doc," Bobby said. "We're coming

up with very little on our end. We're hoping you had a miraculous insight or two."

"I did," said Tancredi. The three people in Amanda's office exchanged glances and huddled closer to the speaker. "Unfortunately, none of them is having anything to do with your case. People in search of the perfect martini, however, are being very pleased."

"I know you're in a hurry," said Amanda, trying to hide her disappointment, "but is there anything that might give us another plausible motive?"

"Possibly, but it is doubtful. Was my report not clear enough?"

Amanda pressed the "mute" button and looked up at Schuyler, who said, "They came in late yesterday afternoon. I had copies made for the whole team."

"I didn't get one," said Bobby.

"Me neither," said Amanda.

"They're probably in your mail slots. The rest of us have ours, and Jacoby picked hers up last night."

"Hallo?" Tancredi came over the speaker.

Amanda punched the button again and said, "Sorry, Doc. They came in last night and we haven't picked them up yet."

"No hurry," said Tancredi. "There is not being little new except long shots. And you were right about the female officer. Not plausible."

While Pamela's candidacy as a suspect had not been a spoken issue for several weeks, it had intruded on their collective consciousness in the absence of a better lead. This news from Tancredi was welcome but also underscored their lack of progress.

"Okay, Doc," said Bobby. "Thanks. We'll read the details and call if we have any questions."

"Sorry I am not being of more help, Bobby," said Tancredi, sensing his disappointment. "But sometimes killers are just not having the decency to cooperate. Please keep me informed if there are more hopeful developments." He rang off.

"Damn," said Bobby.

Amanda sat upright as she caught herself slumped back on

her chair, remembering that it was her duty to stop the team from getting discouraged. "Let's go get our copies, Parks. Schuyler, we'll see you in briefing in a couple of minutes." She walked briskly out of the room, and Bobby got up to follow.

Schuyler waited until Amanda was a few paces out the door, then stood quickly and grabbed Bobby's arm. "Hang on a minute, Parks," he said quietly.

Bobby turned to him in surprise. "What's up?"

Schuyler kept his eyes on Amanda's retreating back before responding. It seemed to Bobby that he did so a bit longer than he needed to, as though reluctant to begin this conversation. He waited until Schuyler turned his face back to him.

"Didn't want to bring this up in front of the captain before running it by you first, Bobby." He looked pained, and it was evident that something had been on his mind for a while. Bobby caught the look and motioned him back to the chair.

"Okay, Josh, I'm listening."

Schuyler cleared his throat. "I been talking to Mike, going over what we have. You know, blue-skying just to make sure we're seeing it all."

Bobby nodded. He understood the process well. Take all the pieces and try to construct logically consistent alternatives, no matter how off the wall. From such exercises insight often came.

"So, the more we talk, the more we keep circling back to something. Like a magnet, y'know? And after a while we fit more pieces, and then after some more while it starts to sound good. Only . . ."

Bobby stayed silent and didn't move, knowing it would come in its own good time.

"Bobby, nobody wants to finger a cop, especially when other cops are involved, but I think this fag angle with Murdoch is off the mark."

Bobby looked confused. "Then why worry about fingering a cop?"

"Because it isn't about that, but it's about something. I think like, maybe, it's about the captain."

Bobby tried to keep his face immobile. He was hearing Schuyler give voice to something that had been fluttering in his mind but that he hadn't quite realized until that very moment. As it revealed itself to him now, he could feel his stomach start to tighten. He cleared his throat quietly. "A revenge killing."

Schuyler raised his eyebrows in surprise. "You thought of it already?"

Bobby shook his head, declining credit. "Not until you started talking."

Schuyler looked away and continued. "If you keep thinking about it, pieces start to fall into place. Not just the captain, but Jacoby, too. It's a brilliant hit."

"He gets back at Jacoby, that much is clear, although nobody would consider that someone would commit murder over a minor embarrassment. And the captain—"

"He makes her look like the world's most irresponsible and incompetent fool," Schuyler finished for him, "since there's little doubt that Jacoby's psychiatric treatment while on the force is going to come out. Putting Jacoby on the investigating team was pure icing. An extra treat."

"It gets worse," said Bobby, "the more you play it out. A cop's boyfriend gets brutally murdered practically under her nose. We can't even protect our own, much less the public. And who gets all the shit for running a lousy force?"

"You got it."

Bobby stared off as the beauty of such a scenario continued to sink in. "I gotta tell you though, Josh, it doesn't feel right." He was the only other person who was aware of the intense guilt Amanda had suffered following her takedown of Murdoch so many years before. In addition to his police duty of trying to evaluate the new scenario, he couldn't help but consider the personal effect on his friend.

"How so?"

"I've known Dennis for a lotta years. Not my favorite character, but I just can't see this." He spoke idly, still looking away.

"Me neither."

"And how do we prove it?"

"Don't know that yet. The cleanup foots with an experienced cop, but that's circumstantial. We could confront him and hope he cracks."

"But if he doesn't, our job gets tougher." Bobby looked back at Schuyler. "We have to tell the captain. You know that."

Schuyler nodded and got up to leave, having accomplished his primary goal of pulling the head investigator into the theory. " 'Course. Just wanted to tell you first so you could tell me where it was wrong. Lemme go see if Jacoby's here yet."

"I better get to the mailroom."

He walked slowly and met Amanda coming out holding a large manila envelope. "How come every time we talk to Tancredi I get the feeling that he knows more than he's telling us?" she said.

Bobby thought before responding. "It's in his training, I think. Always keep facts and opinion clearly separated. If he really knew for sure, he'd say. Otherwise, I think he likes to drop little hints here and there. It pays to listen carefully."

As they rounded a corner, Bobby started to speak. "Captain, let's go back to your—" He stopped as Officer Annie del Gatto came into sight, carrying a fresh cup of coffee from the machine. "Del Gatto," he called as they strode past, relieved at his slight reprieve. "Have you seen Jacoby around?"

Del Gatto looked up in mild surprise. "Yeah, she hit the streets a little while ago."

Amanda and Bobby stopped and turned to her. "Patrol?" asked Amanda.

Del Gatto, taken aback by the effect this news seemed to be having on them, answered hesitantly. "Yeah. That a problem?"

"Thought you took her off patrol," Bobby said quietly to Amanda. They both took several steps in del Gatto's direction.

"I did." Then to del Gatto when they were all together and out of earshot of anybody else: "Annie, she shouldn't be out there. I didn't authorize return to regular duty. And she's missing a meeting."

An exaggerated look of consternation came over del Gatto's face. "Hey, Captain, it wasn't my turn to watch her, y'know?" She was shorter than either Bobby or Amanda, and their close proximity accentuated their towering advantage. None of this fazed her, though, since her license to be acerbic had been earned through an enviable performance record on the line and her accepted status as a station-house character.

"It's okay, Annie," Amanda said, smiling and putting a hand on her shoulder. "We know you're friends. Come and talk to us for a minute."

"Sure," said del Gatto. "Can I take my coffee?"

They reconvened in Amanda's office. Del Gatto relaxed and hoped some of the other officers would notice her calmly drinking coffee in the captain's office.

"How's she been lately, Annie?" asked Bobby.

Annie looked up without speaking.

"Nothing specific," Amanda added. "We don't want to pry into her private life, just help if we can."

Annie nodded and said, "Not so hot lately, to tell you the truth."

"Not so hot how?" asked Bobby.

"Well," Annie started, settling onto the chair, "After, y'know, it happened, she took it pretty good. A real trooper. I think working on the case helped. Then she got a little down, then a lot down. I don't know: staring into space all the time, stuff like that, y'know?"

"Did she say anything?" prompted Amanda. "Anything that might tell you what was going on?"

"No, not really. I just figured, hell, if somebody took out my boyfriend, it'd put a damper on my day, too. And she's seeing that shrink, y'know? Two, three times a week. I think that fucks up—oh, 'scuse me. I think that has a lot to do with what kind of day she has."

Amanda and Bobby listened intently, nodding occasionally. "What about today?" Amanda asked.

Annie brightened considerably and sat upright. "Oh, today was a great day."

"How do you mean?" asked Bobby.

"Well, yesterday she looked like hell. Rock bottom, y'know what I mean? This morning she sees her shrink and she comes in like all chipper." The experienced Annie shook her head in cynical remembrance of Pamela's cheerful demeanor. "Regular Pollyanna."

Amanda looked up at Bobby, who returned the glance. "What do you mean, Annie?" Amanda asked.

Annie looked at her, confused. "Nothing, really. She was

just in a great mood. Top of the world. I figured, Hey, this is terrific. Maybe she's gonna snap out of it." She noticed the look of growing alarm on both their faces. "What the hell, Captain? What's going—"

"Where is she, Annie? Quickly!"

Annie was confused and starting to get scared on top of it. "She grabbed a set of keys and said she was hitting the streets. Captain, what in the hell . . . ?"

Before she could finish, Amanda snapped to Bobby, "Find her . . . *now!*" but he was already half out of his seat and reaching for the phone on her desk.

He punched the button marked "DISP," waited a few seconds, then yelled into the mouthpiece, "Ruth? Parks. We need to find Jacoby. Fast. She's out on patrol but may not be right in the car." He stopped and listened, then said, "Yes. And put out a priority APB on the vehicle." Pause. "Shit, I don't know." He held his hand over the mouthpiece and said to Annie, "Which car, del Gatto?"

She furrowed her brow and held a hand to her head. "Lemme think. Kangas and Loconto are out, Bernacchi and Simpson . . . Wait: Lietsch and Fullinwider pulled graveyard on the peeper thing and came back in before six."

"One fifty-seven," Bobby said quickly into the mouthpiece. "Get it going and call Pearsall in the pool to confirm." He stopped and listened, then said, "No, call the location in to me and tell them to look for her if she's not in the car. We'll be mobile," and slammed down the receiver.

Amanda had her jacket on and was outside the office, giving instructions to the attendant on duty at the desk. Bobby pointed his finger at Annie and said, "Move it. Let's go," and was out the office door.

Amanda saw him on the move and fell in behind him. Annie followed the two of them out past the front desk and into the street, to Amanda's reserved spot. Bobby started to get into the driver's side, but Amanda yelled, "Let del Gatto!"

"Yeah," he said, and stepped around the car and into the front passenger seat. Amanda took the rear.

Annie closed her door and pulled the lap belt around her,

giving it a sharp tug into its tightest setting. She looked over at Bobby and said, "Tight, Lieutenant," as she turned the key. Bobby didn't need to be told. "Which way?" she asked.

Bobby turned to look at Amanda. "East on Newkirk," she said, looking back at him.

Annie looked in the rearview mirror and saw Geoff Pearsall in the middle of the street, arms outstretched in both directions, holding up traffic. Without checking further, she punched the accelerator and sent the car out into the street. When they were well clear of the other parked cars, she turned the wheel sharply, slammed on the brakes, and tapped the selector into "Drive." The front tires of the car lost traction, and just as they did so, she took her foot off the brake and pressed the accelerator. Before either of her passengers could even regain their orientation, Annie had the car pointed perfectly in the right direction and rapidly picking up speed.

When her skillful display had ended for the moment, and there was nothing to do but drive straight ahead, Annie said, "That's her place, isn't it? Pamela's. I mean, Jacoby's."

"Yeah," said Bobby. He pointed past the steering wheel to a panel on her left. "Beams and screams."

Annie reached under the dash and flipped two switches, turning on the red-and-blue flashing lights and the siren. In the car there was no Doppler effect, and the rise and fall of the siren was constant, without the added ups and downs in pitch that stationary bystanders would be hearing.

"Gimme the mike," Amanda said. Bobby pulled the microphone up and out of its holder and handed it to her. She keyed it and said, "Grant here. Say status."

"Word's out, Captain," Ruth Velasquez's voice rasped in return. "Doyle's coordinating a grid search on second frequency. What's going down?" Her voice was clipped and professional, but the suppressed tremors came through over the radio.

"I'll tell you later," Amanda said.

"Roger. Stay on one and I'll squawk when we hit."

Amanda keyed the mike without speaking and let the button go. The click in Ruth's earpiece would acknowledge that she'd heard. Annie took the last turn at high speed but confidently kept the tires a hair away from drifting and maintained control throughout the turn.

"There!" shouted Amanda, her hand coming over the backseat, pointing through the windshield. Bobby spotted the squad car at the same time and moved his head back and forth as they neared it, trying to see in.

Annie's younger eyes saw no sign of anyone in the car. "Empty," she said, then added with less self-assurance, "At least nobody sitting up."

Bobby reached for the mike. "Ruth, we need an ambulance at five forty Ditmas, on the double. Situation unknown." *Just get the ambulance here and we'll figure it out once it's on the way.*

"Roger," Ruth replied, and clicked off, momentarily incommunicado while she ordered one of the secondaries to get on the hospital frequency. Then she was back on. "Need assistance?"

"No," said Bobby, "just the wagon."

Annie pulled up next to the squad car, leaving enough room for the doors to open. She had switched off the siren as they'd gotten closer but left on the flashing lights.

Bobby was out and peering into the cruiser before they had fully stopped. He looked up at the apartment house and broke into a run, Annie and Amanda close behind. "What floor?" he yelled.

"Second," Annie yelled back. "Up the stairs, first on the left, just under the light."

Bobby took the stairs two and three at a time. As he neared the top, a door opened to his right and an elderly woman emerged but drew back as he reached the top at high speed. "I saw the police car, the lights," she said, "Outside ..." It sounded like "ootside" in her slight brogue.

"Have you seen Pamela Jacoby, miss?" Bobby asked, panting slightly.

"Yes, sure," the old lady answered. Each sentence seemed to end on an upward inflection, like a question instead of a statement. "She come in a little while ago." She indicated with her head and pointed to the door on the left. A hall ceiling light glowed just above it.

"Was she all right?" Bobby asked.

"Oh, my, yes. She was just fine. Is there sumthin' the matter with her, then?"

Bobby didn't answer but turned to Pamela's door and knocked as Amanda and Annie reached the top of the stairs. "Jacoby!" he yelled, and knocked again. No answer. He tried the knob. It was locked. He backed up and looked at the door, turning slightly so one shoulder was facing it.

"Here, here, young feller, no need for that," said the lady, turning to reenter her own apartment. She emerged dangling a key from a paper clip and handed it to him.

He took it, and Amanda said, "You're McGillicutty, aren't you? You gave us a statement."

"That's right," she said, smiling for the first time, then throwing a more reproving look at Bobby. "She could be gettin' dressed, or tekkin' a shower or sumthin'."

Bobby was already fitting the key into the lock. "I'll go in first," Amanda assured her.

The door swung open and Amanda stepped in tentatively, followed by Annie. "Pamela!" she yelled. She passed through the neat living room, noticed the picture on the bureau, and entered the small foyer that led to the bathroom and bedroom. The bedroom door was open. She looked in. Pamela's uniform jacket was on the bed, her holster and gun laid neatly on top, her cap close by.

She turned to her left, facing the closed bathroom door, and knocked. "Pamela?" She tried the doorknob. It was locked. She banged on the door with the flat of her hand and yelled louder. "Pamela!" Still no answer.

She put her ear to the door, thought she heard the sound of running water.

"Parks, get in here!" she screamed back into the living room. Bobby came running and saw Amanda pointing to the bathroom door. He hit it hard with his shoulder, and it seemed to buckle slightly but stayed intact. He backed up and ran at it again. A little more give this time.

"Hold me and I'll kick it," he said. Amanda took up a position to one side of the door and about four feet away from it, then motioned Annie to a spot directly opposite and facing her.

Bobby put one arm around each of their necks, took a step backward and then flung his legs toward the door, Amanda and Annie holding him up by the shoulders. He connected hard, and the door frame buckled. A panel where his right foot had hit was broken through. The sound of water was louder now. He punched a wider hole with his fist, reached through and turned the knob from the inside. The door was stuck in the bent frame, but he shoved with his shoulder and it swung in and banged against the wall.

He stopped in the doorway, and Amanda and Annie stepped to either side of him and looked in. Pamela sat in the tub, fully clothed in her uniform. The water reached her chest. It was pink and hadn't overflowed, but streaks of a deeper, more viscous red dropped down the side of the tub where her slashed left wrist had lain before she'd submerged it. Tears streaked her cheeks.

Fresh tears.

"Jacoby!" Bobby yelled as he regained himself and knelt beside the tub, two fingers on her neck. The pulse was fairly strong. Her head rolled to face him, her cheek resting against his arm.

"Oh, Jesus, Bobby," she said weakly. "Oh, Jesus Jesus Jesus."

"Easy, kid, easy." He slid his arm farther under her head, lifting it away from the hard porcelain. She pulled her right hand out from under the water and reached for the side of the tub. Blood dripped from it onto the tile.

"It was me, Bobby," she said, crying now.

"What the hell are you talking about?" Bobby said, not really asking a question but just trying to keep her talking. With his free hand he had taken a handkerchief out of his pants pocket and held it out to Annie, motioning to Pamela's wrist. Annie wound the cloth into a long band, wrapped it twice around the cut and started to tie it. "Tight," Bobby said, and Annie tugged the loose ends, made one overhand knot and tucked the ends under the cloth. "Find something for the other one," he said, but Amanda had already gone into the bedroom and found a pair of panty hose. Annie wrapped it around the other wrist. A siren sounded in the distance.

"It was me. I'm the one. Oh, God, please, let me die."

Bobby stopped and looked at her. Amanda was leaning over his shoulder. "What are you saying, Pamela?" she asked.

Pamela turned her eyes to Amanda. Her voice was growing weaker. The siren was closer now. "I did it, Captain, I killed him. I killed Mac." The effort took its toll, and she closed her eyes and rolled her head away from them. "It was me." She passed out.

The siren had stopped, and sounds of heavy boots on stairs came in through the apartment. Annie said something. "Whaa?" said Bobby, lost for a minute.

"Her vitals, Lieutenant. The EMS guys're on the way up."

"Shit," Bobby said, and put his fingers back on Pamela's neck while looking at his watch. He could hear Amanda's voice talking to the paramedics.

One of them came in and said, "I'm Hauser. What've we got?"

"Pulse fifty-five, breathing labored," Bobby said in as calm a voice as he could. He was afraid to try to get up and stayed down with his arm still under Pamela's head. "She was conscious until a minute ago."

Hauser clapped him on the shoulder twice. "Let us get in here, Lieutenant." He reached down and put a small, inflatable plastic pillow underneath Pamela's head while Bobby slipped his arm out. At the same time he reached to the opposite end of the tub, put his hand down into the water and turned the drain cock. As he pulled his hand out he also turned off the tap that was still letting new water in. The gurgle of water going down the drain was loud in the small room.

"C'mon, Bobby," Amanda said, and he stood slowly. The other paramedic stepped aside to let him out.

"We need a drip, stat," Hauser said to his partner, pulling a small flashlight out of one of the many zippered pockets in his overalls. "Large-bore IV and forget the glucose. Make it D5

Ringer's." He opened one of Pamela's eyes, shined the light directly in and said, "Normal contraction. Look around for pills anyway."

His partner was unwrapping the IV kit and, when nobody moved, looked at the three cops standing just outside the door. "He means you guys."

Rank notwithstanding, they knew the medics were in charge in situations like this, and they hurried to comply, Amanda and Annie in the living room, Bobby in the bedroom, all grateful for some way to help. They checked the garbage for empties as well. Another siren drifted in.

"Here's something," said Annie, handing Hauser a brown plastic bottle.

He looked at the label, then opened the top and shook a few pills into his hand. "Xanax," he said, confirming the label and showing off a little at the same time. "Easy tranq. That wouldn't do it. I think we're okay on drugs."

The other siren stopped, and soon another set of paramedics was up the stairs and in the apartment. One stuck his head inside. "Hauser, how you doin'. What'sit?"

Hauser knew the voice and answered without looking up. "Hey, Searns." He inserted the IV needle into the anticubital fossa vein near Pamela's elbow and taped it back against her skin so it couldn't jog out of place. "Police officer."

"No shit?" said Searns.

Hauser looked around to see if any of the cops were listening. He turned to Searns and said in a half whisper, "Do-it-yourselfer." The last of the water disappeared from the tub. A red stain covered the porcelain up to the water line.

"No shit," Searns said again.

"No shit," Hauser repeated. "We're gonna need the gurney. And call General. Tell 'em about twenty minutes."

The radio on Hauser's belt issued a burst of static. He stopped unwinding the panty hose from Pamela's wrist and reached for it. "EMS three-three, go."

"Hauser, is Captain Grant nearby?" the radio squealed.

"Damn," Amanda said to herself in the living room. Then louder, to Hauser, "Keep your line clear, I'll phone in."

She picked up the phone and dialed. Several seconds later

she said, "Dispatch," and waited again. "Ruth? Captain Grant. I'm sorry, things hit the fan over here. Stand down the all-points on the squad car, we're at Jacoby's now." She paused, then said, "We don't know yet." Paused again. "There was an accident, no time to go into it. Put me through to Atkins." She waited and then said, "Okay, Schuyler, then."

Searns and his partner returned hauling a collapsed gurney. Searns had a plastic sheet under his arm.

"We're here, Hauser," he called into the bathroom. "Say when."

Annie wandered into the bathroom. "How's she doin'?"

Hauser spoke while working. "Vital signs are pretty stable. It looks worse than it is. Not as much blood gone as we first thought." He looked up at Annie. "You guys got here pretty quick. What'd she do, call first?"

Annie looked at him without answering. He shrugged and started on Pamela's other wrist. He already had a cannula in her nose, the other end hooked into a valve on a green bottle that was hissing softly. "What's that?" Annie asked, pointing.

"Oxygen," said Hauser. "With some blood gone and decreased pulse, we want to get as much in her as possible. Avoid brain damage. She probably doesn't need it, but why take a chance? Yo, Searns!" he called loudly.

"On the way," Searns called back in.

Annie stepped aside to let the paramedics in. They left the gurney collapsed and set it on the floor next to the tub, then started the process of lifting Pamela out. Amanda was still on the phone. Annie went into the bedroom and found Bobby sitting on the edge of the bed with a small sheaf of papers in his hand. There were about eight sheets, stapled, the first several folded back, exposing one of the inside pages. He looked up as Annie entered. He tried to smile and said, "How you holding up, del Gatto?"

She leaned her back against the wall, then slid down its length until she was resting on her haunches. She wrapped her arms around herself, suddenly cold and alone, and tried to smile back. It wasn't very successful. "Ben Casey in there says she's lookin' good."

Bobby pursed his lips and tilted his head slightly. Amanda's voice, indistinct but in control, filled the background. Metal-on-metal clicking sounds could be heard in the bathroom. "How'd you know, Lieutenant?" Annie asked.

Bobby looked up from Tancredi's report. The gurney went by in the doorway. Black fabric straps secured its passenger. Plastic peeked out where the medics had put a sheet of it to keep her from soaking their underpad. A pole holding the IV solution poked up from one corner of the metal frame, a plastic tube running down and under the sheets. Drops fell slowly from beneath the clear plastic bag and into a small catch-pool atop the tube.

"About Pamela, I mean. You knew. How?"

Bobby waited until the gurney passed completely from view. He looked at Annie and stood up, dropping Pamela's copy of the report back on the bed about where he'd found it, putting his hands on the small of his back and stretching painfully. "It's a classic red flag, del Gatto." He looked back at the bed, reconsidered, and sat on the floor against the wall opposite her. "Someone's depressed, or shocked, or hurt in some terrible way. Moping around and feeling like shit." He looked toward the doorway.

"Then one day they come in acting like they just won the goddamned lottery. Smiling, happy, bubbly." He looked back toward Annie. "Good sign they're gonna do themselves pretty soon."

"What?" Annie sat up straight. "I don't get it."

"Don't they teach you anything in cop school these days?" Bobby asked, not unkindly.

"C'mon, man, I don't get it."

"It means they've decided, Annie. They picked the time, the place, how they're gonna do it. It's all settled. No more worries, no more problems. Like a big lead weight you didn't know was there got lifted off your chest. Like . . ." He paused, searching for the words, looking around the room. "Like you just don't have to put up with any of this shit anymore."

Amanda's voice had stopped. She appeared in the doorway. "Looks cozy." Annie started to scramble to her feet, but Amanda put up a hand and stopped her. "It's okay," she said, and took a seat on the edge of the bed. She ran her hand absentmindedly over Pamela's jacket. Bobby was looking at her. "What?" she asked.

Bobby reached behind her and picked up the report, still opened to the page where Pamela had stopped her reading, probably the night before. The bed was made. *Tidy up loose ends before you go.* Pamela was always a stickler for neatness. He handed the report to Amanda and sat back down.

Amanda started at the top of the page, ran her eye quickly down the cited references and other formal rigmarole, and settled in on a plain English paragraph near the bottom:

> There are similarities in this case to crimes committed by women who were sexually abused at a developing age, but these are rare and virtually always sloppily carried out in fits of rage; the careful cleanup in the aftermath of this crime makes this scenario a virtual impossibility and inclines more to a compulsive, female-role homosexual.

CHAPTER 27

She thought she heard a crunch of gravel on the footpath outside, and the elderly woman froze, her hand in midair about to set a teakettle down on the stove. She stopped breathing so the rush of air wouldn't interfere with her ability to pick up the slightest sound.

There it was again. And again, louder this time. A cat, maybe. But it wasn't the sound of an animal scratching at the loose rocks. It was the sound made by pressure that compressed the stones together. From something heavy, like a boot. . . .

There was more than one, and this time the low murmur of secretive voices was mixed in with the sound of steps. Heat filled Bronya's head and chest and shot down through her arms in a burst of adrenaline, a gift of surplus energy, but there was no outlet for its employment. Nowhere to run. And too much energy to let her gently place the kettle down without its making a sound. She laid it on the soft padding of a chair.

The gravel sound was louder now, less careful. The men were confident, which meant that the little cottage was likely surrounded. Bronya looked around frantically, landed her eyes on the curtained rear door and watched a shadow cross the window, then return and remain in place. Her breathing resumed when she could hold it no longer, but it sounded to her so loud that surely they would hear it. She eyed the trap-door in the floor leading down to the potato cellar. An obvious and potentially fatal dead end, but her mind was now so panicked that it saw the door only as a way to leave this room, right now, and failed to assess the consequences.

She had taken only one step forward when the explosion hit her door. Once, then again. It felt like a grenade after the quiet stillness, but it was only a rifle butt, and the door held. Bronya couldn't move. Images filled her eyes with a physical presence. The door to her childhood home caving in, brown-shirted storm troopers spilling into the neat kitchen, a homemade truncheon ruining her mother's sweet and beautiful face. A grinning and maniacal animal, yesterday a delinquent facing trial for beating and robbing elderly pensioners and today a hero of the new order, picked up her gentle young brother by the ankles and swung him until his head . . .

Another crack and she knew the door couldn't possibly hold. She was rooted to the spot in suffocating terror. German voices, harsh, guttural and frenzied, knifed into the room from all directions. "Whore! Jewish slut!" Glass rained to the floor from the breaking rear window, and a bayonet tore at the curtains. "We've got you, pig! No way out!" A hand reached in and grappled with the knob. Bronya slid slowly to the floor and grabbed her knees, hugging them to her chest. "Mrs. Tancredi! Mrs. Tancredi!"

She lowered her head and tried to lift her shoulders over her ears to drown out the sound. The banging on the doors seemed to recede. "Mrs. Tancredi, please!" She risked a side-ways glance and saw that the hand was no longer reaching in through the window. The German voices were fading.

"Mrs. Tancredi, please, please, it's Ahmed." She dropped her eyes, and the glass was gone from the floor, the curtains restored. Sun groped its way through the pane behind them and lit the ground at her feet.

"Please, Mrs. Tancredi, Ahmed. Look at the wall. Above the stove. Look, Mrs. Tancredi," the boy's voice pleaded.

She lifted her eyes and found the stove, wondered where the

teakettle had gone. "The calendar, Mrs. Tancredi. Look at it. Please."

The calendar hung from a single nail. "Scenes from the Holy Land" was printed in large letters over a picture of Jerusalem, one of twelve color photographs. She remembered this one. It showed a thin blanket of snow covering the Holy City. The legend over the numbered grid of days read "December." At the bottom, the Hebrew year was printed, 5732, and beneath that, the conventional numbering used by the rest of the world: 1972.

Bronya Tancredi blinked hard several times, reading and rereading the number until the wavering border of reality slowed and solidified. When she thought she could trust herself, she let go of her knees and put her hands on the floor, rolled forward onto the balls of her feet and stood up slowly.

"Mrs. Tancredi?"

She looked toward the door and automatically reached for her hair, patting both sides of her head to push down any strays. She started for the door, then turned quickly, picked up the kettle off the chair and placed it on the range. She walked to the door and opened it.

An Arab boy of about sixteen stood on the step and looked up at her. "Salaam aleikem, Mrs. Tancredi." He reached down and picked up a large cardboard box and started to carry it into the house.

"Shalom, Ahmed," she answered, and stepped aside to let him pass, but not before casting a barely noticeable, furtive glance past him. She turned and followed him. He set the box on the kitchen table and turned to her. "Something good today?" she asked, and reached to straighten a hair that had fallen down over his eyes.

Ahmed smiled kindly and turned back to the box, opening the cover and pointing inside. "Beautiful tomatoes. And grapefruits straight from the pardess only this morning."

———•———

"Long memories," said Dr. Tancredi after he'd stopped talking for a few minutes. The forgotten glass in his hand tilted precariously.

Amanda waited, not wishing to intrude on what had started

as a story but had evolved into a reminiscence told mostly to himself rather than to her. When she finally did speak, he seemed momentarily surprised that she was there and had been listening.

"How long did it go on?"

He took a sip of his straight Scotch on ice, keeping his eyes on the sun settling below a stand of trees at the far end of the yard. "Until the day she died. Maybe once, twice a month. Always the same. She is snapping out of it herself, usually, or someone is coming along."

The sun was below the tops of the trees, like a canvas on which were painted the silhouettes of leaves, perfectly motionless in the still air.

"Long memories," Amanda said, echoing Tancredi's observation. "Did anything in particular make it happen?"

He shrugged and looked down at his drink. "Hard to say. Probably. Her teakettle seemed to be figuring in. I am believing she maybe was holding one when the Gestapo is storming her father's house."

"And otherwise?"

He looked at her and said, "Perfectly normal. You would not believe it. Just this one mishegass, this one craziness." He shook his head, remembering. "We know now that the survivors who are suppressing the memories, who try to forget and get on with their lives, these are being the happiest and best adjusted. The ones who are feeling compelled to talk about it all the time and keep the images burning, the ones who are going to support groups, these are a much more miserable lot. The book is saying it should be otherwise." He held up his hands in a helpless gesture. "What the hell am I knowing? But for sure is this: We can suppress, but we can never forget. Always it is down there somewhere. And once in a while . . . ?" He flicked his fingers upward and made a "phfftt" sound.

"Pamela," Amanda said.

"Who knows?" he said, turning back to his drink and the dying sun. "But this whole thing is having a long memories feel about it. When is the hearing?"

"Prelim's Tuesday. No judge. We need to get it past the DA first."

Tancredi nodded. "I cannot imagine he is being a problem. What about the lawyer?"

Amanda was surprised by the question. "Why would her lawyer be a problem?"

"What if he is deciding to make a case out of it?"

"She." Amanda shook her head. "And I can't imagine it. Not with Pamela's own doctor ready to certify her."

Tancredi's gross misreading of the case sat between and around them like a mist, ephemeral but ever present, sometimes barely discernible but never completely gone. Neither one of them had brought it up. Still, Amanda appreciated his help and his almost clairvoyant sensitivity to her need to see him this day, and she needed to soften the blow.

"Can you come? I wish you would."

"I will try," he answered halfheartedly.

"How did she die? Your wife?"

Tancredi was quiet, and Amanda was instantly sorry she asked. Earlier that afternoon, when Pamela had been safely admitted and was out of physical danger, a phone had rung at the nurse's station. "It's for you, Captain," the nurse had called, holding up the receiver.

Amanda had taken the phone. "Grant," she'd said into the mouthpiece.

"Hallo, cutie-pie," the voice had answered.

"Dr. Tancredi," Amanda had said.

"I heard. Come have a drink. My place, if you are trusting me."

She'd driven alone to his house and had been sitting with him in the backyard for most of the afternoon. He turned to answer her question about his wife. "Let us just be saying the other side is playing from a different set of rules."

Amanda looked at him, horrified, but held her curiosity in check. So that was what drove a super-spook to drop out and pursue a more bucolic life psyching out blackmailers, extortionists and serial killers and tending occasionally to the psychic wounds of police captains who felt cheated and betrayed by life and circumstance, and who should have known better by now.

CHAPTER 28

For starters," Helena Faustus said, and reached across the table and grabbed the court reporter's hands, pushing them down onto the keys, "I'm not agreeing to anything"—the court reporter, whose whole life revolved around the commitment of the spoken word to paper, struggled to lift her knuckles far enough into the air to shift her fingers onto the right keys and back down again—"that goes on here," Faustus finished.

The reporter was now frantic; she was pretty good at catching up if she got behind on maybe five or six words, but here an entire sentence was floating around in space, and her fingers were still pinned in place. "Miss Faustus!" she pleaded, her eyebrows arched in fright, too intimidated to express anger at the lawyer's draconian censorship. Faustus had just walked into the room and hadn't even taken a seat yet.

"Helena," LaBelle said, affecting a schoolmarm's rebuking tone, "will you please behave yourself?" Then, to the court reporter, "We're off the record, Michele." He flicked his fingers in the direction of the recording machine keyboard, and Faustus released the reporter's hands, glared at LaBelle and sat down.

She looked around the room. Her eyes landed on Jake Nostrand. "This guy her doctor?" she asked nobody in particular.

"No," said Brixton Ferrin. "I am. That is Dr. Nostrand, friend of the deceased."

"Just fucking swell, Libel," said Faustus to LaBelle. "You got the dead guy's pals sitting in on the prelim while my client's got tubes dripping Christ knows what into her, you start Van Cliburn over here"—she indicated the reporter—"tapping away before I even show up. . . . This meeting's over, boys and girls," she said, starting to rise, "and I'll let you know—"

"Miss Faustus!" Amanda said sharply. When she had Faustus's attention, she said icily, "Sit down."

"Listen, there's no fucking way—"

"I said, sit down."

Some small, heretofore insignificant and long-forgotten piece of Faustus's self-preservation mechanism forced her to comply.

"I take it you didn't have a lot of time to prepare for this meeting," LaBelle said.

"Time? They handed me the file and the message at the same time."

"But you already know the case." Everybody did. "Let us continue, and if you don't like the way it turns out, we'll wait a week and start again, de novo. Fair enough?"

Faustus looked around the room. Everyone nodded agreement. "Okay," she said, considerably subdued. "Sorry, Michele," she said to the reporter.

"We're going to ask the DA to decline charges if your client voluntarily commits herself," Amanda explained to her. "You certainly have the right to talk to her about going to trial, but she's already confessed—"

"Did you read her her rights when you found her in the tub?" Faustus interrupted before she could stop herself, zeroing in reflexively on a possible technical flaw.

"What the hell are you, on autopilot or something?" LaBelle demanded angrily. "We're trying to help your client. We've got her involved with the dead guy, we placed her at the scene within an hour of the murder, we've got corroboration on the timing, and she confessed, *after* she was Mirandized. She told her doctor," he continued, indicating Ferrin across the table, "that he could release whatever part of her records he wanted. If he says what I want to hear, I'll go to the DA and tell him to accept an insanity plea. Your client goes to Giggle Central, end of case."

"She can always refuse the deal," said Bobby. Faustus knew that was true.

"Let's go back on the record," Amanda said, gracefully rescuing Faustus from the requirement to publicly back down a second time. The reporter's keys clacked softly as she logged the lawyer's entrance and noted a return to the record. Faustus took out a business card and handed it to her to get the spelling right for the official record. "Michele, where were we?" asked Amanda.

The reporter reached in back of her machine to the bin holding the narrow strips of fan-folded paper. After locating the right spot, she read the phonetically coded markings and translated out loud, flatly and with no inflection. Later a computer would read a cassette tape from inside the machine and print the transcript automatically. The paper was for backup, in case the tape was spoiled, and to allow her to immediately read back what had been said previously, if so requested.

"Dr. Ferrin: 'Of course I knew almost with a certainty that Jacoby had killed Graham, but doctor-patient privilege forbade my coming forth until now.' Mr. LaBelle: 'Why now, Doctor?' Dr. Ferrin: 'I advised Pamela to waive the privilege.' " Michele looked up. "Then my fingers got stuck," she said without looking at Faustus, "and we went off the record." She dropped the paper back in the bin and sat with her hands poised over the keys.

"So why now, Doc?" LaBelle asked. "If you knew all along, why not advise her to waive it before?"

"A partial waiver, please. Because it wouldn't have been in her best interest. Until we went to the scene, Pamela had absolutely no idea that she'd done it."

In the sudden quiet, Jake Nostrand put his hands on the table and leaned forward. "You're kidding."

There was a knock at the door. Jake leaned over and opened

it, and Edan Tancredi's head poked around from behind it. "Sorry I am being late," he said.

"Come in, Doctor," said Amanda. As he entered she said, "You already know LaBelle and Parks. This is Helena Faustus, Jacoby's lawyer, and Dr. Nostrand, Graham's friend . . ." Tancredi shook hands as he was introduced. "And this is Dr. Ferrin, Jacoby's psychiatrist."

Tancredi's hand paused on its way to Ferrin's. "Brixton Ferrin?" he asked.

"Why, yes," Ferrin said tentatively.

"My, my, this is indeed a pleasure," said Tancredi, gripping Ferrin's hand firmly. "I am hearing you lecture in Tel Aviv."

"Tel Aviv?" Ferrin looked confused. "But that was—"

"Sshh, sshh," Tancredi hissed comically with a finger to his lip. "Hush-hush, yes. Well, I am assuring you I was authorized."

"Have a seat, Tanc," said Amanda. "Dr. Ferrin was just telling us that Jacoby—"

"Is having no idea she did it," Tancredi finished for her.

Jake looked at him wide-eyed. "But how did you know?"

"It must be so. There could be no other way," said Tancredi.

Ferrin turned to look at Nostrand. "It was total suppression, Jake. Almost total. I believe some part of her knew and was trying to get the message to her conscious mind. I think that's why she felt she had to go to the scene, even though the thought terrified her."

Sensing a mounting skepticism, Ferrin felt the need to back up his thesis. "There is sound precedent for this. Recently, a twenty-two-year-old murder case of a young girl was solved after her best friend suddenly remembered seeing the murder happen."

"Yes, yes," said Tancredi, nodding. "For so many years was the memory suppressed, hidden it was in a secret place. Then, poof, up it is coming."

"Huh?" LaBelle looked unconvinced. "How come the woman couldn't remember in the first place?"

"Because the murderer had been her own father," Ferrin explained calmly. "He'd made sexual advances toward the

friend and his own daughter, and then killed the little girl
because he was afraid she might talk. He didn't realize his
daughter was watching, and the shock shut down a part of her
and made her forget."

Tancredi underlined the point for Ferrin. "The psychological detachment is having a name, even. Dissociation. Altered
perceptions of time, identity, often such memory gaps. Followed years later by spontaneous recall."

"Wait a minute, wait a minute," LaBelle said sarcastically.
"I'm willing to believe Jacoby went nuts, but you're telling me
she really had no idea? How the hell did she manage to clean
the place up and then forget about it?"

"She's a cop," Ferrin explained patiently. "You asked Miss
Faustus before if she was on autopilot. Maybe Pamela was on
autopilot and covered her tracks, covered them well, as only
a conscientious cop would know how to do. I don't know for
sure about that part. I'm just guessing."

"That's the part you forgot to factor in," said Amanda to
Tancredi. "That she was an experienced policewoman."

Ignoring Amanda's observation, LaBelle continued to protest, less stridently this time. "But her neighbor saw her when
she came home. She didn't see any blood, and we know the
killer got covered with it."

"She was naked," Amanda said without thinking, suddenly
starting to see the pieces fall into place and beginning to understand something of the secrets Pamela had been harboring
since childhood.

"And that's why the shower," Bobby added, snapping his
fingers. "She took a shower afterward to wash the blood off. It
comes off easily. No residue."

Faustus was also starting to understand where this was heading and why all of these people were untroubled by the obvious
breaches in procedure. "So what you're saying, Doctor, is that
my client legally has no culpability, because she doesn't—
didn't—know she was the killer."

"Exactly," said Ferrin. "Putting her in jail accomplishes
nothing, although she is a potential danger to others and to
herself, as she has already demonstrated. She needs help. She

is intelligent, and she knows she needs help. In an ironic way, this incident is technically a major breakthrough, as it forces her to confront the totality of her neurosis and its causes."

"You gonna stick with her, Doc?" asked Bobby.

Ferrin looked at him and said, "Yes, Lieutenant. Whatever it takes."

"Has she in fact confronted it?" asked Amanda.

"That's an important question, Captain. She's been under a lot of sedation and it's difficult to be precise, but I don't think we're there yet. She knows she did it, but it was in a schizophrenic fog, and she cannot remember the details, only the blood and the wounds. I don't think she can visualize the scene or dredge it up and replay it. Until she does, she's still trapped. There are too many powerful and conflicting emotions."

"Like what?" asked Jake.

Ferrin elaborated. "The morning after it happened, she was confused because her boyfriend was dead, yet she felt better than she had in weeks."

Amanda nodded. "That's true. She was almost cheerful. It was very disconcerting."

"That's because, in a strange way, it was an immense relief. The intense pressure she had voluntarily put herself under had reached the breaking point. In a manner of speaking, killing Mac relieved the pressure, but in the ensuing weeks the guilt caught up with her."

"Until . . . ?" Amanda asked.

"Until she read Dr. Tancredi's report," Bobby interrupted, a faraway look in his eyes as he remembered the document left open on her bed.

"I think so," said Ferrin, nodding in agreement.

"Wild Bill," Bobby murmured as the puzzle got clearer still.

"What about Wild Bill?" asked Amanda.

"Her father abused her, Captain," said Ferrin. "Sexually. For years. Her mother was too afraid to intervene. When Pamela got old enough to assert herself, she cut him off and estranged herself from him. He went from an object of adoration to something she loathed and reviled. Except that we don't make such mental leaps that easily, and the resulting confusion was overwhelming."

LaBelle shook his head in disbelief. "I gotta tell you, Doc, somehow this doesn't wash. Lots of kids get abused, some pretty badly, but they don't wind up killing people."

"I say, Mr. LaBelle, I didn't kill the man," said Ferrin, starting to get irritated by the ADA's belligerence. "I'm just trying to be helpful."

LaBelle, surprised, looked around the room and then back at Ferrin. "I'm sorry. Really. It's just my style to play devil's advocate."

Ferrin seemed to consider something for a moment, already thinking past his annoyance with LaBelle, and then said, "Can we go off the record?"

LaBelle felt that they had enough to accomplish their purpose. The conversation had drifted more to curiosity and morbid fascination than legal necessity. He looked at Faustus for assent, and she nodded at the reporter, who lifted her hands from the keys.

Ferrin glanced at Tancredi, who was fingering his lower lip and staring at the tabletop as he listened, then looked back to Labelle. "When her father would climb into her bed and rape her—which is what it was, make no mistake—she would shut her mind down until it was over. Being had, in that fashion, could be a passive activity on her part, and she could take her mind somewhere else.

"It was harder when he started making her perform other acts, but she learned to disconnect from those as well, even though she would remember later and cry herself to sleep, without the comfort of a mother or even a strong sibling. She was able to retain some shred of dignity by virtue of her recognition of the outrage that was being committed against her.

"But the last time they were together, something awful and unspeakable happened, or so it seemed to her, and the shame slammed a door in her mind, a door so heavy it hasn't fully opened yet."

"What is so terrible?" asked Tancredi, although he had already guessed.

Ferrin paused and then said, "She had an orgasm."

"It is being quite a surprise, seeing him," Tancredi said quietly when Ferrin was out of earshot at the coffee machine.

Bobby, Amanda and the two doctors had decided to take a short break in the courthouse cafeteria over coffee before reconvening to work through lunch and possibly finish all the loose ends by early afternoon. Faustus had gone along with the overall approach, LaBelle was satisfied that no greater justice would be served by prosecuting Pamela Jacoby, and it was now down to formalities.

"What was that about a lecture?" asked Amanda.

"It actually is being hush-hush," Tancredi replied. "Better left that way. He was quite brilliant, in a young sort of fashion. All theory and experiment, little real-world experience, but compelling indeed. Very convincing."

"But you looked more than just surprised, Doc," said Bobby. "You looked a little startled, as though it didn't make sense for him to be here."

"Very observant, Bobby. What are you being, a cop? The last I am hearing of Brixton Ferrin he had disappeared from sight, vanished, poof, up in smoke."

"Why?" asked Amanda.

"I believe his father died, and it is affecting him greatly." Tancredi grew serious. "He really was being quite highly regarded, and we tried to get him back for some additional consultations. The university officials are telling our representative that he is taking the shock quite hard, he left his position, left unfinished work. One of our agents is checking further, and it seems they were getting ready to throw him out anyway."

"Throw him out?" asked Bobby, getting lost in Tancredi's scrambled tenses. "What happened?"

"Apparently, he was difficult. A good doctor, an excellent researcher, but brash and arrogant. Basically a pain in the *tuchis*. It was a small department, and they are not wanting to put up with him any longer. Nothing against his skills or practice, no, no. This we know for sure. Quite a loss, especially considering what we were doing in Mossad at the time."

"There are a couple of things I don't understand about him, what he was doing," said Amanda.

"So ask," said Tancredi.

"What?"

"Ask him."

Ferrin was returning to the table, gingerly handling a cup of coffee that was nearly overflowing. "But I'm not sure . . ." Amanda protested, whispering in strained tones under her breath to try to stop Tancredi from embarrassing her.

Too late. "Doctor," said Tancredi, "Captain Grant is having few questions, for you specifically, off the record."

"Certainly. Ask away."

"There're two things that are bothering me, Doctor," Amanda said hesitantly, already annoyed with herself for presenting this extended and unnecessary preamble, "and I didn't want to bring them up in front of everybody else."

"Let's hear it, Captain," Ferrin said with sincerity.

"How come you didn't spot Pamela's upswing in mood? Before she tried to take her own life?"

He seemed genuinely startled. "Excuse me?"

"She came into the station after seeing you that morning," Bobby said. "One of our officers reported that she was nearly manic. That's when we went after her. Another hour or so and she might not have made it."

"But I had no idea," said Ferrin, obviously disturbed by this news. "I had been pushing her very hard. The time we spent at the scene had been punishing for her. She was as down that morning as I have ever seen her."

"It is very likely that she is making her decision after she leaves you, Doctor," said Tancredi. "Her method requires no great preparation. There was time." He looked sad. "She is reading my report the night before, apparently."

"She didn't mention it to me," said Ferrin.

"It's funny," said Bobby. "If she had killed Graham intentionally, your report would have let her completely off the hook, thrown the whole investigation off track. As it was . . ." His voice trailed off as he suddenly realized how insensitive he was being to Tancredi.

"As it was," Tancredi said, "it is probably pushing her over the edge."

"You shouldn't kick yourself, Doctor," Ferrin said. "Under different circumstances it could have been the epiphany that rescued her soul. I wonder if Nostrand and I did the right thing in setting the two of them up. If we hadn't, maybe Mac Graham would be alive today. Or maybe someone else would be dead. What is important is that we believed we were doing the right thing and behaved responsibly." He paused and looked at Amanda. "You said there were two things."

"Yes. Would you have let her kill someone else? Because of the privilege?"

Without pausing to consider, he said, "No. I don't know how I would have intervened, but I would have done it. That's why it was so important for me to make something precipitous happen, rather than the slow, tedious method we had been pursuing. Her idea of visiting Graham's house provided the opportunity."

"I guess I did some pushing of my own on you, Doc," Bobby said apologetically. "About the privilege and all that."

"We were both doing our jobs, Lieutenant. Rather looks like you did yours better than I did mine."

They fiddled with their spoons, stirring coffee that had no sugar or cream.

"Dr. Ferrin," Tancredi said, "is that being the last time Jacoby is reaching a climax with a man?"

"Sorry?" asked Ferrin, not used to Tancredi's sudden segues.

"With her father? Is she ever having success after that?"

Ferrin seemed confused and uncomprehending, not certain of whether the fault was his or Tancredi's. "But, I'm not sure you—"

"It seems relevant, somehow, since she obviously is coming to see Graham not only as substituting for her father, but abusing her the same way her father did, and I am wondering if possibly the unexpected approach of an orgasm triggered—"

"No, no, you don't understand, Doctor," said Ferrin, beginning to apprehend the mistake.

"Somehow the memory, the long memory, is unearthed in that moment," Tancredi was continuing, intent on his analysis and not mindful of Ferrin's animated protest, "and this is what—"

"Doctor!" Ferrin said sharply, and Tancredi stopped and looked at him. Ferrin searched Amanda's and Bobby's faces and realized they'd all missed it.

"She didn't climax when her father was having her," he said slowly and carefully. "It was when he was shot. While he was dying."

BOOK
3

CHAPTER 29

Captain Amanda Grant stared at the blinds, eyes focused in the distance, and winced as the hot coffee burned her tongue. She'd never really known before what the phrase *struggle for perspective* meant.

The complex investigation of a major crime was, she imagined, probably much like childbirth. It was an all-consuming endeavor that dominated completely the lives of its protagonists, filled as much with doubt and fear as it was with great expectation, and the outcome was never a certainty, only a hope. Fanfare and congratulations surrounded its successful conclusion and, often as not, the elements of caprice and chance were as important as skill and planning.

Unfortunately the metaphor was applicable afterward as well. Postpartum depression was as common in police work as it was in procreation. The aftermath of many months of intensive work was rarely a relaxing bask in the afterglow of public adulation. After the paperwork and the inevitable debriefings, the officers involved often sank into melancholia as they were reabsorbed into the largely tedious reality of precinct life. Good police managers knew this syndrome and took pains to quickly assign the repatriating heroes to another tough case. But like the alcoholic who drinks to get rid of a hangover, they became investigating junkies, which was not necessarily a problem on a large police force with plenty of major crime but was the scourge of smaller operations.

The problem for Amanda was doubly acute. The highly publicized investigation of the death of Mackenzie Graham was brought to a definitive close, but the murderer was a cop. One of their own, a sister, the daughter of a visible and popular veteran who had died in the line of duty. Sworn to protect and serve, she'd taken the life of one of the very citizens with whose care she'd been entrusted.

Local journalists had not been kind. Pulitzers were not generally awarded for the kinds of reporting indigenous to minor metropolises, so the rare opportunities to hit the big time were seized upon with a vengeance. Like all people involved in a cause, the local reporters were concerned with their own self-interests first, carefully hidden behind a mountain of self-righteous and self-serving platitudes. In their case these were "the public's right to know," whether the public gave a damn or not, and "freedom of the press," meaning my freedom, since I am the press. After threats of defection to other papers, the type sizes of reporting bylines were expanded three points in height, and reporters whose pieces made it to the wire services strutted like high school football players scoring touchdowns. The thirst for scandal and higher mounds of precinct filth was unquenchable, and those reporters who valued their integrity above all else found themselves under enormous pressure to readjust their worldviews.

The wire service professionals and the veteran hands on the big-city newspapers had seen all of this before and were vigilant for it. They carefully sifted the substantive from the merely sensational and hoped that their lack of attention to the latter would soon result in the diminution of the inevitable tide of speculative trivia. It would not, of course: nobody ever lost money overestimating the hunger of the public for this kind of news. The tabloid sales would rise as a function of the local misery quotient.

Coupled with a national atmosphere of civil rights bloated

into unrecognizability, where vilification of police was a pastime, the public outcry was as predictable as it was devastating and demoralizing. The police under Amanda's command stood helpless as the citizenry took up arms against them, figuratively and, in thankfully rare instances, literally.

Simple wisecracks were the easiest to handle. A rookie writing a simple traffic ticket hears, "Yer not going to kill me and cut my nuts off, are ya?" It soon became a common theme.

More difficult were the recalcitrant perpetrators of minor crimes who resisted arrest violently and prepared their courtroom defenses well in advance. Mike Atkins fought hand to hand with a shoplifter who performed for the gathering crowd. "How I know you not gonna kill me, man, huh? You gonna cut me up, muthafucka? Who the fuck're you to bust me, yo' ass belong in jail, not mine!" And endless variations of the same replayed on a daily basis.

The most serious single incident involved Al Emley, who narrowly avoided losing his life trying to break up a domestic squabble, a typical Saturday night occurrence not normally a terribly serious occasion. He and Dennis Murdoch had banged on the door and announced themselves as dictated by procedure. The noise within died, and they knocked again. "Police officers! We've had reports of a disturbance. Please open the door."

"Fuck you man, you take care of you' own, then you come and gi' me shit! Get the fuck outta here!"

"Open the door, please, sir," said Murdoch. "This is the police. Just take it easy and we won't have any trouble. We can settle this right here."

The door flew open and a twelve-gauge poked out and came to rest against Emley's neck. "Fuckin'-A right we can settle it! Right here, man! You wanna cut me up?"

Murdoch knew the Jacoby reference was just a smoke screen, an excuse to rattle and embarrass the police, but with a shotgun poised to kill his partner, he was not going to start talking politics with a crack-spaced maniac. "No problem, man, no problem. Just point the piece somewhere else and we're outta here, nice and easy, just like you say."

Murdoch saw the indecision in the junkie's eyes and sought to push him in the right direction. "We just walk away, man, like it never happened. C'mon, you don't need this, we don't need it, everybody walks away, okay?"

Emley was holding still, his hands visible. The junkie looked at Murdoch and, his reluctant decision made, started moving the muzzle of the gun away. When it was pointed between the two cops, Emley grabbed it with both hands and pushed it up in the air, steeled himself against its going off, then let go with his right and drove his elbow into the man's face. He fell on him and began pummeling him mercilessly, blindly, the brush with mortality fueling his anger and giving him strength.

Murdoch knew that it wouldn't be trouble. Crack junkies were often brought in badly bruised. The drug made them difficult to subdue, and the arresting officers often found themselves fighting for their lives as much as for the collar. But Emley risked getting out of hand, and this was not a good time to open themselves up to charges of brutality. When Murdoch was sure the perp was out, he put his arms around Emley and lifted him into the air and back out into the hall. The shotgun attack would excuse a good deal, and they would bring the guy directly to the emergency ward and avoid the specter of a bloody suspect being marched into the station. Why give the Fourth Estate a free pass to another front-page exposé?

Like incipient raindrops looking for a speck of dust around which to coagulate, settle, and drop to earth, the hue and cry circled and hovered for a while, then came to rest on Amanda Grant. Like any survivor, she knew better than to ignore it. Maybe she could deflect it, maybe meet it head on, but deal with it she would. This one wasn't going to go away. And while she diverted energy and attention to the necessary task of her own self-protection, there was no doubt that the department was going to suffer. Maybe it would emerge stronger. Certainly her own self-doubt and second-guessing about her conduct robbed her of some of the self-confidence that was necessary to mount a fully effective counterattack.

However it would eventually turn out, these were not happy times. She considered this as she sipped idly at the coffee, now grown cold and rancid.

———◆———

A tapping sounded on the glass office wall. Amanda found herself trying to stare through the blinds, forgetting that she had drawn them shut, only the second time she had done that in many years.

She stood up and twisted the clear plastic control rod and saw Annie del Gatto standing uncertainly outside. Despite Amanda's avowed open door policy, it was relatively rare for younger staff to seek a personal audience. She opened the door and motioned Annie inside. "Slumming, del Gatto?" she asked as airily as her mood would allow.

"Yeah, I guess," said Annie. Amanda noticed that her normal spunk and swagger was somewhat diminished, and the young officer seemed to carry an air that was, if not quite morose, at least in stark contrast with her normal, genial surliness.

Amanda took a seat on one of the free-standing chairs and motioned Annie to the couch opposite. She left the blinds drawn; if she opened them, the station veterans would recognize the seating configuration as standard for a Captain Grant counseling session, and Annie was clearly looking for private comfort to speak what was on her mind.

"How are things going, Captain? I mean, with the reporters and all that."

"About what you'd expect. Trashing the force is more fun than debating the dog poop ordinance, so . . ." She passed off the rest of the sentence with a hand wave.

"Yeah," said Annie, "we were good for six columns this morning alone."

"It's funny, you know. . . ?" Amanda began.

"What?"

"This is the most bullshit I've heard out of Anne Marie del Gatto in four years." Annie looked up, surprised. "So what is it?" Amanda asked gently, with a pretty good idea of what was coming.

Annie leaned forward, rested her elbows on her knees and scratched her head with both hands. "I don't get it, Captain. This shit with Jacoby. It doesn't figure."

"How doesn't it figure?"

"Well, all I know is what I hear around the station and what's in the paper, right? And we all know what crap *that* is."

We do indeed. "So?"

"So, Jacoby goes berserk with a guy because all this terrible shit she's hiding about men pops her bubble in the saddle. Is that it? Is that what it's supposed to be?"

"Well, I wouldn't have put it quite like that, but that's the basic picture."

"That's a crock, Captain. Pamela didn't hide it like some goddamned chain-saw maniac. She used to joke about men all the time. She was always giving me shit about fooling around, but friendly like, y'know? And she was always saying how she wished she could fool around, too, and have a good time, but it was a problem for her. Does that sound like 'a time bomb waiting to explode'?" She used the pet phrase of the lead reporter of one of the sleazier local rags. (He had interviewed countless "Jacoby intimates," like the gas station attendant who filled her car once two years ago and never spoke a word to her. "You could see it in her eyes, y'know," he said. "Something strange about that one," said a beautician from Mr. Michael's. Pamela had never visited Mr. Michael's, a small error corrected three days later on page twenty-four.)

"Did she ever mention her father, Annie?"

"Her father?" Annie creased her brow in concentration. "I don't think so, now you mention it. But I heard that things weren't so hot between the two of them. I heard . . . well, some pretty bad things. She never brought it up."

"I don't imagine so. Her doctor thinks she might not really remember some of those things. It might have figured in."

She was playing devil's advocate with Annie. Amanda knew better than to dismiss her observations out of hand. Behind Annie's unpolished facade was a sharp-eyed judge of character, who more than once had made the right call in tight situations. More important, her no-holds-barred analysis of Pamela Jacoby mirrored Amanda's own, and she wondered if the other nagging doubts also figured in, the ones about—

"Right. The shrink. What'sizname, Ferrin?" She knew perfectly well what his name was. "I gotta tell you, Captain, I don't trust that guy worth a damn. Always shovin' her around like a freakin' lab rat. Hey, before she hooked up with that guy, she was fucked up like the rest of us, right? Then he gets ahold of her, and all of a sudden she's a serious wack-o. I'm tellin' ya, Captain, she wasn't so bad before."

This was interesting. More than interesting. Amanda was tempted to voice some of her own doubts, but she didn't want to artificially lend credence to Annie's own thoughts or prompt her beyond where she had already taken herself. "What do you mean?" she asked simply.

"Pamela was really freaked by men. Okay, so she was great looking and built real good, guys were probably hitting on her all the time, that can get to you. But she was really *freaked*. Scared. She wouldn't go out, even to a movie."

"I didn't know it was that bad, but . . . ?"

"But, this Ferrin is all the time pushing her to go out with Mac. So she does it and tosses her cookies, it's so bad, and he keeps on beating on her to keep doing it. She looks like shit the next morning, she lost work time . . . you knew that, right?"

"Yes, but not always that it was after a date."

"Every time. Almost every time. It was terrible for her."

"Maybe he thought it was like getting back on a horse after being thrown. Keep doing it until you're used to it."

"Uh-uh. No way. And she wasn't getting better, she was getting worse."

"It's sort of a judgment call, Annie. He probably knew what he was doing." What else did Annie have?

"Well, what about taking her to Mac's house? That was nuts. She was really falling for the guy, and he takes her to see his blood and brains all over the walls. What the hell was the point?"

"But that was Pamela's own idea. To see if she might remember something."

"Remember something? Remember what? Christ, she didn't even know she was there when he got whacked."

"Ferrin seemed to think some part of her remembered."

"It's psycho-mumbo-jumbo bullshit. She was freaking out

all over the place. And what about the pills he was feeding her? What the hell was in those?"

"Pills? Those were just a mild tranquilizer. Even the paramedic said so. They're swallowed by the millions every day."

Annie seemed disappointed at this. "Maybe she was allergic to them or something. How should I know? They were supposed to calm her down, and she kept goin' loony."

"They were harmless, Annie. He was trying to help her, not drive her crazy. She didn't even really need them. Dr. Nostrand told us they were just an excuse to get her to his office."

Annie sank back on the couch. She looked beaten. "I know," she said morosely. "I know all that. It just doesn't figure. She just wasn't that bad."

It was time to change the subject. "Have you seen her? Visited her, I mean?"

"Every day. Have you?"

Amanda was surprised at both Annie's answer and her question. "No," she answered, "I haven't had the time." She reconsidered, electing to award Annie's openness with some of her own. "That's not true. I just can't seem to bring myself to go see her."

"You should, Captain. I think she'd like that very much. They've got her on a lot of downs. She looks like hell."

"I'll try. I will. I suppose the tranquilizers are to stop her from hurting herself."

Annie shook her head in objection to this observation and got up to leave. She paused at the door and turned. "Tell me something else, Captain. What the hell kind of shrink can't tell when one of his patients is gonna try to knock herself off?"

CHAPTER
30

Amanda stared idly at her door after Annie disappeared. Discomfiting how the young officer refused to accept the realities of the situation. Disconcerting how she let her feelings and instincts run counter to the facts and evidence at hand.

Vexing how closely Annie's intuition matched her own.

The door had hardly closed when the sound of knuckles rapping once again intruded on her thoughts. "Del Gatto?"

"Not quite," said a familiar voice. *Oh, shit,* she thought as the face of Mayor Walter Zipkin appeared. Normally, and in contrast with most people in her position, she would be happy to see him, but in the current atmosphere she sensed that this would be other than a pleasant visit.

"Good morning, Walt," she said as easily as she could, trying not to overdo it and betray the wariness she really felt. She had known for days it was only a matter of time until he showed up. "You not a senator yet?"

"Too much stress. I'm thinking of going back to lube and oil jobs. Get the feel of grease back under my nails."

Sure, Walt. Zipkin owned a statewide rolling lube service, the automotive equivalent of fast food. It was a brilliant concept. His fleet of full-service trucks camped in corporate parking lots and performed oil changes, lubes and other minor services, charging great premiums to customers too busy to bring cars in to a fixed facility. Amanda guessed he had never been under a car. He sat down heavily on a chair facing her desk and avoided her eyes. "How's it going?"

Amanda waved her hand and looked directly at him. She wasn't going to make things easier for him. "Going? Just great. Sergeant Gumer's in the ER with a head wound from a thrown bottle, just reward for the nerve he had to write a speeding ticket this morning. I got a call from the *Herald* wanting to know what plans I had for instituting a psychiatric testing program for prospective police officers. It was the same reporter who gave us so much crap for administering polygraphs to vice applicants two years ago. How's it going? I'm supposed to be protecting the peace, and I can hardly protect my department."

Walter nodded absently, in that manner politicians adopted so that their gestures, however noncommittal or insincere, were at least technically appropriate. "I imagine it's not easy," he said.

She wished he'd cut to the chase, but she didn't want to rush him. "And you?" she asked.

He shrugged and looked up at her briefly before turning to the window, pretending to be distracted by something outside. "Not unlike you, really. I've got my own wolves to keep at bay."

She nodded with the same insincerity, knowing that he couldn't be having an easy time of it either. She tried to guess what he had come to see her about and decided it was some kind of public statement, or a meeting with the board of supervisors, or some other display that would be uncomfortable for a few days and then blow over. Her refusal to enter into public debate over the Graham killing had frustrated a public and press with too much leisure time.

"Mandy," he started, then hesitated.

This isn't fair to him, she thought, and got up, heading for the door.

"How about a couple of coffees?" she said to the desk clerk. "Both black." She shut the door and sat on the couch, facing Zipkin. "What is it, Walt?"

He turned his chair toward her. "The board is under a lot of pressure. They hoped it would die down, go away, be replaced by some other piece-of-shit problem they could use to look important and useful." He looked down at his nails, then up at Amanda, gesturing as he spoke. "It's not going away. The local rags won't let it. I think they write one story, then cut it up into little pieces and run one every day. Makes them look like real reporters."

Amanda felt a new discomfort starting to grow.

"They've started to run out of novel ideas," Zipkin continued. "Now what they need is a more specific target. Something to lend focus to a lot of free-floating accusations."

The discomfort was evolving now as the point of the conversation started making itself evident. "Me," she said.

"Supervisor Doyle has a friend on the *Herald*. Personally I think it's a typesetter he's been putting it to for the last seven years, but usually reliable." His attempt at lightening things up fell flat in the context of Amanda's growing dismay and his own nervousness.

"And?" she prodded him.

"And, they know about Jacoby's participation in the investigation. They know she'd been seeing a shrink. They're going to make a big stink."

"With me at the center."

"Apparently."

Apparently, hell, she thought. *They're going to crucify me.* "Swell," she said. "That's just terrific. The impact on morale ought to really pick things up around here." She stood and walked to the window, then to a corner file cabinet and back again, unable to contain her anger. "What the hell are they trying to do, maybe get a few of my people killed? Doesn't anybody out there understand what's going on?"

Zipkin stayed silent. She would have thought that getting this out on the table would have relieved some of his anxiety, but he appeared not to be any less agitated than when he'd first arrived. Her previous sympathy vanished under the pressure of her evolving predicament. "What about the board, Walter? Didn't anybody come to my defense? Didn't anybody call the *Herald* and try to explain the background, the details, tell them to talk to people on the investigating team, anything? Anything at all?"

Walter said nothing, only stared at his hands, his left knee jittering up and down in rhythm with his tapping foot.

"Holy shit, Walter. That's not all, is it?"

Nothing.

"What?" she demanded, her voice rising despite her effort to regain control.

He looked up. "The board got in touch with the county. Internal affairs. Asked for some help."

She froze, unable to speak, only able to stare at him.

"Don't worry about it, Amanda," he rushed to explain. "It's not a formal thing, nothing on the books. The board feels it's too much for them, they're not used to dealing with stuff like this, they needed help. The county guys'll talk to you, you'll explain, it'll all go away."

Amanda found her tongue and made it work somehow. "IAD?" she managed to ask. "IAD is going to talk to me? About how I conducted the investigation?"

"I told you. It's off the books, just to get your side, by an expert instead of some goddamned reporter trying to make his bones."

Amanda stared at him, dumbfounded. "You sonofabitch."

He looked surprised. "Why are you getting so excited, Mandy? It's no big deal, I'm telling you. This is a chance to make it all go away. If IAD squashes it, that's official, nobody'll bother you anymore—"

"I thought you said it was unofficial," she interrupted. "Off the books, you said."

"Yes, yes, of course. I only meant . . . I mean . . ."

"What do you mean?" she pressed relentlessly, unwilling to let him off the hook. "What do you mean, Walter? What's IAD going to do? Off the books? So they're coming down as a favor to the board? Is that the kind of thing they do these days, favors for local governments?" She felt herself getting hysterical and knew she'd regret it later, but she seemed unable to stop as recent events snowballed in her mind and threatened to overwhelm her. "And where the fuck were you, Walter? Where

were you when this brilliant plan was hatched? Did you call
the county yourself?"

Zipkin looked at her, gripped the chair arms and rose to
his not inconsiderable height, now uncoiled from the slightly
hunched position he had adopted subconsciously to try to
diminish his presence when he'd first walked in. He stepped
toward Amanda, who stood with her fists clenched at her sides,
anger evident in her entire posture.

"Now you listen to me, lady." He pointed at her and spoke
with controlled menace. "I put you in this job, so don't give
me any of this crap. Half this fucking town jumped on my ass
for pushing a broad for police captain, and I stood fast and
that's why you're here. I got you more cops, better equipment
and a bigger station house. And I never, *ever*, questioned your
judgment, even when you put a murder suspect on an investigating team. So don't you dare give me any shit now about
letting you down!"

His pointed finger was trembling from the force of his emotion, and she stared at him, stupefied, unprepared for his sudden outburst. She had misread his discomfort as weakness and
his embarrassment as guilt, when unease at having to deliver
the news was all that it was. In that moment she understood
how hard he had probably fought for her, how bitter he was
that he had lost the battle. He had probably insisted on deliv-
ering the news himself, telling her in his own way and suffering with her rather than letting someone else gloat. And every
word of his spontaneous diatribe was true. She was instantly
sorry for taking out after him and hoped that he would understand.

"Gee, Walter." She took on a look of comical concern. "Do
you feel very strongly about this?"

It took a few moments, but he smiled. " 'Course not. Why?"

Her sholders slumped and she turned back to the window.
"What am I going to do, Walt? How am I supposed to do my
job and save my ass at the same time?"

Zipkin sat back down. "You're going to explain yourself to
the IAD guy, charm his pants off, and send him back smiling.
You're not going to get in any pissing contests with reporters,

supervisors or anybody else. You'll let your record speak for itself."

She turned and sat back down on the couch as he continued. "You're going to take the high road, Mandy, just like you always do. When this is all over, and it will be, people will think back on it, and everybody else will look like schmucks and you'll be the one with grace and style. Just don't crumble on me."

She stared down, seeing nothing. "IAD. Christ Almighty."

"It's an opportunity. But it won't be easy." She looked up at him. "You made some questionable calls, Mandy. I'm not saying they were wrong. But you've got to appreciate how they might look to people outside, people who aren't familiar with the details or the background."

"If Jacoby hadn't been on that team, we might not have her locked up now," she said.

Zipkin nodded vigorously. "Right. So tell IAD that. They're professionals, they'll understand. It'll be a lot easier than trying to sell some jerk Cub Scout reporter trying to get a byline."

Yeah, she thought, *like IAD investigators get a lot of points for coming up empty.*

CHAPTER
31

Joshua Schuyler wondered what it must be like to be interrogated in this room.

A simple, metal-topped table, blank walls, plain chairs. Nothing at all, not even a wall-covering pattern, to provide some distraction, to take a suspect's mind a few degrees outside the fear. The room was purposefully designed to drive home the immediacy of the present predicament, to subtly accentuate the reality that nothing else mattered right now but the problem at hand, your problem. No escape. All these people around the table, staring at you, had only one purpose. There was nothing else in their lives, only you, only now. It could take a minute, it could take a day. But look at these walls, this table. *There is nothing there that can speak up and help you until we know it all, know everything.*

The door had a flimsy dead bolt slide latch. It could be locked from the inside to deter the casual interruption but was easily broken by a strong push from the outside, in case a detainee, sitting alone awaiting questioning, decided to lock himself in.

Schuyler looked at Bobby Parks, the only other person in the room. "Any idea what this is all about?" he asked.

Bobby appeared not to hear at first, lost in his own thoughts.

Finally he said, "Not for sure." He shifted on his seat. "But I've got a rough idea."

The door opened and Amanda walked in, not with her usual purposeful stride, but slower, less confidently. "Hi," she said, and sat down.

Bobby and Schuyler nodded and waited as Amanda put a writing tablet in front of her. There were handwritten notes on it, but neither of them could read anything from their positions opposite her, although the format looked like a list. She looked from one to the other and took a ballpoint pen from her pocket, as close to fidgeting as either could remember from her.

"This is off the record," she began, and waited for acknowledging nods. "I've got a couple of problems with Brixton Ferrin."

Schuyler stole a glance at Bobby. Amanda caught it but said nothing, although the subtext beneath the conversation was obvious to all three of them. It was common knowledge that Captain Grant was in trouble. Among her fellow officers, this was treated as just another of the travails of a highly visible community official, and there was little doubt around the station that she would carry this off with typical aplomb.

But the pressure had increased, not abated. Lines were starting to appear in her plate-glass exterior. Schuyler's glance to Bobby was a question: Was she going to try to deflect the pressure somewhere else, or to several places, starting with Pamela Jacoby's psychiatrist?

"What kind of problems?" asked Bobby.

Amanda looked down at her notes. "Couple of things. Mostly about the way he treated Jacoby. Either of you ever see a psychiatrist?" she asked without warning, looking back up at them.

"No," they answered simultaneously, and she could tell from their continued easy manner that neither of them ever had.

"Me neither," she went on. "But we all know people who have. It's not like in the movies. It's like police work, in a lot of ways. It's not filled with drama and startling revelations. It's long, slow and tedious. Progress comes in drips, not floods.

The psychiatrist doesn't pummel the patient mercilessly until she confesses her horrible secrets in a screaming fit. It doesn't work that way. Who would go if it did?"

Her sentences picked up speed as she made the point, and she stopped to catch her breath and to see if they were following where this was leading.

"Ferrin was a little unconventional," said Schuyler. "That's not news." Openly criticizing superiors on investigating teams was not only tolerated in Amanda's organization, it was actively encouraged. Truth first, protocol second, nobody took offense.

"A little is one thing, Josh," she said. "Incompetent or negligent is another."

"Whoa," said Bobby, sitting upright. "That's pretty strong. What are we talking about here?"

"I'm not sure yet. Mostly a feeling." She considered, for the hundredth time, the paucity of hard evidence and started to regret the strength cf her opening diatribe. It would be difficult to realign the two.

"But a couple of things," she continued. "First, I wonder how smart it was to take someone as screwed up as Pamela Jacoby and set her up with someone as screwed up as Mackenzie Graham."

"But he didn't do that. It was Jake Nostrand's idea." Schuyler had practically memorized the case details during the investigation. "It was days before Ferrin agreed to go along with it."

"But Nostrand wasn't a professional psychiatrist. Pamela wasn't his patient. He didn't even know her. Ferrin knew it was a risky idea, and he relented anyway. He was the pro, he should have known better."

"That's a stretch, Captain," said Bobby. "Hell, it was just a blind date. What's the big deal? Nobody forced her, she could have cut it off at any time."

"That's not true! Ferrin encouraged her to see him. That was part of the whole arrangement. And free will doesn't enter into the psychiatrist-patient relationship. The influence is too strong."

"Transference," said Schuyler. "The patient sees the doctor as someone else. A father, maybe."

"Exactly," said Amanda. "You can imagine how much self-determination Pamela was able to exercise in Ferrin's presence." *Especially since her therapy was a condition for her being on the force,* she didn't say. *My condition.* "We know she threw a fit every time she went out with Graham, and yet she kept on doing it. Why? What kind of therapist puts his patient through that kind of grief?"

"So he pushed her hard," said Bobby. "Psychiatry's a judgment call. Where are we heading with this?"

"There's more. And let's try to remember that she committed a murder while under his care."

Bobby didn't need to be reminded and took Amanda's comment as a sign that she was annoyed with his resistance. Another symptom of her inner turmoil. He let it pass.

Schuyler sensed the tension and sought to ward it off. "Technically, you know, it wasn't murder. She didn't commit a crime."

Amanda snapped her head toward him and said, "But maybe he did."

Schuyler tried to keep his voice level. "What do you mean?"

"If Ferrin was incompetent, or strayed from accepted methods, doesn't he share some liability for her actions?"

"Holy shit, Amanda, are you serious?" Bobby asked without thinking or taking the time to be polite. "How can you hang this on Ferrin?"

"I'm not hanging anything on him, at least not yet. But I think—"

"You said there was more, Captain," Schuyler broke in again. "What else have you got?"

She looked back at her notes. "Taking her to the crime scene. Was that necessary? He had to shoot her full of tranquilizers just to calm her down. There's a good chance it led to her suicide attempt."

"It also led to her confession," said Bobby. "Otherwise we'd still be chasing useless leads."

"He says he did it because he knew it was her, to get her to see it," said Schuyler.

"But his first obligation was to his patient," protested

Amanda. "How did that help her? And then he gets her on his couch and confuses the shit out of her some more, when she's still reeling."

"Wait a minute here," said Schuyler. "I thought you were trying to prove that he had some responsibility for Graham's death. Everything you just mentioned was after the fact."

"But it's evidence of his methods, don't you see? Just like when he injected her with Thorazine the night of the murder—the homicide," she said.

"What was wrong with that?" asked Bobby.

"Injecting her? Nothing. It's *leaving* her that bothers me. Shouldn't he have been there when she woke up? What if she was still out of it? What if she went out to kill someone else?"

"But he didn't know at that point that she'd killed anybody at all yet," said Bobby.

"That's not her point," Schuyler jumped in, starting to get Amanda's drift now. "The point is that Ferrin knew she was having a severe attack, and he left her alone, to wake up scared and possibly still schiz'ing."

"Right," said Amanda. "It was sloppy and irresponsible."

Bobby fingered his lip and grew thoughtful. "Okay. Maybe. So what are we looking at?"

She slumped slightly. "I don't know. I haven't gotten that far. Maybe malpractice."

Bobby shook his head. "Nope. That's civil. Her mother could sue him for damages, maybe go after his license, but that's it." His FBI experience had given him a good feel for what was possible within the criminal justice system.

"Criminal negligence?" asked Amanda.

"Better," said Bobby, "but you're on mighty flimsy ground here, Captain. You know that."

She nodded. "I know. I was just testing a concept."

"Why don't we just get her records?" asked Schuyler. "Didn't Jacoby authorize it?"

"Only at Ferrin's discretion," Bobby said. "And only to help her case."

Schuyler looked up sharply. "She said that?"

"So Ferrin tells us. Why?"

Schuyler drew his eyebrows together and turned his head slightly in an expression of intense suspicion. "Awfully clear thinking for an incarcerated head case."

"Regardless," Amanda added, "I don't want to alert him to anything. It could complicate things, maybe give him a chance to destroy some records, I don't know. And I don't want to taint him with an investigation if there's nothing there. We're looking at this from five thousand yards through heavy lenses, and I don't want to hurt him unless we're sure, unless we've got a lot more to go on."

"Fair enough," said Bobby, relieved that she wasn't about to try to destroy Ferrin to save her own neck, but also that she wasn't going to ignore his potential culpability because it might make her look self-serving. "So what now?"

Schuyler also understood and saw the wisdom of keeping it low-key for the time being. "Suppose I do a little unofficial checking around on Ferrin, just light background. Maybe you can call in some Bureau favors, Lieutenant."

"Do you have any?" Amanda teased Bobby.

"Actually, no, come to think of it. So I'll owe a few instead. But, Captain, we're all three of us babes in the woods on the shrink business. Shouldn't we get some professional assistance? From someone who can keep it quiet?"

"Absolutely. I'll put in a call to Tancredi. He's feeling a little bad about the whole thing, he'll be glad to lend a hand."

———◆———

"**No way,**" said Tancredi.

Amanda was too surprised to do other than ask, "What? Why?"

"Already I am making a mess of this case," he said, referring to his miscast diagnosis regarding a likely perpetrator. "Now you want I should help make a mess of a good psychiatrist?"

"But everybody makes mistakes," she said, tightening her grip on the phone and getting ready to mount a reasoned argument.

"Exactly!" Tancredi said triumphantly, drawing the word out slowly. "Ex-act-ly! Everybody is making mistakes. I make mine, he makes his, what makes him worse than me?"

"Yours threw us off for a day or two. His may have caused a murder."

"Tell me, smart lady. I am running a stop sign, the *shamus* is giving me a ticket. Somebody else is running the same stop sign, kills three children and their dog. Same crime. Different results. Who is worse?"

"Tanc," she said in exasperation, "we need some help on this. None of us knows enough to go it alone."

"So if you are all being so ignorant, how come you are being so smart to say he has guilt in this?"

Good question. "We're not. Yet. It's just a suspicion."

"Some suspicion."

"Major investigations have been won on less."

"Comfortable I'm not, cutie-pie. Doesn't feel right. Every doctor, especially a psychiatrist, is all the time making judgments. Used to be they would worry only about the patient. Will this help? Will that hurt? Is this working maybe for somebody else before?"

"Tanc—"

"Sshh. Listen. *Now*, first thing they are thinking, Am I going to get sued? Every time somebody comes to question judgment, the doctor is getting more worried. You complain because too much useless testing is done? Hah! They are afraid *not* to test. Better to charge a million than forget some little stinky test and somebody dies.

"Now you want to punch this one in the nose because you don't like how he treats your friend. Maybe a little too rough, maybe not so neat. . . ."

"It's more than that. Why did he force her to go out with Graham when he knew it was eating her alive?"

"Forced her? How forced her? She couldn't say no?"

"You know how strong his influence was."

"I know nothing. *You* know nothing. Maybe she forced herself. Maybe he told her no, but she said yes."

"I don't think so. And what about taking her to see Graham's blood splattered all over his bedroom?"

"Excuse me, miss, excuse me. Who said she could go?"

Jesus. "Me. But that was because he seemed to think it was a good idea."

"Yes? So maybe it was."

"I don't think so."

"Sure. *Now*. Smarty-pants. And if so stupid even you could see it now, how come you are letting her go then?"

"It was his professional advice. I didn't like it, but I believed him."

"And without him you would have no confession."

"Without him I might not have a murder." She was losing this and needed to press. "And what about when he left her on Thorazine, didn't even wait to see how she'd be when she woke up?"

"Stupid. Dumb. But criminal?"

"C'mon, Tanc, she tried to kill herself three hours after leaving his office, what kind of—"

"Why don't you look at the records, *mein* Captain? Of all the suicides?"

"What do you mean?"

"Look at every suicide. How many were seeing a psychiatrist?"

"I don't know."

"Look, then. You won't believe it. If this was a crime for a psychiatrist, put them all in prison."

Really losing. "Doctor, we're keeping this low-key, off the record. We're only going to ask some questions. Very quiet. If there's nothing, we drop it and nobody's the wiser."

There was silence at the other end. Amanda held her breath. She heard his long exhalation. "Questions only? No big deal?"

"No big deal. I promise."

"Mmm, mmm," she heard him mutter as he considered. Then, "I know a professor," he said at last. "Knew Ferrin very well. In the university."

"You *know* a professor? This is a hell of a coincidence, Tanc."

"Not exactly maybe know them, maybe more like—"

"Them?"

Pause. "There are two such people in the university."

It was Amanda's turn to pause, and Tancredi went on unbidden. "I looked them up through the professional societies. One I spoke with, he is very nice. Maybe even helpful . . . ?"

"Jesus Christ, Doc, why didn't you tell me before!" she exploded.

"Ahhh," he said resignedly. "Why? For what reason?"

She understood and smiled, then got angry, then both at the same time. "You sonofabitch. You sonofabitch—"

"Easy, lady, you will be popping a—"

"This isn't news, is it? Everything I'm telling you? Here I am thinking how smart you are, how fast you're thinking up counterarguments, and—"

"Sweetie-pie—"

"Sweetie-pie my ass, Tanc, you've thought of all this before! And more, I bet. Why didn't you tell me? Why are you hanging on to it?"

He paused before replying. "Same as you, lady. I open a mouth, everybody says, sure, give a zetz to the shrink so Tancredi doesn't look so bad." He paused again. "You, too, have tsuris, hah? Trouble? So you open a mouth and what?"

She rubbed her eyes with two fingers. "Will you set me up to see them? The professors, I mean, or one of them, at least?"

His voice was sympathetic now that his points were made, and his empathy for her was plainly evident. "No problem. But for background only, yes? You promised. Don't let's break his back too soon. We are not storm troopers."

"Agreed. Will you at least talk to me about this? Off the record?"

"So who's stopping you from picking up a phone once in a while?"

———◆———

It felt like a flock of birds, somehow. Not robins or blue jays, but African starlings. Jet black, a black so impenetrable you couldn't see individual feathers, with streaks of iridescent blue and violet that flashed like lightning when they shot by the insides of her eyes.

But mostly they hovered in the distance, waiting, or so it seemed. Reminding her of the vulnerability of her mind, whose solidity she had taken for granted, but which now suddenly seemed tenuous. Here, surrounded by the tide of shattered psyches and failed defenses, the beating wings of the black birds didn't seem new: it seemed that they had always been there, she'd just never noticed before. Were they all hers? Or would her impending proximity to the psychologically damned leave her naked before the onslaught, helpless, as the unholy creatures stormed her citadel and pecked at the gates of her soul?

"She's on a lot of medication, Captain. You understand that, right?"

"Wha—?" Amanda jumped at the sound of the voice. "I'm sorry? Medication, yes, I understand."

"Good." The nurse offered no apology for her intrusion into Amanda's thoughts. Over the years she had seen every manner by which this place could frighten people, and she no longer had any sympathy for it. "Dr. Ferrin wanted me to remind you that she's very fragile, and that I'm to interrupt if she gets upset. Which I will," she added sternly.

Amanda considered this without offense, sensing a protective rather than officious motivation. "You like her, don't you?" she said to the dour-faced nurse, whose expression appeared to change to one of surprise at the question.

"I like her well enough." She looked away, embarrassed at what could be taken for a lack of professionalism. "Everybody likes her. She's very sweet. At least as much of her as we can see when the meds aren't so heavy."

"When's that?" asked Amanda.

"When *he* comes," she answered, referring to Dr. Ferrin. "Can't have her tranq'd during therapy, can we?" She turned before Amanda could ask any more questions, and they walked toward a small holding area.

"When did you see her last?" asked the nurse.

"Before she . . . before she came here," answered Amanda. *Before she murdered her boyfriend.*

"May look a little different now. And remember: nothing about . . . that night." She opened the door and motioned Amanda in, then followed and stood off to the side.

It wasn't as bad as it might have been. Pamela had lost some weight, and her complexion was sallow and unhealthy looking. Her hair, once a justifiable source of pride, hung limp and lifeless, the ends curled in places where her fingers had idly toyed with it. She sat without discernible posture on a plain chair, hands folded in her lap, eyes focused at a distance in a room only ten feet square.

"Hey, champ," Amanda said quietly to Pamela, who had not appeared to notice the door opening.

She turned her head and looked up slowly. As soon as she saw Amanda, she smiled. "Captain. Oh, Captain . . ." The words came labored and slurred, but her pleasure was unmistakable. Amanda stepped farther into the room and sat on a low cabinet opposite Pamela, who leaned forward with whatever eagerness her tranquilized body could muster. "Jeez, you look great, Captain. You . . . I . . . I'm so glad to see you?" she made it sound like a question.

Amanda nodded. "You look like shit, Jacoby." It was a test, albeit a harsh one, and the nurse began a protesting motion.

Pamela laughed, but it seemed to require an effort. "D'hell y'expect, goddamned cover girl?"

Amanda smiled back at her, then watched helplessly as Pamela's sleepy laughter transformed into quiet crying. She took her hand and they sat without speaking, until Pamela broke the silence. "I'm sorry." It was barely a whisper. "So sorry. . . ."

"Easy, easy." Amanda turned to the nurse. "Do you mind if we're alone for a little while?" To the doubtful look she got, she added, "Trust me, please. I'm on her side."

"But Dr. Ferrin said—"

"It'll be all right, I promise."

The nurse looked at Pamela, who had turned pleading eyes upward in her direction. She walked over and smoothed back some of Pamela's hair where it had fallen over her eyes. There was affection in her movements. "Just a few minutes, then, okay?"

"Thank you," said Amanda. "Thanks very much."

When they were alone Amanda asked, "How is it going, Pamela? With the doctor?"

Pamela shrugged and sat back, turning her head to the side. "It's hard," she said eventually.

"I bet."

More silence, then Pamela turned back to face Amanda and look into her eyes. "I can't remember it."

"What? What do you mean?"

"I try, and I try, and I can't remember it. Any of it." Short breath, then more softly, "Killing Mac."

Amanda was startled at the candid reference but tried not to let Pamela notice.

"It's okay, Captain, I don't mind talking about it." She leaned forward again. "I did it. I know that. My brains felt like they were scattered over a square mile, but I'm still responsible."

Amanda nodded and tried hard not to ask any of the thousand questions that her police instinct told her were relevant.

"It's just that I can't remember any of it. Doing it, I mean."

"What do you remember, Pamela?"

"It was like the other times. Remember?"

"Do I ever." They both smiled at the memory of their back-alley conversation. *I don't get it, Pamela. You're not a crazy, not like these other people in here. You're not drooling or talking to the walls. You smile when you're supposed to, you cry when it makes sense.*

"Even the pills Dr. Ferrin gave me didn't help."

"You took one?"

Pamela smiled conspiratorially. "Took two," she said. "I was so damned scared?" To Amanda's look of concern she said, "Didn't matter. Didn't do any good, anyway."

Amanda heard the birds again, circling in the distance. *You know what this is about, Amanda, don't you? Think! It's not about Pamela. Or even about Mac Graham. It's about—*

"It's just that, even if I was crazy, why did I do a thing like that? I could have just left, gone away. I could even have smacked him on the head, but . . ."

The black birds were massing for a coordinated attack. Amanda put her hands on either side of Pamela's face. *I don't know why, Pamela. I wish I did. Why do any of us do the things we do?* "Take it easy. Easy."

"I didn't mean it. . . ."

CHAPTER 32

Amanda Grant had missed being valedictorian of her high school class by a hundredth of a point. Accepted by all five of the colleges she had applied to, including two Ivy League institutions, she chose a small liberal arts school in the Midwest to pursue a five-year master's program in psychology.

Packed and ready to leave home for the first time in any way more significant than summer camp, she found herself alone with her father for a few minutes. He had been more silent than usual for the past several days, and she knew he was heartbroken at her leaving. His feelings mirrored her own, and she assumed this was why he was not as full of advice and counsel as he would normally be in the face of a new undertaking.

They sat side by side on the front steps, and she poked at him lightly. "So. Here I am leaving the nest, looking to my wise pop for guidance, and what do I get? The silent treatment."

"I never went to college, big shot. What the hell do I know?" He reached for her nose and twisted it, enough so it hurt but not too much. "You'll be pregnant and a drug addict in six months. They'll blame it on me because I didn't give you a lollipop when you were two."

"And they'll be right, you know. Not my fault." She leaned

her head on his big shoulder. "You went away once, Dad. To the army. To the war. Isn't there anything you wish someone had told you beforehand?"

He put his arm around her and hugged her close, and thought quietly for a few moments. "There is, but you'll laugh."

"No, I won't," she said, and sat upright. "I promise."

He looked at her and said, "Yeah, you will."

"What, Dad? Please, tell me," she pleaded.

He waited a few seconds and then said, "Get enough sleep."

She stared at him, eyes grown wide in disbelief. "Say what?"

"You heard me."

"Get enough sleep? That's it? I'm going to college and all you have to say is 'Get enough sleep'?"

"Yep."

It proved to be sage counsel. Whether it was genetic, psychological or a combination of the two, she never figured out. But when she was rested, she was relaxed and alert and felt that there was little she couldn't cope with. At those times when sleep had been scarce, when she had spent too many late night hours studying or talking with her dorm friends, most of whom made it up by missing morning classes, she had frazzled easily, blown trivial matters out of proportion and generally met the world ill-equipped to deal with its demands.

She learned the lesson quickly. While her friends made a great show of cramming all night for a final exam, Amanda got a good night's sleep, regardless of the state of her preparation on the subject matter. Occasionally she would even take a room at an off-campus motel to get away from the noise of the frantic dorm study sessions, which seemed to require a gathering of as many students as the rooms would hold.

Captain Amanda Grant pondered this one morning a few days after her "unofficial" meeting with Bobby Parks and Joshua Schuyler on the subject of Dr. Brixton Ferrin and wondered where her discipline had gone. She found herself consumed with the accumulation of evidence, most of it speculative or, at best, circumstantial. She had taken to keeping a notebook on her nightstand, entering nearly indecipherable scribblings at odd hours following bouts of insomniac mind racing, much to the consternation of her husband. In the morning most of the pages wound up in crumpled balls on the floor as the harsh glare of daylight revealed the lack of substance underneath what had seemed brilliant insight in a half dream.

Amanda knew that the resultant lack of sleep would soon make itself evident in the traditional ways. Irritability and the energy it drained would lead to listlessness and loss of appetite, which would further deplete her resources and make sleep even more difficult. The self-destructive spiral would eventually reach her face, and no amount of makeup would hide the dark bags or drawn features. Every look in the mirror would add to a growing depression, and all because of Ferrin. This was his fault, and she was damned if she was going to allow that bastard to—

"Captain?"

She looked up suddenly, startling Bobby Parks, who had stuck his head in when his knocking went unanswered. "Sorry," he said, "I wasn't sure you were in here. Didn't mean to interrupt whatever you were—"

She waved it off. "No, no problem. I was just thinking about something. Come on in." Bobby was sharp, challenging. Maybe he would take her mind off Ferrin.

"About Ferrin, I'll bet," he said as he sat down.

She nodded and looked away.

"If it's any comfort to you, Mandy, it's starting to bother me, too."

"How's that?"

"I'm not sure, really. Just something about his manner. Maybe he should have been more upset."

There was very little Bobby could come up with that Amanda hadn't already considered, in endless variations, and filed away in the right mental pigeonhole. "Tancredi said that was a possible psychological defense mechanism, a way for compensating for his guilt."

"What guilt?"

"When a psychiatrist's patient goes off the deep end during therapy, it's a great failure. Like a driving instructor having an accident." *Or a cop committing murder.* "Maybe he's really stricken by it, and he's acting icy and in control to ward it off."

"Didn't seem all that damned stricken to me," said Bobby.

"That's the point. By not acting that way, he tries not to feel that way." She flipped a hand idly in the air and let it drop to her lap. "Shit, I don't know. Every time I think I understand something, I've got experts giving me eighteen reasons why it could be otherwise."

Bobby nodded in assent and waited.

She turned her attention back to him. "So what's up?"

"Maybe nothing. I've been talking to Annie del Gatto here and there."

"She's still upset?" It was more of a statement than a question.

"She is. She's been visiting Pamela regularly. The more she goes, the madder she gets."

"Anything we can use?"

Bobby shrugged. "Hard to say. They've got Pamela on a lot of drugs."

"I know. I've been there, remember?"

"Oh, yeah, right. I forgot. So you know, her mind seems to wander, and she gets lost in the middle of sentences. Annie says it's a pain in the ass to try to talk with her for any length of time."

"That's funny. Didn't seem so bad when I saw her."

Bobby seemed not to hear. His own pain in describing the condition of their former colleague came through in his voice and manner and was obviously distracting him. "She's still going on about those pills. Annie, I mean."

"How so?"

"I told her what they were. She said she knew that, she was there with the paramedics when we found Pamela. But it still bothers her. She told me that Pamela said that one night, when she double-dated with Jake Nostrand and his wife, she forgot to take a pill like she was supposed to. And everything went fine. She felt okay."

"So Annie thinks it supports her notion that the pills were to blame."

"I guess. I told her what Ferrin said, that it was four people all together, nice and safe, nothing threatening. Pamela went home alone that night, nothing heavy. So, the pill made no difference. Nice and neat."

"Except that Pamela took two of them the night of the murder."

"What?" That got his attention. "What the hell are you talking about? She tell you that?"

Amanda's eyes narrowed, and she stayed silent. Finally she said, "So what do you think?"

He considered for a moment. "Truthfully? Not a whole lot. But as long as we're clutching at straws—and we are, you know . . ." Amanda nodded in agreement, much as it distressed her to admit it. "Why don't we check the pills out? They're still down in Property. It can't hurt."

It can't hurt you, she thought. *It could make me look like a cornered rat*, grasping at wisps of gossamer "evidence" a first-year cadet wouldn't bother with, an hysterical female panicking and looking for a way out rather than facing the music with a straight back.

"Okay. Let's do it. But with a private lab, not the county."

Bobby stood up. "Turns out I've still got a friend at the fed. He says they'll help with no fuss, and get it done in a few days."

She couldn't hide her surprise. "You asked him already?"

Caught, Bobby managed a slight smile and said, "I'd thought of it, but it didn't seem justified until now. Figured you wouldn't mind."

"I don't like someone under my command knowing me that well."

"Too late, Captain. You lost that option in a bar one night."

Amanda remembered Bobby carrying her home the night he was referring to. She had scored perfect marks in a crucial criminal-law exam and had gotten dead drunk, the first and only time in her life. When she'd challenged two truckers to a bare-knuckle fight, Bobby had decided that there were one or two things even Amanda Grant might have trouble handling, and he'd made the problem disappear.

"So you're going to bring *that* up again. Go away. Keep me posted."

He shot his friend a smile and left.

CHAPTER
33

It's the law, you know," said Daniel Emmerich, Ph.D., as he leaned back in the ancient leather chair and lit his pipe. "All college professors have to smoke pipes."

"Would have been disappointed otherwise," said Amanda. "No tweeds? Elbow patches?"

"Those are the theoreticians. I'm an experimentalist." He plucked at the lapel of his white lab coat. "This is a better cliché, anyway."

Amanda and Bobby appeared to relax in Emmerich's affable presence, but they were in fact trying to gauge the correct amount of preliminary small talk. Edan Tancredi had warned them that most academic backbiting was confined within the family, and the professor would not be instantly amenable to airing dirty laundry to outsiders. Not enough verbal foreplay, and Emmerich might harden to any meaningful discussion about Brixton Ferrin, his former student. Too much, and he would see through the insincerity and be put off by it.

"Dr. Tancredi spoke very highly of you, Professor," said Bobby. "He said you did brilliant work, but most of it's classified, so you don't get the recognition you deserve."

"Actually," replied Emmerich, "I do shitty work, and it's a

damned good thing it's classified or these old farts around here would have gotten rid of me by now."

Amanda laughed and said, "I don't believe that for a second. Tancredi doesn't suffer fools easily, Dr. Emmerich."

"Dan, please," he said. "And the Tanc has suffered a lot of fools in his day. Has he told you much about himself?"

"Not really, come to think of it," said Amanda. "But I feel like I know him well anyway."

"He had that effect on me, too. Ask him someday." Emmerich tapped his forehead and said, "I did a little checking of my own."

"Did he tell you why we're here?" asked Bobby.

"He said it was about Brixton Ferrin. But he didn't say why. Has he done something?"

"Is there any reason why you think he might have?" Bobby asked.

"Listen, you need a therapist's license to answer questions with questions," said Emmerich. "Never bullshit a professional bullshitter."

"Dan," Amanda jumped in, "we'll be glad to tell you what's going on, but this might work better if you let us ask some questions first."

Emmerich considered this for a moment, then said, "I understand. But it's completely off the record until I know the reason."

"Agreed," said Bobby. He knew this arrangement was more than just symbolic. Emmerich would be within his rights to deny anything he said off the record and could not be compelled to any testimony that relied on those comments as its basis. However, should he decide to go on the record, he wouldn't have to repeat himself but simply retroactively declare it so. None of this was in the law but was a canon among professionals of all persuasions. It was rarely violated.

"Tell us a little about him in general," said Amanda. "What was he like as a person? How did his colleagues view him?"

His earlier protestation notwithstanding, Emmerich needed no great persuasion and seemed eager to unload on them. "He was brilliant, he was arrogant, nobody liked him and nobody was sorry when he left." He watched their eyes for some reaction and was surprised to see that they were not taken aback in the slightest. "How come I get the feeling this isn't news to you two?"

"Neither of us actually knows him well," said Bobby. "He doesn't seem very likable, but he sounds pretty smart."

"Why wasn't he liked?" asked Amanda.

Emmerich sat back, realizing that the price of his dramatic opening was an obligation to provide details. "Ferrin was unusual, in that he was both an experimentalist, a researcher like myself, as well as a clinician. He saw patients, as all our postdocs do." He paused to relight his pipe.

"It seemed to some of us that he was more interested in the theories of therapy than he was in his patients. I'm not saying he treated them like lab rats, although others might be less kind. But psychotherapy is intensely interpersonal, and when done without compassion . . ." He pursed his lips and shrugged. "You can't administer therapy like an injection and watch for the results. You have to throw yourself into the fray, become a very part of the process. That's why all pyschiatrists are themselves analyzed first."

"Was Ferrin?" asked Bobby. "Analyzed, I mean?"

"Yes, but not here. In England. And I daresay probably not very well. Don't see how he could have been. . . ." Emmerich trailed off and seemed to get lost in memory.

"So, what does all of that add up to?" asked Amanda.

"He liked to try unconventional approaches. Sometimes, frankly, they worked quite well. Other times it was hard to tell. But the patients weren't volunteers for an experiment. Some of them were deeply troubled, not only with superficial emotional disturbances, but with deep-seated anxieties and, in some cases, full-blown schizophrenia. If his methods were to have backfired . . . well, there could have been some problems."

"Did they backfire?"

He seemed disappointed, but admitted that they never had.

"Didn't any of the other staff call him on it?" asked Bobby.

"Sure. At first. But Ferrin was a powerful personality and

quite vengeful. He was also patient, and could carry a grudge for a long time before giving it full vent. Pretty ugly at times, to tell the truth."

"Like when?" asked Amanda.

"I'll tell you a story." Emmerich settled back on his seat, clearly not indisposed toward smearing Ferrin a little. "You know that he was a foremost researcher in the area of psychomimetic substances," Emmerich began.

"Psycho-what?" asked Bobby. "Tancredi said he was into hallucinogenics. LSD, stuff like that."

"Popularly called hallucinogens because that's the part that recreational users like. Ferrin wasn't a thrill seeker, he was a serious researcher. He was interested in those substances because they induced what appeared to be temporary psychoses." He stopped in light of the perplexed looks on the faces of his audience.

"It's actually not important to the story, which, let me warn you in advance, suffers from a good deal of speculation and what you law enforcement types would probably call 'circumstantial evidence.' "

"How so?" Bobby asked as he and Amanda both clicked on the assume-twenty-percent-is-bullshit filters that all experienced cops carried in their heads.

"Problem is, the events themselves don't really tie together cohesively unless you understand what probably went on in Ferrin's mind, which none of us knows for sure. But I'm pretty confident, from what people who knew him well tell me, that I can call it pretty close."

He squirmed himself deeper onto the chair. "Best place to start is a couple weeks before a major conference some time ago, at which Ferrin was due to present. He wasn't quite ready. In fact . . ."

———●———

Brixton Ferrin was at the end of his rope. The conference was two weeks away, and he was nowhere. Number one in his field and he was going to bomb at this gathering of eagles, when he was supposed to be the star attraction.

He stared morosely at Egbert, his last hope. No researcher liked to be under pressure to produce results. Such a condition had prompted more than one scientist to test the boundaries of propriety in presenting dubious results.

His graduate student, Felice Botrell, watched as Ferrin slipped on a pair of rubber gloves, reached for a vial on the counter, opened the top and scooped out a tiny amount of the white, crystalline powder. He laid it on the pan of an electronic balance and added a few grains at a time until the scale read 5.5 micrograms, an amount carefully calibrated against Egbert's body weight. He then dumped the powder into the chamber of a syringe containing distilled water and shook it until the powder disappeared in solution.

He reached toward Egbert and picked up the white mouse out of its cage by the scruff of its neck, placing it on the surface of the table. Then, immobilizing it with one hand, he squirted a few drops of the liquid straight up into the air, eliminating any bubbles that might cause an embolism, and plunged the needle into the fleshy knob above Egbert's left thigh. The mouse jerked at the initial contact and then lay still as Ferrin pressed the plunger and emptied the liquid into its body.

He wiped away a tiny spot of blood where the needle had entered and put the mouse back in its cage and checked the clock. The unwitting Egbert had about five minutes before the lysergic acid diethylamide solution, better known by its nickname, LSD, started blowing out its little mouse neural synapses. Egbert was by now an experienced tripper, and Ferrin and his graduate students had carefully measured his physiological responses to the mysterious drug. They could tell exactly where he was at any point on the six- to eight-hour curve that defined the duration of the drug's effects.

When Egbert started rolling on his back in between bouts of running the floor of his cage in the now familiar back-and-forth pattern, Ferrin turned to Felice and said, "Okay, he's ready. Put him in the twin with Harold." Felice picked up the cage and left the room.

The "twin" was a specially constructed cage that held two mice, separated by a space of about three inches. They could see each other but could make no physical contact. Ferrin was studying the phenomenon of the "contact high," reported anecdotally by frequent users as well as drug abuse counselors. They all swore that you could get a mild buzz just by being with someone on LSD. The breath, they said. Inhale the user's exhalations and you get high. The more mystically inclined felt it was induced telepathy.

Up until this point, the telepathy theory had been subject to the usual ridicule in scientific circles but had never been actually tested under the rigors of a laboratory setting. Ferrin didn't believe there was a shred of merit in it, and the current experiment was designed to lay the matter to rest, at least if one believed that the telepathic potential of white mice was roughly akin to that of people. Now he could make a definitive statement, by observing Harold after sharing "mental space" with Egbert for an hour or so. Of course, if there *was* a real effect—but that was too fantastic an idea to play with, although he did allow himself the momentary fantasy of imagining how he would present those results to a stunned audience.

Time passed slowly, and Ferrin took advantage of the interval to torture himself some more with thoughts of failure. He would need at least fifty experiments to hit the mandatory ninety-five percent confidence level on his statistical analysis, and that was assuming clear-cut results absent the usual behavioral ambiguities that plagued these kinds of studies. What if the proximity to Egbert without the ability to touch agitated Harold and elicited behaviors mimicking the drugged state? Many such possibilities swam through Ferrin's head. He could be left high and dry in two weeks with nothing to say.

He looked at the lab timer. Fifty-eight minutes. Close enough. "Botrell," he called without looking around. No answer. He turned and saw her on the opposite side of the room in low, giggly conversation with a lab technician, an hourly employee of little consequence whose interruption of his smooth procedures annoyed him. "Botrell!" he said loudly, and she turned toward him, a loopy grin still on her face. "Bring him in now," he commanded, pleased to be breaking up what he assumed was the idle chatter of unworthies.

Embarrassed at having to accede to his imperious tone in front of the lab tech, Botrell lowered her eyes and walked into the next room, returning a minute later with Harold in a cage. She set it down on the table and walked away, declining to look at it in petty rebellion.

Ferrin, who had been staring at her reprovingly, turned his attention to the cage. What he saw made him draw his breath in sharply and forget about her.

————•————

Emmerich stopped and looked into the bowl of his pipe, then turned it upside down and began tapping out the cold ash, unaware that Amanda and Bobby had moved forward slightly on their seats.

"Again," he said, continuing to fiddle with his pipe. "I don't know for sure what went on in Ferrin's head, but I know what would have gone on in mine. Felice Botrell believes she knew him well enough to understand, and it fits with what happened later."

"What does?" asked Bobby. "What happened?"

"Actually," the professor said, and Amanda was sure his expression contained a trace of less-than-charitable self-satisfaction, "nothing much."

————•————

Harold, who had been sitting quietly in the twin an hour ago, was on his back writhing from side to side. As Ferrin watched, the mouse righted itself and ran to one side of the cage, turned without pausing, ran back to the other side, then into a corner, then to an opposite corner. After a few more iterations of this back-and-forth pattern, he returned to the center of the cage, dropped into the depression in the cedar shavings left by previous cycles, and once more flipped over onto his back and started the process all over again.

Ferrin felt himself grow dizzy as he watched this impossible display. Keeping his voice as steady as possible, he called to Felice again. "Are you certain the air shield was in place, Botrell?"

"Yes," she said curtly. Her answer was definitive, but the voice sounded tentative.

"Go check it," he said, and didn't even notice the purposeful half-second pause before she started to move into the next room. She returned shortly and said, "It's in place, secure on all sides," referring to the rubber gaskets surrounding the plate-glass shield.

Ferrin didn't acknowledge her reply but watched, fascinated, as Harold continued the pattern. The mechanism by which the effects of LSD transferred themselves from Egbert to Harold without any physical contact would keep serious researchers busy for years. His own career would be assured, as the discoverer of one of the most astonishing finds in years. Maybe they would call it the "Ferrin effect," and he would enter a hallowed ground reserved for those whose very names fell into the everyday lexicon. Mesmer, Pavlov . . .

He reached for his dictating machine. Future chronicles would record this day, and they would marvel at how he maintained his professional demeanor even in the face of his excitement and forced himself to make careful observations as history unfolded before his eyes. He held up the dictating machine and began: "Control subject B-seven exhibits behavioral patterns clearly analogous to those observed in primary subject C-thirty-six and established previously as representing reproducible evidence of lysergic acid–induced agitation."

He felt a quavering in his voice and clicked off the machine until he could take a few deep breaths and compose himself. He turned it back on as he watched Harold. "Subject B-seven crosses the cage several times and then returns to the center, where it stretches full length and rolls onto its back. . . ." He was careful to try to remember the words he used in dictating his observations of Egbert. Professors would hold up both sets of transcripts and declaim triumphantly to their students how they matched, the first evidence of the reality of the Ferrin effect. He had to get this right. "Both hind legs extend fully"— he bent closer to peer through the glass side of the cage— "straight up in a pedaling motion that seems to—"

He stopped. His head was still bent toward the cage, and he

blinked his eyes several times. The miniature tape reels in the now forgotten dictating machine kept turning.

Felice, observing from across the room, turned toward him at the sudden cessation of his voice. "What's the matter?" she asked with as much disinterest as she could muster.

Ferrin didn't answer, didn't hear her, in fact. He opened the top of the cage slowly and deliberately, then reached in and tried to wrap his hand around the still struggling mouse. The wriggling creature managed to evade his grasp, and he cruelly slapped his open hand straight down, pinning the helpless mouse beneath it. He reached in with his other hand and put his fingers around its neck, lifting it up and out of the cage. His grip was tight, and the mouse craned its neck upward to try to breathe, emitting a distressed squeal as it did so.

"Hey!" Botrell yelled in consternation, but Ferrin ignored her. He held the mouse a few inches from his face and turned it over. There. On its tiny haunch above the left leg. A small but definite spot of blood.

Ferrin rose unsteadily and walked quickly into the next room and there, on the countertop, in the right side of the twin, sat Harold, calmly sniffing the air. Ferrin had been observing Egbert. The wrong mouse.

Botrell appeared at his side. When he could regain himself, he said calmly but with unmistakable menace, "You brought me the wrong mouse."

Botrell looked from Egbert to Harold and then back again. "Oh. Sorry," she said, and took Egbert from Ferrin's now limp hand, put him back in the twin, removed Harold and held him up to Ferrin. "Here you go."

He made no move to take the mouse, which quite obviously was not experiencing any signs of the Ferrin effect, but only stared at Botrell.

By the next morning he had her out of the lab and had done it without saying a word to her or even acknowledging her presence as she packed up. She never knew exactly what had incurred his wrath and assumed that since no other immediate consequences seemed to ensue, the incident was over and forgotten.

——•——

Emmerich paused to relight once again.

"I take it," said Bobby, growing impatient with the theatrics but captivated nonetheless, "that it wasn't over at all."

Emmerich grinned. "What gave you your first clue, Sherlock?"

"C'mon, Dan," said Amanda. "What happened?"

"Okay. Months went by without another word about anything. When the end of the year rolled around, Felice Botrell drove herself into near exhaustion prepping to defend her Ph.D. thesis, last step in getting her doctorate. She'd been obsessed with that goal for four years. Even more, actually, since in truth she'd been planning for it since high school.

"On the day of her orals, she was so keyed up that she went to an afternoon movie just to relax, then showed up outside the examining room twenty minutes early. Just as she thought she had it all under control, she walks into the room and damn near faints to see none other than Dr. Brixton T. Ferrin sitting on the panel."

"Oh, boy," said Bobby, and Amanda nodded.

"Indeed. The rest was a nightmare of epic proportions. She blubbered somewhat, but the examiners were used to that and always cut candidates a great deal of slack, taking pains to sift the substance out of the nervousness. But it was Ferrin who almost made her give up on the spot. His interrogation consisted of a series of vicious, verbal grenades that landed on her with devastating effect. Unlike the others on the panel, he had read every word of her written thesis. He had spent hours in the research library tracking down virtually every existing reference to her chosen topic. He had filled himself with every study, every anecdotal reference even marginally related to the subject matter."

Emmerich made a throwaway gesture. "Hell, it was easy. Felice Botrell had deliberately chosen an area of great controversy, a set of leading-edge theories unproven in the field. Ferrin had no trouble grinding the theory to dust, and doing so in ways that she couldn't possibly refute without risking head-to-head argument, normally acceptable if one had the supporting evidence and could present it well, which was in this case impossible. His challenge was ingenious and shrewd, vastly more so than Felice's original presentation."

"And?" prodded Amanda.

"When she left, pale and shaking, I'm told, the other examiners were so cowed by the force of Ferrin's performance that they felt powerless to do other than deny Felice Botrell her dream. They voted her down."

Emmerich stopped talking, pleased at the effect his dramatic rendition was having on Amanda and Bobby. "Long memory," he said between puffs of his pipe.

"Jesus," said Bobby. Then, after a pause, "You mean to tell me one guy could nuke her degree just like that?"

"Course not. Her thesis adviser came unglued and, a few days later, when everybody calmed down, pointed out that Botrell had made no claims for the theory's veracity, but carefully cautioned professional restraint and suggested only that further clinical studies be conducted. The point of the work was not to prove that the theory was correct, but only that it merited serious study."

"Did it?" asked Amanda.

"Nope," Emmerich said. "But that's not important. What *is* important is that the thesis was beautifully crafted, well researched, sober and worthy of publication. Botrell went out on a limb, did a good job, and deserved her degree. So we revoted and gave it to her."

"How did she turn out?" asked Bobby.

"Why don't you ask her yourself?"

"She's here?"

"About four doors down. And here's the best part. After Ferrin left, guess who took over his research?"

———◆———

"Why not?" asked the diminutive Dr. Botrell. "It was fascinating stuff, he was gone, so I took over the lab."

"I take it from Dr. Emmerich that you were not fond of him," said Amanda.

"Fond? The bastard tried to ruin my life, and would have if

Daniel hadn't stepped in. Is he in some kind of trouble, I hope?"

"Not clear," said Bobby, seeking to evade disclosing too many details, as he and Amanda had agreed. Tancredi had made the point strongly: People like these would go down fighting to protect doctor-patient privilege but were the world's worst gossips otherwise. University laboratories were notorious hotbeds of rumor and scandal, real or imagined. The worse the research was going, the better the hallway intrigue. "Was he a good scientist?"

"A genius," Botrell answered without hesitation. She saw their surprised looks and said, "There's no denying it. A prick, but a genius. He had a lot of creative approaches and ideas. Of course, he wasn't the best one to sort out the idiotic from the useful, but he broke a lot of new ground, especially in psychomimetics."

"Emmerich used that word," said Amanda. "What's it mean?"

"Literally, mimicking psychosis. Drugs like lysergic acid induce a state remarkably similar to that in severe schizophrenics."

"Why would you be interested in that?"

"Because," said Botrell, "if you can make it happen, you might learn a lot about how to make it stop. Medical research is based on models. If you can discover a general rule for the way something works, you then understand it and can exploit that knowledge in all kinds of useful ways.

"Let me give you an example," she continued. "You start with a powerful painkiller, and nobody knows how it works, but it's very effective. Only trouble is, people get addicted to it. Then you figure out that what it does is block nerve signals, which are electrical, and you make a little black box with a battery that does the same thing, and you hook it up to patients, and voilà: the pain stops. No drugs, no addiction. Because you found the model of how it worked."

"So if you find a drug that makes somebody psychotic, and learn the mechanism, you might be able to find a cure," Bobby finished for her.

"Exactly. If the cause is chemical. In some cases we know it's not. But Ferrin took it further. He thought that administering hallucinogens to psychiatric patients might reverse the effect of chemically based schizophrenia."

"How would that be possible?" asked Bobby.

"It's complicated, but there's no sense going into it because it didn't work. However, he had another theory that says such substances can expedite therapy in basically healthy but mildly troubled people. We're still looking at that one. Nobody really wants to get into it until we understand the mechanism better."

"After all this time you still don't know?" asked Amanda.

Botrell scratched her head. "Not really. These are very strange substances, especially LSD. Do you know that by the time it starts to work, it's gone? Completely metabolized, no trace left. We don't even know why it stops after a few hours." She seemed lost in her thoughts.

"So what else can you tell us about Ferrin?" Bobby prompted her.

"He turned his attention to toxic psychosis for a while. 'Bum trips,' they're usually referred to, recreational abuse gone bad. He was the first to advise against using chlorpromazines to stop them."

"What's a chlorpromazine?" asked Bobby.

"Class of strong tranquilizers. Thorazine and stuff like that." Amanda sat up straight at the mention of Thorazine. "Ferrin didn't like it," Botrell continued. "He taught that stopping the trip in midstream was psychologically damaging, that the user had to resolve all the issues that surfaced while coming down from the trip. Stopping it suddenly would leave all that stuff in the air."

"You say he was opposed to Thorazine?" Amanda asked tensely.

"Sure was. Why?"

"He gave it to one of his patients," said Bobby. "On at least two occasions that we know about."

"Really? That's pretty unbelievable," Botrell said, tapping her finger on the side of her nose. "What was going on?"

"She was having a psychotic episode," said Amanda, controlled excitement evident in her voice.

"Oh," said Botrell, waving her hand downward. "That's different. Perfectly appropriate. It's only a bad idea in drug abuse cases. You've got to give it to someone who's naturally schiz'ing badly, or they could really get screwed up."

Amanda slumped back on her chair involuntarily as another possibility once again vaporized. "I've disappointed you, haven't I?" asked Botrell.

"Not you, Doctor," Amanda managed insincerely. "You've been very helpful. Really."

Botrell doubted it but let it pass. "Then I'm disappointed," she said. "I was hoping that if he was in trouble, I could help nail him."

———●———

"So what did you think of her?" asked Emmerich behind a cloud of blue smoke.

"She was very cooperative. We learned a lot," said Bobby.

"But not about what you really wanted, I bet."

"She seemed to talk about hating him, but there didn't seem to be a lot of bite behind the words," said Amanda.

"Well, she softened up a little because of the circumstance surrounding his leaving. He was very distraught when his father died, and up until that time, I don't think Felice ever thought of him as human. Maybe that explains part of it. Did she tell you he was his own best experimental subject?"

"You mean he took LSD himself?"

Emmerich nodded, drawing on his pipe. "That may have been the crowning touch to his demise here."

"Why?" asked Bobby. "Seems a fairly noble thing to do."

"Noble?" Emmerich leaned forward, his eyes suddenly gone hard. "Here was a therapist entrusted with the mental health of his patients. The therapeutic process is based on the doctor maintaining a solid grasp of his own persona. Dropping an immensely powerful chemical disrupter like lysergic acid into the middle of his brain hardly constituted noble medicine."

Emmerich's face had reddened with anger over the memory, and he leaned back and tried to calm himself. "Tampering with your psychological support systems is not the same as flying your own experimental airplane. Personally, I think it

interfered with his ability to handle some of his later troubles."
*And the nasty sonofabitch wasn't in such hot shape to begin
with,* his sense of propriety prevented him from adding.

Bobby mulled this over. "I understand what you're saying,
but at least he wasn't a coward, trying it on himself like that.
As far as you know, did he ever not do right by a patient while
he was here?"

"Tough to say," Emmerich answered between puffs. "Therapy sessions are very private. But I frankly doubt it. If anything
untoward had occurred, I can't imagine we wouldn't have
gotten wind of it. We do judicious follow-ups with each patient
of a postdoc. All we got were the standard complaints about
how long everything takes. We get those in over three-quarters
of our patients."

"Nothing you can think of? An incident that might have
seemed small at the time?" Amanda was practically pleading.

Emmerich turned toward the window, trying to come up
with something, feeling bad about what was clearly turning
into an unproductive visit for his guests. "I'm sorry," he said,
turning back toward them. "I just can't think of anything. Like
I said, we didn't like him very much, and he was colder than
we were comfortable with, but there's just no faulting his work
technically."

Neither Bobby nor Amanda could hide their disappointment, although they thanked Emmerich profusely for his time
and cooperation. "Can we call on you again?" Bobby asked
when they were partway out the door.

Any anxieties Emmerich might have had about committing
a professional indiscretion were gone in light of the obvious
uselessness of his information. "Absolutely," he said affably.
"Anytime at all."

CHAPTER
34

Leaning back slightly on her chair, legs crossed, Amanda had her hand on the table, index and middle fingers tapping an insistent but patternless rhythm, one of only two sounds in the featureless room.

Bobby Parks sat on the adjacent side of the table, his chin dropped onto one fist, which sat on top of the other fist, which sat on the table, forcing his back forward and lending emphasis to his posture of expectancy. His right foot tapped idly on the floor, the second sound in the room.

They had been this way for some minutes, staring hard at Assistant DA Scott LaBelle, saying nothing, letting him think. LaBelle had his feet up on the table, arms crossed over his chest, slumped precariously back on his chair and staring intently at nothing on the ceiling. Every so often he scratched at the side of his face with the back of his curled fingers. Finally the results of his intense cogitation were issued as a formal pronouncement as he shook his head slightly and mumbled, half to himself, "I don't know. . . ."

Amanda and Bobby said nothing. He looked from one to the other and said, "Actually, I do know. I'm just trying to be polite."

Amanda glared at him. LaBelle noticed that it wasn't one of

her normal looks of steely determination, icy calm or incisive penetration or any of her standard repertoire of impressive and intimidating glowers. This one was a bit too electric. Her eyes darted from side to side too rapidly, a sure sign of emotional pressure approaching the limits of control, which, coupled with the taut tendons visible in her neck, contributed to a look of wildness not altogether appropriate for a municipal official charged with the public safety.

LaBelle had no wish to add to her rucksack of ills, public or private, but there was the law. And he loved the law more than he loved his colleagues, his career, or perhaps even himself. "Let me guess," his division chief had once asked him sarcastically, "it's all that's keeping us from anarchy, right?"

LaBelle had replied, evenly and with conviction, "No, it's all that's keeping us from ourselves." The part of ourselves that clawed and scratched at the insides of our civilized outsides, as it seemed to be doing to Captain Grant right now.

LaBelle looked at her. "Would 'flimsy' come to mind as a description of the evidence?"

She was in no mood for his whimsy, and Bobby tried to ward off a confrontation, not so much to avoid contention as to save his captain from embarrassment. "No argument there, LaBelle," he said. "We're just trying to understand the potential here, know where we're heading."

"Is that all you were trying to do when Officer Murdoch was a suspect?"

Amanda's voice turned cold. "You're out of line, LaBelle. Every investigation with multiple suspects ends up with all but one of them perfectly innocent." *Albeit sometimes with their reputations damaged. Need to square that one away somehow. . . .*

"Just playing with ideas, Scott," Bobby said. "What do we have legally if we have something forensically? What's important and what's not? If we get a better handle on that, we know where to spend our time."

He was trying to placate LaBelle, draw him into the speculation and away from his legal objections. Bobby tried to shoot the drift over to Amanda telepathically, that is to say, by his tone of voice, body language and the force of their years of mutual trust. The transmission appeared to have arrived at its destination relatively unscrambled.

"Standard procedure," she said, speaking with a calm that belied her feral look. "You know that as well as we."

Scott looked at them both, a sardonic smile playing around his mouth and eyes. "You guys are very good," he said with genuine, if ironic, admiration.

"That's why they pay us the big bucks," said Bobby, stretching out the amiability, drawing the ADA onto their side of the fray.

"And do these big bucks, and the saving of same thereof, have anything to do with the present discussion and the best use of my time?" LaBelle shot back.

Bobby started forward, but Amanda intervened quickly. "Let's all calm down here," she said, sitting up straight and moving closer to the table. "I won't bullshit you, LaBelle," she said, looking directly at him. "It wouldn't hurt me right now to have Brixton Ferrin come up dirty in this thing. But if you think I'd go after him just to save my own neck, then you can take a walk, now or anytime."

LaBelle stared toward her but past her, trying to gauge all the subtexts, political, legal and personal. He'd never known Captain Grant to be anything but straight, but he'd seen better and stronger people come apart under this kind of pressure. And it was often impossible to tell exactly when somebody crossed over that amorphous line separating competing agendas.

Bobby broke into his thoughts. "Who's to say what exactly motivates any of us at any time? What do you think about during a trial, Scott? How about during the Eschbach case? Were you thinking about the righteous wrath of God?" He had LaBelle's full attention and worked it. "When you stood up to make the closing argument, what was on your mind? How the public good was to be served by locking away a vicious killer?" He nailed LaBelle with his eyes. "What did you toast to the night of the verdict? Justice?"

No, thought LaBelle. *I toasted myself. And I didn't think about God, I thought about winning. And I did win. And one amoral sociopath was no longer on the loose. I did the right thing. But not for them. For me.*

Bobby's question was rhetorical and demanded no answer. His point was well made. "So what are we looking at?" asked Amanda.

"Assuming you get more than you've got now . . ." LaBelle started, and waited for assenting nods.

"Malpractice is out, right?" asked Amanda, trying to demonstrate that she was thinking clearly and dispassionately and believing that if she could get LaBelle started in the right direction, he would find a way to get the law to conform to her notion of what it ought to be rather than what it was.

"Right, Captain, that's a civil charge. Her family could bring it, but we can't."

"Okay. So what have we got on the criminal side for the same fact pattern?"

"Well," said LaBelle, now satisfied that there was some legitimacy in the pursuit of this matter and regretful of his heavy-handed manner in assessing it, "there is always criminal negligence." Amanda and Bobby looked up at him simultaneously, and he was pleased at their reaction, hopeful that they caught not only his legal expertise, but his willingness to be on the team if they really had the goods.

They didn't need to prompt him to continue. "He had a professional obligation to adhere to a higher than normal standard of care. If he abrogated it, and such abrogation led to a grievous consequence—"

"Like a murder," added Bobby.

"Like a homicide," LaBelle corrected, "then we might have something actionable from a criminal-law perspective."

"I like it," said Amanda, careful not to sound too eager in front of LaBelle, whose little lesson in legal precision with respect to murder versus homicide put them on notice to start worrying as much about a case as about an investigation.

"Further," said LaBelle, warming to the task, "if we can demonstrate that the potential for grievous consequences was somehow apparent to the accused, we have extenuating circumstances and an even stronger case." He stopped, satisfied with himself and hoping for some of the devil's advocacy Amanda Grant was famous for. Like all good attorneys, Scott LaBelle liked nothing better than the raw intellectual challenge of heated debate backed up by real-life crisis. Argument, like sex, needed no rationale for itself beyond its own existence.

Amanda was on her feet now, pacing with her head down. "We have no way of knowing if Ferrin saw something like this coming."

"He didn't have to see *this* coming," said LaBelle, "just *something* coming, something dire." *Good lord, she's got me arguing her side of the case now. Be careful. . . .* "How much could he have seen? How badly had Jacoby been reacting to her dates with Graham?"

"Tough to tell," said Amanda. "I know what she told me—"

"Hearsay, if she doesn't testify herself," said LaBelle.

"I know that. It may not be evidence, but it is a lead. May point us to something harder."

"You know what we're dancing around here, don't you?" asked LaBelle.

"Wait a minute," said Bobby. "We can't tell"—he looked at Amanda—"or at least we can't prove, that Ferrin should have known something was boiling up inside Jacoby. But what about after the mur— the homicide?"

Amanda looked at him, puzzled. Where others who didn't know him so well might have dismissed his comment out of hand, she knew better, and she thought hard. "Of course. Her attempted suicide."

"Exactly," said Bobby, then to LaBelle, "He might not have had enough clues to her killing Mac before she did it, but after that, when she spiraled into a mental black hole, shouldn't he have known she was a danger to herself?"

LaBelle shook his head. "She hadn't confessed at that point. He didn't know she— Wait!" He could tell from their faces that they were well ahead of his thinking, but he spoke it out loud anyway. "He *did* know. *We* didn't know, but *he* did. He said so. That's why he took her to the scene. To force it out of her." He looked at Bobby approvingly.

"Right," said Bobby. "He had to have known she was exploding inside, wrestling with demons we can only begin to imagine. Is a suicide attempt so farfetched for someone like that?"

Amanda had sat back down, one elbow resting in an open palm, stroking her chin in expectation as LaBelle mulled this over.

"No good," he said at last.

"Why?" asked Amanda, already disappointed since she knew that LaBelle was well into the process and no longer testing them.

"Because nobody's going to give a shit about his failure to predict a suicide attempt that didn't work anyway. It's not about the homicide anymore when you put it like that."

The obviousness of his conclusion made further argument along this avenue useless. Amanda and Bobby sat quietly, working back through the preceding dialogue to see if there was another thread worth picking up.

"Dancing around what?" said Amanda.

"Huh?" LaBelle said.

"Before, you said we know what we're dancing around here. What?"

He remembered the point he had been trying to make that had gotten lost. "The transcripts. Or at least the tapes. From his sessions with Jacoby."

"What about them?" asked Bobby.

"Why don't we just ask him for them?" said LaBelle. "See what happens?"

Amanda shook her head. "If he's clean, there won't be anything there. If he's not, he'll destroy them."

"So we'll declare him a suspect and get a warrant for his arrest and his records. He won't give them up, maybe he'd even get a hearing on the issue, but now they'd be official evidence. If he destroys them, he's obstructing justice. A felony."

"I don't think he'd give much of a damn about that, if he's suspected of abetting a homicide," said Bobby. "Right now he's probably not concerned with the records, because there hasn't been a hint of suspicion around him, at least that he's heard about. If we alert him, he might go underground and take the records with him." There was one thing that had always amazed Bobby about lawyers and continued to do so no matter how many times he saw it: they always believed at first that everybody under oath was telling the truth, that they would follow court orders, that they would toe the line when informed of the rules of evidence and other procedures. It always came as such a shock to them when someone was discovered lying.

"Let's think about later, then," said Amanda. "When we have more. The privilege is supposed to protect the patient, not the doctor."

"Yeah, but the patient is *non compos mentis*," said LaBelle, "and he's the physician, and he's got a lock on her records. You have to have a basis for getting them opened. Something against *him*."

"He took an extremely troubled patient and pushed her to the edge," Amanda suggested.

"Wait a minute," said LaBelle, "I thought your whole contention was that she wasn't that bad before he got hold of her. He made her that way."

"Not totally clear."

"But then your whole basis evaporates if she was a mess to begin with."

"Okay, then he took somebody who was basically okay and turned her into a homicidal lunatic."

"Prove it," said LaBelle, only to be met by silence from Amanda, who could prove nothing at this point.

Bobby tried another approach. "What about this method of pushing her into social situations he knew was causing her tremendous anxiety?"

"The defense will pull up a hundred examples of where that technique was spectacularly successful. I can see the lawyer telling the story of how, when he was jes' a little feller, well, he got throwed from his horse and, by golly, I jes' pulled mahse'f back up onto thet thar horse and dang if I din't do it better the next tahm."

"But it didn't work in this case. It didn't work in lots of cases."

"Nobody ever said psychiatry was a precise science."

Bobby nodded at LaBelle's logic. "We don't even have enough to get them sealed," he said, referring to a procedure by which the records could be protected even if they couldn't be opened just yet.

"No, we don't," said Amanda, standing up and terminating the meeting with a command decision. "I think he fucked her up. I think Mac Graham would be alive today if Ferrin hadn't interfered, and I want the strongest case possible. No mistakes. We're hands off Ferrin until we get something better, and when we do"—she made a fist and tapped her knuckles on the table several times—"we'll nail his ass to a wall."

———◆———

As he opened the interrogation room door, Bobby nearly ran into Annie del Gatto, who stood with her fist in the air ready to knock. "Message from the lab, Lieutenant. Thought you'd want to know."

"Thanks," he said as he took the piece of paper. Then, turning to Amanda and LaBelle, "This could be it."

"Let's call from my office," said Amanda.

"Let me know," LaBelle said as he started in the opposite direction. "I'm due in court."

"I called them, but they wouldn't tell me anything," said Annie. "I didn't have the code. There's a written report ready, but they said they'd give you the basics over the phone."

The "code" was a four-digit number each lab customer provided as an identifier. This way the lab would know if the caller requesting results was genuine. Or so they said. The real reason was to protect the anonymity of people requesting tests for HIV and to let them get their results by phone so as not to prolong the agony of not knowing.

Bobby picked up the phone and dialed and gave his code number to the attendant on duty at the results desk. The attendant was not a lab technician, just a telephone operator who read verbatim from the summary report and could answer no follow-up questions. Bobby listened and then said, "Hold it, hold it. Start from the top and repeat that." He punched the button for the speakerphone and put the receiver back on the hook.

Annie and Amanda huddled closer to the source of the tinny voice rasping into the room, as though their increased proximity could affect the words coming out. "Gas chromatography, mass spectrometry and chemical binding analysis performed on three full caplets and traces from remaining eleven disclose chemical composition consistent with known components of the benzodiazepine alprazolam—that's Xanax, 'kay?—according to manufacturer's published specifications. No anomalous substances of appreciable proportions were found in any . . ."

"Nothing," said Annie, staring at the speakerphone as the attendant droned on. "Nothing at all." She looked up at Amanda apologetically.

Amanda nodded her head slowly, vastly more upset than Annie but trying not to let it show. "It was a good call anyway, del Gatto. We knew it was a long shot."

When Annie left, Bobby looked at Amanda, who had her head in her hands and an attitude of resignation in her downturned shoulders. He tried to find words of encouragement, but none were forthcoming. He hit the disconnect button on the speakerphone, cutting off the attendant in midsentence.

CHAPTER 35

Therapy is taking many forms. Some not so obvious. The best is when one does not even know he is being therapied. Am I inventing a word?''

"I think so."

Amanda forced herself to take a bite of the salad she hadn't ordered but that had come with the meal anyway. The loss of some seven or eight pounds didn't hang well on her frame, as her husband had finally admitted under her direct questioning. Eating by itself wouldn't solve the problem, she knew, only go right to her thighs and rear and leave her face thin and drawn. Ordinarily a disciplined exerciser, she hadn't been to the gym in weeks and had stopped taking Jack Krakowitz's chiding phone calls altogether. *What the hell,* she thought, *after tomorrow I'll probably have plenty of time to work out. To shop, travel, and all those things I couldn't give a tinker's damn about.*

"An example," Tancredi continued between forkfuls. "Lady cop asks old *cocker* to dinner. She wants to be talking about funny drugs, brainwashing, the usual pleasant dinner conversation. But she doesn't listen." He took a sip of wine. "So, now the *doctor* isn't supposed to know he is doing therapy. Perfect! Something new!"

She smiled in spite of herself. Was there no hiding anything from him? Maybe that's why she enjoyed his company. The inability to put anything over on him resulted in a relaxation of the effort to try to do so.

He reached across the small table and put his hand over Amanda's, stilling the idle scratching of her fork on the table-cloth, and squeezed. "What is it, cutie-pie?" he asked softly, holding her with his pale blue eyes that had seen so much but were nevertheless capable of great compassion. Maybe *because* they had seen so much. "Why so much trouble?"

Damn! she thought as the burning started in her eyes and her throat constricted involuntarily. Weeks of repressed emotion threatened to burst like a far-gone aneurysm. She looked into Tancredi's eyes as his face disappeared behind the foggy window of her tears, but she didn't dare to speak for fear of dissolving into heaving sobs.

Tancredi patted her hand and suddenly let go, inexplicably, and returned to his plate, picking up his knife and fork and resuming the attack on his meal. "You know," he said when his mouth was full, "when you cry you are looking like a flounder."

The laughter flew out of her before she could stop it. "What?" she cried. "How can you say such a thing?"

"Because it is true. A flounder which is wearing mascara." He gestured toward her face with his fork.

She buried her face in her napkin and wiped her eyes and cheeks. She lowered the napkin slightly and peered at him over the top of it. "Better?" she asked.

"Difficult to tell. Let me see the rest." She lowered the napkin completely. He looked for a few moments, then turned back to his plate. "No. Still a flounder."

But she had stopped crying. "I thought the rule was to encourage people to cry, that it was healthy, a release. Something like that."

"Sometimes," he said. "But not in public. Ruins everybody's dinner and is making you feel like a *putz*. Especially a visible somebody. Imagine the headlines." She could, easily. "Eat," he commanded.

She tried again, with a little more success. After a while she said, "Tell me about LSD, Tanc."

It was his turn to get flustered, or his own version of it. His knife stopped moving, and he grew still. It only lasted a moment, and then he resumed his previous motions, saying with practiced nonchalance, "What the hell am I knowing about such things?" not believing for a second that he would get away with it.

"What was Brixton Ferrin doing in Tel Aviv?" she asked.

"Lecturing."

"I know that. About what?"

"His area of special expertise."

"I assumed that. Hush-hush, I know."

Tancredi knew that continued subterfuge would only buy him, at most, a few more minutes before this woman wheedled it out of him. He didn't have the heart for it. "He is not being so special, this one. Just one of many people we invited to come talk to us."

"About what?"

"About hallucinogens. Mind-altering substances."

Pieces started falling into place. "For espionage," she breathed. "You were going to drug people in your intelligence work."

"Not going to," he corrected. "Considering it. As we considered many things. As did your country. Only you went much further."

"And Ferrin?"

"Told us to give it up. Too complex, too difficult to control. And too cruel."

Amanda sat in shock. "Give it up?" she said with effort. Every clue, every avenue they had tried to pursue, had dried up and withered away. Now this, too, was threatening to crumble in her hands. Was there nothing for it but to conclude, even as her instincts raged against it, that Brixton Ferrin did his best under trying circumstances and that Pamela Jacoby had fallen into a psychotic abyss of her own making before taking the life of Mackenzie Graham?

Tancredi was nodding, his meal forgotten, now giving his

full attention to Amanda. "He is being a little bit afraid, I thought. He is saying that the drug is too volatile, too unpredictable. The effects are so different in different people as to defy our ability to . . . to make categories—"

"Categorize," she corrected mindlessly.

"Just so. To categorize and predict response. Some are telling you secrets, some are screaming for their mommies, some . . . well, some, they are never coming back."

She looked up at this. "What does that mean?"

He tilted his head to one side, a sad expression on his face. "Occasionally, a permanent psychosis. No one knows why. Except that, so it seems, giving the drug to someone who doesn't know it is coming? Devastating beyond words. No way to describe the terror, so I am told. The only road for some is madness. This is why its use is dying out so quickly in the seventies."

"And you weren't prepared to take that risk?" Amanda asked.

"Our people are tough. Some would say too tough. But torture is not for us, physical or mental. Our agents are flatly telling us, No, we will not do this." He looked at her reprovingly. "We are not Nazis, Amanda."

Chagrined and embarrassed, Amanda held her tongue as he continued. "Besides, as a practical matter, our enemies are having a habit of becoming our friends. Damaging their brains is not a good style." He smiled, having made his point.

"Where did you fit in, Tanc?" she asked, a question she had been burning to ask since the first time they'd worked together, but had never dared to, for fear of turning him off.

"My specialty?" He answered as directly as she had asked. "The psychopathology of terrorism. Climbing in the minds of maniacs masquerading behind political motivation. Looking here and there for little-bitty clues to great big monsters."

He lowered his head slightly and looked up at her from beneath his full eyebrows. "And little-bitty clues to why the pretty captain is having dinner with me and not her long-suffering husband, who is being a fool to marry such a one in the first place."

She had almost forgotten why herself. He helped her remember, continuing, "Tomorrow, a little informal chat, nothing official, nothing to worry about . . . something like that, yes?"

"Something like that."

"I will tell you this, cutie-pie. You won't believe it, of course." He leaned forward, his face serious. "It is not so bad as it looks."

She stared in amazement at this unexpectedly banal utterance. "Thanks, Doc. I needed that. You give lollipops, too?"

His expression didn't change as he continued to look at her. She returned his gaze and said, "You know something I don't?"

In fact, he knew nothing about her upcoming IAD interrogation. Except that she risked great damage if she went in skittish and unsure, and she stood the best chance of walking out whole if she was as self-assured as possible. He felt the trade-off against the risk of being *too* relaxed and confident was worth taking, so he took it upon himself to mislead her.

"Trust me," he said. "Like a dentist visit. The drill is almost a relief after the sound in the waiting room."

" 'Almost' is the operative word here." She wondered if he was in on something that allowed him to know that her concerns were unfounded. The possibility gave her some small comfort, a comfort that would soon seed itself and grow as the only armament against another fitful, tortured and sleepless night.

CHAPTER
36

Amanda hefted the handful of medals she had dumped from the cigar box in her bureau drawer. Three for exceptional bravery. Sharpshooter levels one and two. Self-defense level three, the first ever by a woman on the force. She had never worn any of them, even on occasions calling for dress blues. Her modesty had backfired, and the absence of the coveted medallions elicited an admiring rundown of all of them by the covering media.

She threw them back into the box, which she slid into the drawer, then put her uniform back in the closet as well. *To hell with him. Business as usual today. Nothing changes.*

She had awakened at five that morning, purposely this time, and gone into the gym, much to the surprise of the early morning regulars. She hadn't known what to expect, but the reception was gratifying, not because it was warm, which it wasn't, or bully-for-you, slap-on-the-back bolstering, which it also wasn't, but because it was perfectly normal, perfectly ordinary. Steve Doyle, a swimming alternate on the Olympic team fourteen years earlier, struggled to keep up in their standing calisthenics competition and puffed his way to a narrow victory as Amanda punished herself mercilessly.

"What's with you today, Captain?" he asked. "Training for a marathon?"

As she stood, bent over and gulping huge breaths, she replied, "In a manner of speaking."

But the tactic worked, at least to a limited extent, and some of the gnawing tension of recent weeks eased a bit. The healthy fatigue of a tough workout calmed her, aided no doubt by a relatively decent night of sleep. She had come home intending to make notes, to anticipate his every question, prepare a response for every avenue he chose to follow. She'd gone to bed instead.

She had insisted on a nine A.M. meeting. No way was she going to flay herself alive for half a day and walk into the arena in the afternoon. She ate a big breakfast at eight, low in sugar but high in carbohydrates, and drank only decaffeinated coffee. She saw to it that a lot of powdery doughnuts and strong coffee were waiting for the IAD guy. *Let the sonofabitch pump his blood sugar up through the ceiling:* it would drop like an anvil by eleven, making him irritable and disoriented and ravenous for lunch, which she would insist be deferred until they were finished.

She arrived promptly at nine. Bobby spotted her and inclined his head toward the room where IAD was waiting. *He's here,* his eyes said, *and good luck.* Head high and with purposeful stride, Amanda headed for the lion's den, opening the door and ready to greet the beast.

Barry Simkins was young, almost laughably so. In fact he was thirty-two, but looked barely in his twenties, an ambiguously beneficial characteristic. As a line cop he'd had trouble convincing the citizenry to take him seriously, on occasion necessitating a slight excess of force, of which he had plenty, to help them to understand. As an interrogator, he was unparalleled, consciously exploiting his youthful looks to lull detainees into a false sense of experiential superiority.

I'm going to be interviewed by a goddamned teenager, thought Amanda. *I don't believe this.* She also didn't believe the neat pile of deadly doughnuts, standing untouched next to the small plastic container of freshly cut fruits Simkins had apparently brought with him. He stood as she entered and, while shorter than Amanda, gave away nothing in the athletic body department. He stepped toward her, betraying a very slight limp, and she knew the whole story without asking. Permanently disabled, maybe in the line of duty, mustered off the streets and into this thankless pit of a job where the misery of cops was his stock-in-trade.

"Captain Grant?" he said in a confident voice, holding out his hand. "Barry Simkins."

Barry Simkins what? Sergeant? Lieutenant? What? "Amanda Grant," she responded, taking his hand. His shake to a woman was perfect. Not a limp imitation of manly ritual or a bone-crushing squeeze supposedly communicating deep understanding of feminine liberation, but just enough pressure to show respect.

He caught her glance at his gimpy leg and smiled sheepishly. "Still recovering from the county marathon Sunday, I'm afraid. Got into a little bit of a contest with some bozo from the DA's office. Stupid, really. Ran on it sprained for the last seven miles. Uh, would there happen to be any decaf around?"

Oh, fuck. "Sure, right here," she said, indicating the silver plastic serving thermos she had carried in for herself.

"Great. Please, sit down," he said, gesturing to the table at large rather than a particular seat, which denied Amanda the small victory of sitting other than where he wanted her to.

"Listen, Captain, I brought a tape recorder. I'm terrible at taking notes, and it really helps. I promise you no one but me will ever hear it. If you don't want it on, just say the word and it's gone."

This was getting worse by the minute. Amanda was a master at depositions because she never forgot that the only thing that survived the questioning was the written record. No inflections, no facial gestures, no long pauses while considering a response ever made it to the printed page. Unless a really smart defense attorney put it on the record. ("Would you mind explaining that gesture, Captain?" or "Is there some reason why you're taking so long to respond, Captain?" to which she would respond, "Gesture, Counselor? What on earth are you talking about?" or "Taking so long? You've barely finished the question.")

Now, his promise of confidentiality notwithstanding, Simkins could take away most of the advantages of a purely written record. She thought fast and said, "Fair enough. But I keep the tape and supply you with a transcript."

"Done," he said amiably, "and I verify the transcription. In your presence."

She nodded her agreement, a little taken aback by his ready acquiescence.

"You know," he said, "there's really no need for all of that. This is really quite off the record. Just a little chat."

"Good," she said calmly, starting to get annoyed at his cloying condescension, "then let's have no tape and no notes at all. Unless that's how you usually have a little chat."

"Touché!" he cried, and seemed genuinely pleased at her display of wit. She kept her poker face intact, despite the temptation to find him ingratiating, reminding herself that it was his job to disarm her. His turning on the tape recorder made the reminding easy.

"August eight, nine-fifteen A.M., Amanda Grant, captain, Detective First Class Barry Simkins, county IAD designee," he spoke in the direction of the microphone.

Detective first class? "Designee?" she asked.

"Oh, yeah, didn't I mention? Sorry. Out of the field a week or two until my leg heals."

A professional detective, Amanda thought. *Terrific.* "So this is a sideline with you?"

"Well, not exactly. I've been trained, and I come in from time to time."

Bum leg like hell, she realized. *Since when does that keep detectives out of the field? You're here because you're the best they have, and I'm a full captain. Stay cool, miss, you can do this.* "So let's hit it."

He nodded. He began with the preliminaries, taking her through a fairly dry recounting of the known facts of the case, touching at first only incidentally on her conduct of the investigation. As she spoke, he by turns nodded, frowned, scratched his head, look puzzled. He rarely asked full-blown, carefully considered questions but rather grunted acknowledgment, indicated with hand gestures the parts he was interested in, raised his eyebrows and muttered the occasional "Oh?" to indicate that she should emphasize a point. She realized after an hour and a half that what had felt to her like a fifty-fifty conversation had in fact been borne almost entirely by her. She felt spread-eagled on the table, and Simkins had given virtually nothing away, and it was impossible for her to tell what he was thinking. The tape reels continued their inexorable turning.

They came to a natural pause in the flow, and she needed badly to put out a feeler, to see if she could take his pulse. "Incidentally, you're free to talk to any of my people, without my prior permission. Anytime, just do it."

He seemed surprised. "I thought this was supposed to be a secret."

She couldn't resist the opportunity to display her greater experience. "A secret? Detective, a secret between two cops is a secret when one of them is dead."

Properly chastened, he admitted the truth of this observation and asked a series of questions about Pamela Jacoby. Amanda trod cautiously as the issue of her judgment slowly rose to the surface of the conversation. It wasn't long before it appeared.

"You let a murder suspect visit the scene of the crime?"

Like it's a big surprise, asshole. Isn't that the whole point of this meeting? "She wasn't a real suspect. I mean, she was technically a suspect, but no one really believed she did it." *Get a grip, she told herself. This line doesn't work anymore. What are you going to do, make a real powerful case for why that was such a great piece of police thinking?* "It seemed prudent in light of the circumstances."

He stared at her and said nothing.

"Her doctor was with her," she added. "And a police officer."

"A detective? Someone assigned to the case?"

You know damned well who, why toy with me like that! Stay cool. . . . "No, a sergeant. A good one."

"And did you trust the doctor?"

"There was no reason not to."

"Then why are you investigating him?" Simkins asked without changing inflection.

She failed to hide her surprise and asked, "How the hell did you know that?"

"A secret between two cops . . . ?"

She wanted to choke him but forced herself to good sportsmanship instead. "Touché yourself."

"Thank you," he said, accepting her good grace without gloating. She was now going to realize, however, that the point of that line of questioning was not petty retribution, but preparation for a serious inquiry into her motivations.

"Captain, what is it about this psychiatrist that warrants an investigation, official or otherwise, into his background?"

"One of my officers," Amanda began, purposely emphasizing the currency of her command, "killed an innocent civilian while under the care of a psychiatrist."

"And going after him takes some of the heat off you?"

She leaned forward, anger flashing from her eyes. "I'm a police officer. Sworn to pursue anyone transgressing the law."

"No need to get defensive, Captain," he said.

That does it. She rose and put her hands on the table. "Now you listen to me," she began. He had used one of the most unfair dialectical tricks in the interrogator's lexicon, and she wasn't about to let him get away with it. Not at her expense. "Defensive? What in hell does that mean, Detective? We both know why we're here. My entire participation in this interrogation is for the purpose of defending myself. So don't accuse me of something and then complain when I defend myself that I'm defending myself!"

He stayed calm and said, "Nobody's accusing you of anything."

"Is that right? So how come they take a hotshot like you out of the field and send you all the way down here to have a little chat with a precinct captain?"

"We're just trying to get at the truth," he said evenly.

"Bullshit," she said, and sat back down. "If you wanted the truth, they would have sent you down to help us figure out

Brixton Ferrin's role in this thing rather than try to bust me to make the media circus stop."

"What is it that bothers you about Ferrin?"

"His methods are unconventional."

"How so?"

Amanda postponed her indignation and outlined for him all the evidence. Her goal in this exposition was not to convict Ferrin, but to demonstrate the reasonableness of her judgment in conducting the investigation. A preponderance of evidence, however circumstantial, might not fly in a courtroom, but it might persuade Simkins to give her a clean bill of health.

She noticed as she spoke that he was engrossed in her recitation and that his probing questions had shifted away from her role to the details of the investigation itself. *Some had it in their blood,* she thought, *for some it was an addiction.* Simkins couldn't help himself. He drank details like a camel drank water. She fed him all that he wanted.

When he had exhausted his inquiries and sat musing to himself, almost forgetting where they were and why, Amanda risked a question of her own, hopeful that his mood of involvement might work to her advantage. "So how does it look, Simkins? For me, I mean."

He looked up at her, a faraway look in his eyes, his chin resting in his hand, one finger tapping the side of his face. His eyes refocused suddenly, and he said, "I think you screwed it up, Captain Grant. You had the only reasonable suspect right under your nose, she was the only one you could put at the scene, she was already under psychiatric care and she gives you a ridiculous story about going conveniently psychotic. Christ, if the damned shrink hadn't forced her confession for you, you'd still have a killer on the loose."

The striking simplicity of his conclusion and the directness of his delivery left her stunned, unable to speak for a moment. "What are you going to do?" she managed finally.

"I don't know," he admitted. "Just because I disagree with how you handled it doesn't make you wrong. You said Sergeant del Gatto suspected the pills Ferrin gave Jacoby. What about that?"

"I had them analyzed." He nodded in approval and turned

off the tape recorder. "Negative," she added. He shrugged and began to gather up his things. She was starting to get angry. *Don't tell me you're going to leave me in limbo!*

"What about the in-and-out?" he asked casually. "Did you—"

She cut him off. "Look, Simkins, do me a favor, okay? Don't tell me how to do my job."

He threw up his hands and continued his packing. He really was going to just leave. "If you don't mind, I'd like to be kept informed as your investigation proceeds."

I don't believe I'm hearing this. "Would you like written reports?"

"No," he said, refusing to fluster. "The occasional phone call will do."

She stared at the door after he had gone, sitting alone with her hands in her lap.

In-and-out, my sweet butt! she fumed.

She casually fingered the papers sticking out the side of the case file she had brought with her.

Fuck you, in-and-out!

She then turned to a flimsy pink sheet, the fifth of six copies of a multicolored form. She ran her finger down the right-hand side, stopping about two-thirds of the way down.

———◆———

Bobby kept an eye on the door after Simkins had left, unable to read anything from his face, wondering how long it would be before Amanda came out. Without warning, the door blew open and slammed into a file cabinet adjacent to the jamb. Amanda strode out and yelled to him, "Parks, with me!" and headed into the corridor.

Not good, he thought, and followed her, quite aware of the surprised stares that followed both of them.

"Where to?" he yelled.

"Property," she called back over her shoulder.

Sergeant Sean O'Malley was leaning against a pillar, reading the racing form, and didn't notice the two of them in time to put it away. "O'Malley!" Amanda's voice caromed around the echoing, subterranean room. He jerked upright and dropped the form on the floor and was not at all comfortable with the look on his captain's face.

"Yes, ma'am, what brings you down—"

She didn't wait for him to finish. "I'm having a little trouble reading this carbon," she said, waving the pink sheet at him. "Have you got the original?"

He took the sheet and held it at arm's length, unable to make out the small lettering. He reached for his glasses and put them on, then looked again. "Oh, sure, Captain, it's for the—"

"Get it," she said. "Please."

Mindful of her anger, O'Malley pulled open an ancient and creaking file drawer, prayed to the god of manual record keeping, thumbed through a haphazard jungle of white paper and finally managed to extricate a wrinkled and dirty sheet. "Here it is," he said with relief, handing it over.

"Go get the box," Amanda said, and O'Malley took off, grateful to get away, if only for a few moments.

She took the original and held it slightly to one side so Bobby could look on. She ran her hand down the left side of the page, stopping at the entry that read: "Pill bottle, prescription, Xanax," and then moved her finger to the right, pausing at the column labeled "Out." The handwritten entry read "August 6: count 10." An inch to the right, under the heading "In," another entry was plainly visible. It read "August 10: count 11."

Bobby took the sheet from her and used his own finger to hold his place as he read the entries again. On August 6, the property department had sent the bottle, presumably containing ten pills, to the lab as instructed by Lieutenant Parks. Four days later eleven had come back.

"It's all wrong," he said, flipping forward the attached lab report on top of the white property sheet. "The lab destroyed three of the pills doing the analysis, and said they scraped eleven others. How the hell did they do that with only ten to start with?"

"I'll tell you how," Amanda said as O'Malley returned carrying a standard file box. She reached in and found the bottle, opened the top and shook all the pills into her hand, counting them as she put them back into the bottle. "Eleven," she said, "just as the lab indicated." She read the label and then turned to O'Malley. "Did you check these in originally?"

"Yes, ma'am," he said.

"Did you count them?" she asked. O'Malley didn't answer but rubbed his head, as though trying to remember.

"You didn't, did you." It was a statement, not a question. "You just copied down the label information. You never looked inside."

O'Malley started to stammer. "It's s-so busy down here. There's never time. I mean, Jesus, it's just a bottle of pills. There's no time—"

"So how come you've got time to torture female rookies with the wrong flak jackets?" she shot at him, ignoring his reaction as she turned to Bobby. "It's a physician's sample bottle. It was packed with ten pills. By machine, not by hand. No mistakes. Somehow fourteen pills wound up inside, all legitimate product."

Bobby nodded in understanding. "At *least* fourteen. Jacoby might have taken some."

"True," said Amanda. "Now how the hell do you explain that?"

Bobby took the bottle from her and held it, as though it contained an answer. "I don't know. But it's not right. Somehow, somebody put them there, maybe somebody in a hurry." His agile mind zigzagged among various possibilities. Amanda stayed silent and let him go. This was his specialty, inventing scenarios and discarding them, winding up with one or two that might fit the facts at hand. "Maybe somebody who just emptied out whatever was in there originally," he continued, "refilled it with the real thing and didn't bother to count the replacements." He stopped, the merit of this conclusion now obvious.

As they turned and headed out of the property room, Amanda looked around to see if anyone was listening, then leaned in closer to Bobby and said, "Listen, do me a favor. This Simkins guy from county? I'd just as soon you wouldn't say anything to him about the in-and-out, okay?"

CHAPTER 37

The late summer sun had crushed all movement out of the air. Trees, birds, even insects surrendered to heat-induced somnolence that created an atmosphere of expectant surreality as though something, faintly malevolent, sat poised and waiting to spring from hiding. The three people occupying this supernatural tableau moved their drinks slowly, as though the clink of ice against glass might waken a sleeping demon to tear against the silence.

Amanda's one other visit to Tancredi's backyard, the afternoon of Pamela Jacoby's attempted suicide and subsequent confession, had been, by mutual and unacknowledged assent, an opportunity for her to escape the constrictions of the precinct house. Her shock and mortification had been mitigated to a great extent by Tancredi's easy style and unhurried manner and by his natural aversion to such inanities as "Do you want to talk about it?" which he knew were surefire ways to get people not to talk about it.

It occurred to him in retrospect that, as much comfort as he had offered Amanda, was she not doing the same for him? His out-of-hand dismissal of the possibility of Graham's murderer being an abused female had haunted him, especially in light of the ready availability of a suspect. His own shock at the investigation's dramatic denouement had rivaled Amanda's, and he had torn at himself with the possibility that, had he put the pieces together correctly and made a timely phone call, an attempted suicide might have been averted. Since that day, he had spent countless hours trying to re-create his thought processes, trying to figure out what personal pathology had blinded him to the obvious.

Their mutual support that afternoon had helped them both, but the need had not been so terrible. Now she was in serious trouble, the present crisis threatening to destroy her career, and the pressure had caused her to question her own judgment, transforming what had been a bedrock of self-confidence into a well of self-doubt. Tancredi couldn't stem the surge of his own guilt—how much of this could he have prevented?—and was determined to help if he could.

"Thanks again for setting this up, Tanc," said Bobby Parks, the lack of enthusiasm in his voice betraying not only the effects of the heat, but the conviction that had been slowly draining from him for several days. He had stuck by his captain, his friend, and would continue to do so for as long as she chose to pursue her current course, but the procession of nonevents that railed against his police instinct made him wish for an end to it, as much for her sake as for his own. Like a mountaineer scraping toward the summit low on oxygen, it was difficult to judge how far forward to struggle, knowing each step toward an uncertain goal made retreat more difficult.

"It is the least I can be doing," replied Tancredi.

They sat on the vinyl-webbed lawn chairs and waited, speaking only enough to avoid the embarrassment of admitting that they were not very interested in each other at this moment. This was a last-ditch attempt to draw some meaning out of the swamp of their suspicions and the dry hole of the evidence.

A doorbell rang, and Tancredi got up immediately to answer it, disappearing inside the house. Amanda noticed his lengthened shadow and realized that most of the day was gone, spun away from her as so many things seemed to be doing these days.

Muted but friendly voices came from inside the house, and

soon Tancredi reappeared with Dr. Daniel Emmerich at his side. As they stepped through the sliding glass door onto the patio, Emmerich looked toward Amanda and Bobby and stopped in his tracks, staring at them, the hand that had been stirring the ice in his glass now stopped.

Bobby leaned in toward the puzzled Amanda and said in a low voice, "I'll be damned. Tancredi didn't tell him we'd be here."

She nodded slightly and whispered back, "Probably the only reason he came."

Emmerich had recovered himself and turned to look questioningly at Tancredi, who took his elbow and propelled him forward. "Come, come, be polite and say hello. Too damned hot to be doing otherwise."

Emmerich went reluctantly and shook hands with Amanda and Bobby in turn, mumbling polite courtesies but unable to keep the irritation out of his bearing. Having neither the time nor the inclination to stumble around idle niceties, Amanda took it upon herself to try to clear the air when they were all seated.

"It would seem that you're a reluctant participant in the good doctor's little garden party," she said with what little warmth and humor her present temperament would allow her to muster.

"So it would seem," he answered dryly. He wasn't so much angry as surprised. He had heard of Tancredi years before getting the phone call from him about Ferrin, and he had not been a fan, even knowing full well that the vagaries of the intelligence profession often demanded actions traditionally at odds with the expectations of polite society. Over the years he had come to realize that there were things that many intelligence agents valued above blind obedience to duty, and he had decided after some preliminary probing that Tancredi's priorities in that arena meshed well with his own.

"We need you to talk to us, Dan," Amanda said. "It's important." *Please don't ask me for whom.*

Emmerich took a small leather pouch from his pocket, unrolled it and withdrew his pipe from an inner fold. "Let me guess," he said with mild sarcasm as he dipped the bowl into a tobacco holder sewn into the soft leather. He tamped down the moist, brown shreds, struck a match and held it over the bowl. "Ferrin again." He glanced briefly at Tancredi and said, "Now that you've got me here, don't you think it might make sense if you gave me some clue as to what this is all about?"

Without hesitation Amanda said, "We think he may have been experimenting on one of his patients."

Emmerich turned his eyes to her without betraying surprise and put the pipe in his mouth. She watched the flame being sucked repeatedly into the tobacco as it caught fire, glowing red and sending small puffballs of smoke straight up into the still air. The smell was sweet and pleasant and lent texture to the oppressive heat. Emmerich seemed to be thinking of nothing as the blue tendrils drifted across his face, until he said, "And what leads you to that conclusion?"

Bobby said, "We think he was feeding her an hallucinogen, maybe LSD. Small doses, here and there, maybe trying to short-cut his way in her therapy. There's a chance that it could be what drove her to commit a murder. You probably read about it."

Emmerich nodded. "Graham," he said, then added, "Then it could also be what drove her to confess it, right?"

Amanda and Bobby exchanged glances. "How much do you already know about this case?" Amanda asked him.

"It is working both ways, both directions," Tancredi jumped in. "You want his help, my help? *Quid pro quo.* Too many veils, too little progress."

She realized he had discussed the case with Emmerich, and she had no choice but to agree with his decision. Tancredi was certainly within his legal right, being a sworn peace officer and officially involved in the case. As to his judgment call, who was she to argue? Besides, she was gratified to know that he had seen enough merit in the case to warrant his complicity in bringing Emmerich in. There was little sense in holding back now.

"Ferrin prescribed a mild tranquilizer for her, to be taken in stressful social situations, like being out with Graham. I spoke to her myself several times after those dates, and her descriptions of her mental state were appalling."

"Extreme dissociation, inappropriate affect, visual and auditory hallucinations, somatic synesthesia," Tancredi said, exploiting the precision and effectiveness of professional jargon. Emmerich nodded in understanding as Amanda continued.

"One of Jacoby's friends on the force has been visiting her regularly at the institution. Ferrin's still treating her. They've got her on heavy medication—neuroleptics, I think they called the stuff—all prescribed by him. It makes it difficult for her to communicate, but her friend told us that she's pretty sure that one night Jacoby forgot to take the pills and had a relatively relaxed evening."

"Identical circumstances?" asked Emmerich.

"No," Bobby said, "there were more people around than just the two of them."

Amanda could tell from Emmerich's expression that he was already formulating less sinister explanations for Pamela's behavior. "I know what you're thinking, Dan. But listen some more. The night of the murder, we're pretty sure she took two of the pills, and her description of what went on was the worst of all."

"There is the possibility that she fabricated the stories of her attacks," Emmerich proposed.

"But there's no motive, Doctor," said Bobby. "There's no reason for her to have committed murder."

"None that you understand, you mean," said Emmerich. "You're used to dealing with revenge killings, botched robberies, marital disputes. This might be different. Her abuse as a child constituted trauma you and I can't begin to understand." He was getting professorial, and this wasn't the direction they wanted to go in.

"Dan, you get physician's samples of drugs all the time, don't you?" asked Bobby.

"Sure, tons of 'em. Why?"

"How often do the bottles contain the wrong number of pills? Over by one or two, say."

Emmerich looked at Tancredi and laughed. "You must be

kidding. Over? For a prescription drug? Never. The filling ma-
chines make it physically impossible to overfill a bottle, those
guys are so paranoid about the FDA."

"We recovered Jacoby's bottle of Xanax at her apartment. It
was a physician's sample. There was plenty of extra room,
where the cotton had been removed, and there were fourteen
pills in it. And that's not including the ones she had taken
already. The preprinted label said ten."

Emmerich looked at Bobby without speaking, his mind racing through the various alternatives that would justify more
than ten pills in the bottle. Maybe Ferrin thought ten weren't
enough and added some more?

"Maybe he wanted to give her more than ten," Bobby said
before Emmerich could speak, having gone through the same
exercise already. "Why would he open one bottle, remove the
cotton, then open another bottle, take out a bunch of pills, and
add them to the first? All he had to do was hand her two fresh
bottles."

"Maybe Jacoby did it herself," offered Emmerich.

Exercising his considerable skills in interrogation, Bobby
chose not to offer a logical rebuttal, but to force Emmerich to
his own conclusions. "You figure that's the explanation?" he
asked.

Emmerich took a moment and then said, "I don't know."

"This friend who visits her says Pamela told her Ferrin only
gave her one bottle," Amanda said.

Tancredi asked, "But what would it mean? Surely Ferrin is
not counting on Jacoby to chance on a few planted pills among
many genuine ones? The statistics are too risky."

"No," said Bobby. "That makes no sense, and doesn't account for the evidence anyway. There were fourteen genuine
Xanax tablets and no anomalies. Somebody put extra Xanax
in the bottle. That wouldn't have been necessary if she was
supposed to take a few bogus pills accidentally."

"What, then?" Tancredi asked impatiently. Obviously
Bobby would not be persisting in this line of questioning if the
issue wasn't important.

Bobby looked back to Tancredi. "We believe that the bottle

Ferrin gave Jacoby contained only LSD, and nothing else. Every time she took what she thought was Xanax, she got the hallucinogen. No hit or miss, no probability, just certainty."

There was no need for Tancredi or Emmerich to ask him about the obvious flaw in this line of reasoning. "After what happened," he continued, "Ferrin panicked and knew that he was in great jeopardy if those LSD tablets were ever discovered. Aside from the propriety of administering them to a patient, and without her knowing it to boot, they're illegal. Somehow, and we don't know how, he got hold of the bottle and replaced the pills with the genuine article, but wasn't careful, either in his haste or because he didn't think about it, and overfilled the bottle. Which is the only way we can account for it."

Emmerich still wasn't convinced. "It's a stretch and you know it."

Bobby nodded in frank agreement but said, "Not any more so than any other scenario for finding too many pills in a machine-packed bottle."

"Maybe not," said Emmerich, "and before you ask, no, I can't think of one off the top of my head, but that doesn't mean I couldn't if I tried. Or you couldn't if you tried."

"I have tried, and I can't." Bobby backed off after that, knowing from the lack of conviction in Emmerich's argument that the professor was beginning to find credibility in the house of cards they were building. Academics were suckers for reason and logic. It was time to switch gears, get Emmerich's mind off this isolated mystery, get him to circle the fringes of a larger picture and make a new contribution to the unfinished quilt. A crucial square was missing, composed of knowledge that only Emmerich, maybe Felice Botrell and a handful of others possessed. Out of context, it was so much incomprehensible psychobabble. Extruded through the die of their painstakingly crafted, half-completed theory, that knowledge could assume the shape of a key.

"Professor," said Amanda, "tell us about LSD."

She could tell that Emmerich had been expecting the inward spiral of their questions and ideas to eventually iris to a point

on this area. What she didn't know was that the topic of hallu-
cinogenic substances was one both he and Tancredi were reluctant to discuss and which they hid behind the partial truth
of government classification.

"Tell them, Daniel," said Tancredi. "Not what they can be
reading. What you are knowing, in such a way they can use
it."

Emmerich seemed to consider the request and took a moment to relight his pipe, which had grown cold during the
repartee with Bobby. "I'll be glad to give you a synopsis of
what I know or, more correctly, a theory I believe, but I don't
think you're going to find anything useful in it. You may not
even find anybody who agrees with it."

"We're running on empty," Amanda admitted, "ready to
give up and go home. Give us a few minutes, then maybe we
can forget about the whole thing and fry up some of Tanc's
steaks."

Emmerich refilled his glass from a nearby pitcher. "To understand this stuff—and I'm talking not about its pharmacolog-
ical effect, but what it means—you need to begin with a model:
a newborn baby.

"For obvious reasons, we know virtually nothing about how
little babies think. We can't ask them. There's not much we
can do to test them. All we can do is guess and sometimes
work backward from the great body of developmental psychology that exists for older children. But a couple of things are
fairly obvious and probably true.

"The newborn has no way to block out incoming sensations.
Its brain hasn't developed any methods of interpretation for
what its eyes see or its ears hear. It's all raw input, streaming
in at an alarming and terrifying rate, with no way to sort it all
out, no mechanism to place things in categories that can be
processed usefully."

"I don't get it," said Bobby. "It sees a crib, or its mother,
what's to categorize about that?"

"Plenty," Emmerich said. "Let me give you a particularly
striking illustration. You've heard about cases where people
who have been blind since birth get some miracle surgery that
gives them normal sight? All very touching, but what you don't

read about is what it's like for these folks when they first open their eyes.

"They haven't *learned* how to see. They have absolutely no way to relate the sensations pouring in to any sense of their own reality. The newly sighted patient can't tell the difference between black and white, up and down, or green and red. They can't tell their doctor's face from the hospital wall. They don't know the difference between an ant on the sheet and a tree outside the window. They simply haven't learned. There's nothing to relate to."

"You're kidding," said Amanda.

"Not at all. But they learn quickly, because they already have a well-defined sense of reality. They know what a chair is, so now it's only a question of learning to relate the new sensation to what they already know to be a chair from what they've felt and talked about for years."

"You keep talking about reality like it's a personal thing," said Bobby. "A chair is a chair. That's reality. I just have to learn what to call it."

"Oh," said Emmerich, leaning forward, rising to the challenge, "but a chair is *not* a chair. A chair is whatever it appears to be to you, and only you, which may have very little to do with what it looks like to me. In a very real sense, reality is not an absolute. It is a thing we create in order to allow us to interact with a very small subset of the world, which we can handle, rather than all of it, which we cannot."

"No wonder Felice Botrell thinks you've gone round the bend," said Amanda.

Emmerich took the gibe in good humor. "Let me ask you something. See this glass?" He held up his drink. "What color is it?"

Amanda eyed the cobalt glass and, fearing a trick question, answered tentatively. "Blue."

"I agree," said Emmerich. "It's blue. Now, do you have any idea what it looks like to me?"

"Blue, I imagine."

"No, I didn't ask you what I call it. I asked you what it *looks* like to me. How do I perceive it? How do I see blue?"

Amanda considered this and said, "I don't know."

"Of course you don't. How could you know unless you were inside my head?"

"I can understand that for colors," said Bobby. "All kids wonder about that, it's a kind of game. But how does that relate to individual realities?"

"Because it goes much further than colors. How do you know what heat feels like to me? How do you know what a violin sounds like to me? Take it a step further. How do you know that the way a Beethoven sonata sounds to me isn't exactly the way a grapefruit tastes to you?"

Emmerich paused to let the point sink in. "These questions have no answers. There is no empirical basis for ever assuming that we experience things the same way. That little baby receiving raw input from the world hasn't learned how to deal with any of it, and is completely overwhelmed. The only knowledge it comes equipped with is how to eat. If left alone, it will die. In all likelihood, it cannot even make a distinction between itself and the world at large. For all practical purposes, it has no self.

"From the minute it emerges into the world, its only task other than immediate survival is the construction of its own personal reality. Sorting out the sensations, discarding most of them, creating neat pigeonholes for the rest. It does this by building filters for its senses, then later for its very thoughts. The filters are shaped by its genes and by its environment both and, for the most part, stay intact for life. Taken together, they define what the person is. They are the very definition of the self. As they form, the organism begins to draw a distinction between itself and the world, eventually coalescing into a personality."

"Are you saying that my personality, who I am, is defined by the way I've learned to view the world?" asked Amanda. "These filters, as you call them, define me?"

"Absolutely," Emmerich replied. "That's your reality, and only yours. It consists of the rules you personally have built to help you negotiate a very small part of a larger experience, which if it hit you naked would rock you into babbling incoherence."

Amanda and Bobby both sat back and considered this extraordinary philosophy. The forceful logic of it was at odds with their own sense of an objective, rather than subjective, reality. "I find it hard to believe," said Bobby, holding up his hand, "that this hand is only what my mind says it is."

"And I don't blame you," said Emmerich. "But let me feed you a few micrograms of LSD and I'll change your mind."

"But that's a powerful drug," Amanda objected. "How can you claim that what you experience under its influence is in any way credible?"

Emmerich smiled and said, "Because you have just made a very important, albeit unconscious, assumption about what it is that LSD does. You assumed that it randomly scrambles signals, like too much vodka or a bang on the head."

Amanda realized the truth of that and also understood that all of this had a point. It was important for them to understand the philosophical foundations underlying Emmerich's ideas in order to understand what was to follow. She felt as though curtains were being parted on some great truth, but she had no idea what that truth might be.

"So what *does* it do?" Bobby asked.

Emmerich tried to consider the best way to explain it in nontechnical terms. "It blows out every filter in your personal universe. Sends you back practically to the moment of your birth. You stand naked before the millions of worlds your mind has been carefully rejecting for you all your life, and you've not only got no way to stop it, you've got no way to relate to it. Every mechanism you have spent all that time constructing to help you wend your way through the world has been smashed into powder." He stopped to puff on his pipe.

"Jesus H. Christ," Bobby said softly.

"Is that what Dr. Botrell meant when she talked about it mimicking psychosis?" asked Amanda.

"Exactly," said Emmerich, "although she would have couched it in less flowery terms than I did. But the principle's the same. It's roughly analogous to what Freudians refer to as defense mechanisms, although they're talking about how to cope with your mother and your boss, and I'm talking about

how to cope with the whole world, on a much more primitive
and profound level."

"What about the hallucinations?" asked Bobby.

"Astute question. Everybody talks about LSD causing hallucinations. I disagree. It doesn't so much cause them as allow
them to occur. They are not manufactured by the drug but
released from within the user. And there are two sources. One
is the newly unchecked sensations that you never even knew
were there until the drug let you see them. The other, and more
important to your case, is those that arise from the release of
trauma-based thoughts and images subconsciously suppressed
for many years.

"You see, there are many frightening experiences in early
childhood, some of them so painful that they would cause
great damage if left unchecked. Part of our natural survival
mechanism is simple denial. A neighbor shoots your dog, you
find your mother in bed with a stranger, maybe you were kid-
napped or raped. Your mind makes them go away. At least at
the surface. But they're never really gone. They're down there
somewhere. They leak around the edges and make you sensitive or callous, brave or cowardly, sometimes mildly neurotic
or severely psychotic. But they never completely disappear.
To a large extent, our mental health is defined as our ability to
keep the demons at bay.

"Some people undergo psychotherapy, usually over a period
of many years. The process of self-revelation is an extremely
painful one, even though one usually barely pokes a pinhole
into the seething cauldron of repressed memories. Yet swallow
a tiny pill containing enough LSD, and the whole inferno
comes slamming down the chute like a river of molten lava. It
is very difficult to distinguish from a full-blown psychosis,
except in one important respect: In most cases, at least where
the drug was taken consciously, the effect disappears in a few
hours. The tornado goes back in the bottle, and it's all over
except for some lingering aftereffects. The realization that it
will end is what enables the recreational user to ride out the
storm. For the psychotic, there is no such comfort."

Emmerich leaned back, his presentation finished. The sun

approached the treetops, its low angle gradually robbing it of its ability to warm the earth. As the ground temperature dropped slightly, the cooler air at its surface began to mix with the warmer air above it. Leaves rustled softly in the resulting movement. Amanda found it difficult to tell whether it was the light breeze that made her suddenly shiver or the glimpse at an unseen world that Emmerich had been talking about. She fought to draw back from her fascination and relate this to the topic of immediate concern.

"Did you arrive at all of this yourself?" she asked. "From personal experience?"

"No," replied Emmerich. "In truth, most of it came from Brixton Ferrin. I told you when we first met that he was his own best experimental subject."

"Did he also push its use in psychotherapy?" asked Bobby.

"At first he did. But then when he began to realize what this stuff was really about, he dropped that idea."

"More than dropped," Tancredi put in. "Actively opposed."

"That's what he was doing in Tel Aviv," said Amanda.

Now it was Emmerich's turn to be surprised. He looked questioningly at Tancredi, who shrugged and said, "Was old news already, Daniel."

Bobby pressed it quickly before Emmerich could be put off by what he might perceive to be an indiscretion on Tancredi's part. "What was the point in the first place?"

Emmerich decided that maybe his built-in aversion to openly discussing classified material was misplaced in the present context. "The original notion was fairly straightforward. If LSD could pop the locks on the mind's secret compartments, why not use it as a therapeutic shortcut? It seemed simple enough. Drop a few micrograms, and all the things you've been keeping submerged come bobbing to the surface, open to view."

"What's wrong with that?" asked Bobby.

Emmerich smiled. "It's difficult to describe in words how wrong that thinking is. Let's say a man goes to a psychiatrist because he can't stop scratching the side of his face. After about a year he finally discovers a memory of being attacked by a pigeon when he was six years old. It takes him another year to dive far enough back into the feeling of having his face pecked to relive the pain he had been successfully repressing and make the problem go away. So you might figure, what the hell, give him some LSD and let's get right to the heart of the matter and get it over with.

"The problem is, his little pigeon incident constitutes a vanishingly small percentage of all the things he's got locked away, starting with the trauma of his very birth and escalating from there.

"Well, the drug doesn't discriminate. It goes after everything, and you can't control it. Even in tiny doses you can't target it."

"An analogy," Tancredi interrupted. "You want to drink a glass of water from behind a huge dam. A pinprick is what you are wanting. But this what Daniel is talking about would be like dropping a hydrogen bomb on the dam."

Emmerich nodded vigorously but said nothing further, waiting for the significance of it all to dawn on the two police officers. Bobby spoke first: "And Ferrin himself realized all of this?"

"I'm afraid so," said Emmerich. "The therapists were interested in using LSD to unlock the hidden mind. The researchers in the lab were using it to try to simulate schizophrenia so they could understand the disease better. What Ferrin did was consider these both together and remind the therapists that there was a damned good reason why those secrets were repressed in the first place: it was the mind's way of protecting itself. Release too many too fast, and you have an induced psychosis, the very thing the patient's subconscious was trying to avoid when it created the neurosis to mask the pain of the memories."

The implication for their case was evident to all of them by now, and Amanda took it upon herself to verbalize it. "So what you're saying is that Brixton Ferrin would be the last person in the world to be using it on a patient."

Emmerich's enthusiastic manner dimmed as he realized the effect of his analysis on Amanda's hopes. "I'm afraid so," he said apologetically. "When Ferrin beat up on something, he never reversed himself."

An unseen bird chirped tentatively, as though to test whether the heat had died down enough to warrant the effort involved. One or two others soon joined in. The sudden lull in conversation made Emmerich uncomfortable. What had been for him a dispassionate dissertation on a topic of intellectual interest was for these people a much more personal concern. He went on, primarily to just make conversation, and said lightly, "I can tell you that poor Felice Botrell never brought up complementary neuroses again."

Bobby jerked his head up, the abruptness of the motion jarring his arm and making him spill a few drops of his drink onto the concrete patio. "Never brought up what?"

Emmerich, surprised at the tone of Bobby's voice, looked up to see him sitting upright, his mouth partly open, his face a mask of confusion. "Complementary neuroses. That was the theory Felice wrote her thesis on. Not worth bothering to discuss, really, it was—"

"We already know about it, Dan," Amanda said in a hesitant voice, her face betraying as much puzzlement as Bobby's. She had come fully upright on the lounge chair and set her bare feet on the ground. "Jake Nostrand—Graham's friend—said that Ferrin spoke to him about that theory. It's why he arranged for Jacoby and Graham to meet. Nostrand thought they might be able to help each other."

"Not possible." Emmerich was shaking his head as Amanda spoke. "Not possible."

"I'm telling you," said Bobby, "that's what Nostrand told us. He said Ferrin resisted at first but then gave in and agreed to go along with it."

"True, Daniel. It was just so," Tancredi added.

"It doesn't make a lick of sense," Emmerich said almost scoldingly. "The guy trashed the daylights out of that theory, what in the world would he be doing talking about it?"

Amanda was on her feet and pacing. "I don't get any of this," she said, her voice louder than usual and uncharacteristically strident. "He goes on the record, a classified record, telling government officials how useless and dangerous LSD is for therapy or as an intelligence tool. Then he uses it on a patient."

She held up her hand, palm facing Tancredi and Emmerich.

"I know what you said, but I'm telling you, he used it on Jacoby. I'm certain of it. I don't know if he changed his mind, or tried an experiment, or what, but goddammit he fed it to her. Then he blows smoke at Nostrand with this cockamamie psycho-bullshit theory that he once blew away, again on the record, and he never even mentions that it's been officially discredited."

She stopped and looked at them, her eyes glassy and wide, the pupils darting furiously. "What in the hell is going on here? What are we missing?" She looked directly at Bobby. "It's out there, Bobby. I can feel it, like an animal, looking at us."

Bobby returned her gaze, helpless in the face of conflicting evidence. "Let's bring him in, Amanda. We're over the edge on this one. I can't put it together."

She stared at him a few moments longer, then her shoulders slumped as she was no longer able to sustain the energy to keep them tensed. The breeze had picked up, and the neighborhood birds were now risking flight.

Bobby wasn't ready to let it go yet. "We'll bring him in, confront him with what we've got, threaten to indict, the whole nine yards. We've got enough to seal his records pending forced disclosure, we'll get another doctor for Jacoby, someone who'll consent to opening her transcripts up. . . ."

"We've got nothing," Amanda said dejectedly, and dropped back full length onto the lounge. "Nothing. Just vapor. We can't indict him on gut feel. My God, it's so confusing I'm not even sure anymore what I'd want to indict him for."

They sat for a while longer, letting the light wind wash around them. Tancredi refilled their glasses and said, "So who is hungry?"

Nobody spoke at first, then Amanda said in a tired voice, "I'll pass, Tanc."

"Me too," said Bobby, then to Amanda, "What do you say we pack it in?"

She nodded her assent and sat up to hunt for her shoes and take a last sip of her drink. "I appreciate your help, Dan," she said. "You may have saved us from a great deal of embarrassment."

Emmerich admired her ability to be gracious under trying circumstances. "I wish I could give you something better, but . . ." He shrugged helplessly.

She dismissed his apology with a wave of the hand as she drank from her glass. Tancredi offered one last suggestion. "Is there some possibility, maybe slight, that Ferrin losing his father, at the same time fooling with such drugs, drove him *meshugge*? So now he's taking dumb ideas out of his closet and washing them off?"

Emmerich looked skeptical. "How did he seem when you met him?" he asked Amanda and Bobby.

"Normal," said Bobby. "Rational, in control. Normal. Would be mighty tough to make him out a loony."

Tancredi sank back on his chair. Bobby bent over to tie his shoelaces and said casually to Emmerich, "By the way, how *did* his father die?"

Emmerich was in the process of filling his pipe with a fresh plug of tobacco. He raised his eyebrows in surprise. "You didn't know? I'm surprised."

The nascent breeze disappeared for no apparent reason. The new stillness emphasized the heat once again. The soft rustle of the leaves stopped, as did the sounds of the birds singing and fluttering among the branches.

Emmerich struck a match and held it over the bowl, inhaling and drawing the flame down into the tobacco. "His father was a union organizer"—he puffed the flame in—"and he was working a job site"—another puff—"and he stepped under a crane carrying a load of I-beams." Puff. "The hitch slipped and dumped the whole load right on top of him."

Puff, puff.

"He died instantly."

Puff.

CHAPTER 38

A grotesque chemical ballet by a deranged choreographer began in Amanda's brain, set to music by a demonic composer and performed on its unwitting host by a company of glands, cells, hormones and other physiological instruments. Cacophonous and discordant, the piece assaulted rather than soothed, the notes competing with each other for primacy, any hope of harmony crushed under the weight of the cataclysm triggered by Emmerich's innocently delivered grenade.

For a brief moment the adrenaline onslaught threatened to overwhelm her ability to deal with external reality.

"Mandy . . . ?"

She couldn't move. Or, more correctly, chose not to. Her mind retreated involuntarily to earlier, traumatic memories that may have triggered similar visceral reactions but found nothing comparable to the Richter magnitude of the freak newness that seized her at this moment. She felt as though all her cells were conspiring to rub her mind into the scene being played out before her, the one central solution that had instantly replaced all the confusing subsections, and the feeling was so all-consuming that she tried desperately not to ruin the spell, at least not until she'd had a chance to explore it.

"Amanda!"

It was no use. As quickly as it had come, it was going, vaporizing into ephemeral wisps that rose and dissipated behind her eyes. She concentrated hard, shutting out her immediate surroundings, wishing it back, knowing that as long as she lived nothing could ever shock her so deeply as to trigger its return.

"Captain Grant!"

Hands gripped her arm and shook it. She opened her eyes and the concrete patio swam into view, broken shards sparkling at the center of a spreading stain where she had dropped her glass. She looked up and saw Tancredi and Emmerich. She shook her shoulders once, hard. *Enough self-indulgence. Time to act like a police captain.* "Where's Parks?" she asked, her voice deep and throaty.

"He went in to use the phone," said Emmerich, concern clouding his face. "Are you all right?"

She blinked hard once, then again, trying to clear her head and concentrate. Mac Graham killed Brixton Ferrin's father, however inadvertently, and now Ferrin had killed Graham, however indirectly. "Yes, I'm fine," she said. The evidentiary Rosetta stone had been unearthed. As with that linchpin hieroglyphic artifact, it would take time to mine the wealth of linkages it provided, but the most vital of enabling factors in any crime was now theirs:

A motive.

"You can't let me down, Tanc," she said calmly but with force. "He made her do it and you've got to help me prove it." Tancredi stood quietly, arms across his chest, rubbing his chin and lost in his own thoughts. He barely heard her. "This isn't about professional courtesy anymore," she went on. "He has no right to be practicing. You can't turn your back on it."

Emmerich, annoyed at standing in one conceptual place while everyone else seemed to have shifted astral planes, said, "What in the hell is—"

Bobby came out of the house, interrupting Emmerich and casting protocol aside as he grabbed Amanda's arm and put his face next to hers. "Snap out of it, Mandy. We gotta move."

"I'm there, Bobby." She rose immediately and fumbled for her shoes with her feet. "We need LaBelle."

"Just called in. They're trying to find him."

She turned to Tancredi. "Think about it, Tanc, but don't take too long."

"Will somebody *please* tell me what in the bloody hell is going on here?" yelled Emmerich.

Tancredi took him by the arm and led him away from Amanda and Bobby, who needed to leave without standing on a lot of delaying ceremony. "Let us be saying, maybe our Dr. Ferrin's motivations are extending somewhat beyond therapy, hmm?"

————◆————

Bobby called in again from the car as they were nearing the station. The clerk of the court promised to beep LaBelle through police liaison but warned that he was preparing for a major trial and would not be pleased. Just as Amanda and Bobby were settling themselves into the small conference room, LaBelle threw open the door and strode in, carrying a stack of red file folders under one arm and a briefcase in the other. "This had damned well better be—" He stopped when he'd had a chance to see their faces. "It *is* good, isn't it?"

Bobby smiled slightly and raised an eyebrow. Amanda was still recovering from the shock of Daniel Emmerich's casually delivered revelation and was not yet trustful enough of her own reactions to fully believe that the light at the end of the tunnel was not a train coming from the other direction. Rather than risk LaBelle's detection of any premature jubilation in her voice, she let Bobby start the process.

"Do you remember Dr. Nostrand's deposition, the part where he described the accident that led to Mackenzie Graham's dropping out of med school?"

"Of course," LaBelle said impatiently, still standing and clumsily dropping his papers onto the table. "He dropped a load of girders on some union guy. They investigated, somebody put the fix in, he walked." He put out his hand to draw back a chair. "So what are you telling me, he knew in advance it was a setup?"

Bobby shook his head. "No. The guy he killed was Brixton Ferrin's father."

LaBelle's hand stopped dead on its way to the back of the chair. After a second he slowly turned his head toward Bobby, then toward Amanda. Quietly he said, "You're shitting me." Amanda looked at him but stayed silent. "Jesus," he breathed, then, "Jesus Christ," and he slowly sat down.

Bobby gave him a moment and then said, "It seems that—"

But LaBelle held up a hand. "No. No, let me think about this for just a second." He rested both elbows on the table, lowered his head and rubbed his temples, staring only at the tabletop, his eyes jumping back and forth. "He made Jacoby do it."

"So it seems," said Amanda, not pushing it so as to avoid appearing self-serving.

"Or didn't stop her from doing it," said LaBelle, recovering now and thinking like a courtroom tactician.

Here we go again, Amanda said to herself. "Don't even start that crap, Scott. Take another minute to think about it. How many thousands of towns in this country, and Ferrin shows up here six months after Graham does. Six months after that he's got a patient dating the guy that killed his father. Six months after that and the guy is dead, killed by his patient. Some fucking coincidence how all that came together."

Momentarily taken aback by her uncharacteristic public vulgarity, LaBelle looked at her, then kept staring, making her uncomfortable, until she realized he wasn't seeing her at all but had simply settled conveniently on her face while his brain raced through alternatives. He drummed his fingers, and Amanda and Bobby sat quietly, until he said distractedly, "You're right." He thought some more, then stopped drumming, sat up straighter and said more definitively, focusing on her now, "You're right."

"Good," said Bobby. "So?"

LaBelle stood and began walking around the room. "First thing, let's not get overconfident. Remember that the jury didn't do the investigation. They didn't plod through mountains of clues and then see the skies open on crucial information. They'll get it all methodically, with the defense blasting hell out of all our witnesses, doing everything they can to defuse the drama. And we've got two goddamned huge problems."

Pausing first to determine how best to articulate his thoughts, he went on. "Help me out here. Every crime of this type has three elements, right?"

"Motive, method and opportunity," said Bobby.

LaBelle nodded. "We're golden on motive. Couldn't ask for better. Method? This is tough. Most prosecution proofs of method are based on precedent. People get shot, they die, this we know. The only question is, did the accused do the shooting, and if so, is he criminally liable? In our case, the method probably has no precedent. So, first we have to demonstrate the method, then prove that it occurred, and only *then* prove that the accused is liable.

"Which brings us to opportunity. If we do well on method, opportunity is still not so obvious. How did he premeditate this? What was the opportunity? Jacoby didn't even know Graham beforehand. How did Ferrin pick Jacoby?"

"I think that's easy," said Bobby. "He didn't. He waited patiently for the opportunity. He gets a female patient, deeply troubled, open to suggestion and manipulation. He sets up a blind date with the victim—"

"But he didn't," LaBelle interrupted. "It was Nostrand's idea. Ferrin only went along with it."

Amanda's eyes were flashing now, and she leaped. "More news, Scott. Ferrin gave Nostrand a load of nonsense about a therapeutic theory, planting a description of a patient that perfectly matched Graham. Nostrand fell for it and walked into the trap."

"How do we know it was nonsense?"

"Because a couple of years ago Ferrin went on the record *saying* it was nonsense. He denied a Ph.D. candidate her degree based on it. Transcripts of her orals were taken. We can get them if we need them."

LaBelle considered this, fascinated as much by the story as by the case. "Wow."

"Indeed," said Bobby. "There's more. We still need time to assemble it all and make a cohesive story."

"So," said Amanda, repeating the line she had used so often with LaBelle in tricky situations, "what are we looking at here?"

"Good question," he said candidly. "We don't get a lot of homicides around here, especially weird ones."

"Is he an accomplice?" asked Amanda.

"No," said LaBelle. "That concept's pretty much gone by the wayside. These days a person is a criminally responsible party to a crime if he has criminal responsibility for the conduct of whoever committed the crime."

"Spoken like a true lawyer," said Amanda. "What did that all mean?"

"If I heard it correctly," said Bobby, "I'm on the hook if I made you do it, as much as if I did it myself?"

"That's the idea. It's always made sense, just took a long time to get the system to come around."

"But," said Amanda, "technically, there's been no crime. No accused, no arraignment, no finding of guilt."

"I'm impressed, Captain," said LaBelle. "But that's not a problem. The law was designed so that innocent or nonresponsible people don't have to suffer prosecution for us to be able to get at the real criminals."

"So we're okay, then, right?" said Bobby.

"Not right," said LaBelle.

"Why not?"

"Because," Amanda answered for him, "we haven't figured out what to charge him with yet." LaBelle nodded his assent.

"But I thought you said he was criminally responsible," said Bobby, confused.

"Yes," said LaBelle, "but for what crime?"

"Murder, I'd imagine," said Bobby.

"Maybe," said LaBelle, "but this is why I gave you the 'let's be careful' speech." He paused to gather his thoughts. "The idea is to put him away for as long as possible, right?"

"And to clear Jacoby," said Amanda. "As much good as that's going to do her."

"Agreed," said LaBelle. "Murder One is the hardest thing to prove. It requires premeditation, total sanity, knowing right from wrong, everything. In this case, where Ferrin didn't actually do the killing, the defense is going to throw the issue of reasonable doubt at the jury like herring to seals."

"What reasonable doubt?" Amanda asked indignantly. "The motive is a huge smoking gun. How could they ignore it?"

"They don't have to," answered LaBelle. "Okay, picture this. We go after Murder One. Assume Ferrin never took the stand in his own defense, so we never got to question him. I'm the defense attorney, and here's my closing:

" 'Ladies and gentlemen of the jury, I'm not going to kid you. Mackenzie Graham killed my client's father. My client would have liked nothing better than to see Graham dead. No argument there. And when his patient started dating Graham, maybe, just maybe, my client saw a crisis coming. And maybe, just maybe, he thought there was a possibility that his patient might kill Mac Graham. And he stood by and did nothing, and he let it happen. I'll grant you that all this is possible.

" 'Ladies and gentlemen, my client may be guilty of *something*, but it isn't murder in the first degree. He didn't premeditate the murder. He didn't set it up. The prosecution would like you to think he did, but have they proven their case beyond a reasonable doubt? Have they proven absolutely that he tricked Jake Nostrand, a well-educated and intelligent doctor, into engineering a romantic relationship? Have they proved, beyond a reasonable doubt, that he somehow got a woman, a cop, no less, with no criminal record, to stab her lover to death?' "

"Okay, I get the point," said Amanda. "But I think we can prove most of those things."

"If you don't," said LaBelle, "he walks."

"Are there other charges, easier to prove, that can also lock him away?" Bobby asked.

"Yes," said LaBelle, "and I think we should seriously consider those. We might have to get creative, bank on the fact that we can get a jury to believe he's a class A creep and wink at some of the legal niceties."

"How about assault with a deadly weapon?" asked Amanda. "He messes with Jacoby's mind, sneaks drugs into her. Can we make a case for an hallucinogen being a deadly weapon?"

"Not deadly weapon," said LaBelle. "Dangerous instrument. The wording includes a substance that can cause injury or death. But it won't work. There was no physical injury to Jacoby."

"But we're not going after him for hurting Jacoby," Bobby reminded them. "It's Graham he got killed. What if Jacoby was the dangerous instrument? Under Ferrin's influence, and the drugs, she was capable of causing great harm, so she's a dangerous instrument, right?"

"Creative," said LaBelle, "but any time you get too creative you automatically stand a fifty percent chance of losing. I don't like it. We need something more conventional. Maybe we could stretch voluntary manslaughter. It's supposed to require sudden passion at the same time as the act, but we might be able to get around that." He snapped his fingers suddenly. "Wait a minute. There's another one. Criminal solicitation."

"Solicitation?" asked Bobby. "Sounds like he called her up and asked her to do him a favor."

"Never mind what it sounds like," said LaBelle. "Legally, it means he attempted to cause her to commit a felony, and a capital felony at that. That makes him a felon. And we can combine that charge with one or two others, and nail him without risking Murder One."

"Good," said Amanda. "What now?"

"Not so fast," said LaBelle. "We still need to craft a story that hangs together, and there are too many flaky pieces still around. Right now we have a terrific fairy tale and a shitty legal case." He watched as their faces fell, betraying disappointment. *Good*, he thought, *now let's get professional.* "Outline the basic theory for me," he said, taking off his jacket, unbuttoning his cuffs. "Just the broad brush to start with."

Amanda indicated Bobby with her upturned palm, and he stood up and removed his jacket as well, starting a back-and-forth walk as he spoke. "Ferrin freaks after his father's death, especially after a bullshit investigation and hearing. I'll bet we'd find him on the record of that case, if they even kept records. We'll have witnesses, at least.

"Ferrin has patience. He doesn't hurry revenge. We know this from his university colleagues. He follows Graham after he resurfaces, after Nostrand rescues him, and sets up practice here, and he waits for a way to get even.

"Pamela Jacoby presents the perfect opportunity. She's a psychological mine field, desperately in need of a father figure to look up to, very vulnerable to suggestion. Once Ferrin figured out what her childhood had been like, he starts in trying to dredge up those memories. But any premature revelations would have ruined his plan. So he slips her small doses of LSD every time she's in a position to start remembering. These cause low-level hallucinations and intense paranoia and anxiety that not only damage her sense of her own sanity, but heighten her aversion to realizing the truth about herself until Ferrin is ready.

"I don't know how we do this without the transcripts, but let's say Ferrin somehow gets Jacoby to confuse Graham and her abusive father. He forces her into making parallels. Finally, the one night she tries to solve all her psychosexual problems at once, she takes a double dose of LSD, loses it completely, confuses Graham with her father and kills him."

He stopped. LaBelle sat with his arms folded across his chest, motionless, listening. Amanda looked at LaBelle, looking for a sign, some clue as to what was going through his mind, knowing he was trying to think like a jury. After what seemed an interminable interval, he spoke.

"Horseshit."

Amanda and Bobby exchanged looks. "Horseshit what?" asked Bobby.

"I can believe he played with her head. I can believe he slipped her mind-altering substances. But how are we going to convince a jury that he actually got her to bash the victim's head in and then take a knife and mutilate him?"

Through the slightly open door, Amanda saw Annie del Gatto. She was leaning against a file cabinet, facing the meeting room, too far away to hear anything going on inside but intent on the proceedings anyway as though, if she concentrated hard enough, some vibrational message might reach her.

"We don't have to show he got her to do those specific things," said Bobby. "She could have picked the method herself. All we have to show is that he made her want to kill him."

"No," said LaBelle, "we also have to show something else. That she expertly covered up the crime while under the influence of a powerful drug. That she had enough presence of mind to wait until he was asleep before she whacked him, even though it's supposed to be a crime of intense, irrational passion. Now how the hell did he get her to do all of that?"

"She didn't," answered Bobby. "What did he care about the method, or if she covered it up or not? Come to think of it, that strengthens our case. He could have let it go unsolved, but got Jacoby to confess so that we'd close the case and stop investigating. Otherwise we might have ended up on his doorstep. This way he gets a nice, clean ending."

LaBelle was shaking his head. "Too damned circumstantial and incredible, Parks. It doesn't play. And you haven't answered the part about waiting for him to fall asleep."

Amanda's eyes met Annie's. The young officer started to straighten reflexively, then caught herself as she realized that her observation of the meeting room might be detected.

Bobby was speaking. "Okay, let me think." His eyes searched the ceiling for inspiration. "Here: They went to an early movie, so there was plenty of time for him to fall asleep."

"What if she was lying about the time?" asked LaBelle.

"Lying? For Chrissakes, Scott, she confessed! What's she gonna lie for?"

LaBelle took the rebuke in stride. "Good point. Keep going."

"So he falls asleep, and meanwhile this drug is still running through her. Maybe it took a while for it to really take over and drive her to the edge."

"Were there any traces in her blood?"

"You're not going to believe this," said Bobby, "but the stuff disappears right away. Completely metabolizes in about thirty minutes."

LaBelle rolled his eyes. "This is getting worse. I believe Ferrin is connected, even responsible somehow. But this just isn't hanging together. Too complicated, too many elements would have to work perfectly."

But Annie couldn't avert her eyes, try as she might. They locked with Amanda's, and any pretense of disinterest on her part dissolved in the lengthening stare. Later, Amanda would replay the moment in her mind and it would seem to her, as it did now, that they were actually conversing.

"Maybe he hypnotized her?" said Bobby, much less confidently. "Laid out all the details for her to follow?"

"No. First of all, from what you guys have told me about this drug, hypnosis under its influence would be about as effective as a fart in a windstorm. Second, why program her to clean everything up, just so he has to go through all the trouble of getting her to confess later? Why not have her go screaming into the night, bloody and naked?"

Out of ideas and his frustration mounting, Bobby turned to Amanda, who had been silent and barely paying attention, lost in her own thoughts. "What about it, Captain: you got anything to add to this?"

She seemed not to have heard, and he was about to question her again when she blinked away from Annie, looked up suddenly and said, "I want to see McGillicutty."

LaBelle looked at Bobby questioningly. "Who?"

"The neighbor?" asked Bobby, clueless as to what this was all about.

Amanda nodded. "Now."

"What the hell are you talking about, Amanda?" he asked.

She ignored him. "Call Dispatch and have Ruth set it up. Tell McGillicutty to stay there and wait for us."

Bobby glanced at LaBelle before getting up to make the call.

"Captain . . ." LaBelle started.

"You too, Scott. We'll take my car." She got up to leave, clearly brooking no argument, out the door before they could protest further.

———◆———

In the car, Bobby driving, he and LaBelle sat in embarrassed silence, too intimidated by Amanda's inexplicable behavior to speak. After some time, and without preamble, she said softly, "Bobby, you once started to tell me that you had a problem with the scenario, the night Pamela killed Mac."

"Yeah?" he said.

"You said you couldn't quite put it together. What did you mean?"

He had forgotten about it and tried to reconstruct his thoughts. "I'm not sure. I tried to picture how it went down, you know, like I do?"

She nodded without speaking, and he continued. "They try to have sex, but she couldn't do it, so they stop. Now what? Graham is a good guy, but he's only human, he's gotta be frustrated. We used to call it 'blue balls' in high school. Make the girls feel sorry for us, y'know?"

"I know," she said, smiling for the first time in hours. "Some of us believed it, too."

"Anyway, here he is, thrown out of the saddle, so what does he do? Does he go to sleep? Not likely. Not only is he frustrated, but his girlfriend is fritzing out all over the place—"

"So she says," LaBelle threw in.

"So she says," agreed Bobby. "But we know he never ejaculated." Amanda looked at him in surprise. "I had the coroner check it out specifically," Bobby said. *Thank you, Dr. Tancredi.* "I forgot to mention it when the results came back because it didn't seem relevant anymore. Don't make me give you all the details here, but the ME said Graham hadn't climaxed, and he was positive. In fact, everything Pamela told us checked out perfectly. It's all in the autopsy report."

"So now what?" asked Amanda.

"Right. Now what? If he doesn't go to sleep right away, when does he? It's a virtual certainty he was hit on the head while sleeping—"

"What if he was just lying with his eyes closed?" asked LaBelle.

"He would have had to have them closed while she got up, went to the fireplace, grabbed the poker, walked back and hit him."

"But that's possible," said LaBelle.

"Under normal circumstances, yes, but there wasn't anything normal about this night."

The conversation was interrupted as they pulled onto Ditmas Avenue. "You gonna tell us what this is all about pretty soon?" asked Bobby. Amanda said nothing, only pointed to an empty spot in front of Pamela Jacoby's apartment building. As soon as he nosed the car in, she was out the door and heading for the entrance, Bobby and LaBelle running to catch up.

They walked quickly up the stairs, and Amanda knocked on Mrs. McGillicutty's door. It opened, and the diminutive but feisty lady, not waiting for introductions, said, "They told me you was comin', and I said I already told you everythin' I knew."

"Thank you for seeing us, Mrs. McGillicutty," Amanda said. "May we ask just a few more questions? It won't take long."

"I suppose so," she answered, moving aside as her Old World manners overcame her suspicion.

But Amanda stepped back instead and walked to Pamela Jacoby's door. She looked up at the overhead lamp shining down on the mat in front of the door and placed herself under it. The yellowish light flooded her hair, illuminating it as though she were being positioned for a portrait.

"Do you remember the night Pamela came home late?" she asked. "The night her boyfriend was killed?"

"Of course I do," Mrs. McGillicutty answered. "An' I been over it a hun'erd times with the police, I have. I was watchin' me TV an' I heard—"

"No, please," interrupted Amanda. "I'm sorry. You don't have to go through it again. Just tell me: What did her hair look like?"

Momentarily nonplussed, Mrs. McGillicutty repeated the question. "Her hair?" she asked, mystification in her voice.

"Yes," Amanda said patiently. "What did her hair look like?"

Mrs. McGillicutty thought for a moment, then said tentatively, "Well, it looked fine. Parfect, in fact. 'Twas always parfect, and that night was no different."

"Are you sure?" Amanda pressed.

Somewhat indignantly, Mrs. McGillicutty answered, "Well now, of course I'm sure. She always kept her hair so nice, I would have been noticin' if somethin' was amiss, now, wouldn't I 'ave?"

"Not wet? No loose hairs blowing around, like it was recently dried?"

Mrs. McGillicutty put her hands on her hips in defiance. "I'm tellin' you, nothin' like that, it was—"

"No blood?"

The little woman drew back in horror, bringing her hands up to her face. "No, no, my goodness! Blood? No, no! I read the papers, to be sure, I know what they're sayin', but sure'n there was no blood!"

Amanda looked at her for another second, as though considering whether to ask any more questions, then took both her hands in her own and squeezed them gently. "Thank you, Mrs. McGillicutty. You've been very helpful."

"Well, I don't know," she said, still confused by these questions.

"Thank you," Amanda said again, then turned and led Bobby and LaBelle back down the stairs. As per procedure, Bobby waited until they were out of earshot and out of the building before he tried to address Amanda. But by that time she was in the car and had her hand on the microphone.

"Ruth," she was saying, "get me a patch to the courthouse. I want to speak with David." She released the button.

"Roger," came the reply. "Stand by, one."

"Earth to Grant," said LaBelle. "You want to throw a few clues our way?"

He had resumed his seat in back, and Amanda turned to him. "Bobby's little problem with the schedule of events the night of the murder," she said. "And you, poking holes in our theory."

He nodded. "Yes?"

"New scenario, Scott. New theory."

"I'm listening."

"Me too," said Bobby.

"We missed—" A static squawk from the radio cut her off.

"Clerk Frerer here, Captain. The judge is in court and can't be—"

"Tell him I want him now," said Amanda, keying the mike, forgetting that the clerk wouldn't hear her until her own mike button was released.

"I'm sorry, Captain. Say again?"

"Tell him it can't wait."

"Well," said the clerk, exasperation evident in her voice. "Hold on."

Rather than resume her conversation with Bobby and La-Belle, Amanda waited. Shortly the clerk was back. "He's on his way," she said.

"Now that's what I call service," said LaBelle.

"Yeah," Bobby said sarcastically, "someday I'm gonna marry me a judge."

"It has its advantages," said Amanda, "so long as you don't go to the well too often."

"Dammit, Mandy," the radio exploded, "what in the Sam Hill is so goddamned important it couldn't wait?"

"Easy, sweetheart," she said. "You're on the air and I'm not alone."

"Shit," Judge Grant said, "so sue me."

"I need a warrant, Dave."

"For what?"

"The arrest of Dr. Brixton T. Ferrin."

"The shrink? You're kidding."

"And I need it fast. With a premises search thrown in."

"You got probable cause?" he asked. "Something better than what I've been hearing day and night for two solid—"

"David," she cut him off, and waited a moment to be sure he was listening. "Do you remember the last time I asked for a warrant and then blew the collar?"

There was a long silence, and then he answered, "Actually, no, I don't."

"Right," she said tartly, "so trust me on this one, will you?"

"All right, all right," Judge Grant replied. "We need a DA on the line to do a telephonic warrant. Hang on a minute. Frerer!" he yelled to his clerk.

"Got one right here, Dave," Amanda said into the microphone, then handed it into the backseat.

"Hiya, Judge," said LaBelle.

"That you, Libel?"

"Yeah. And please don't sign it yourself, Your Honor," he said, looking at Amanda, "or there might be an appearance of conflict. Is there another judge on—"

"Hey, Libel, I might be ornery, but I'm not stupid." Sounds of scrambling for paper and pencil came over the radio. "Okay. Charges?"

Amanda reached back for the microphone, took a deep breath, gripped it with both hands and pressed the key. "Murder in the first degree, with special and extenuating—"

Bobby went for her arm, but LaBelle had his hand over the seat like a shot. "Jesus Christ, Grant!" he yelled, and grabbed the mike out of her hand. He and Bobby talked frantically over each other. "Are you crazy or what? We just talked about this hardly an hour ago!"

She looked at LaBelle evenly. "It was him." She reached for the mike, but LaBelle drew it farther into the backseat, stretching the cord.

"I understand that, Captain, but if you overdo these charges, you're gonna blow the whole case. We went through this. At the most we have solicitation, manslaughter—"

"Amanda," said Bobby, trying to calm things down, "take it easy. Let Scott lay out the charges." The radio squawked angrily as Judge Grant tried to find out what was going on, but they ignored him. "We've gotta have stuff that sticks, or else we're—"

"You *don't* understand," said Amanda, her voice perfectly calm, displaying a degree of control neither of them had seen in weeks. "She didn't do it."

They looked at her, dumbstruck. LaBelle's hand went limp as her words sank in, and she took the microphone back from him. "It was Ferrin," she said. "He killed Mac Graham. With his own hands.

"Pamela Jacoby wasn't even there when it happened."

CHAPTER 39

Antipathy toward police notwithstanding, no self-respecting cop could ignore a flaming red Corvette doing eighty-five, especially one sporting out-of town plates.

The young Bohemian behind the wheel saw the flashing red roof lights and was faced with the kind of instant decision that could affect the outcome of his entire life. In this particular instant, he chose wisely.

The sports car slowed and pulled onto the shoulder. Being hardly a novice to such situations, the driver stayed inside and didn't reach for his back pocket, or the glove compartment or any other interior location not immediately visible from the outside. Instead he placed his hands at the top of the wheel and splayed his fingers open.

The officer emerging from the squad car saw the driver's hands and relaxed a notch. Coming up to the window, hand on the butt of his holstered service revolver, he checked to be sure his partner was in position at the right rear quarter, then bent toward the window and twirled his finger in the air. The driver obediently lowered the window.

"Thanks for keeping your hands where I can see 'em," said Dennis Murdoch.

The driver flashed his most charming smile and said,

"Well, Officer, I come from a family of cops. I know the score."

"That so," said Murdoch, not believing him. "License and registration, please."

"In the glove compartment," said the driver. Murdoch nodded, and the boy leaned over to retrieve the documents.

"Know how fast you were going?" Murdoch asked.

"To tell the truth, I knew I was a little over. Was it a lot?"

"I had you at eighty-five."

"Gee," the driver said, "I wasn't aware." He handed the license and registration over. "Well, you got me fair and square, Officer."

Murdoch displayed no reaction. Sweetheart ploy. *I'll make your life easier and you give me a break.* Usually worked, too, given the abuse people normally heaped on him.

But not today. Not this month. Not Dennis Murdoch. He'd had to learn from a street informer that he was a suspect in the Graham murder, holding his face immobile and pretending he already knew. And that pissed him off. Everybody around him was paying for it. And that bitch of a captain? Damned if he'd so much as nod at her for the next fifty years.

"Good," said Murdoch. "Then there'll be no need to see each other in court."

The radio in the squad car crackled. Procedure called for it to be turned up loud when they were outside the vehicle. Al Emley went back to answer the call.

"Five over the misdemeanor limit, son," Murdoch was saying as Emley withdrew his head from the passenger window of the squad car and yelled:

"For you, Murdoch!"

The boy was into his pleading harangue when Murdoch turned without apology and walked back to the other side of the squad car. "I think it's the captain," Emley said fiendishly, knowing how much Murdoch would welcome this.

"Shit," said Murdoch, slowing down deliberately. "What in the flaming hell could *she* possibly want from me?" Emley smiled broadly, and Murdoch slammed his ticket book and the driver's documents on the hood.

"Why don't you can the shit-eating grin and finish writing this up, asshole?" he said.

He picked up the mike and waited until Emley started walking away. He donned an earpiece, reached in to turn off the speaker, pressed the button and said, "Murdoch," as gruffly as he could make it sound.

Emley by now was at the driver's window of the red Corvette, still smiling idiotically at Murdoch's annoyance and discomfort, amused at the deliberately disrespectful, slouched posture his partner had adopted, one arm flung over the roof of the squad car.

He turned back to the ticket. In his peripheral vision he saw Murdoch's body move and looked up to see him straighten his back, then turn toward the car. He strained to hear what Murdoch was saying.

"Yes, ma'am. Yes, ma'am. I understand."

It sounded about three octaves too deferential for his buddy Murdoch, and Emley started slowly back toward him. Murdoch reached into the car for a spare notepad, placed it on the roof and began writing. "I got it," he said excitedly. "Yeah, I mean yes, I got it, Captain."

Emley stepped up to him and shot a quizzical look, but Murdoch waved him away, put his fingers to his earpiece and concentrated. "You got it, Captain. No problem. We're on our way." He pulled out the earpiece, threw it into the car along with the microphone, and yanked the ticket pad and documents out of Emley's hands.

"What the hell—" said Emley, but Murdoch was on his way back to the Corvette. Emley lingered, rooted to the spot because there was nothing to tell his feet to move, his brain being fully engaged in trying to figure out what bone the captain could possibly have tossed Murdoch that would be big enough to warrant moving the mountain of carefully accumulated enmity.

Murdoch threw the license and registration into the window and said to the driver, "Son, this is your lucky day."

"No shit?" the boy said even as he cranked the ignition.

"No shit. Now get going."

The boy let out a grateful whoop, pulled out and was gone.

"I'll drive," Murdoch said to Emley, handing him a list of police officers. "You get on the horn. Round up these guys and give them this address. Tell them to be there in one hour."

————●————

A knock sounded at the front door. Brixton Ferrin, annoyed at the interruption, rose and left his study to answer it.

He opened the door to see a very large, very black policeman standing with his blue cap in his hand. "Well, this is a surprise."

Alberon Jolicoeur appeared nervous and upset and turned his cap continuously between his fingers. "Doctor, may I please speak to you? Please?"

Imagining that Jolicoeur was still distressed at having witnessed Pamela Jacoby's breakdown at the scene of the crime, Ferrin stepped back and said, "Why, certainly, Officer. Please. Come in."

He came in and stood to one side. As Ferrin started to close the door, Jolicoeur put his huge foot between the door and the frame and stopped it from closing.

"What—" Ferrin started to say, but by the time he got the one syllable out, Jolicoeur had his right hand around his neck, all trace of nervousness miraculously vanished, and was lifting the smallish psychiatrist into the air. Ferrin's hands gripped Jolicoeur's wrist as he tried to struggle free of it. Jolicoeur seemed not to even notice, as he also did not seem to notice Ferrin's legs flailing helplessly in the air.

Through his choking, Ferrin heard Jolicoeur begin to sing, a soft, slow elegy in a strange and mellifluous tongue. For some reason this frightened him more than the implacable hand around his throat.

Through the open door he saw half a dozen police cars suddenly appear on his lawn, lights flashing, officers emptying out. One who appeared to be in a leadership position came through the door.

Dennis Murdoch tapped Jolicoeur on the shoulder as he walked past without stopping. "Easy, Al," he said. "How many times have I told you not to play with your food?" He didn't look back to see if Jolicoeur had even heard him, much less complied with his admonition. Ferrin stepped up the intensity of his flailing as blood filled his head and veins in his face threatened to pop. He twisted his head to the left and saw Murdoch enter the study. More cops came into the house.

Jolicoeur let him down slowly and eased the pressure on his neck but left little doubt as to his ability or inclination to hoist him back into the air if he didn't cooperate.

In the study, a reel-to-reel tape machine was turning. Murdoch looked for a button to turn it off and, not recognizing one, reached over and pulled the power cord out of the wall. Ferrin's voice, strained and rasping, came in through the door. "Everything in there is privileged and confidential! You have no right!"

Murdoch came out and signaled to the other officers, three of whom went into the study. "Your privileges have just been revoked, Doc," he said.

Ferrin was recovering and fought down panic and the inclination to lose control of himself. "I assume there is a charge, Officer?" he said to Murdoch.

"Nah, no charge, Doc. This is a free service." He laughed at his own joke and then said, "Yeah, sure, we got charges. You're wanted in connection with the murder of Mackenzie Graham."

"You're out of your fucking mind."

"That a professional term of art, Doc?" Murdoch asked him, smiling.

"You can't touch those records," Ferrin persisted. "You know damned well you can't."

"Who's touching 'em?"

"Then what are you doing?"

"Sealing them," Murdoch said triumphantly. "We can't touch 'em, but neither can you." Annie del Gatto walked out of the study and handed him a thin box containing a reel of tape. Murdoch studied the label briefly and then said to Ferrin, "Well, most of 'em, anyway. Say, mind if I use your phone?"

Without waiting for a reply, he walked into the nearby kitchen, picked up the phone and dialed. After a few seconds he said without preamble, "Got it, Captain. July sixteenth."

His tone toward her was deferential and respectful, grateful acknowledgment of her attempt at forgiveness and reconciliation, which she had expressed by hauling him off traffic duty and handing him what was sure to be the most visible and highly publicized collar of the year.

From the other room, Ferrin was yelling lewd suggestions as to what Murdoch could do with his anatomy, most of which the officer found topologically untenable.

CHAPTER 40

A police precinct, like any bureaucracy, is organized with the objective of maximizing the amount of time available for its line people to do their jobs. While station-house denizens rail angrily against the oppressive forms and procedures, this irritating administrative trivia is vastly preferable to the alternative, which is to have every officer confront a blank sheet of paper and invent a new format rather than check off boxes or wander about trying to figure out whom to contact and what to say in order to carry out simple tasks. The tight establishment of administrative procedure, like the use of professional jargon, ultimately makes life easier—or would, if the caretakers of the paper blizzard didn't so often forget who was serving whom.

Over time, the ebb and flow of the bureaucratic tide takes on the characteristics of a living organism. A stimulus in the payroll department, perhaps in the form of a misprinted check, travels along the synaptic pathways of in and out baskets, and manifests itself as an inflammation in the personnel department, and occasionally flares up in the normally asymptomatic executive suite.

Those who dwell within the beast for any length of time know that truth lies not in the actions of any individual person

or department, but in the effects that ripple throughout the
body and make themselves known as a change in air pressure,
a minor inflection in the sonic cadence surrounding desks and
cubicles, subtle shifts in the patter of heels on carpets and
hardwood (or, more correctly, linoleum in most police sta-
tions).

Amanda sensed it as she walked in through the front door
with Bobby Parks at her side and Scott LaBelle close behind.
The level of banter and jostling in the closely confined hall-
ways was almost nonexistent. Colleagues who would normally
say hello or nod a greeting stared instead and said nothing.
This was standard station-house etiquette in Captain Grant's
precinct after a major break in an important case, as though
not to disturb the concentration of the involved officer. The
crucial moment, confronting the suspected perpetrator, was
close at hand. It was a critical and carefully orchestrated en-
counter, witnessed by attorneys and a court reporter. Improp-
erly handled, it could wreck the case. Amanda's people knew
better than to give rein to their jubilation, risking acute embarrassment to all concerned if it should turn out to be premature.
And the involved officer in this case was their captain.

As Amanda walked in she turned her head slightly to see
Annie del Gatto leaning over a desk, watching as a clerk wearing a set of headphones typed, pressed a pedal with her foot
and listened, then typed again. The headphones were plugged
into a tape transcription machine whose reels turned with each
press of the pedal.

Annie looked up and saw Amanda. She brought her hand
up chest high, clenched her fist and held it shut. Amanda
did the same, completing a barrio salute of shared victory,
provisional for the moment but intense and intimate in its
vindication of personal loyalty. Amanda knew what Annie
was feeling. It was common among police: *Even if the system
fucks up again and turns the scum loose, we did good.*

It lasted only a second, but the precinct organism recorded
it, and the mood of expectant optimism intensified. LaBelle
prayed that they wouldn't have to let anybody down, but his
own confidence was elevated by Amanda's bearing, which

seemed fully restored to its former state of easy grace. Her step carried none of the hesitancy that had insinuated itself in recent weeks, and the commanding presence that had withered under the heat of unbearable pressure spread out from her now like a blanket, comforting the troops who had felt cast adrift.

"He's in C, Captain," said a uniform. "Been there 'bout a half hour."

Amanda nodded, then turned to LaBelle. "My office first." The threesome veered away from the interrogation room and into Amanda's office, the inner blinds still down where she had left them, reflecting the depth of her progressive withdrawal of late.

"I thought we were ready," said LaBelle.

"We are," said Amanda. "There's just one little problem."

Suddeny wary, as though his enthusiasm were about to be drenched in ice water, LaBelle asked, "What problem?"

Amanda walked over to the credenza behind her desk, where a cardboard box sat, its top flap already cut open. She opened it, reached in and pulled out what appeared to be a black shirt with gold lettering. She held it up by the shoulders and shook it out full. "These," she said ominously.

LaBelle, confused and worried, looked at the shirt and tried to understand. "I don't get it." He looked over at Bobby, who had pursed his lips and was nodding his head slowly, in apparent comprehension of what Amanda was driving at.

LaBelle looked back at Amanda, who was casting an eye over the shirt. "What?" he demanded loudly.

"Uniforms," she answered.

"I can see that. What's the problem?"

She looked at him as though mystified at his confusion. "You don't see the problem?" she asked.

"What the hell are you talking about?"

"These are the new shirts for our softball team. They're black with gold letters." LaBelle merely stared, so she continued, drawing out her words in controlled anger. "They were *supposed* to be gold with black letters!"

"Damn!" Bobby said angrily. "Can you believe those incompetent idiots?"

Too stunned to speak, LaBelle looked back and forth at the two of them. Amanda returned his look and said, "Okay, okay, let's not panic here. We can fix it."

"Fix it?" LaBelle croaked in mindless echo.

"Absolutely." She smiled in triumph. "We've got a contract. You're a lawyer, it's a good case, right?"

LaBelle looked to Bobby for some help, but got none as the lieutenant said, "Yeah, that's right. A contract. Now all we have to do is get them to redo the shirts before the first game."

LaBelle felt as though someone had mounted the wrong reel of a movie. "Are. You. Guys. Fucking. Crazy?" he finally managed to sputter.

Amanda gave him a quizzical look and then turned back to the shirt and held it out at arm's length. "Why? You think gold on black is better?"

Openly angry now, LaBelle stood up and confronted Amanda. "He's been in there for an hour already and—"

"No," said Amanda, cutting him off. "It's been less than forty minutes."

Bobby, standing now, put a gentle hand on the ADA's shoulder and pressured him back onto his seat. "Easy there, ace. Let's give him another few minutes." LaBelle turned to him as he went on, Bobby letting him in on the private joke. "He was probably rattled half to death to start with. Then he hears we're in the building and figures it'll get started right away. Now he's coming more unglued with every second."

LaBelle turned back to Amanda, who was now seated behind her desk, taking a pad of paper out of a drawer. After a few moments he got up and walked over to the desk. He picked up the shirt where she had dropped it, opened it full and held it up. "Definitely black on gold," he said seriously, nodding slowly. "Better let me have a look at that contract right now."

———•———

It worked, in a way. When they walked in, he was on his fifth cigarette, hair disheveled from repeated run-throughs by his hand, knee up and down like a piston driving his heel into the floor.

That was his lawyer, Paul Daniels. Brixton Ferrin himself sat as though contemplating a painting in a museum. Essentially motionless, relaxed, two fingers lightly supporting the side of his head, a third tapping idly and unhurriedly at his lip.

Daniels was on his feet before the door had even completed its opening swing. "Captain, my client has been kept waiting here for over an hour." He turned quickly to the reporter and pointed his finger at her keyboard, making an up-and-down motion.

"Hold it, Michele," Amanda said to the reporter. "We're not on the record yet." The reporter didn't need to be told. Her hands remained folded primly in her lap. "Hello, Paul," Amanda said to the attorney. "How are you today? You're looking well."

"That's very charming, Captain Grant. I'm fine. We're all fine. Do you plan to honor us with the graciousness of your participation at this point?"

The two practiced adversaries eyed each other's faces carefully for preliminary clues as to who was holding the most cards. Off the record, Paul Daniels could be quite civil. When the reporter's machine was transcribing, however, he reminded Amanda of a ventriloquist. Keenly aware of the limitations and opportunities offered by a purely written record, Daniels was an expert at mixing verbal and nonverbal signals. He could smile unctuously and exude warm feelings even as his words were eviscerating an ill-prepared prosecutor, the true potency of his venom apparent only upon a later reading of the transcript. Or he could mount thunderous rage and fuming anger, leading the unwary to accuse him of inappropriate behavior, only to have a bemused judge declare that the written record reflected nothing but genteel civility and elegant manners.

"I am terribly sorry for any inconvenience we might have caused you or your client, Counselor," Amanda said, looking at Ferrin for the first time since she had entered the room. "I assure you it was unintentional, and we will do our best to expedite these proceedings. By the way, Dr. Ferrin, that's a very nice haircut. Are you wearing it longer these days?" Ferrin looked up at her as she continued. "I seem to recall that it was much shorter when we last met."

Oh, this is going to be good, thought Bobby. *Time enough, and evidence, too.* Amanda nodded to Michele, and the reporter dutifully began collecting the names and exact spellings from everyone in the room, then swore Ferrin in.

"Captain, do you mind?" Daniels said with mounting impatience.

Without bothering to respond, Amanda said, "This is a preliminary interrogation of Dr. Brixton T. Ferrin, conducted with his consent and with the advice and presence of counsel. We are on the record. Dr. Ferrin, have you been advised of your rights?"

Ferrin spoke for the first time, looking directly at Amanda. "Yes," he said, then looked away again.

"Very well, but let me remind you of a couple of things, just to make certain. You are already represented by counsel, and I assume that you are satisfied with your representation?"

"Yes," Ferrin replied. His hands were out of sight, below the table. Amanda guessed that they were on the verge of shaking and that he didn't want to give the appearance of being in less than full control.

"Good. If at any time that should change, you have only to tell us and we will postpone these proceedings and allow you to engage the services of another lawyer."

"Captain," said Daniels, "as you said, Dr. Ferrin is represented, and he knows his rights. Can we move along? Maybe to the charges?" As soon as he finished speaking, he tried to adopt an air of studied indifference, as if to demonstrate that all of this was too insubstantial for him to harbor any serious concern as to his client's jeopardy.

Amanda ignored him. "And you know that anything you say can and will be held against you in a court of law?"

"Yes," Ferrin said casually, knowing that all of this was designed to heighten his anxiety. He wasn't going to let it work.

"One other thing," Amanda went on. "If, at any time during this proceeding, and only during this proceeding, you would like to go off the record, I will ask the reporter to stop recording.

Anything you say will be privileged, and it will not be used against you."

Daniels looked up, suddenly interested. "Excuse me?"

"You heard me. I'm willing to go off the record."

"Why?"

"Do you have an objection, Counselor?"

"None. No objection. One second, please." Daniels leaned over and whispered into Ferrin's ear, blocking his mouth with his hand. Ferrin nodded and resumed his study of the tabletop. Daniels nodded at Amanda.

"You are charged in connection with the murder of Mackenzie Graham," said Amanda, and waited for a reaction.

Ferrin looked up without surprise. Amanda realized that Daniels had had time to prepare him. With the skimpy charge list she had given Murdoch, they had already started to put together a defense, and it would be affirmative rather than a simple denial and a shifting of the burden to the prosecution.

The commencement of the proceedings were to Daniels like the gun going off in a foot race. Nervousness drained away as he entered his element and stood up. "LaBelle, I object to the entire proceedings. I am going to enter a motion to quash the search—no: to *traverse* the search warrant on my client's files on the basis of unsubstantiated speculation and reckless accusation."

"Paul—" LaBelle began.

"Furthermore, these proceedings are improper." He was yelling now. "Why in hell are we being interrogated by a cop instead of the DA? And since when do cops run an investigation like this?"

"You through now? I ceded the interrogation to Captain Grant, who has cooperated with my office in the conduct of this investigation—"

"Bullshit, LaBelle, it's cops protecting their own, and you're letting them walk all over—"

Ferrin reached up calmly and put his hand on his lawyer's arm. "Paul . . ."

Daniels kept his eyes on LaBelle for a moment, then looked at Ferrin.

"It's okay, Paul. Sit down." Daniels did so, and Ferrin turned his attention to Amanda. "I understand my rights, and I've no objections to this questioning."

Daniels leaned in to Ferrin's ear to begin an impassioned plea for him to keep quiet. Ferrin held up a restraining hand.

"You have nothing," he said to Amanda evenly. "Nothing but a deranged and dangerously psychotic police officer." He waited, then continued, drawing bravado from Amanda's non-reaction. "The best you can make is that I pushed her too hard, which may be an error in judgment but is certainly not a crime."

Amanda pretended not to hear him. "Specifically, you are being charged with murder in the first degree for the premeditation of the crime—" She paused to gauge Ferrin's reaction, which was nonexistent.

But he smiled for the first time. "How can you prove I made her do it?"

Amanda cocked her head to one side, as though confused. "Whatever makes you think I believe you made her do it? I don't remember saying anything of the sort."

Ferrin's smile froze in place, no longer a mirror to feigned mirth, but a mechanical artifice. "You're accusing me of abetting a murder, are you not? That's considerably more dire than my simply failing to prevent one."

"Give it up, Doctor. You *wanted* us to think you were abetting a murder." She caught Daniels's look of amazement. "As I was saying," she went on, "murder in the first degree"—another pause—"and aggravated assault upon Police Officer Pamela Jacoby with intent to commit grievous bodily harm."

In contrast with his client's equilibrium, Daniels was immediately back on his feet. "What bodily harm? There's not a scratch on her she didn't put there herself! And what is this 'first degree' bullshit?"

"Bodily harm to Mac Graham," Amanda said calmly. "Your client used Officer Jacoby to kill him."

Ferrin still betrayed no alarm, although it seemed as though the effort to do so might be increasing. Daniels, panting slightly from exertion, struggled for something, anything, to say. "How do you get first degree?"

"Because your client killed Graham himself. Yes, he used

Jacoby, but only to cover it up. He wanted us to suspect that he made Jacoby do it because he knew that was an easy one to beat and would deflect us from the truth."

Ferrin swallowed before chancing speech but did so quietly. "You're insane."

Amanda marveled at his composure. Bobby was frightened of it. "No, you are," said Amanda. "But we'll get to that later. Did you have a reason to kill Mac Graham?"

"No, I did not," said Ferrin, reaching for Daniels's cigarettes, as much to show the lack of tremor in his hands as to get a smoke.

"Are you sure?"

He put the cigarette in his mouth and spoke around it. "Of course I'm sure." He took the lighter with equal poise, flicked it casually and brought it up to the cigarette. "And how in heaven's name would I accomplish such a thing?"

"First you set her up with the victim. You fed a local physician a lot of nonsense about a theory you had demolished years earlier. Then, knowing how deeply anxious those encounters were making her, you fed her small doses of LSD to heighten her distress, cause her to doubt her own sanity, and clear the way for you to confuse her into thinking she committed murder."

Daniels, who had been taking notes frantically, stopped and looked up from his pad. "You can't be serious about this."

"Did they find any in her blood?" asked Ferrin, exhaling, before Daniels could grab his arm to make him stop. First rule of cross-examination: *Let them make their own case.*

"No," said Amanda. Daniels relaxed his grip on Ferrin's arm and appeared pleasantly surprised by Amanda's answer.

"Pity," said Ferrin, tapping the ash into the tin ashtray in front of Daniels. "Can we go now?"

"Not quite yet, if you don't mind. Why would you ask me about finding it in her blood?"

"Well," said Daniels, confidently answering for Ferrin, "if you are accusing my client of feeding illicit substances to your police officer, shouldn't it have shown up in her blood, which was taken the day she was admitted following her attempted suicide?" He sat back with a self-satisfied look.

"Well, Counselor, that would seem a reasonable question," said Amanda, reaching into her leather attaché and withdrawing a bound report. "Recognize this, Dr. Ferrin?" She watched his eyes narrow and his fingers stiffen. Turning back to Daniels, she said, "The reason I'm a little confused is that your client used to be one of the foremost researchers on LSD, and in this report—let me see, here—oh, yes, here it is: he says that the substance is completely metabolized within thirty minutes and no trace is left in the blood." She looked up. "Now, why on earth would you suppose that he would ask me if we found it in her blood?"

Daniels, realizing that he had been tricked, said, "Perhaps he forgot. That research was done years ago."

"Did you forget, Doctor?" she asked.

"Apparently I did," Ferrin said, his chin lifted slightly in the style of the newly embarrassed wishing to retain their dignity.

"Sounds to me like you're on a fishing expedition here, Captain Grant," said Daniels. "Do you have anything better than this?"

"We have an eyewitness."

Daniels sat up straighter. Ferrin shifted his shoulders. "Who?" they asked simultaneously.

"Pamela Jacoby."

"You are mad," said Ferrin, turning away dismissively.

"Professional diagnosis?" Amanda asked with only mild sarcasm. "You were waiting in your car when Jacoby came out of Graham's place. She looked up and saw your face in the dome light before you had a chance to turn it off. She had been hallucinating, so you had us all convinced it was part of some transference effect. But she saw you."

"Saw me? What the hell kind of bloody eyewitness is that? She was high on—"

"Doctor!" yelled Daniels, cutting him off.

Ferrin paused, mindful of the sudden stridency in his voice, and reconsidered. "Or so you say," he said to Amanda, equanimity quickly restored. "Your conclusion, not mine."

"You're going to look bad in court, Captain," said Daniels, anxious to reestablish himself in what was narrowing into a duel between his client and the captain. "You're either going to have no eyewitness or one high on drugs. You can't have it both ways."

"Are you saying that she wasn't high on LSD?" Amanda asked Ferrin.

Daniels wouldn't let him answer, starting to distrust both his client's haughtiness and the facts that were beginning to unfold. "You've got no way to connect my client to the administration of any hallucinogens."

LaBelle decided that this was a good moment for him to jump in. "Good. Then she's a reliable witness, isn't she?"

"No," said Ferrin. "You seem to forget. You all seem to forget. She was having a psychotic episode."

"According to whom?" asked Amanda.

"According to me," Ferrin replied. "I confirmed that when I went to visit her. After she called."

Amanda nodded thoughtfully, as though she realized she was stuck at a dead end. "And what did you do about it, Doctor?" she asked casually.

"I administered twenty-five milligrams of Thorazine."

"Mm-hmm," Amanda murmured. "I see. And then?"

"Then I rang up Dr. Nostrand."

"Nicely establishing your presence."

"There's no need for such innuendo, Captain," said Daniels.

"I apologize."

"So where is all this LSD I was supposed to be giving Jacoby?" asked Ferrin.

Bobby leaned forward and said, "You told her it was Xanax. You put LSD tabs in her pill bottle."

"Ah," said Ferrin. "And did you have the pills analyzed?"

"Yes," Bobby said. "Straight Xanax."

"Naturally. So why are we here?"

"Because there were fourteen pills in the bottle."

"So?" asked Daniels.

"So the label said ten." Bobby turned back to Ferrin. "You told Nostrand you checked her pills that night, to make sure you didn't overdose her with tranquilizers. The real reason was so you could take out the LSD and put Xanax back in. But you were nervous. You lost count.

"And then you shot her full of Thorazine. Only she wasn't psychotic, she was tripping on LSD. You stopped those trips with a powerful tranquilizer, which damaged her even more. All her demons dancing loose, and she never had a chance to fight them because you bottled them all back up.

"You fucked her up, Ferrin. She started off with troubles like the rest of us and you drove her over the edge."

Bobby was on his feet now, and Ferrin stood slowly and faced him. "You have no proof of that!"

"Oh, yeah? What did you do after you phoned Nostrand?"

A tremble came to roost in his voice. "I left."

"Did you think it was safe to leave your patient?"

"As you said, Thorazine is a strong tranquilizer. I knew she would sleep."

"I'm not concerned about her sleeping, Ferrin. What I'm worried about is when she wakes up." He paused to let the point sink in. "What happens then?"

Ferrin stayed silent. "What happens when she wakes up, Doctor?" Bobby pressed. Ferrin, realizing with surprise that he was standing, sat down as Bobby continued. "What if she's still having an episode when the Thorazine wears off? What stops her from hurting herself, or somebody else? How could you leave her alone not knowing what kind of shape she'd be in when she woke up?"

"You're badgering my client," said Daniels.

Ignoring him, Bobby said, "You knew because she wasn't at all psychotic. She was high on LSD. It would all be over by the time she woke up. You knew that and—"

"Nonsense," Ferrin said weakly, his hands now gripping the edge of the table.

"You knew she was tripping, Ferrin," Amanda said. "It's the only way you could have left her without worrying about the tranquilizer wearing off. And you refilled her pill bottle with straight Xanax because you knew she wouldn't be going out with Graham anymore. Because you just came from killing him."

"Stop it!" Ferrin yelled.

But Amanda didn't stop. "That's why she couldn't get you on the phone for so long. You needed time to get home from Graham's house to answer Jacoby's call."

"That's not true! It's not—"

"Doctor," Bobby said suddenly, "are you all right? Do you need a break?"

Amanda looked at Bobby as if he'd gone mad. They had Ferrin on the ropes and bleeding, and Bobby was offering a break?

Ferrin stared uncomprehendingly at Bobby, who said, "You should feel absolutely free to request a few minutes to yourself, if you feel you need them." Amanda started to protest, but Bobby waved her back. "We surely don't want to cause you any unnecessary anxiety."

"I . . . I'm fine," said Ferrin, his voice tremulous and low.

"I don't think so," Bobby said. "You appear to be under great stress." He glanced at the reporter to verify that she was taking down every word. "We want to be sure that you're clearheaded before we proceed."

Desperate not to appear anxious or flustered, Ferrin hissed through clenched teeth, "I told you, I'm fine."

"Counselor," said Bobby, turning to Daniels, "I'd like to recommend that we take a short recess to allow your client to recover himself."

"I see no signs of stress at all in my client," said Daniels, equally conscious of the reporter. "He appears to me perfectly composed and capable of resuming with no recess."

"Are you certain?" asked Bobby.

"Let's go on," said Ferrin, nervously banging the side of his hand on the tabletop. "Enough delay."

Amanda looked at Bobby admiringly. Ferrin was indeed on the verge of breaking down, but now Bobby had made it impossible for him to request a break without appearing to concede that they were making a good case. His distress, already acute, would escalate with no letup, maximizing the likelihood of careless mistakes.

Daniels knew all of this and would do his best to protect his client. "The best you've got here is negligence. There's no motivation whatsoever for—"

"We know about your father," Amanda said to Ferrin, letting the sentence hang in the air.

"What about his father?" asked Daniels, determined to prevent Ferrin from implicating himself inadvertently.

"Your client thinks Mac Graham killed his father," answered LaBelle.

"He *did* kill him!" Ferrin blurted out.

"It doesn't matter," said LaBelle.

"What the hell is going on?" Daniels demanded.

"Mac Graham was running a crane when a load of girders fell on Ferrin's father," said LaBelle. "There was a sham investigation, and Graham was let off the hook. That's why your client came after him."

Daniels shot Ferrin an icy glare for violating the cardinal rule: *Tell your lawyer everything.* Then he pondered how to deal with this new information. "Still, Officer Jacoby killed Graham herself. You have a confession. At best you've got some lesser charge than first degree murder."

"Meaning that he made her do it?" asked LaBelle, rocking back and forth as though a new thought were entering his head. "Okay. How'd you get her to do it, Doc?"

"Hold it," said Daniels. "Nice try, Libel, but let's lay off the cheap tricks, okay?" LaBelle shrugged his shoulders.

"You have very little beyond clever speculation," Daniels said, turning to Amanda. "There's nothing hard here. So if that's all, why don't we break this up and we'll see you in court?"

"That's a good idea," said Amanda, to Daniels's surprise. "But, I suggest we go a bit longer. Otherwise your day in court might get a little ugly."

Daniels looked at his watch in exaggerated exasperation. "If you insist."

"I didn't insist. I recommended. It's up to you."

Daniels made a waving motion with his hand. The reporter glanced at Amanda and raised her eyebrows: *Don't you want a verbal reply on the record?*

Amanda let it pass and continued her questioning. "What was Officer Jacoby's mood when she left your office the morning of her attempted suicide?"

"I'm not at liberty to discuss matters—"

"Just generally, Dr. Ferrin. No specifics. Was she afraid, happy, anxious, cheerful . . . ?"

"Take your time," said Daniels. "Think all you want." *Why is she asking that?* he was trying to communicate to his client. *Be careful.*

"She was very depressed," Ferrin said after a long pause. "Shaken after the visit to the crime scene."

"Are you sure, Doctor? I remind you that you are under oath in these proceedings, as though you were testifying in a court of law."

"I need no such reminder. She was in great distress."

Amanda nodded thoughtfully. "Did you have any reason to believe she was suicidal?"

"There were no such indications. She had been in darker moods before with no untoward consequences."

"I see. We believe differently. We think she was in a state of euphoria, a classic symptom of impending suicide."

"That's not true!" Ferrin said, his voice now clearly betraying the frayed edges of his nerves.

"We believe you knew she was suicidal and did nothing to discourage it. Maybe you even egged her on."

"He already stated what went on," said Daniels. "There's no need to browbeat and intimidate him."

"There's a taped record, Counselor," said Bobby. "Why don't we simply open it up and then there'll be no dispute. It's in your client's own interest."

Daniels cast an inquiring eye at Ferrin, who said, mechanically and without conviction, "Those records are privileged communications between doctor and patient. To open them up to public scrutiny might do damage to my patient, and I will not allow it."

"Your client is already damaged, Doctor," said LaBelle. "Maybe beyond repair. I think maybe Jacoby herself will give permission to open them up."

"Nonsense. She's profoundly schizophrenic and unable to exercise rational judgment. As her physician it's my call, and I won't violate her privacy."

"Her new doctor might see things differently," said LaBelle.

"You can't do that. I'm her doctor and—"

"Well, there's the question of her mother."

Ferrin stopped and stared at LaBelle. "Her mother . . . ?"

LaBelle nodded. "I hear she's been standing on a table screaming for a new doctor, and we have little choice but to comply."

"When did all of this take place?" asked Daniels.

"Off the record?" asked LaBelle, and waited for an answering nod from Daniels. He motioned to the reporter, who typed in a notation, then took her hands off the keyboard.

"Tomorrow afternoon, best as I can tell," he said.

Daniels glared angrily. "More cheap tricks. You've got a bullshit case here, LaBelle, and your bullshit tricks aren't going to work. Furthermore, a judge isn't going to take too kindly to your wasting the court's time, especially in a sham trial designed to deflect attention away from shoddy police work. I also suggest—"

"Tell us about her hair, Doctor," Amanda said suddenly.

The room went quiet, the silence enhanced by the absence of clattering from the reporter's machine. Amanda sat with studied calm, her hands folded lightly on the table, staring at Ferrin without letup.

Ferrin returned her look, suspicious of her non sequitur, not knowing what to make of it. "Her hair?"

"Yes."

"What about her hair?" asked Daniels.

Still addressing Ferrin, Amanda replied, "How did it look that night you went to see her?"

Ferrin, wary now, could find no reason not to answer, but he spoke cautiously. "All right, I suppose."

"Normal?"

"I suppose."

"Any blood in it?"

Thinking fast, he tried to hedge. "I didn't really notice."

"Dr. Ferrin," Amanda began, her tone both commanding and rebuking, "I ask you again: You visit a patient quite familiar to you and, by your own testimony, in great distress. Did you look her over for any signs of physical problems?"

Realizing that not to have done so would be grossly irresponsible, he answered, "Yes."

"So was there any blood in her hair? Take a moment to
think."

"No, there wasn't."

"Are you sure?"

"Captain," said Daniels, "I think what my client is trying
to say is that blood on her hair is not something one would
specifically check for, which was why he was momentarily
sidetracked by your question. Isn't that right, Doctor?"

"Yes," Ferrin said quickly. "Yes, that's correct."

"I understand completely," said Amanda. "So you're positive now that there was no blood on her hair, correct?"

"I am positive," he said confidently, grasping at the approval
this answer seemed to evoke from his attorney and starting to
believe that this was the answer Amanda did not want to hear.

"Her neighbor didn't see any, either. So tell me this: We
know the killer was splashed with blood from the cut artery.
How is it possible for Officer Jacoby to come home with perfectly clean hair if she just got finished slicing up her boyfriend?"

Daniels jumped in immediately. "Just a minute, Captain. My
client is not a detective or a forensic scientist. It is not up to
him to figure out the details of a crime."

Amanda turned to Daniels. "Too late for that, Counselor.
Your client is the one that told us all about how this competent
police officer covered up her tracks, some bullshit about her
subconscious guiding her through the motions. He provided
that critical bit of analysis, so let's hear him put together the
rest." She looked down toward the end of the table and said,
"And I want this back on the record, Michele." The reporter
entered the notation and positioned her fingers on the keyboard.

"She took a shower, didn't she?" said Ferrin.

"Maybe," said Amanda, "but she sure as hell didn't have
time to wash all that hair. And before you embarrass yourself
further, there was no hair dryer at Graham's place. Or enough
time had there been one. And even if it dried on her way home,
which was hardly likely, it would have looked like hell."

"Perhaps she wore a shower cap?" offered Daniels.

"When, Paul? During the murder? Mac's hair was short. He didn't use shower caps. Are you saying that Jacoby brought one with her, anticipating that she would become psychotic and kill her lover, remembering to put on a shower cap to keep her hair clean?"

"No," said Daniels, seeing an obvious way out. "She wore it afterward, during her shower. She brought one with her because she knew she might stay over and would want it for the morning, to save time before going to work."

"That would have kept the blood on her hair, Counselor. She would have been covered with it." She turned back to Ferrin. "There's no way around this, Ferrin. Pamela Jacoby could not possibly have killed Mackenzie Graham. She wasn't there, plain and simple. You pushed her into a false confession.

"You killed him, and you were doing it while she was trying to get you on the phone, which is why there was no answer." Amanda rose and began to pace, continuing her soliloquy as much to herself as to Ferrin.

"The night of the murder, you stepped into Mac's porch and took off all your clothes. You waited until he was asleep, grabbed the poker, knocked him out and then mutilated him, making it look like a sex crime. You knew it would be perceived as a homosexual revenge killing but also knew it looked like the act of an abused female, and that someone would figure it out eventually. You took a shower afterward to get rid of the blood, and patted yourself dry with toilet paper and flushed it down the toilet. You dampened a few towels to make it look like the killer had taken a shower, to explain the lack of tracings leaving the house. You took the shower, not Pamela."

Not willing to give up, Daniels kept up his defense. "Isn't this a bit of a coincidence, that my client would be waiting close by on the one night she happened to freak the worst?"

"It would be, except that we know that she was never able to get him on the phone right away when she needed him. He had been following her around for weeks, waiting for the right chance. The one night he saw her running out of the house, knowing that her original intention had been to spend the night, he saw his opportunity."

She stopped her pacing and addressed Daniels, purposely ignoring Ferrin to emphasize her dismissal of him or anything he had to say. "It took us a while to figure out the phone records, because we forgot that the date changes at midnight. Pamela finally reached your client a full hour after the time he said she called."

"But it was Nostrand's idea to get them together in the first place," Ferrin whined.

"No, it was yours," said Amanda. "The theory of complementary neuroses was crap. Christ, you tried to stop a Ph.D. candidate from getting her degree over it. You brought it up in front of Jake Nostrand knowing it was bullshit, and you listed a set of characteristics you already knew fit Mac Graham perfectly. If Nostrand hadn't picked up on it, you would have found another way."

"I—I found new merit in the theory," he said lamely.

"And in LSD?" asked Amanda.

"I admit I administered LSD. But it was purely for her benefit. As a therapeutic agent. I was afraid to admit it because the drug is illegal."

Amanda shook her head. "Sorry, Doc. You lectured against its use in therapy. Edan Tancredi will testify to that. You used it to steal her mind, a crime as bad as murder. I don't know how we're going to frame *that* charge just yet, but I assure you we will make it stick."

Daniels felt backed into a corner, on the one hand by Amanda's seemingly endless parade of evidence, on the other by what he perceived as his client's betrayal of the attorney-client relationship. But he was a professional, and he wasn't ready to quit the game just yet. "I'm not buying it, Captain. You've created one scenario out of a mountain of purely circumstantial evidence, but there might be other alternatives."

"Like what?" she asked.

"I haven't got the slightest idea, but I will by the time this gets to trial, and I assure—"

A knock at the door interrupted him. The door swung open and Dennis Murdoch walked in. Ferrin shrank back reflexively. "Okay to come in?" Murdoch asked deferentially, holding a plain manila folder in the air.

Amanda waved him inside and took the folder from him. She opened it, exposing half a dozen sheets of paper, which she glanced through rapidly. "It's rough, Captain," said Murdoch. "Anna did the best she could in short order."

Amanda looked up at him. "Thanks, Dennis. This'll do fine for now."

Murdoch touched his cap in salute, then looked at Ferrin and smiled. "Hiya, Doc. How's it goin'?" he said, then left the room.

When the door had closed, Amanda took one sheet of paper from the folder and slid it across the table to Daniels. "Better have a look at this."

———————●———————

Excerpt from transcript of Pamela Jacoby clinical therapy session 54, July 16, 8:00 A.M., analyst Brixton T. Ferrin, M.D., Ph.D.

I've never seen you like this.
Can't explain it, Doc. I feel terrific.

Bloody marvelous, I should say.
Don't know what it is. The whole world looks better. Maybe I just needed some shock to pump the tubes clean.

Could be. Could very well be.
To tell you the truth, I really don't feel much like getting into anything important today, know what I mean?

[Pause.] Tell you what. Let's play hooky today.
Hooky?

Yes, hooky. I hate to see you miss out on a good day of feeling so well. Let's call it off today, shall we?
You mean it?

Absolutely. Go off and have a good time. Enjoy yourself.
I love it. I'll do it.

And Pamela ...
Yeah?

Whatever you had planned, go for it.
[No response.]

[Spoken slowly] Don't be afraid. Follow through.
Everything will turn out well. I promise.
[Quietly] *Okay, Doctor.* [Pause.] *Good-bye.*

Good-bye, Pamela. [Sound of door closing.]

———————●———————

"I asked the transcriber to put annotations in square brackets for now," said Amanda. "We'll play the actual tape back in court."

There was no response from Daniels or Ferrin as Amanda continued. "You just said under oath that she was depressed, Doctor. Distressed to such a degree that you called off her therapy session. In fact, you pushed her toward her suicide attempt."

"That document is inadmissible," Daniels said. "Those tapes are privileged, and you can't—"

"We're changing doctors, remember?" said LaBelle.

Angrily Daniels got to his feet, feeling a need to quell the drama that had built up in his adversary's favor. "The tapes are still privileged communications between doctor and patient. You can't use them and you know it, Grant."

"Oh, yes, she can," said LaBelle. "C'mon, Paul. The patient's already confessed, so the privilege is moot. Besides, we have her permission, and we don't need the doctor's. The privilege is for the protection of the patient, not the doctor—"

"Hold it, Scott," said Amanda, placing a hand on his arm. She picked up the transcript, tore it in half, tore it again, and pushed the pile of scrap toward Daniels. "We don't need it anyway."

As Daniels sat back down, his face a mirror of his failing confidence, Amanda stared directly at Ferrin and said, "We're going to have you committed, Dr. Ferrin. For your own good, of course."

Ferrin looked up at Amanda, and it appeared to her that it took a great deal of energy and will to do so. His eyes were flat and dead, and if there was any defiance left, it was undetectable. She felt for a second as though she were looking at the husk that remained after life had fled, and it occurred to her that she might have a difficult time engaging his interest in any sort of deal. That the prosecution would win in court was no longer a question in her mind. A court victory, as well as satisfying in a professional sense, would also restore the fallen star of her career and public image. But however sweet, the victory would be only Pyrrhic; nailing Ferrin was no longer the objective. She was counting on the fact that his revenge, now consummated, was turning sour, and some comfort in his remaining years was all that was left to him.

"I won't be institutionalized, Captain Grant," he said, his voice soft and monotonic. "It was premeditated—" Daniels started to protest the impending confession, but Ferrin patted his arm in a gesture of resignation and looked at him, saying, "Please, Paul."

Before he could resume, Daniels said to Amanda, "We're off the record, okay? Your offer. I want it now."

Amanda considered for a long moment, then shrugged and said, "Sure. I've got all I need, anyway."

Ferrin picked up where he had left off, the tone of his voice now giving away that he had played this scenario before in his mind. "It was premeditated. I am easily proven sane, and I can demonstrate that I know the difference between right and wrong. I'll plead guilty of murder in the first degree, not wasting the court's time, and there is little doubt that I will not be executed, but will serve my time in a conventional prison."

"You'd be a real hero in straight prison, wouldn't you?" Amanda asked in a conversational tone. "You took out a cop, you made an entire precinct look like a bunch of idiots. Damn near ruined a captain." She put her elbow on the table and rested her chin in her hand. "Well, this is your lucky day, Doctor. You won't have to suffer the embarrassment of being found guilty of a capital crime. You're going to be committed to the state hospital for the criminally insane."

Some small spark crept back into him as Ferrin realized that his contingency plan was about to go dangerously awry. "You can't do that. I have to agree to an insanity plea."

She shook her head. "You're too crazy. We'll handle all that for you."

Ferrin looked at Daniels pleadingly. "They've got to have me examined by a psychiatrist, don't they?"

Before Daniels could answer, Amanda said, "Of course, by all means, properly court-appointed. Would you like to meet her?"

"Her?" Ferrin stared in confusion as Amanda walked up to the large mirror on the wall facing him and made a flicking motion with her hand. A light switch was turned on inside the observation booth, illuminating Edan Tancredi's face and, sitting next to him, Felice Botrell, who appeared ghostly and surreal through the half-silvered glass. She held up her hand and waggled her fingers at Ferrin. Amanda walked back to the table and sat down.

"You're going to love it in the nut house, Ferrin," she said. "I hear tell that the attendants just love psychiatrists in there. Treat 'em real well. And Jacoby's attendant friends are real fans of yours."

Ferrin tore his eyes away from Felice Botrell and looked around him frantically, recalling the contempt that surrounded him during his visits to Pamela Jacoby in the state institution. She was a favorite patient among the staff, nearly all of whom disliked him intensely. Now betraying his desperation for any hope of rescue, his eyes settled on his attorney. Daniels leaned in toward him, cupped his hand over his mouth, and whispered something in his ear. Ferrin drew back and looked at him, but Daniels only shrugged and averted his eyes.

Ferrin's head jerked back around toward Amanda. As they

locked eyes, Amanda saw growing defeat and hopelessness. He looked down at the table and said in a barely discernible voice, "What do you want?"

Amanda looked at Bobby and then LaBelle, then turned to throw a glance at Tancredi. She stood slowly, placed her hands on the table and leaned forward. "Dr. Ferrin, I don't really give a flying fuck about you or what happens to you. You can burn in hell or walk out free for all I care."

Ferrin looked up, mystified.

"I want my officer back," Amanda said.

Daniels, slouched on his chair, now perked up and said, "What do you mean?"

Amanda turned to him. "I want all her records. I want your client to tell Dr. Tancredi precisely what he did to her, including during her therapy while she's been institutionalized. All the details. All the transcripts annotated."

She turned to LaBelle, watching his face to make sure she was getting it all right. "We'll hold him for psychiatric observation, with his written permission, witnessed by his lawyer. When Tancredi tells me that we've got everything and don't need your client anymore, we'll let him plead guilty and get him into a standard prison."

Daniels turned to Ferrin, who indicated his consent by not moving, then said to LaBelle, "You can do that?"

Amanda leaned back, let out a long breath and answered for him. "We know a good judge."

EPILOGUE

CHAPTER
41

Amanda turned her face toward the morning sun, whose warmth drifted over her casually, in contrast with the hard concrete bench beneath her. In the false peace of this depressing setting, she tried to let her mind drift, with no particular place to go, as she had been doing for the past week as part of a program of enforced relaxation.

She opened one eye slightly to see Bobby Parks doing the same. "Working on your tan, Lieutenant?"

Without changing position or looking at her, he took his time in answering. "Yeah. Don't want to overdo it, though. People might think I don't work hard enough."

"I hope we don't have that to worry about anymore. At least for a long while. And the worst sunburn I ever saw was on a certain black guy who fell asleep on a certain beach."

Wincing at the memory, Bobby turned his head away from the sun. "You can really be a pain in the ass, you know that?" He looked at his hands, then at his watch, for the fifth time in as many minutes. He looked up at the main entrance, but still no sign. "Where the hell is this guy?"

Amanda looked at her own watch, then turned back toward the sun. "Relax," she said. "Enjoy the weather. Tancredi isn't here yet, anyway."

"Place gives me the creeps."

"Wait'll you go inside."

Bobby threw his arms back over the bench top and drummed his foot on the ground. "I never did get to ask. What did you put together about that night?"

Without opening her eyes, Amanda answered, "Not me. You. You had it pretty much figured out. Just needed to take it one more step."

"How so?"

"I assumed that they had gone to bed together. There was no way to tell for sure, but Pamela had no reason to lie." She shifted position slightly and crossed her legs. "We know that Graham never climaxed, because of the autopsy. We have Tancredi to thank for making us check that."

Bobby stopped tapping his foot and thought for a moment. "We have Tancredi to thank for a lot."

She nodded slowly. "He was right all along. Just had no way of knowing it. So what happened when they stopped doing it? Like you said, it's doubtful that he just nodded off to sleep. Not only was he frustrated, but his date was freaking out all over the place.

"Yet we know for a certainty he was killed in his sleep. Did she leave and then sneak back in? That hardly squares with an unpremeditated act of psychotic passion. Maybe he tried to rape her and she got away, sneaking back later to kill him? More likely that she would try to get as far away as possible.

"And this business of her cop subconscious guiding her to cover up the crime? What nonsense, but I had no way to argue with a renowned psychiatrist. Then I remembered the first meeting of the investigating team. Do you remember us discussing the details?"

"I think so," said Bobby, trying to recall as much of the roundtable discussion as he could. "What about it?"

"Pamela Jacoby was a beat cop. She didn't know a damned thing outside the classroom about homicides, crime scene investigations, none of it. She didn't even know what a 'wipe' was."

"I remember," said Bobby. "So, bottom line, the whole thing didn't fit together."

"There was no way it could all fit together. But that was hard to see because there were no other explanations on the table. Is that him?"

A portly man, slightly balding, was hurrying out the front door toward them. "Jeez," whispered Bobby, "you mean to tell me they really do wear white coats?"

Amanda smiled. As the man neared them, he slowed his pace, glancing back and forth between their faces. Amanda and Bobby had the same thought. It wasn't the first time. They decided to let the game play out, have a little fun with him for being late. *Who's the captain, the woman or the black?*

"I assume one of you is Captain Grant?" said the white-coated man.

Nicely handled, Doc. Two points for you. "I am," Amanda answered, rising and offering her hand.

"Ah," said the man, taking her hand in his. "Well. You are a credit to your gender. I'm Dr. Crawford. And you, sir . . . ?"

"Lieutenant Robert Parks. Bobby. And you are a credit to yours."

Crawford laughed good-naturedly. "I am very sorry to have kept you waiting. Slight emergency that couldn't wait."

"Not a problem," said Amanda, warming quickly to the jovial physician. "How do you maintain your sense of humor in a place like this?"

"A place like what?" he shot back quickly.

Amanda stammered, suddenly embarrassed at her insensitivity. "I mean . . . I meant . . . it's where, you know, people, uh . . ."

"Hah! Next time don't make me guess who's the captain!" Crawford smiled delightedly at his jocular revenge. "You mean it's full of crazies and loonies and who the hell do I have to talk to who's normal, right?"

Reddening visibly, Amanda said, "I'm sorry, Doctor, I didn't mean—"

"You made her blush, Doc," Bobby interrupted. "Never thought I'd see the day."

Crawford laughed loudly and took their arms in his, leading them back toward the entrance. "We'd better go to my office first. Have a little talk. And don't be so serious, Captain.

There's enough misery here already without you adding to the pile."

Bobby disengaged his arm from Crawford's and stopped walking. "Uh, if you don't mind, I'll just hang out here for a while."

"Bobby?" asked Amanda, surprised.

He shrugged, saying, "I don't know. Just rather not, that's all."

"Come, come, Lieutenant." Crawford walked back and took Bobby's arm again, urging him forward. "It's not as bad as all that."

"Please, Bobby," said Amanda. "I really need you to be with me."

Reluctantly Bobby followed them into the building, worry creasing his forehead as he looked around for the telltale signs he remembered from bad movies and comic books.

"Tell Dr. Tancredi to come right in when he arrives," Crawford said to his assistant as they entered his office and closed the door.

When seated, he became serious as he addressed Amanda. "I don't mind telling you, Captain, I do not approve of this business of withholding her medication."

She nodded. "I know you don't. But I'm taking full responsibility, and—"

He waved her off, shaking his head. "That wasn't for the sake of shifting liability or any nonsense like that. As a physician, I don't like it."

"What's the big deal?" asked Bobby.

"The big deal is that she's had about enough shocks for this lifetime. Technically, her therapy is succeeding. She now realizes that she killed her lover and is starting to come to grips with that fact."

"But she didn't kill him," protested Bobby.

"That doesn't make any difference." To Amanda's confused look he answered, "Look. When you're trying to understand how somebody feels, really feels, it doesn't make any difference whether that feeling is appropriate to the reality of the situation. When you were a little kid and your pet turtle died, that certainly didn't rank up there with having another kid's whole village disappear in a landslide, but to you, it may have been just as devastating. That's why I hate it when someone tries to convince somebody else 'It's not so bad' or 'Look at so-and-so, they have it much worse' or junk like that. Never judge psychological impact using the objective reality of the situation as a criterion."

"So what's that got to do with taking her off the drugs?" asked Bobby.

"Like I said, her therapy, however misguided, was making progress. Now you're about to tell her that her psychiatrist is a lunatic and she didn't kill that guy after all. The rug gets pulled out from under her once again, and once again her sense of reality is blasted into dust. There is a real danger of her going catatonic. Without some medication to soften the blow . . ." He let his voice trail off meaningfully.

Amanda considered this plainspoken explanation. "I understand. Truly. But to be honest with you, psychiatrists are not exactly number one on my personal hit parade these days." She held up a hand as Crawford started to protest. "I know, I know. But I don't want her to be carefully coached back to the real world over a period of years, most of which she'll spend trying to figure things out through a drug-induced haze. It's not fair to her."

"But Captain—"

"Please, Dr. Crawford. I'm firm on this."

Crawford leaned back in his chair and eyed her carefully. He knew that her wishes in this case weren't capricious or sloppily considered. "And Tancredi? What does he say?"

She smiled as one might in a confessional. "He agrees with you. As a professional diagnosis. But he thinks I'm right in how I want to handle it."

A knock on the door preceded Tancredi's entrance. "Hallo, Harvey," he said, striding forward to shake hands. Studying Crawford's face, he said, "So I am seeing a meeting of the minds is not being such a happy occasion. Who won?" He looked around at Amanda and Bobby.

"We're going to do it like we said, Tanc," said Amanda, no trace of victory in her voice.

Turning back to Crawford, Tancredi said, "How is the patient without the happy pills?"

With only mildly grudging admittance, Crawford answered, "Not too bad, actually. Very tense and anxious. Fidgety, but her affect seems appropriate, and she's eaten two normal meals."

"So, then," said Tancredi, "away we go, yes?" and he strode out of the room without further preamble.

As they walked down the hall, Amanda took Bobby's hand in her own and squeezed it tightly.

"Hang in there, lady," he said softly. "You're doing the right thing. I think."

"She's in a holding room," Crawford said as they walked. "Just two chairs and a table. You can have the attendant in or out, it's up to you. Dick Salit. He's a good man and has been a good friend to Pamela."

"I'll go in alone. She hasn't been violent, has she?"

Crawford shook his head. "Never. The drugs weren't for that. Only to ease her pain."

Amanda reflected on Crawford's sensitivity to one of so many patients and asked herself, as she had endlessly for the past week, whether what she was about to do was right. She tried to keep her resolve, sensing more than knowing that she had to be strong when talking to Pamela. Only through the force of her own conviction would she be able to communicate the truth to Pamela. Only by supplying a confident substitute for the anchor that was her doctor could she hope to get through to her.

Amanda stopped and faced the door to the holding room. There was a small, shuttered window in the door frame. Crawford swung it open and said, "Dick? They're here. Would you come out, please?" A surprisingly elderly man emerged and looked with some suspicion at their faces. Crawford clapped a hand on his shoulder and said, "Dick will be right outside the door. Pamela trusts him completely, so if there's a problem, let him take over. Agreed?"

Amanda nodded without speaking. Bobby gave her hand a final squeeze and let go. "I'll be here, too. Good luck."

As she went in Tancredi said, "Stick to the plan," and Crawford pulled the door shut after her. The four men looked at each other and took up positions, Bobby leaning against the wall close by the door, the attendant walking to a folding chair and sitting down, Tancredi and Crawford milling about aimlessly. Crawford pulled out a pack of cigarettes, drawing a disapproving stare from Tancredi. He shrugged and said, "What the hell. We all have our little imperfections."

"True," said Tancredi, reaching for the pack and taking a cigarette. "But for a practicing physician, a terrible example." He stooped toward Crawford's lighted match.

Bobby paid no attention to them but fixed his eyes on the small window, straining for a sound, any sign of what was taking place within. Suddenly the silence was violently broken by the sound of a chair hitting a wall at high speed, the clattering, crumpling noise banging out as much through the surrounding walls as through the door. "He did what?!" shrieked a female voice.

Dick leapt to his feet as Bobby reached instinctively for the doorknob, only to find Tancredi's hand clamped around his own. "The sonofabitch did what?!" Pamela's voice said again. Tancredi put a finger to his lips and wiggled it back and forth, urging Bobby to restraint. He relaxed his grip on the doorknob but stayed close.

After a moment of silence inside, a sound came out that could have been fists banging on a table, banging very hard. "I'll kill that prick, that scumbag!" Pamela's voice thundered through the small corridor. "I'll *really* cut his nuts off, and I'll shove 'em down his fucking throat, I swear to God I will, that— that shithead!" And on and on.

Tancredi, who likewise had been leaning in close to the door, looked up at Bobby, a crinkle starting at the corners of his eyes. He took Bobby's arm in his own and started to lead him away, much to the confusion of the frightened lieutenant.

"Come, my friend," Tancredi said, turning his face toward him. "I am thinking maybe our young police lady is going to be just fine, yes?"